DIARY OF AN IT BOY

By

Gavin Lambe-Murphy

Copyright © Gavin Lambe-Murphy 2017
This book is sold subject to the condition that it shall not, by way of trade or otherwise, be lent, resold, hired out, or otherwise circulated without the publisher's prior consent in any form of binding or cover other than that in which it is published and without a similar condition including this condition being imposed on the subsequent publisher.
The moral right of Gavin Lambe-Murphy has been asserted.
ISBN-13: 978-1976321139
ISBN-10: 1976321131

DEDICATION

This book is dedicated to the believers – shine on!

This is a work of fiction. Names, characters, businesses, organizations, places, events and incidents either are the product of the author's imagination or are used fictitiously. Any resemblance to actual persons, living or dead, events, or locales is entirely coincidental.

Gavin Lambe-Murphy came to the attention of the media in the late nineties as the original 'It' boy, when he chose to turn his life into a well-documented journey with the help of a PR agent. From regularly appearing in weekly gossip columns, to moving on to write them, he also became a popular face on television both in Ireland and the UK, taking part in shows such as Young Posh & Loaded (ITV1), Celebrity Farm (RTE1) and Celebrity 5 Go Dating (Channel 4), to name a few. An outspoken columnist, he has written for a number of international newspapers and magazines, including the Sunday Times, Social & Personal and the Daily Mail. Diary of an It Boy is his first novel.

CONTENTS

Introduction *1*
Chapter 1 .... *3*
Chapter 2 .... *23*
Chapter 3 .... *47*
Chapter 4 .... *59*
Chapter 5 .... *71*
Chapter 6 .... *87*
Chapter 7 .... *107*
Chapter 8 .... *138*
Chapter 9 .... *154*
Chapter 10 .... *171*
Chapter 11 .... *184*
Chapter 12 .... *201*
Chapter 13 .... *225*
Chapter 14 .... *243*
Chapter 15 .... *261*
Chapter 16 .... *282*
Chapter 17 .... *303*
Chapter 18 .... *320*

Introduction

Super social, in demand and on the all the right guest-lists with all the right people, Oli seems to have it all. A member of an international jet-set scene, where lavish lunch parties become hectic nights of debauchery behind the velvet ropes of the world's most exclusive parties. Bed hopping with both men and women are mixed with missed opportunities and lost moments due to an increasing appetite for excess. Having been catapulted into the media spotlight following a rather clever PR stunt, life has rapidly gone into overdrive, and as he ventures forward the glamour brings with it the challenges that face an addictive personality. Oli finds himself completely dependent on cocaine, publicity, the vacuous party scene, and his one true secret love, Marco. However, love isn't enough, when he discovers that the one addiction he craves most isn't all he seems to be. Private jets, Fashion Week parties, living in the best hotels and waking up in compromising situations have all become the norm, but as his journey unfolds the more messed up it gets. A life filled with self-induced drama is usually resolved by those around him, as they pick up his tabs, clean up his messes and hold him up as he rapidly spirals downwards.

Everyone wants a piece of his lifestyle and as he tries to please every audience, he becomes a caricature of himself fuelled by daily alcohol and drug binges. TV appearances go drastically wrong, and his real friends step aside as they witness the It Boy coming to town. From Dublin to London, to New York and beyond, he floats from one high society bash to another, yet fails to remember the vital details which he must file in order to get his popular weekly newspaper column to print. While he appears to be everywhere, he is fact utterly lost and on the brink of collapse.

Oli allows us to glance at diary snippets of his life, which are funny one minute and tragic the next. His high-octane lifestyle remains on track, but when he realises the truth about his partner Marco, will it be too much to handle? With the eyes of the media starting to notice his manic behaviour, can he manage to keep his love life and drug addiction on the down-low?

Chapter 1

May 19th 2014, Somewhere above New York

"Excuse me, signore, please can you wake up! Signore?" exclaims the handsome Emirates steward. "Signore please, you must wake, as we are about to land in New York!"

I'm dead to the world in a Xanax dream, unaware that the entire first-class cabin-crew has gathered and is beginning to panic. As I snooze, the captain has already requested medical assistance at JFK International, and while the stewards try various methods of waking me, nothing works. I just lie there, soaked in champagne and covered in copies of *GQ*, *Tatler* and *Vanity Fair*. Perhaps if I wasn't a priority passenger they could simply chuck a glass of cold Evian over my head, but alas. While most passengers have been soaking up the luxe that is the Airbus A380, I've managed to miss everything. That's the thing about flying on a regular basis, you become immune to it. No matter which airline, no matter which wine-list, no matter which celebrity chef has created the meals, it is all the same – just a chore. Many years ago a therapist told me that the best way to beat the travel blues is to pass out on departure and wake up fresh in surroundings new. That said, I never travel without my stash of Xanax to make sure flying is relaxed, if not sometimes completely missed, due to me passing out as soon as they've offered the first glass of champagne. On this occasion I was in need of more than a tranquiliser pill, I needed to remain asleep, for a very long time.

Allow me to explain. Just hours earlier, I found myself in possibly one of the most compromising situations imaginable. Waking with the morning sun on my face, I stretch out and feel the cool Frette bed linen as I reach for my BlackBerry. It's going be a great morning, having had a perfectly amazing Milanese night with Marco the night before; dinner at Cracco and dancing at Byblos. Yeah, I know, perfect date night, right? We'd been seeing each other for what seems like an eternity, albeit of the on/off relationship sort, having met by chance at a party during London Fashion Week almost a decade ago. Having just moved to London from Dublin, I was a guest at every show and party taking place during the week-long circus that is Fashion Week. Long days met by longer nights, air-kissing, drinking heavily, and then trying to remember it all for a feature I was commissioned to write for the *Sunday Times*. Yes, every show – well, I was young and eager. These days the thought of sitting through just one fills me with dread.

It all came out of nowhere, or rather he did, and following our first date I just knew he was the one. Yes, cheesy I know, but that's how it is. He's pretty much close to perfection; tall, dark, strong and stereotypically Italian, as in he gets extremely jealous when I flirt with others and let's just say he knows how to work it in bed. We've spent the past year really getting to know each other and for the first time we've managed to go for months on end without as much as a cross word. Both fiery and hot headed, we've managed to keep our tempers under wraps and spent our time together smiling rather than scowling. Finally, we were at a place where I was sure we were ready to live together full-time, even if it meant I had to relocate from Rome to be with him in Milan. Having taken a few years to adjust to the Roman way of life, I was now about to learn what it was to be Milanese, which believe me, is a world apart. Where life in Rome is every bit the romantic adventure one would expect – long lunches met with cocktail parties and evenings filled with wonderful dinners, dining al fresco in a city that feels like a movie set – Milan is far more fast paced and serious.

I often feel as if I've been transported from Italy to Germany, just by stepping off a plane in the north. I loved my life in Rome; having snapped up a great flat on Via della Croce several years ago, just after meeting Marco, it soon became my new home. I'd kept my mews house in Dublin, but I was spending less and less time there, quite simply as I longed to be close to Marco. It was a time in my life where I was ready for a change of scenery and well, he lived in Rome and there was no sign of him leaving. So, if the mountain won't come to Mohammed and all that. Sure, we spent most nights together, but with our constant fighting and all-round drama, we were still holding on to our respective flats, just in case. Well, at least I was. I don't think Marco had ever envisaged moving into my place. That's one of the things I find most attractive about him, he's very headstrong and determined. Quite the opposite of me, I must admit. I'm known to be somewhat flighty, and possibly fickle. Ever since my report cards at school told me so, time and time again. Anyhow, he lived just a stone's throw away on neighbouring Via Bocca di Leone, so even when we did fight, we would still bump into each other on the street. It's all slightly comical, looking back. Crazy over-the-top fights and break-ups would result in us ignoring each other as we sipped espresso at separate tables at Caffè Greco, or pretending we hadn't seen each other at the bar of Hotel de Russie, even when barman Gianluca would let us know of the other's presence. Plus, within forty-eight hours we were usually back together, even if it meant I had to be the one to back down and apologise first.

Marco comes from a rich Italian-Swiss family and as an only child, he's very used to getting his own way, a trait that's followed him into adulthood, and one that I believe is his downfall in many ways. Having been brought up on Lake Como and schooled at the ultra-exclusive Le Rosey, he certainly is pampered, if not spoilt. When we fight he can hold out for days without as much as saying hello. When we make up we laugh so much at our childish behaviour and spend days on end in loved-up bliss, until the next fight and then we do it all over. Destructive, rather like the way an alcoholic claims it won't happen again after one of their blowouts, we're electric and we know it. Despite our tempestuous relationship, I knew that I was happy to be in Rome as I was close to my man. I'd moved there to be with him, something I used to lie about. When people would ask what brought me to Italy, I'd say that I needed an adventure, and Rome just felt right. These days I'm not so embarrassed to say that I followed my heart. I'd come out rather publicly in the Irish and UK media for him, and in a way I'd given up my old life for a new one in Rome. Well that was the plan, until Marco announced casually over dinner that he was relocating to Milan for work commitments. Heading up a creative team of designers at one of Italy's leading architectural firms, everything about him screams 'stylissimo', from his Brioni suits, to his Maserati Granturismo, to his perfect manners. In fact, as it was once noted by a female colleague of his, if he wasn't Italian he would most certainly be gay. Go figure! Anyhow, I'm always happy to visit him in Milan, and I believe that by living apart from Monday to Friday it keeps our relationship sharp. On top of this he has amazing taste, so staying at his Corso Venezia penthouse is rather like staying at a glorious five-star hotel, but without any of the hassle. Seriously, I don't think I've ever met someone more organised or in control. Sometimes when we're lying in bed on a Saturday or Sunday morning, I try to think of obscure things to ask for, like I don't know, maybe a certain brand of facial scrub, or some random herbal tea. Things that are so specific it would be strange if they were in his place. Almost every time he has what I want, and if not, it's purchased within days and presented to me as a joke, usually gift wrapped in packaging that costs more than the contents.

After years of 'will we, won't we?' the time had arrived and we were just about ready to take that step to live together, and it felt so right. Besides, as I said, we haven't had a proper fight in months, so what's stopping us? I've managed to find a perfect French couple to let my flat to, and they've already moved in, so I've come to Milan with a purpose.

Waking slowly to find that he's already left for work, leaving me to welcome the new day over espresso and a flick through some of the stack of magazines left on the bedside table, everything feels right. Seriously, this pad is divine, wall-to-wall Farrow & Ball with dottings of B&B Italia furniture and a continual scent of Tom Ford Oud Wood candles, which seem to be lit eternally. A perfectly designed duplex with two terraces and a private roof garden on one of Milan's most exclusive tree-lined streets. The perfect city pad, which Marco inherited from his family's vast estate just a few months ago. Following a tedious and laborious interior design project, it's finally perfect. I think the fact he was trapped in the middle of a rather messy and drawn-out divorce from his, and I quote "total fucking bitch whore ex-wife", only further slowed the design process, but he sure was picky. The drawing room has been painted and repainted three times, just to achieve the exact shade of white. Yes, white! Who would believe that there are so many shades of white? From All White to Wimborne White and beyond, I think he must have looked at over twenty shades of the same colour! While fabrics were ordered and returned on more occasions than I can recall, there always seemed to be something wrong.

Marco rarely speaks of Alessandra, unless he's had too many glasses of Barolo and slips into a rage over something she had done while they were married.

Their divorce, like most things in Italy, had taken longer than usual to become a reality, mainly as she wanted everything and was refusing to go anywhere until it was in writing. What she wanted most was their stunning home on Capri, well Anacapri to be exact. There was no way Marco or his mother Gabriella, who at almost eighty and still a force to be reckoned with, were letting go of their beloved island home. While I waited patiently in the wings for things to dissolve, he assured me that the marriage was well and truly over even before it began.

Unlike Marco, Alessandra worked hard to become the person she is today. Born into humble beginnings in Naples, she soon realised that she needed to escape her roots and land herself the perfect husband and social position. She's the sort that had left her old life behind and wasn't going to give up her new, much sought-after one at any cost. I know you're probably thinking I'm just being bitchy, but I'm not. After all, I have little interest where she comes from or where goes next, as long as it's far away from us. Plus, I'm simply filling you in. In writing terms, I think they call it character development. Anyhow, their settlement had finally come through, roughly six months ago, and while it was pretty substantial from where Alessandra sat, much to her annoyance she didn't get her hands on Capri, but settled impressively in picturesque Fiesole, Florence.

Once the dust settled we were ready to come out of the shadows and be a proper couple. Oh, don't get me wrong, we were very much together, well at least to those who knew us. However, we were still guarded about things to the outside world. A part of our relationship which hurt me from time to time, I must admit. There had been times when I would be introduced as his "friend" and times when he would become this uber-macho, rugby-loving bloke, if we bumped into certain friends or work colleagues of his. Looking back, it's all rather funny and totally stupid, as when you try to be something you're not, even the slowest people pick up on it. I mean, there's something rather odd about a guy who is all but thumping his chest to prove his masculinity, while on the table in front of him is an open copy of *Arena Homme Plus+*.

Anyhow, I digress. My perfectly calm morning is what should have happened. What did happen is utter hell. Lying here, flicking through my phone to check emails and Facebook, I can hear voices coming from downstairs, loud female voices, which seem to be getting louder and coming closer very quickly. There's nobody home apart from Marco's trusted housekeeper, Federica, and she would never enter the room until I was already at breakfast. As I reach for a t-shirt the double doors into the bedroom are flung open and there standing in front of me is Alessandra. I've only ever seen her in photographs but it's her for sure. She really is beautiful, stunning in fact. Dressed head to toe in Loro Piana and with a waft of Hermès she storms towards me, removing her oversized Chanel sunglasses before pulling the duvet from the bed and throwing it aggressively to the floor. "What the fuck is going on here? Who are you and what are you doing in my home? In my bed?" she barks in broken English.

You know when people say they're completely lost for words, wishing to speak but nothing comes out?

Well, that's me. I actually always believed it to be a myth, I mean, there must be words. There are always words, but no, there are no words, just a dry mouth, a hangover and a sinking feeling. "Sorry, what? Who the hell are you?" I ask, although I realise the truth. Coldly and with purpose, she reaches into her Kelly for her iPhone and voice commands it to call Marco. As the handset begins to call his number on speaker phone, I stand up, noticing that I'm wearing just a t-shirt – one of Marco's Dolce & Gabbana ones with Mickey Mouse on the front. I grab for the bed sheet but before I can the call is diverted to voicemail and all attention is back to me.

"So? Who are you? Do I need to call the police or the concierge to have you removed from my fucking home?" she continues, and it's clear to see that she's every inch the girl from the tower block in Naples.

"I'm a friend of Marco's and I've stayed here overnight, because… because we were very drunk and I…" I stutter.

"Shut the fuck up! Shut the fuck up right now, I can't stand it!" she snarls as she inches her way around the massive bed towards me. "I know you are the reason my marriage is such a mess, I know all about you, Mr It Boy from Dublino!"

If there were no words before, it seems that now there are too many and once I begin to speak I can't stop. "Your marriage is so over, darling! Marco has told me everything about you, the way you slept around and cheated on him with one of his best friends. How he had to fight to keep the scandal out of the gossip pages. Oh yes, Alessandra, I know all about it. I know that you were a nightmare to be married to and even worse to divorce. So don't you dare come in here shouting and screaming at me, just because you messed up and now I am making Marco happy!" I'm totally flustered but remain in control as I quickly dress myself. Somehow last night's Gucci fitted shirt, Dsquared2 tuxedo pants, and Stubbs & Wootton velvet slippers look like the wrong outfit choice for this situation, but what ya gonna do? I stand awaiting her response to this hideous scenario and then she laughs so loudly that my hangover goes from bad to terminal. As she screeches, I look around the room at the debris from the night before. On the side table there's an empty bottle of Veuve Clicquot Rosé and some strawberries, by the bed an open packet of condoms, lubricant and Marco's Ralph Lauren boxer shorts. There really is no way this can be covered up.

"You really are an idiot. At least there are two of us, tesoro," she laughs while also typing into her phone. "For your information, now listen, as I know you blond boys can be quite dumb. I am married to Marco, we are heading to Geneva this evening to stay at our house with friends for the weekend. Our marriage is not over. It may not be perfect, but we remain together and will not split because of something like... you!" she snaps through gritted teeth. "You are nothing more than a disgusting gay piece of shit that has got to go and go now!" She inches closer towards me again, holding her phone to her ear as it dials a number.

"Marco has told me that you are no longer together, he has told me that you left him," I say in a genuinely shocked tone. The truth is I am shocked, completely shocked. Marco had told me over and over again that he was single. That he had divorced her and that their marriage was a joke from day one. Was this tale all lies? As I look around I feel that this perfect example of Italian style is rapidly becoming as dreadful as my hangover, which is getting decidedly worse. Alessandra walks out onto the terrace and closes the doors behind her.

In the hallway I see Federica looking worried, as if she's about to deliver some dreadful news. She gestures to me to leave the room and come downstairs. I'm so confused that I just walk towards her, leaving my bag and belongings behind. Suddenly I feel as if I'm a child again, being taken to the school headmaster's office. I'm not sure if it's the hangover, the shock or the fact that she may be telling the truth but as I reach the final few steps of the staircase I faint and tumble into the hallway, tearing the knee of my trousers and banging my head against the foot of a table. Federica rushes to my aid and once she's steadied me she takes me into the staff kitchen, which is separated from the main kitchen by a screen door. "You really must leave now," she tells me as she dabs my head with a wet towel. She looks worried but sympathetic at the same time. "Alessandra is not a good woman and I do not think I have ever seen her so angry," she says sternly, looking into my eyes to stress the point. As she stares into my eyes and clasps my hand I feel the pain of my hangover mix horribly with the pain of my fall. Surely this fashion-obsessed size zero couldn't be that scary – she looks as if she may snap in half if she answered her phone too quickly.

"What do you mean, Federica?" I ask as I open a

bottle of San Pellegrino and reach for a sleeve of Nurofen Plus.

"Well, let me just say that not very long ago one of her best friends bought a handbag that she wanted and she made her life over. Really over!" She pulls a spooky face.

"What? She killed her? Over a handbag?" I ask as I spill water all over the granite counter top.

"Oh, dear boy, you really are still sleeping? No, I mean in society... she made her life end. No more parties, no more charity gala, no more anything – all because she jumped the list at Hermès. It is a serious story!"

I'm beginning to wonder if I've fallen through the looking glass, or perhaps I'm just dreaming. I pop three headache pills and sip on the water, which now contains a slice of lime, provided by Federica. "Ok, so she is a fashionista who can't be beaten by others when it comes to her Birkin collection, I can handle that. Everyone I know would do the same." I'm beginning to feel very light headed and as if I'm going to faint again when the intercom sounds, cutting like a blade through my skull. It's Alessandra ordering Federica to come to the drawing room.

"You stay here. Do not move!" she says.

I'm thinking I should run. "But, what if she comes in here?" I ask as I place my head onto the cold counter top.

"In here? Are you crazy? She will not come in here, she has never been in this kitchen. She doesn't enter kitchens ever!" she says as she fixes her hair in the mirror and applies some deep pink lipstick, before walking out of the room, closing the doors behind her. I sit with my head pressed against the cold granite and then I realise I must contact Marco to let him know. I must hear it from him – what is the truth?

In the panic to leave the bedroom I'd left my phone by the bed. Pulling back the dividing doors into the main kitchen, I can smell fresh croissants and coffee, which normally would stop me in my tracks, but I'm so distracted that I don't stop. I creep slowly up the main staircase, trying to hear what's going on behind the closed doors of the drawing room, but all seems silent. Once in the bedroom I decide to make a dash for it. If Alessandra really did wipe people out for something as simple as stealing her place on a handbag waiting list, what would she do to the one who had 'stolen' her husband? I don't want to find out, so I gather my things and take the elevator to the ground floor, calling Marco as I do so. He doesn't pick up, but instead he sends a text to say: 'Get out of there and wait for me to contact you. We are in serious shit!!! Take the car and go where you need to.' The tone of the text makes me feel that I'm in the wrong. It makes me feel cheap and ashamed. Why am I feeling this way when it's Marco who has lied to both his wife and me?

Outside, the weather is warm and the great feeling that summer has finally arrived is in the air. A woman smiles as she walks by with her two young children, beautiful children, just like a Tommy Hilfiger commercial. Cesare, Marco's Romanian driver, is waiting at the front of the building in a black Mercedes S600. "Where to, champion?" he says in a deep macho voice. Cesare is possibly the hottest guy

I've ever seen, 100% pure muscle with a tough guy attitude. He's much more than a driver, in reality he's security. Despite his super macho image, he really is a pussy cat. He has zero problem with my relationship with Marco, in fact he actually enjoys the fun when we we're all in the car together heading to some party or another.

"I need to go to the Bvlgari Hotel and then straight to the airport. Can you check flights to New York for this afternoon for me please? Use Emirates as I have air-miles," I ask, half flirting with him from the back seat, as I open a cold can of Coke.

"I hear there is a trouble in the paradise bello," he says, staring at me in the rear-view mirror.

"You have no idea. I just need to get away from here," I say, suddenly realising that this may very be the end of life as I know it. It also makes me think of how stupid I've been to believe someone who could lie so easily. How, over seven years could I have been so dumb? There's only one person in Milan who could make sense of everything and if not, at least he would make me laugh. My dear friend Paolo, who to most is a bit of an ice queen, a title he enjoys playing up to. He's on every guest list from London to Monte Carlo and beyond, but only attends the most lavish parties with the most stylish party people. Seriously, he manages to pop up on the social pages of *Tatler*, *Vogue*, *Vanity Fair* each month and lands on the *GQ* Best Dressed year in, year out. Something he laughs about, but I know he secretly thrives on. In my opinion he deserves to be there, as his immense sense of style is something to be admired. The reason he can be so choosy and sometimes snooty is due to the fact that his father is a serious name in private banking circles and his mother, who hails from one of Europe's richest 'old money' families, is a leading charity fundraiser and also owns a string of race horses. Everything their boy wants, he gets, including access to homes in Milan, Bel Air, Monaco, Paris, London, and New York. Paolo's days are spent pampering himself and working on his jewellery business. I think he's the only guy I know that visits the hair salon three times a week. The fact his jet-black hair shines like ice he attributes to "great genes and financial means."

Arriving at the hotel, I'm in a daze as I'm greeted by the concierge whom I've known for many years. Handing me a large, beautifully packaged parcel, he escorts me through to the garden terrace, making small talk as we walk. Nowhere in Milan has the same feeling as the garden of the Bvlgari Hotel. It's a little piece of heaven, where I must admit I have sought sanctuary on more than a few occasions over the years. While I await Paolo's arrival, I open the parcel which is clearly from Brunello Cucinelli. As I open it I already know what's inside; a chocolate brown cashmere sweater which I'd bought a few days ago as a surprise for Marco. I had it delivered to the hotel as I wanted to give it to him over drinks tomorrow evening. Very little in his super structured life is unplanned so I felt an impromptu gift was in order. As I look at the sweater I feel sad for the first time in months. I stare at it and think of his great smile if he had been given the chance to open it. One thing he loves more than anything is cashmere. As I sit there a Bellini and an espresso arrive at the table. That's the thing about great hotels; they know what you want before you need to ask.

Sipping the perfect Bellini, I can first hear and then smell Paolo coming through the bar out onto the terrace. He's forever chatting loudly into his mobile phone and he only wears one particular cologne – Ambre Topkapi – which as I am sure you know is one of the most interesting scents imaginable. With a waft of his signature scent and a, "Ciao ciao, baci baci," into his phone, he lands. As we greet each other he quips, "Only time to kiss one cheek today, darling, what the fuck is going on? I need to know everything. Alessandra is going like cray-cray all morning looking for you. What the fuck? I told you this was a bad idea, darling," he says while gesturing to the waiter. "Is it too early for a cocktail? Not one of those things, a proper cocktail!" He's pointing at my Bellini and making a disapproving face. "Oh, to hell with it, darling we'll have two Negroni. If we are going to try solve this mess peach puree is certainly not the answer!"

Already I'm laughing. He truly is a tonic for every situation, even the most dismal. After a number of rounds of drinks I receive a text message from Cesare to say that he will take me to the airport to catch a late afternoon flight to New York. "I'd invite you to stay with me, but I think it's best you vanish for a while, at least until things settle. You must take these for your journey. It's just some Xanax, but they are no ordinary ones. They are super strength, like 3mg. I got them from a Brazilian dancer I met at Ceresio 7. Seriously, you should have seen him, all muscles and rough as…"

I cut across him as I the last thing I need is to hear about his ever-fantastic love life. "I really must go, the car is waiting and I think you're right, I shouldn't be in Milan right now." I'm slightly scared at the prospect of Alessandra on the warpath. En route to the airport I'm certainly tipsy, hardly surprising after five cocktails and no breakfast, but I know I need to get on with things and board the flight. I'm greeted by the ever-charming Emirates ground staff who walk me through to the VIP Lounge, which at Linate is rather nice. You know the way some lounges feel like you should be typing into a laptop or reading the *Financial Times* in order to fit in? Well, here it's more about copies of *Vogue* and taking advantage of the bar. However, instead I choose to freshen up and change my clothes before having a dry Martini with ice. I try to call Marco again but it's now diverting to voicemail. I don't leave a message. While waiting I watch other travellers as they chat into their phones or munch on bar snacks. I think of everything I'm leaving behind and it scares the shit out of me. I'm aware that my New York trip is more of an escape than relocation, but it's a surreal feeling. It's the first time I'm making the journey without contacting any of my New York friends to let them know I'm coming. As I sit sipping my drink I feel totally alone and for the first time in months I'm feeling genuinely lonely. I won't lie to you, sitting here I have that terrible feeling, when you need so badly to cry but you have to hold it in. I try so hard to hold back the tears but they silently stream down my face. I can feel the eyes of others on me which only makes the situation worse. Never been one for wearing sunglasses indoors, but to hell with it. I sit crying behind my large Tom Ford aviators. I guess the scene is imitating my life; all fine on the outside, but behind the lense sits a mess.

Once on board I settle into my seat and following a brief introduction to my private cabin space, I'm left to unwind pre-take off. I stare at a stack of magazines and newspapers which are there for my amusement, but which only make me feel anxious. As the plane begins to taxi I decide to snap myself out of my mood and treat this journey as an adventure. Who knows, I may even meet someone wonderful in the King Cole bar of the St Regis. Isn't that where all the best romances begin? I smile at the pretty air stewardess as I take one of the Xanax which has a strange deep purple, almost blue colour. I wash it down with a chilled glass of champagne, Billecart-Salmon, I think? I sit waiting for a transformation. I want to feel numb. I want to sleep and never wake up.

I stare at a copy of *Tatler*, which offers a guide to being an 80s Sloane. As I read it and look at the fashion trends of the 1980s I wonder if the drugs are already working, as this is bad taste in full colour print. How could the people at Condé Nast think that this is a good idea? To revisit an era of hellish fashion and obnoxious behaviour is wrong on every level, I think as I argue the pros and cons in my head. I am not usually one to give an article in *Tatler* much thought, but you must understand that I'm in a state of utter shock. Twinning this with being half pissed and half stoned and you get the scene. I still believe that I'm not feeling any effects from the tranquilisers. Reaching for another pill, I pop it with the remainder of the champagne. A few minutes after that I don't remember anything at all, I'm wiped. The next thing I recall is being woken in a room at JFK Airport, while on a stretcher and surrounded by worried-looking medics. "Are you ok, sir?" asks a smiling Asian nurse. "You gave us all quite a fright. Do you know where you are?" she asks while fixing my hair.

"New York, I hope," I say with a dry mouth. I feel as if I've the worst hangover ever. My head is banging, I'm beyond dehydrated and like every terrible hangover there's that sinking feeling which is realised once I wake further. Remembering the drama in Milan, I'm unable to control myself and projectile vomit all over the place. I begin to cry uncontrollably, so much so that the nurse seems unsure what to do. Reaching for some water, she asks what seem like two-hundred questions. "Look, please can you stop with the questions! I took some Xanax and had a few drinks. It's not a big deal, I'm alive and I'm sorry for wasting your time," I say, trying to crack a smile, although crying maniacally.

"Are you a nervous flyer? Can I call anyone for you?" she asks as she holds my hand.

"No, I'm not scared of flying, never have been. I am scared of life. I am scared of everything the future holds," I say, sounding slightly crazy and removing my hand from hers. Once I've had chance to sip some dreadful coffee and splash some cold water on my face I'm allowed leave. After what feels like an ordeal, I finally find myself in the back of a Range Rover whirling towards the Mercer Hotel in SoHo. Usually I would be super excited to be in one of my favourite cities, but all I want to do is climb into bed and sleep for days. Suddenly my phone signal kicks in and it beeps as a string of text and WhatsApp messages come through. Flicking through them I stop when I see Marco's name. 'Everything will be OK. I've told her everything and it's over. Truly over, I swear. I'm free and all I want is to be with you. Do you still want to be with me? Should I pack for New York? X'. I read the message like twenty times, and each time I'm shocked. As the jeep inches its way through the Manhattan afternoon traffic, I'm silent.

I sit looking up at the skyline, then at the phone. I call his number and although it only calls two or three times, it feels like eternity until he picks up. "Ciao baby," he says in his usual sexy tone, although he does sound nervous. "I am so happy to hear from you. Cesare tells me you left town for New York. Do you think I should follow you?" he asks quickly, sounding very unsure of my answer.

I pause and then simply let my heart do the talking. "Yes, come… I will be waiting at the Mercer. If you hurry we could have late dinner." And just like that, life is about to reboot and start over. But before that, I think it's only fair to let you know just how I met Marco. So I'm going to take you back to where the whole thing began…

Chapter 2

September 17th 2007, London Fashion Week, Claridge's Hotel for Luella

"Darling, she's had so much work her face is like a balloon, so don't expect to see her at any of the shows this season. Plus, she's no longer living with him in Cadogan Square, kicked her out weeks ago and changed the locks apparently. He even took the Aston back! She may be spotted riding the 22 any day now, can you imagine!" Paolo whispers excitedly.

"Who?" I ask, squeezing through the crowded ballroom of the famed London hotel. The thing about Paolo is that he expects everyone, including me, to understand what he's talking about without as much as an explanation. Having grown up in a world where people never say no and hang on his every word, he gets ever so irate when things don't go his way.

"Oh Dio, you're really not listening to me are you? I've been talking but you're not listening and that makes me so mad. Plus, it also means that you've missed out on the hottest gossip of LFW, so good luck making small talk at the après show!" he jokes in his most bitchy voice.

He's right, I'm not listening, as I'm miles away, due to the fact that I'm still reeling from last night's string of parties and an introduction to an Italian guy called Marco, who I don't mind telling you is playing heavy on my mind. I've tried not to think about him, but he just creeps back in. "Hey, did you meet Marco last night?" I ask casually.

"I met fifty thousand people last night, bello! Marco who?" he quips as he checks himself in his pocket mirror. I kid you not, he actually carries a Dior pocket mirror with him at all times, and I love him for it.

"That guy at the gallery party. Good looking, I guess, wearing a Dsquared2 t-shirt… Italian, I'd say early forties…" As I remember him I feel excited, even though we'd only spoken for about ten minutes. I was sure he was flirting with me; it was all in the eye contact.

"Oh, I know Marco, everyone knows Marco! He's from Milan, but lives in Rome with the witch that is Alessandra. Super social, but I've heard that their marriage is not so rock solid," he says almost gleefully. As usual he's right and it's true, they're so super social, that everyone seems to know everything there is to know about them and everyone seems to have an opinion. The fact that his marriage is a hot topic of gossip really pisses Marco off, while Alessandra, well, she dines out on it. Plus, when you post every last detail of your life to social media, it's rather like trying to keep a secret at Le 55 in July. "He's quite good friends with the Caten twins so the t-shirt was probably a freebie!" he laughs as he grabs two snipes of champagne from a passing waiter.

Making our way to our seats, it feels as if we're at a nightclub, rather than a fashion show. A club that's rammed with everyone from Poppy Delevigne to Plum Sykes, Erin O'Connor, Melissa Odabash, Lapo Elkann and beyond.

"Hey Oliver! Can I get a shot of you guys for Vogue Diary?" asks a photographer.

"Who are you wearing?" an emaciated girl wearing oversized 'nerd' glasses and sporting a sharp edgy bob asks.

"Surely if you work at *Vogue*, you should be able to tell me, darling!" Paolo says cheekily, as she scribbles things into a notebook. "It's all Saint-Laurent, oh, and the shoes are Tom Ford."

I'm doing my best to sound disinterested. That's the thing with fashion folk, they all pretend to be super bored by everything and everyone, as if being unimpressed is a barometer of cool. In fact, the more pissed off you look or sound, the more in demand you become – sad but true. "It's all Comme Des Garçons and it's all next season and my surname has a double Z, can you try to get it right? I mean, one of the most important families in Europe!" squeals Paolo as he turns to be photographed by another photographer.

I always find it funny the way he speaks to the press. I guess he has the goods to back up his attitude, but still. My fashion attitude, while perfect, is mainly attributed to the fact that I'm really out of it, as the night before was pretty wild. Myself and my other half

Sophia had been to about seven parties in as many hours, finally landing at Funky Buddha at about 2am. We'd really painted W1 red and I'm paying for it now.

"So where did you get to after the Buddha? I lost you guys after that champagne spray with those crazy Arab boys," Paolo says. "One of them dropped me home and he thought I'd be impressed by his Rolls. I mean, it was a pretty lame-ass Phantom, so I just had to burst his bubble and tell him I had just taken delivery of one of the first Drophead Coupés in the land. I'm pretty sure he wanted to come in for more than espresso macchiato, but me having a better car killed his boner somewhat, if you know what I mean!" he says, mock flicking his hair in the air and pouting. Paolo thinks that everyone he meets wants to go to bed with him. Personally, I'd say it's more of a 70-30 split in his favour.

"Oh, you're so lucky you escaped. We ended up back at a party in a suite of the Sanderson. Man, that hotel is trashy!" I say, sipping on the straw of my snipe of Pommery POP and spilling it everywhere. "Someone really should make it known that straws and tiny bottles of champagne do not mix!" I hiss as I shake champagne from my hand.

"What? Who had a party and didn't invite me?" he asks, as if he had been NFId to the Oscars.

"Oh, I've no idea to be honest, some guys that Sophia was chatting to. We were so out of it I could have gone to a party in the East End and not known. I think they thought Sophia was up for it until they realised I was her boyfriend. I still have coke in my pocket if you want some?" I say, discretely showing Paolo the bag.

"Oh, yummy! No show is complete without a little dusty baby!" He grabs the bag and publicly snorts a little mountain off his Porsche key, before offering the same to me. "Where is Sophia today, I thought she was joining you?" he asks, wiping his nose.

"Oh, she's going to get her hair done or nails done, or something done, and to do some shopping for the new flat," I say, noticing I've really no idea. Oh yeah, by the way, I'm happily partnered to Sophia. Well when I say happily, I mean that our relationship suits me. Blonde, hot and all of twenty-three, she's the sort of girl that turns heads easily and I know that most of my friends want her. I know that she loves me even without her saying it. The fact that she says it all the time, only makes me feel more distant from her. It's a strange thing when someone you don't love tells you that they love you. It makes you feel guilty or something, I don't know. All I do know is that the more she pushes the issue, the further away I want to run. On paper she is perfect, no really, she is. Stunning, in an English rose sort of way, and smart, with a History of Art degree under her belt, but most importantly she's well-connected, as her father owns a whole lot of land in Gloucestershire and is friends with one or two prominent HRHs. Anyhow, you'll meet her later. I'm just giving you the heads up, in case you're already confused. Right now, the truth is there are only two things on my mind – the fact I need to file copy for my *Sunday Times* piece and Marco, but why is he on my mind so much? It's like a fascination. He's super handsome, sexy and masculine, the complete opposite to the person I'm sharing my bed with.

"Ladies and gentlemen, please can you take your seats. The show will commence in five minutes. Thank you."

The announcement heralds the return of Luella Bartley to London, having shown in New York for the past few seasons. While there's excitement about the show, everyone really wants that all-important invitation to the party later, which naturally we have and naturally we're attending. The show is fast paced and dramatic, or perhaps that's the effects of the bump of coke? Anyhow, after it I call Sophia and arranged to meet her for lunch at Zafferano. "Do you want to join us or are you going to hang around here and find some fun?" I ask, already knowing the answer.

"Oh, you're buying me lunch? Lovely, I'm starving, NOT! I'll join you for a liquid lunch if you insist," Paolo says in a dreadful fake American accent, pulling me by my sleeve through the crowd. "Oh look, it's Stuart Vevers, isn't he divine!" he gushes. Paolo stops for no man, not even Stuart. "Quick, quick, quick, before we get trapped chatting to fashion bores, or worse, those 'friends' of the designer!" he says as he almost sprints for the door, the latter being possibly the most annoying part of any fashion show. You know the sort; they hang around like groupies, except with more attitude and less fun, believing themselves to be part of the actual show. Idiots!

Outside, Paolo's brand-new Porsche 911 is parked on the street, well, on the pavement to be precise. "How do you never get ticketed?" I ask in genuine awe.

"Oh, darling, they don't bother with people like me. I once told this horrible man who was trying to tow my Range in Knightsbridge that he could have it as I had another. Since then, I don't know why, but no more tickets. I think they must have had a chat, or they know my cars by now or something," he says without a hint of irony. As soon as we get in he takes the coke from my pocket and helps himself. If anyone else did that I'd freak out, but not Paolo. We'd met years ago while skiing in Aspen, at a time when he was hanging out with the Hilton sisters. These days it's a time he chooses to forget. We clicked instantly as I loved the fact that he was so upfront and honest. He's openly gay and not short of admirers, due to his good looks, great sense of fun, and immense wealth. On that trip, we became good friends and since then, great friends. "Look, I want to ask you something and don't get angry, OK? What is going on with you and Sophia? I get the feeling things aren't right since you moved in together," he says before gumming some more coke and speeding through an amber traffic light onto Sloane Street, almost hitting an Asian dog walker and his collection of designer hounds in the process.

"Nothing, we're cool. She's just busy with decorating the new place, plus she has a lot on getting ready to start her new job," I say calmly, trying to sound convincing. The truth is very different and myself and Sophia know it. We aren't sleeping together and that isn't the only problem in our messed-up relationship. As for moving in together, it just feels as if I'm moving in with my sister, if I'm honest. The trouble is that I like the way things are and also love Sophia and don't want to hurt her. On top of this, my career in the Irish and UK media is starting to grow, so a pretty blonde girlfriend feels necessary. All so stupid really, I mean come on, how many 'socialites' do you know that are straight men?

Sophia is in theory the perfect match for me, as she's good looking, smart, social and posh. Having met at a shooting weekend in Hampshire a year ago, we instantly hit it off and have become regulars in the gossip pages on both sides of the water. I've met her family and she's met mine. In fact, most of our friends believe that we're destined to marry, and it's been joked that it will be the wedding to end all weddings if it happens, as our stamina for partying is pretty impressive. She works in PR for one of Chelsea's most happening galleries and her career is just about to rocket. Her work means that she understands my world and doesn't judge it. Trust me, a partner that doesn't judge you for being a socialite is hard to find. After long busy weeks in London, at weekends we usually escape the city and head to her parents' fantastic house in Gloucestershire, where we horse ride in the morning and lunch at great country pubs such as the Gloucester Old Spot. Lunch easily becomes supper, with many of Sophia's childhood friends gathered. Other times we escape to Paris, where she insists we'll retire. She's effortlessly chic at every occasion, even when she wears one of my old Thomas Pink shirts as a nightshirt around the flat early in the morning. You know that time when you wake up and haven't allowed cosmetics or mirrors to change how you look. She looks great then, but sadly not great enough. I've often wondered why she stays with me, as without sex, aren't we just good friends? Yeah, we mess about and of course we seal the deal from time to time, but I've used every excuse in the book; from being tired to being drunk or having taken too much coke. Seriously, who isn't horny after too much coke? Anyhow, she wants to stay with me and while I love her greatly it could only ever be as a friend. Honestly it scares me, as I know that this world I've built up could come crumbling down at any minute, and apart from that, it disguises the real me from the media, so yes, I'm happy. Happy in a way that's hard to describe, but I guess I just enjoy going through the motions of being in a relationship, even if it is flawed.

As Paolo parks on Lowndes Square he hides as low down in his seat as he possibly can. "What the fuck are you doing? Mind that Land Rover!" I urge.

"Forget that old jeep thing, look over there! Getting out of that BMW. It's Lady Vic Hervey! I thought she was supposed to be living in LA these days? My god, she hounds me! You know that she was the last of the 'It' girls, right? She was supposed to replace darling Tara PT. Pretty lame replacement if you ask me," he says as he continues to park, barely peeking out over the steering wheel. "I mean, does she not know I'm a homo? Everyone knows I'm homo… Do you know her? Can you tell her I'm a big Dior-wearing homo?" He screeches with laughter while pulling himself back up in his seat. I do of course know Lady V and I like her. However, I feel it best to pretend that I haven't met her, just in case he goes into a tail spin.

Arriving at lunch, we're almost thirty-five minutes late and Sophia is already sitting at a table with some girls she knows from the Chelsea circuit. "Hi baby, and darling Paolo! Such fun, I didn't realise you were joining us. You know Bella, Vicks, and Milly, right?"

she asks as she half introduces us to her all blonde, all beautiful pals. "I won't be long darling, just catching up on some essential goss!" she says, sounding overly excited.

Once we sit, Paolo orders a Rossini for him and a Bellini for me. "I just think it felt right. You're peachy and I'm tarty, ha ha. Salute!" he smiles cheekily. "Oh, mio dio, bella Sophia, you look radiant! Balenciaga, right? Take a seat, what's the word on the Chelsea streets?" he asks as he air kisses her three times before leaning in close for the gossip.

Over lunch Sophia is distracted. I can tell that something is troubling her, and I know she's unhappy that Paolo has joined us. "Are you OK, darling? You seem, I don't know… distant," I ask sounding genuinely concerned.

"Oh yah, I'm OK, but I'm going to head home tonight to see Daddy. Mummy called this morning to say he isn't feeling too great, so I think perhaps I'll pop by Berry Bros and grab something fabulous to cheer him up," she says, sounding hopeful.

"Oh, it's just that I'm expected at that…" Before I can finish she cuts across me. "I know, darling, but you're expected at the Christopher Kane party. You go, it will be fun and you really should cover it for the paper, no?" she says, making it sound like her word on the subject is final.

"Anyhow, I'll look after him for you, Sophs. We may meet our new friend Marco later. I'm pretty sure he is going to Chris's party too," Paolo says with a smirk.

"OK, well if you're sure you can trust Paolo not to

lead me astray, I'll stay here safe in SW1 as you tackle the M25." I kiss her hand.

"Just try to behave, Oli, it's bad enough that I have Daddy to worry about!" Despite being a good few years younger than me, she can behave as if she's my mother. Perhaps she's just being sweet, but I see it as a very non-sexual sort of caring. The sort that would turn me off, even if I had previously been turned on. "Anyhow, I better leave you boys to it, if I am to beat the rush hour traffic," she says as she wraps her tiny frame in a huge pink pashmina. I watch as she leaves the restaurant, stopping to say goodbye to her friends. All eyes are on her, male and female. She certainly has it, and how I wish I could make it work.

"Shall we order another?" Paolo says, waving his almost empty wine glass in front of me. After a few bottles of Pignolo and very little food, we walk across the street to the Blue Bar at the Berkeley Hotel. We set about making plans for the evening over a blood orange martini and a few lines of Columbia's finest. "You really are on party mode lately, bello, and long let it remain," he says, removing a huge slice of orange from his glass. The fact is I've been partying way too much, so much so that I've been pulled up by my editor over a recent TV interview I did for ITV on which I apparently 'appeared dazed and confused'. Not exactly how I wanted to come across, especially given the subject of the interview being floral prints for men – good thing/bad thing? I know that my drug taking and non-stop partying is getting out of control, but it seems that everyone else I know is in the same boat and I'm not ready to walk the plank just yet.

As myself and Sophie's flat is still unfurnished we're

staying nearby at Sloane Gardens for a few weeks. Walking home along Sloane Street, I stare into the windows of Gucci, Louis Vuitton, and Bottega Veneta, admiring their displays, which really are pretty cool during Fashion Week. I'm in a world of my own and strangely feeling free, fuelled on Martini, cocaine, and the prospect of the night ahead. The fact that Sophia has left town makes me feel that I can really let loose and allow Paolo to lead the way from party to party.

Before going home to change, I stop off at The Oriel on Sloane Square to get an espresso and to take five minutes in order to reply to the zillion emails that have come through during the day. *Boring, boring, boring,* I think as I scroll through endless party e-vites and press releases, then there it is… an email from Marco. How had he found my address, and more importantly what was he saying? As I click on the screen to open the message my stomach flips and I've a mixture of both giddiness and panic at the same time. 'Hey, this is Marco! We met at the V&A party last night. You liked my glasses – thanks again ☺ I'm just wondering what you are doing tonight? I am going to the party at Bungalow 8, are you? Would you like to have something to eat after it? I don't have your number so here is mine. Call me if you like and I will book somewhere fun. Ciao'

I sit holding an empty espresso cup reading the message over and over. Rather than call him, I decide to reply via email. Possibly not the most flirtatious method but one that feels safe.

'Hi Marco, yes of course I remember you. I hope you had a good night after we met. We went on to a few parties and a club. I am going to be at

Christopher's party later with my friend Paolo – you guys know each other I've been told?! Anyhow I have no plans after the party so who knows… Who is going to dinner and where?'

I hit send and then order a martini. Well come on, I need it for my nerves! Before the waiter has time to bring my drink, the phone vibrates on the table with a reply.

'Hey again, well for dinner I was thinking maybe just us, as in you & me ☺ if that's ok with you? Yes I know Paolo he is fun but maybe best if we don't invite him to join us LOL So are we going to communicate by email only or may I have your number?'

I really don't know what to do. I'm excited and yes, I want to go to dinner, but once I do I know it won't be the end of the story. I know that Marco has my full attention and that's dangerous. Without thinking too much I reply with a simple message: 'See you at the party and we'll talk then.' Oh, and I send him my number. I know, but what the hell!

I walk across Sloane Square and look at the evening commuters rushing for the Tube. I look at young couples greeting each other with long kisses and bunches of flowers. I look at my watch and realise I don't really have much time as it's now almost six-thirty and I'm meeting Paolo at seven. Once home I shower, play Dimitri from Paris at full whack, and empty my entire wardrobe onto the floor in an attempt to find the right outfit for both the party and dinner. Yes, of course I'm going to accept his invitation. After two lines of coke and five changes of shirt I settle on a classic option; white Gucci shirt, black Dior smoking jacket, jeans and

Chelsea boots.

"You look great. I love the jacket," I say as Paolo makes an entrance at Claridge's Bar. Paolo never dresses down; even if he's going to get cappuccino in the morning he sees it as a chance to shine. Tonight, he's wearing vintage Versace and boy oh boy does he shine, like a diamond.

"So we show face at Luella's and then what's the plan for later?" He's air-kissing me and waving his hand at the barman. The fact the barman is very aware of his presence goes completely over his head. "May I have a Pimm's Royale? Actually, make that two. You'll join me in some Royale, I'm sure of it," he says, laughing and pulling a silly face. "If I am completely honest, I'm missing my royal terribly. He's not back in Europe for another three whole weeks and all I get are lame text messages each night when I am sleeping and he is partying in LA!" He sips on his cocktail.

Paolo's not one for settling down and at twenty-seven he's known to be a player. He met his match at the Cartier Polo last summer when he was introduced to his secret royal. His royal isn't in fact royal, well at least not anymore, as he's linked somehow to the now defunct Italian House of Savoy. What his link is unclear, but Paolo assures me that his blood is blue. Anyhow, to Paolo he's a king and that secures his self-suspicions of him really being a queen. They're a great couple, although much to Paolo's anger their relationship isn't common knowledge as such. It's one of those secrets that certain people know about but never speak of. Weekends at Paolo's family home in Florence or hiding away at Skibo Castle in the

Highlands are as good as it gets. While Paolo longs for PDAs, and an 'at home' feature in *Vogue Italia*, his royal is more low-key and guarded. Funny really, as Paolo's wealth and social standing far outweighs that of his laid-off HRH. A few months ago they were photographed together for *Paris Match*, just a social shot at some drinks party or another, and the royal went crazy. Paolo was hurt by his reaction, I could tell, but he claimed that he wasn't happy either, as it was a 'dreadful photo'.

"Oh, by the way, I got an email from that guy Marco," I say so casually you'd think I'm ordering bar snacks.

To my surprise Paolo's reply is equally flat. "Oh, what does he want?" he says without looking up from his phone.

"Dinner! He wants to buy me dinner, tonight after the party."

Paolo looks up from his phone and stares me in the eyes. "Seriously, just dinner? Why would he want to buy you dinner? I'm coming with you. I mean come on, that's just weird." He sounds needy.

"Eh, no you're not. Maybe he wants to talk business or something, and anyhow he hasn't invited you, just me." I'm trying to make light of the situation, before Paolo invites himself along for the ride. People like Paolo get everything they want in life so sometimes it's better not to show them what you've got or at least play it down. "Anyhow, I may not even go. I'll see how I feel later as I am kind of tired," I say as I play with a bowl of olives which have been placed in front of me.

"Oh whatever, bello, whatever." He looks genuinely pissed off. "Let's go say hi to Luella and then check out the Bungalow!" I can clearly see that something has upset the queen and if it's my dinner plans, well then I'm more determined to go than ever.

The party is everything we expected it to be – wonderful, just like Luella herself. "Hey Oliver! Thanks for coming," she beams as we greet each other.

"It's my complete pleasure to be here. I adored your show earlier, so great to have you back on this side of the pond and let's face it, this looks like one hell of a party!" I sound ever so slightly sickening. That's the other thing about the fashion scene; everyone is super nice face to face. I mean completely over-the-top nice, which in another situation would be comical. However, I've never really bought into that whole 'once you turn your back they attack you' bullshit, or perhaps I just don't want to believe it. We work the room and enjoy the scene but we know the real fun is happening over at the yet-to-be-opened Bungalow 8 at St Martin's Lane Hotel. There to greet us is the ever-fabulous Amy Sacco, who in case you live under a rock is the only person you need to know in Manhattan when it comes to nightlife.

The place is hopping as we make our way inside; we chat with Henry Holland and Gareth Pugh, who are as usual surrounded by adoring models, including girl of the moment Agyness Deyn. A man in demand, Gareth's just arrived from DJing at Browns for the launch of Camilla Morton's book and is on form. Amy plies us with champagne cocktails and we get lost in the mood. "This really is the only place to escape the fashion week mayhem," Paolo shouts over the pumping 1980s soundtrack, as we stop to chat with Jefferson Hack and Virginia Bates. Escape it? I feel as if we've been transported to its epicentre. While I'm chatting with our host Christopher, who's wearing one of his own creations – an enviable Swarovski-studded vest – I spot Paolo vanishing into a corner to chat with the ubiquitous Hamish Bowles. Seriously I'm sure he's been cloned; how can one man be at so many parties? The place feels edgy, with a heavy New York vibe. Dimmed lighting and black and white striped walls make a strong contrast to the guests, all of whom are dressed in black. Within the first six weeks of opening the club hosts George Clooney, Matt Damon, Prince, the Geldof sisters, Mark Ronson, Kimberly Stewart and so on.

We inch our way through the crowd and as Paolo's chatting with Sophie Dahl about the launch of her first novel, or something, I stand momentarily alone. "I see you're great at the game of smiling and styling…" a voice says into my ear from behind me. It's Marco, who smiles broadly as I turn to say hello, his teeth brilliantly white in the nightclub lighting.

"Oh, wow, hi, how are you? You gave me a shock," I say as I feel my face redden. What the fuck is going on? I feel giddy again and suddenly very warm, like I need to escape for some fresh air.

"A good shock, I hope?" He's still smiling. Dressed in a fitted midnight blue shirt and tuxedo pants, he looks even hotter than I'd remembered. "I'm going to head out for a cigarette, will you join me?" He's offering me one of his Marlboros.

"Yeah OK, I'll go with you, if only to get some air. Isn't it warm in here?" I say, realising I sound slightly rude. On the street the air is cool, like those first few days of autumn when you can just about feel the seasons change.

"So, have you decided if you want to break bread with me tonight?" he asks as he lights my cigarette.

Before I can answer, Paolo appears out of nowhere, as if he's suspended from me by elastic band, springing to my side. Suddenly there he is in between us requesting Marco lights his cigarette too. "What are you two boys plotting?" he asks in a sarcastic tone.

"Oh, we are just talking about how great the party is." I blow smoke into his face.

"Eh, actually I am trying to convince Oliver to join me for dinner, but he hasn't given me an answer yet…" Marco stares into my eyes. Just by looking at me, he sends waves of excitement through me, like nobody has ever done before.

"Oh, I'll go with you, baby. We don't need to bring Oli along if he isn't in the mood." Paolo's linking Marco's arm.

"Actually, I'm still standing here and if you'd allow me to speak, I was about to ask where we're having dinner?" I ask calmly, as I can feel the situation becoming weird.

"Well I was thinking of something old school. Do you like Montpeliano?" He reaches for his phone.

"You're in luck, I love it and I am rather hungry."

"Oh great, I'll round up some others and we will make a night of it!" Paolo squeals in excitement.

"Well, I wanted to spend some time alone with

Oliver if that's OK with you?" His tone doesn't require an answer.

"I'm not sure if you're talking to me or Paolo, but it's fine with me," I say before Paolo can answer. Yes, I realise that perhaps I sound over eager, but what the hell? I'd enough champagne and not enough food to make myself go for it.

As we drive to dinner Marco's so typically Italian; he drives a Maserati, he's dressed perfectly and he's loud, but not in a crass way. "Maybe I'll park the car at home and we can walk to the restaurant. That way I can have wine with you and some fun, what you think?" he asks with a wink. A wink that sent shivers through me again.

"Oh, I do hope you're not trying to get me drunk." I'm sounding like a fool.

"Are you sure? I thought maybe you would like us to get drunk…" He's sounding confident. The fact is I'm already slightly drunk and fear that if I have any more wine I will be drunk and noticeably so. Where is Paolo with his party favours when you need him? We park the car outside an impressive townhouse on Sterling Street, and before we get out, Marco reaches into the glove box, sprays a little Acqua di Parma and fixes his already perfect black hair in the mirror. Interestingly we both use the same fragrance. I'd once been told that if someone uses the same cologne as you they're not the right match. However, I think I was told that by some crazy in a club at 4am, so it doesn't really count.

As we walk along Montepelier Place towards the restaurant, I feel relaxed. Even though we don't know each other, I feel as if I can be myself. A nice change from living the usual lie of myself and Sophie's dream romance, twenty-four-seven. "It's nice to finally be alone with you. I wasn't sure if you would want to join me for dinner," he says, sounding almost shy.

"Why wouldn't I join you? I am interested to hear why you invited me. Is this a business meeting or less formal?" I ask, sounding both stupid and insecure.

"Well I just thought we could get to know each other outside of the party scene. If that's cool with you, Mister Socialite?" Every time he speaks I feel giddy, like a teenager meeting his crush.

"Buonasera, Marco! Fantastic to see you!" exclaims Antonio, the ever-affable owner of the famed Knightsbridge eatery.

"I've been coming here for years and each time he makes me feel super welcome," Marco says as we're ushered to our table in the corner of the dining room.

"Now to get things going, how about some champagne?" Antonio asks as he places two chilled glasses of Veuve Clicquot in front of us.

"Cento anni, cheers to us!" Marco raises his glass.

"Yes, to us!" I say shyly. As we sip the champagne our eyes remain locked on each other. It's just for a few seconds but there it is, that spark. That feeling that this isn't just a casual dinner.

"So yourself and Sophia are moving into your new home next week, right? Very good address, bello." He sounds impressed.

"How do you know where we will live?" I ask.

"Chester Square, am I right? I can't remember

where I heard this, but am I right?" he says, sounding like a detective. The fact that he knows where we are going to live is slightly strange, but at the same time it shows he has an interest in me. Besides, the news has already made Richard Kay's diary in the *Daily Mail*, twice in the past month.

"Yes, we found a great flat on Chester Square which will be fantastic when it's finished," I try to convince myself.

"It's a fantastic area – only the best for the best," he flirts openly. As he flirts he remains somewhat mysterious. "So will you marry her? She seems like a great girl and she's crazy about you, I can see it. In fact, I think many people are crazy about you, no?"

I'm blushing. "They are? Like who?" I laugh.

"Well I see how people want to be around you constantly. I see how some of them look at you." He now sounds slightly strange. Why is he talking like this? My mind is racing, but before I can speak, he does. "You know we met before, right? About three years ago at Paula and David's party in Firenze. You were there with a handsome black guy from New York. Do you remember?" he asks hopefully.

"Eh, I do remember the party and the guy you talk about is Charles, he works with Ralph Lauren. I don't remember meeting you though, are you sure?" I ask, although clearly we met or how would he have so much detail?

"Yes, I am very sure. I even tried to get your phone number but nobody seemed to have it or at least they weren't giving it to me. You know, since we met I think of you a lot too!" He's looking straight into my eyes.

"You do? Why? Should I be scared?" I ask, trying to make light of the situation which is kind of getting heavy and we haven't even ordered food. The fact that he couldn't get my number I do believe, as my close circle are very protective and they clearly knew that if myself and Marco got to know each other it would only lead one way.

The waiter takes our order, smiles and as he leaves the table Marco leans in closer. "I am not sure why I am thinking so much of you but I am. You're in my head since the party at V&A and no, you shouldn't be scared. I'm not a monster, just a simple guy from Italy," he says in a lame attempt to sound humble. It's the strangest feeling, as he's married and he knows I'm in a relationship with Sophia. "Look, I am going to say this and if I am wrong please forgive me, OK?" He sounds very serious. "I like you. I find you very attractive in many ways."

Now I'm seriously blushing beyond control and while I'm flattered, I'm more shocked. While I know what's happening, I can't quite believe it. This perfect guy is hitting on me and I feel as if I'm dreaming. After years of relationships that hadn't excited me, suddenly I'm seeing real life for the very first time. As we sit staring at each other, the waiter places two simple, but very good spaghetti alle vongole, before topping off our wine. He's only there for a moment but following Marco's honesty it feels like an eternity. "OK, well I think I better be honest with you too. I like you, but I am with Sophia and it just can't happen. Also, Paolo told me that you're married! Are you saying you want us to be friends? Or something a whole lot more?"

So, having waited all my life for a moment like this, now rather than go with it, I'm questioning it and putting up barriers. I think at this point I must be clear with you. I've had one or two fun moments with guys but nothing serious. Yes, a few crushes and one or two fun encounters, but what's happening now is very different. This feels very serious and I know that if anything happens between us, life will change forever. "Dio, Paolo is such a gossip! My marriage is a mess, Oli, we're living together for social reasons and also divorces can be very expensive as you know." He's now sounding pissed off. "The fact is, myself and Alessandra haven't shared a bed in nearly three years and she has a life of her own, keeping herself busy with a string of lovers and I am fine with it, as I really don't care about her the way I should. So, if my marriage is a reason for us not to be good friends, then that excuse no longer works. What do you say to a drink back at my place?" he asks before gesturing to the waiter for the bill. He's good. He has the answers and more importantly he has the moves. As he pays the bill I sit looking at him – masculine, well-mannered and boy oh boy is he hot! Within the few minutes I have while he chats with Antonio about Italian politics, I'm smiling. I think of how good life could be by just being honest and not lying anymore. Life with Sophia is good, but why settle for good when life can be great? I don't want to get all philosophical on you, but I believe that those who choose not to be themselves and who live a lie are the saddest people of all. So many guys I know, young and old, follow what they believe to be tradition and marry a woman that they love on some level but not fully. So many of these guys seek out affairs with other men. If you don't believe me, check the dating sites! Anyhow, I certainly don't want to be one of those guys. This is my chance for real happiness and even if it's just a fleeting thing, it's now or never…

Chapter 3

Sterling Street, London

Arriving at Marco's townhouse, I feel as if I'm floating on air. Perhaps it's the wine, or perhaps exhaustion from my hectic schedule over the past few weeks. Whatever it is, I feel like a giddy teenager on his first high. Once inside he shows me into a vast drawing room and insists that I select some music while he goes in search of someone to help with drinks. As I try to figure out the workings of his Bang & Olufsen system, I stand silently pressing every possible button on the remote control, hoping not to break it, as I do most things technical. I can hear him talking to someone in the hallway, before returning with a wide smile and a bottle of Dom Perignon in hand. "Everything OK, my man?" He's doing a little dance to Amy Winehouse's Back to Black which has somehow magically started playing.

"You know, I don't think I've ever been better!" I'm sounding borderline cheesy.

"That is exactly what I want to hear today and always, bello." He hands me a chilled Baccarat glass. "I've let the staff go for the evening so we are home alone, well apart from Magda, who lives here, but she won't come knocking," he says with a wink. I'm beginning to feel like we're up to something naughty, but all we're doing is enjoying a great glass of '85. I stand admiring an amazing red Rothko which hangs at one end of the room and forces your eyes to adore it. "You like Rothko, baby?" he asks, now standing right over my shoulder.

"Yes I do. It would be kind of hard not to love it; it's so strong, so important." Realising how pompous I sound, I cringe inwardly.

"Just like you, Oli, you are a living Rothko!" He's now standing very close behind me. As Amy sings, he pulls me closer and we move slowly together. "You know, for a long time I've thought that I wanted to meet someone like you. Really, for such a long time… But now I see I didn't want to meet someone like you. It had to be you," he whispers.

I'm seriously ready to faint. This has got to be the most romantic moment of my life, but instead of accepting it as I should, I burst out laughing. "What the fuck? You think I was born yesterday? Champagne, smooth music and even smoother lines… How many guys have you tried this routine on?" I'm laughing out loud.

"None. Believe what you want. I am Italian, I cannot help the way I am and as for the music, well that is all your choice." He sounds slightly wounded, before pulling away and sitting on the overly large sofa. What am I doing? This amazing guy who has been on my mind since our first encounter is now opening up and being honest with me and I'm unable to handle it.

"Look, I'm sorry. I'm just very confused," I place my glass on a Fendi Casa table. "Everything is happening so fast and it feels so right, that it must be wrong." I'm so nervous that I can hear my own breath. "I mean, look at you! You're amazing, perfect in fact. Why would you want to be with me? I am flattered…" I'm rambling and I'm aware of it. Meanwhile Marco sits staring at me with a smile. "Why are you smiling? What's funny about this?" Now I'm sounding pissed off.

"You make me smile. I am smiling because you have real spirit, real passion. You are almost Italian, baby." He stands up and walks towards me. "To hear these words makes me so happy, as I can see you feel it too. You have been on my mind since I spotted you chatting with Paolo and his jet-set pets." He pulls a funny face. "Seriously, I'm not joking. You're special and you are unique. You like to live life and you like those close to you feel special too. I want to be close to you and I want to feel the most special. Is that so wrong?" The fact that I wanted the very same thing is in a way scary.

Having spent most of my life with little problem dating beautiful women, why is it so hard to be the real me? Am I conditioned to only open up and flirt with women? Have all those years pretending finally taken control of my ability to be the real me? "OK, I am going to say it as it is. I am crazy about you, but things are so complicated and it scares me." I'm looking deeply into his eyes. The thing is, I'm really scared. My past is filled with dating women and that's allowed me some freedom, as I never really got hurt. There was no hurt, as there's never really been any true love. The thought of falling for Marco is beyond scary. If I'm already feeling this way how will I feel if things move on? Just then, my phone begins to ring from my jacket pocket on the sofa.

"Do you need to get it?" he asks as he steps out of my way to let me get pass.

"Let me see who it is? It's after 2am so it's probably someone looking for trouble… Yes, exactly, it's Paolo." I reject the call. *He really needs to stop interrupting me at such times,* I think to myself, and switch the phone to silent. "Now, where was I?" I turn back Marco who's changing the music at the far end of the room.

"How about Sade? Too much for you? Too romantic?" he asks with a laugh, before pouring two glasses of cognac.

"She's fantastic as long as she doesn't sing No Ordinary Love. I really don't think I could cope!"

We both burst out laughing as he places the glasses down and grabs me to dance with him. "You know, I was very tempted to play Smooth Operator, but then I couldn't cope."

There it is again, that spark. That moment when you realise you share the same sense of humour. That moment that makes you realise that even after sex there can be true chemistry. The sort that lasts longer than you can control. As we dance, we're silent. I can see our reflection in a large mirror and, I feel safe. My whole life's a whirlwind, but right now even though we were dancing, everything stands still. "One thing I need is time," I whisper. "Time to allow things settle and time to talk to Sophia. She deserves to hear this from me and not the rumour mill."

Just then, Marco turns to face me and kisses me. It's a kiss that makes me feel like I'm suspended in the air. "Sorry, but I took a chance, just in case you were going to make me wait," he smiles. That's it, the beginning. We continue dancing and chatting for three more songs. As Sade sings in the background it's as if I finally understood why her music is so perfect. So romantic. "So, will you stay the night? It's late and…" he asks quietly.

"Yes!" I reply, without hesitation. As we make our way upstairs I notice just how perfectly designed his home is. Plenty of grey on grey, with punches of great art from Lichtenstein to Warhol. Masculine yet impossibly stylish at the same time. Either Alessandra had control over it, or he has Tara Bernerd's private number on speed-dial. As we continue up the stairs the sound system plays on all floors. Stopping on the hallway, Marco stares at me smiling, briefly before we kiss again. This time we don't stop, we kiss passionately like two horny teenagers. We rampage along the long corridor, banging into furniture as we rush to the bedroom. There's no stopping us, not even when a table of silver framed photographs crashes to the floor. Once inside we're in a frenzy, clothes being ripped and that feeling when you're not sure what's happening, but everything feels so good. A feeling that nothing else matters, the house could be on fire and you wouldn't notice. You've had that feeling, right? If not, ditch your partner and go in search of it immediately! We're totally and utterly consumed.

Falling onto the bed, I feel my jeans open and I'm ready to explode. Everything's happening at once, so fast, so intense. I can taste the cognac on his lips and feel my body tremble as he kisses and bites my chest. This is what sex is supposed to feel like. This is what I was born to feel. We explore every inch of each other again and again before passing out. Well, we don't actually sleep, but you know those moments after great sex when you just lie there, smoke a cigarette and talk. Those hours when you're still high, wrapped in each other. The smell of each other merged as one. It seems we talk for hours, until the sun comes up. We talk of how great life can be if we run away and start over. I truly believe that he's been living in a sham marriage for quite a while and he needs rescuing. Alessandra is constantly travelling and spending more and more time in the US. Isn't this the way of every successful marriage? The Woody Allen ideal, allowing both partners space to enjoy the things they need to enjoy. Just not so sure extra-marital gay elicit affairs was part of his plan.

"Do you want to grab a shower before breakfast?" he asks as he reaches for a remote control at the end of the bed. He walks to the bathroom just as Sade comes back on, blasting No Ordinary Love out over the whole house. As I'm beginning to think how cheesy the situation is, he pops his head around the bathroom door and is almost collapsing in laughter. There it is again. The reason why I'm naked in his bed. "Help yourself to anything you want from my wardrobe." He's wrapping his muscular frame in a white robe, before heading downstairs. I stand in the shower for longer than usual, simply because I'm having some sort of out-of-body experience. As I feel the hot water rush over my body, and sense the Molton Brown black pepper shower gel, I can see my life already changing. I can certainly see a future filled with this amazing man – sharing every day and night together. I try to get a grip of the situation and switch off how I feel but it's impossible. I wrap myself in a towel and walk across the hall to his impressive dressing room. If there is one thing I love, it's a man who looks after himself and if this dressing room is anything to go by, he certainly falls into that category. The space is divided into different sections from formal wear to gym gear, rows of Tom Ford suits making way for neatly folded Ballantyne cashmere sweaters in every colour imaginable. Gucci loafers, next to Tod's driving shoes, next to Berluti lace-ups… You've heard of the famed *Vogue* closet, right? Well, this is the real deal in the real world.

After twenty minutes of decision making, I emerge and arrive to breakfast wearing a crisp white Gucci shirt and faded Gucci jeans with bare feet. I question why this already feels so natural, so relaxed. More importantly, I question why I keep questioning everything. "I'd ask how you slept, but I already know that answer, baby." He hands me an espresso. Smiling, I take the cup and look out to the perfectly manicured garden, where a burly-looking chap is pruning some trees and whistling Frank Sinatra's Strangers in the Night.

At the far end of the long kitchen, stands a friendly-looking woman busily arranging flowers. "Good morning sir," she beams.

"Outside is Jim, and Oli this is Magda, she is the glue that holds the house together," he says as he places warm croissants on the table. Madga, who hails from Poland, but calls London home, has worked with Marco for over a decade. She really is the perfect house keeper; in fact, I can see that she's more than that. Marco trusts her totally, so much so that she knows exactly who I am from this very first meeting. I'm telling you I feel so welcome, so relaxed. As we sit sipping coffee and nibbling the flakiest croissants, I don't want to leave. I'm scared that if I do, then we may never have this opportunity again.

"More coffee?" Magda asks as she places a vase full of multi-coloured tulips onto the table, before calling Jim for his break. When she turns her back to make the coffee, Marco leans in and kisses me quickly. It's so silly, but it genuinely feels as if we're two loved-up kids messing about.

"Alright if I come in, sir?" asks the gardener as he starts to remove his mucky boots at the door.

"Ah, Jim, how are you? Everything as it should be in the garden today?" Marco asks as he gestures him to come in. "Oli, this is Jim, and while Magda looks after inside, Jim is king of everything outside!" he smiles.

"Pleasure to meet ya, sir," he says in a deep South London accent, laden with traces of too many Benson & Hedges. "It's a glorious day out there today. It's days like this that make me love me job even more than normal," he laughs, as he heaps some raspberry jam onto a croissant at the counter.

As we sit, staring at each other and sipping coffee, I'm very aware that this fantasy needs to come to an end, remembering that Sophia is probably already close to London. "Actually, I really should be going if that's OK?" I say out of the blue.

"Why? What's happened? Tell me?" Marco asks as he stands up. "You're now regretting our evening?" He's slightly worried.

"No, not at all. It's not that, I just have to go as I must be at a meeting at eleven and I've things to prepare and…" I'm trying to make my appointment with my hairdresser for a trim sound like a meeting with the UN. I knock back the espresso in tequila slammer style and place the cup onto the counter.

"So, do you need a car to bring you home? Magda can arrange it."

While we wait for the driver to show up, there's an awkward feeling, similar to that when you wake up dreadfully hungover in the bed of a 'not so desirable in the light of day' stranger and want to escape but can't. The small talk is shocking. Just hours ago we were wrapped in each other's arms and felt so comfortable, so why now does it feel so strange? Why do I feel so bad? As the driver inches the immaculate BMW 750i through the mid-morning traffic towards Sloane Street, Odyssey Native New Yorker plays on the tiny TV screen in front of me. I listen to my voicemail which is telling me I must delete messages to make room for more. Really? Do I want to allow more people to contact me with demands and requests for appearances and interviews? I begin to play the messages. One from the people at ITV's This Morning show asking if I want to be a guest to review the best of London Fashion Week, another from a catering firm wanting to offer me complimentary catering for my next party, one from my agent in Dublin who is 'just checking in', which we both understand to mean she's worried about my partying getting out of control and not making any money. Then after what feels like another twenty or so nondescript ramblings there's one from Sophia, followed by another. "Where are you, darling? I had an awful night with Daddy, he really isn't doing so good. I'm already home and no sign of you. Switch your phone on and call me. Maybe we can have a lazy day? Maybe a quiet lunch somewhere, just us? Love you." Ignoring her request, I switch the phone off and then suddenly the guilt becomes overwhelming. "Stop the car! Please, stop the car I need to get out here, sorry, I must get out!" I shout, shocking both myself and the driver.

"Sir, is everything OK? Can I help in any way?" he asks, pulling the car to the pavement directly outside Harvey Nichols. "No, I'm fine, I just remembered I must meet someone here. Thanks so much," I reply before hopping out of the still-moving car. Standing on the corner of Knightsbridge and Sloane Street, I feel as if the entire world is whirling by. Saudi princesses rushing to feed their never-ending desire for luxury goods, Japanese tourists photographing everything in sight, a gypsy lady attempting to sell me a sprig of heather, all going on around me while I stand still thinking of the night before. I swear to you I think I'm going to vomit or pass out, or both. That feeling of guilt mixed with the hangover which is slow coming, but definitely rising. It may be approaching eleven, but I need a stiff drink before dealing with Sophia. The guilt really is palpable and despite the longest shower in history I can still smell Marco on my skin. A smell that both excites, and at the same time freaks me out. I hail a black cab and with no plan I ask the driver to drive the short hop to the Grenadier pub on nearby Wilton Row. A journey that can be achieved by foot and one which the cab driver certainly finds amusing.

The Grenadier is an institution, well, at least to me. Set just off Belgrave Square, it's one of the best pubs in London, a place where you can hide out, away from the madness of the real world. I sit at the bar sipping a whiskey and soda and watch as the bar staff get things in order for the lunch-time rush. Listening to them chat and laugh at some news story about celebrity chef Marco Pierre White, I'm somewhat distracted from the chaos that is my life. I try to remain calm and switch my phone back on to call Sophia. "Well, well, well... There you are! I was beginning to think you'd been abducted. Darling, where have you been?" She's relieved to hear from me.

"Oh, you know, here and there, hither and thither. How's your father?" I ask in an attempt to divert from my antics.

"Oh, he's not too good at all, darling. I think he's putting a brave face on things, but he really wasn't himself. He's seeing his doctor today," she says sadly.

"Oh, that's terrible... I'm just so..." I stutter. "Last night was slightly wild. I ended up meeting..."

"You met Charlie and Alex, I know all about it. I can only imagine what you boys got up to. Actually, perhaps best I don't. So where are you now?"

Charlie and Alex? What is she talking about? "How did you know I met the boys?" I wave to the barman for a refill.

"I called Paolo and he said you boys were all out together and you went onward with them as he went home. Why, is it a secret that you don't want me to know about?" She's blissfully unaware of the truth.

"No, not at all. Don't be silly, darling. I am just having a much-needed cure at The Grenadier then I'll be home."

"A cure? Oh, baby you must be in bad shape. Well I'm off to the gym now, how about lunch or are you too frazzled?" she asks.

"Give me half an hour and I'll track you down." I end the call and dial Paolo's number.

"OMG where are you? I'm dying to hear everything! Doesn't matter where you are; tell me, I'm on my way!" Paolo sounds like a silly teenage girl excited to see the next episode of The OC.

"Hang on, why did you tell Sophs I was with Charlie and Alex? What the fuck, man? Why didn't you just…?" Before I can finish he cuts across me.

"Darling, calm down! Do you really think I am so dumb? The boys are in on it, nothing to worry about as they weren't out last night so your story will hold up. Now you can say thank you by buying me lunch and telling me everything." He sounds smug.

"I need to meet Sophs in an hour and I need to get changed first." I'm knocking back the last of my drink. Heading outside, I light a Marlboro and stand looking at the leaves which are beginning to turn from green to amber. Things really are changing, and just like the seasons there's very little I can do about it.

Chapter 4

Sloane Gardens, London

Walking towards our flat, I feel I may faint. Dizzy from the night before and consumed with guilt. The fact that Sophia is waiting for me to whisk her off to lunch and spend the afternoon in loved-up bliss makes my stomach flip. Chain smoking, I stand staring up at the imposing red-brick buildings trying to figure out what to do. Should I come clean and end it right away, or perhaps we have lunch and then let it slip out over coffee? Before I have time to decide, I am somehow already inside. "Hey, I'm home!" I say in an overly happy tone. Perhaps if I'm on such good form, I can disguise my shame. Closing the door behind me, I can smell Sophia's Chanel No.5 wafting from the bedroom. "Soph, where are you?" For some reason I'm acting as if I can't find her, perhaps as part of me doesn't want to. Jardin d'Hiver plays from the drawing room and the smell of two large Diptyque candles lighting on the hall table, make me feel even more ill.

"Oh, hi baby boy! I was beginning to think you got lost," she beams, bouncing along the long hallway to kiss me. "Shit, you look dog rough!" She hands me a Cartier 'Love' necklace to close on her neck. It was a gift I picked up for her months ago in Cannes during the film festival. Then it felt right, today it feels as if it's the world's way of making me feel bad. "So, fun was had? Would you like a glass of wine? There's a pretty good Chablis open," she smiles back at me through the mirror.

"Eh, no I'm all good for wine. Actually, fuck it, go on then." I'm sounding ever so loopy. A rotten mix of a hangover, a comedown, and the worst fear I've ever experienced. Not since I was a kid and given the task of looking after my best friend Jack's cat Blossom for the summer, only for her to be killed by a car, have I felt so sick with guilt. Standing in the doorway to the kitchen, I watch as she pours the wine. Dressed in black cigarette pants and a beige halter, both Joseph if my memory serves me well, she looks radiant.

"Here you go, handsome. I'm not sure if it's chilled enough, but I am sure you'll tell me as always," she laughs. "So where are we lunching? I was thinking maybe Rules? Or what about Wiltons?" She's raising her glass to mine.

"I actually haven't booked anywhere as yet… Why don't you choose, while I grab a shower?" I say before downing the wine in one go.

"Hey, hey, hey, easy tiger! You'll be drunk again before we even leave. OK, go freshen up and I'll call Wiltons. What time is it? I hope they're still serving." She takes full control of the situation.

Standing in the shower, I am instantly thrown back to this morning in Marco's place. The sense of the warm water running over my body, brings me right back to his bathroom. Plus, no matter how much Hermès d'Orange Verte body wash I use I can still smell him on my skin and in my hair. What the fuck is going on? I stop the water and step out. Staring at myself in the mirror, I'm filled with shame. I hate myself. Beyond the bathroom door is a hot girl who really loves me. Why have I been so stupid?

"Baby, I got us a table at Wiltons for two-thirty, so get a move on!" she orders from outside.

Fuck, what am I going to do? Surely I can just forget Marco and pretend it never happened. Yes, let's go to lunch and try get things back on track. I mean, it's not unusual to go offside now and then, is it? "I'll be right out!" Again sounding so cheerful, like bloody Mickey Mouse welcoming guests at Disney World. I dress quickly, in a black fine-knit John Smedley V-neck, grey jeans and suede Gucci loafers.

"OK, let's go – I'm starving!" I announce, emerging from the steamy bathroom. The fact that I can't imagine anything worse than food right now, is easily disguised by my demeanour. The stress is unreal. Only those who are faced with coming out will know what I mean, and get half of how I feel. Those of you who cheat on your partners will get the other half. *How do people cheat on a regular basis?* I ask myself. "You look amazing by the way," I say as I hand her a huge cashmere wrap. "I haven't been to Wiltons in an age, good choice! Perfect spot for a hangover lunch,." I check myself in the mirror.

"Chateaubriand!" we both say simultaneously,

followed by a fit of the giggles. Why, if this feels so right one minute, can it be so wrong the next?

On the street, we hail a black cab and as we drive towards Jermyn Street she's holding my hand, as she types into her iPhone with the other. "Are you happy?" I ask. Honestly, I've no idea why I said it, but it just blurted out. Perhaps it's my guilt or nerves.

"Of course I'm happy. In fact, now that we are going to Wiltons, I don't think I've ever been happier, ever! You really are in a bad way, aren't you? Were you playing cars with the boys last night? Rolls-Royces? Mitsubishis?" she laughs.

"No! Well at least I don't think so, I mean, I'd remember taking ecstasy, wouldn't I?" I sound vague. "It's just that, I sometimes wonder what real happiness is…"

She removes her shades and stares, or maybe glares at me. "Darling, are you sure you're OK? You seem, I don't know, a little frazzled. Are you sure you're going to make it through lunch? We can head back home if you prefer. I can nip to Partridges and fix us a picnic in front of a movie." There it is again, the reason why I should marry her. Always putting me first, even though I'm a selfish prick.

"No, I'm fine, I was just making sure you are too," I lie.

On the street outside the restaurant she grabs me close and kisses me for slightly longer than necessary at two-fifteen in broad daylight. "What was that for?" I pull away.

"Am I not allowed to cheer you up? Besides, after lunch I was thinking we could head home and switch our phones off, if you know what I mean?" She winks.

Inside we're led through to one of the restaurant's more private booths, where I sip a Bullshot while she goes for Taittinger. Sitting here, she's glowing, so much so that I'm pretty sure the other diners must think how perfectly happy we look. "So, Chateaubriand, baby? And perhaps some Native Oysters to start? Oh yum, this was a great idea!" she applauds herself. "So where did you get to last night? Are you going to tell me or is it top-secret boys only stuff?" She's smiling the sort of smile that could mean either of two things. She's truly blissfully happy, or she suspects something.

"Top secret? What are you talking about? I was with the guys, drinking and talking shit until all hours. You know what Charlie's like, especially when he's with Alex, we just lost track of time and it was daylight as we opened another bottle. No big secret. God, what do you think I was up to?" I sound guilty, or maybe that's just how I hear it.

"Relax, baby, now you are making me wonder. You sound like you don't want to talk about it… 'Curiouser and curiouser,' said Alice," she says, making fun of the situation. Fuck, my head is racing.

"Excuse me, a bottle of Pommard Premier Cru and two glasses of champagne, please?" I ask a passing waiter.

"Good choice as always, baby. So, did I tell you that the furniture is ready to be delivered next week? A lovely girl from Nicky Haslam left a message on the machine to let us know. Really, we could be in by the end of next week if we get things in order. All that planning and now it's time to do this, I'm so excited. Imagine the fun of our housewarming. Oh, we must get the invitations printed and..."

I cut right across her. "Look, I think we should cool the jets a bit. I mean, we have the rental for another two months, no?" I can tell by her face that I've ruined the afternoon, if not the year. It's rather like telling a child there's no Father Christmas, only worse.

"But, hang on. I thought you wanted to move in as soon as possible? I thought you felt the same as me? You are the one pushing for it." She places her almost empty champagne glass on the crisp linen tablecloth. Seriously, her eyes look as if they may explode with tears – she looks shell-shocked.

"Calm down, I'm just saying that we should make sure we have everything perfect before moving in. You know, I want it to be perfect from the first day. I hate it when we are still waiting for a sofa or certain art to be delivered. That's all," I say as the waiter presents the wine. Shit, if she reacts this way over the moving-in date, imagine what she would say if I tried to explain last night.

As the waiter pours the wine she sits, staring at me, as if waiting for him to leave so she can say what's on her mind. There's a heavy tension in the air and I'm downing my champagne rapidly. Once he's gone she sits back and places both hands on the table. "Look, I'm going to ask you something and don't freak out, OK? When you asked me if I'm happy, it led me to think that perhaps you're not. What's going on? Is it because Daddy organised the new flat for us? Because if it is, you need to stop thinking that way, he did it as he wants us to be set up. Plus, it's his somewhat belated twenty-first gift to me and what's mine is yours and vice versa, right?" She smiles hopefully. I sit in silence, with sweaty palms. In fact, I can feel beads of sweat forming on my face too.

"Can you excuse me for a moment? I'm not feeling too great, if I'm honest," I say before standing up and walking away from the table. The last three words of my sentence ring in my head. 'If I'm honest', I mean come on! Just before I arrive at the restroom door, I turn back. "I think last night has really taken it out of me. I thought I was going to do something that would be completely unacceptable in Wiltons just then," I joke, in an attempt to make light of the awkward situation.

"So, where were we?" I take a large sip from a glass of water, spilling it as I do so.

"You're a mess today, I think a few days off party mode may be required. Perhaps a few days in the country? How about we go see my parents? They would love to see you." She's reaching across the table to hold my hand. As she does, I need to make a dash to the loo, and this time I almost pass out. I am so sick. Violently ill, like the stuff of horror movies. I swear, it's not the hangover, this is pure guilt and it is palpable. As I stand staring at myself in the mirror I can see more sweat forming on my face and while I know that I'm not really ill, I can't control the way my body is reacting. Washing my hands, I feel my phone vibrating in my jean pocket.

'So, is that it? We had one fantastic night together and you vanish? Not even a text message? Call me you crazy guy x'

An SMS from Marco. I read it three times before switching my phone off. Arriving back to the table, Sophia is chatting to someone on her phone, ending the call before I sit down. "Darling, what is going on? You look dreadful, you really do." Again, she's sounding like my mother.

"You know, I think perhaps we should have gone for the picnic in front of the TV option. Would you mind if we leave?" I already know that she'll say yes.

In a taxi, we sit silently as the traffic is at a standstill. "I think perhaps I should go to bed. Maybe it's flu, or something crappy like that… Seriously, we would be faster walking. Let's get out. Stop the cab, please!" I say, passing the driver a tenner.

"Darling, what the hell is going on? If you're not well, you probably shouldn't be walking," she says in a voice that can only be described as annoying. You know the sort, when someone sounds almost childlike in an attempt to sound caring. Man, that does my head in. I can tell she's losing patience with the situation. As we walk silently along Symons Street, the weirdest thing happens. "Look, there's something I need to tell you. It's not something you're going to like, but I have to tell and I have to do it now." By doing so I shock both of us, so much so, she stops and turns to face me, once again removing her sunglasses. "We shouldn't do this here, let's get back to the flat," I offer.

"No, whatever has ruined my lunch and by the sounds of it my week, I want to hear it right now!" Suddenly her caring and gentle voice is replaced with one of anger. "So come on, Oli, what the fuck is going on?" She's just standing there staring at me.

Her eyes look as if she already knows that it's something terrible. Something huge.

"The thing is... It's... Oh Jesus, to hell with it, I've met someone else." Now it's out there and there's no going back. She just stands staring, motionless. "Are you not going to say anything? Sophs?" Now I'm the one sounding childlike and nervous.

"Are you gay, Oliver? Are you?" Out of nowhere, she asks.

"What the fuck? Where did that come from? Sophs, are you drunk?" I laugh.

"No. No I'm not fucking drunk, but come on, answer my question. Are you fucking gay?" She just stands staring at me. I've no idea what to say, I just stare back. Both of us brimming with tears. Minutes ago we were the 'almost perfect' couple and now I can see that love turning to hate. I can actually see it. It's so strange, fuck, I can almost smell it. "Your face says it all. I cannot believe this is happening to me!" She turns and walks away from me quickly.

"Sophs, what are you doing? Come back. What are you talking about?" I call. While it's possibly the worst way for it to happen, she has figured it out without me having to say a word. I run after her, pulling her by the arm to make her stop. "What the fuck is going on?" I ask, and by doing so bring full attention back on me and the dreaded question.

"Just tell me. I knew this day was going to come, I knew it! Just be a man and bloody tell me!" she says, almost begging. "I don't care who you've met, I really don't. Actually, yes, I do, tell me!" Passers-by stare as she shouts at me. "I've felt it for a while now, the way you are when Paolo is around. The way you're so comfortable with his beyond annoying circle of gay best friends. You can't see it, but you've changed. Jesus, we're hardly even sleeping together these days. Not that our relationship was red hot to start with. Fuck, why have I let this happen?" She's starting to freak out.

"Let's go home and talk, this is not the place," I plead. I swear to you my head is spinning.

"No, I don't want to go home. I need a drink," she snaps.

At The Oriel we sit silently. That truly awkward silence that can be felt by others seated close to us. She fixes her scarf high around her neck, as if it's some form of shield against everything that is about to happen.

Chet Baker Almost Blue plays and around us people laugh, phones ring, and life is normal. I don't think I've ever felt so ill. "Look, I can't sit here like this. Just answer my question. If you have any respect for me, answer the bloody question with a simple yes or no," she demands, making a couple at the next table take notice. I stare into her eyes, knowing in one way that if I come clean now and tell the truth, not only will it crush her, but it will also mean that my life-long secret is out there.

A bottle of Saint-Émilion is delivered to the table, presented and tasted, yet still I'm silent. It feels like one of those really drawn-out break-up scenes in a movie. While part of me wants to say it as it is, something inside is scared to. It's like being a child again, that sort of fear which literally petrifies you.

Either way, I am forced to say something. Gay, straight, bi whatever, she has the right to know what is going on. I lean in across the table and try to grab her hand. She pulls away. "Yes, and I am so, so sorry," I whisper. "Sophia, look at me please. This has been killing me. I've wanted to tell you so many times, but…"

She drinks a glass of wine in one go. "I want you out of the flat by tomorrow, do you understand?" She looks and sounds different to ever before – like a stranger. "I have to get out of here, I think I may be sick. Bella hinted at it a few weeks ago and I laughed it off. My best friend could see it, but I couldn't. Or perhaps I didn't want to." She stands up and before she walks away, she turns to me. "You've hurt me like nobody ever before and I will never forgive you, Oli." While she looks strong, I can hear her voice quiver and behind her sunglasses I sense tears. Then just like that, she's gone, leaving me alone at the table. I can feel the couple at the next table stare at me. Nina Simone Mood Indigo starts to play. Jesus, I can't even tell you how I feel, as I don't even know. What the fuck is going on? What has just happened? Jesus, who will she tell? I haven't even told my family, although my brother Alex has always joked about it, but I don't think even he truly expects to hear it. Then of course my mother will need to be told, and the fucking media. Shit! Without realising it, once again I am being that selfish prick, thinking of myself and the outcome for me. Having just shattered Soph's entire world all I can think of is myself. It's just that this is a double-edged sword, it destroys her world and it certainly shakes the shit out of mine. I down a glass of wine, refill it and reach for my phone to call her, forgetting that it's been switched off for the last hour. As I sit there I feel the eyes of the surrounding tables on me, but I don't care. I pay the bill and start to walk the short distance back to our flat, stopping to light and smoke about ten cigarettes as I do so. It's as if by stalling, things will be easier. I have no idea what to say when I see her.

I switch my phone on, there's another text message from Marco. 'Honestly, I really enjoyed last night, but I understand if you have woken with a changed mind. Let me know either way'

Instead of replying, I call him. "Marco, something terrible has happened. Where are you? Ok, see you there in ten minutes."

Chapter 5

Fifth Floor, Harvey Nichols, London

Stepping out of the lift, I can see Marco sitting at the bar, surrounded by a group of rather out-of-date women. All blonde, certainly not naturally, all tanned, certainly not naturally, and all going to be moving along very soon, certainly. As he stands up to hug me, I feel weirdly safe, just by seeing him. "Why are we meeting here, and who are this lot?" I whisper into his ear as he gestures to the barman for a second glass.

"Tesoro, it's the only place that is safe in SW1, no? I mean, who do we know that would come to a place like this?" He winks as the barman pours me a glass of champagne. "Ladies, I must say farewell as my friend is finally here and we must talk," he says assertively to the gathered female admirers. Quickly looking around, he's right; the bar is busy, but with out-of-towners, tourists and middle-aged European women who look exhausted from too much shopping, as they cling to glasses of champagne as if their life depends on them. You know the sort, they seem to have it all, but in reality all they have is a limitless credit card and a drink problem.

"It's been the worst day of my life. Sophia knows everything, well, almost everything. The part about you and me, well, that's still to be announced," I sigh.

"OK relax, sit down and tell me what happened. Are you hungry, would you like to eat?" I know he's trying to be kind but seriously, fucking food, at a time like this?

"It's all so crazy, I'm so tired and hungover that I'm not really sure what the fuck happened. She asked and I just came out with it, all of it, well, after about half an hour of her begging. Out of nowhere she asked if I was gay! Straight out, I thought I'd misheard." I down a glass of champagne which goes straight to my already spinning head. "Anyhow, hang on, why are we really in here? Do you think we should be skulking around? Who exactly are we hiding from?" I'm sounding freaked out, as he refills my glass.

"Nobody, but please can you try calm down. We are meeting here as I was close by. But do you see anyone you recognise? No, neither do I, so it would be a good spot to, how do you say, skulk in, no?"

My phone is ringing on the bar counter and it's Sophia's father, James. "Oh, fucking hell!" I show the screen to Marco who suggests I answer it.

"Hi James, how are you?" I ask, despite already knowing his answer.

"Sophia has called and is utterly distraught. What the hell is going on? I am going to be at the Savoy in thirty minutes. Meet me at the bar," he instructs before ending the call.

"Oh man, I need another drink." I scan a cocktail list.

"Are you going to go along? I think the person you should be talking to is Sophia, no?" he asks as he places his hand on my leg. I remove it quickly. It's not that I don't want him to touch me; it just feels wrong under the circumstances.

"No, I must go. Anyhow, she has told me to stay away. Can you imagine the conversation I'm going to have with James…? Jesus, would you come with me? You could sit at another table or something?" I'm almost begging.

"Of course, we will go together. I have your back, you know that," he says as he replaces his strong tanned hand back on my leg. Just as we are about to make our way to the hotel, I change my mind. Why am I being summoned by her father? What the fuck has it got to do with him? I mean, I know what's happened is dreadful, but I am not answerable to him on any level.

"No, no let's not go meet him. Can we go to your place? Or perhaps I should go home and get my things… she did say she wants me out by tomorrow." I sound as if Sophia is now someone I used to know. Jesus, it's all such a mess.

In Marco's car, we park directly outside Dolce & Gabbana on Sloane Street. He's strumming the steering wheel with his fingers. "I cannot stand this label anymore. Have you seen the amount of Russians wearing it? It's officially over, we must burn all of our D&G today!" he laughs. He's clearly trying to make me smile but nothing is going to fix this mess.

"Why have we stopped here? Drive around the corner to the flat and I'll pick up my things. I don't have much, apart from clothes, as everything is in storage." I start mentally packing.

"Perhaps you should call ahead to make sure she isn't home? Just a thought…" he smiles.

"She's never there at this time of the day, just let's get this over with!" As he parks the car, I see Sophia hopping into a silver Aston Martin, which speeds past us. "Hang on a minute! What the fuck is she doing with Henry? That was Henry's car!" I spin my head around so fast I almost cause myself an injury. As I try to call Paolo the realisation of what is happening sets in. Henry, who's supposed to be a friend of mine, has been creeping around behind my back, shagging my girlfriend. "She knew all along! Sophia knew I was gay, she had to know. Do you think she knew?" I sound crazy.

"Look, she knew, she didn't know, what difference does it make now?" Paolo answers coldly.

"The difference is she just drove by me with Henry fucking Duchamp. So, hang on, I haven't been shagging her… She's shagging him. I knew he'd been acting strangely." It's as if I'm having my eureka moment.

"Oh, please! So now you are flipping this back to her? So now it's Sophia's fault?" He sounds angry.

"No, not her fault, but if she is seeing Henry then my guilt is, well, it's less. Or at least it should be." I'm trying to convince myself before asking Marco to follow them. "Come on, drive! Let's see where they go. Turn the bloody car around, come on, they're getting away!" I shout, as I end the call. Suddenly the whole situation is flipped. I don't care about what has happened. Now it's about seeing what she has been up to. "It's not as if I care, it's just that there have always been rumours. Paolo was always saying if I'm not shagging her, someone else is," I laugh nervously.

We tail them for ten minutes and then Henry's car vanishes into the underground car park at his place off Pimlico Road. We sit quietly for a few moments. "Well, that's that. They're gone inside, so nothing more we can do," Marco says in a defeated, yet relaxed tone.

"No, hang on." I start calling Henry's phone.

"Hello mate, what's up?" comes his overly plumy voice.

"Henry, where you at? Fancy a quick drink?" It really is like something out of a TV drama.

"No bro, sorry I just arrived at the gym, maybe later?" he lies. I end the call.

"Let's get back to the flat while she's out. I'll get what I can and then… Then, I have no idea?" I say as Marco turns the car three-sixty on the narrow street.

At the flat, everything has changed. I mean, it all looks the same, but it feels very, very different. Although we've lived here for over a month, it never really felt like home, but right now it feels like I am breaking and entering. None of it feels familiar. I walk from room to room, as if in search of a solution to this mess. In the kitchen, an empty bottle and a half empty glass of Chablis sit on the counter top, the drawing room curtains are closed and the air feels heavy. Staring onto the street below, I see Marco standing by his car chatting into his phone. *What have I done?* I think to myself over and over. Yes, I am seriously attracted to him, but it's all so sudden. It's all so crazy. I mean, come on, what now? Pack my bags and say hello to my new gay life, with a flat-pack relationship to put together? While everything seems to be happening in slow motion, strangely I pack my things without even realising. All I take are two bags of clothes and a laptop, the rest can be binned. I don't even know if I want anything at all. I mean, it's just stuff and stuff can be replaced. *Shit, even relationships can be replaced,* I think as I stand in the hallway, staring at the flat for the last time. It's a strange feeling, but even under these circumstances, leaving this rented flat feels final and that makes me sad. Why the fuck am I sad? This is all my own doing, even if it is out of my control.

Closing the door behind me, I burst into tears. I don't mean stupid tears, I mean floodgates. Waiting for the lift to take me out of this nightmare, I feel the heavy tears run over my face and I feel ill. My stomach is churning, but apart from that I feel numb, as if someone has died. Honestly, I feel as if somehow, I've died, or at least a part of me.

"What's happened? Are you OK, bello?" Marco asks as he hugs me close. "What is making you sad? Life will be better now, you will see. Come, let's go back to my place and get you sorted," he says comfortingly.

As we drive I start to feel worse. I feel as if I may faint, throw up or both. "Look, stop the car, stop here!" I shout. Pulling in on the Brompton Road, I am utterly confused.

"What's wrong? Did you forget something? Will I turn back?" he asks.

"Stop! Just stop, OK!" I snarl. "I can't do this! It's not what I want!" I'm in utter meltdown. Suddenly, everything feels too much. Within forty-eight hours my life has been turned upside down. I have no home, no relationship and no idea what to do next. "Why are we going to your place? I mean, it's your place, not mine. I've just walked out of my place and it feels like out of my life too. Marco, what the fuck have I done?" Again, I start to cry. The last thing I want is to cry in front of the guy I've spent the past few days trying to land. I can hear my phone beeping in my overnight bag and can imagine it's Sophia's father ready to attack me further so I leave it.

"Let's go to my place and you can think about what you want to do. Everything is your decision, you must not feel pressure. This is the last thing I want to do to you." He places his hand on mine and starts the engine. At Marco's I stand alone in the kitchen, drink Stolichnaya and check emails, voicemails and text messages. None of them good, especially a confirmation email from British Airways for a flight myself and Sophia are supposed to be taking to LA for her friend's wedding. Everything feels huge, even the smallest things. Closing the laptop, I down the vodka and call Paolo.

"I feel like I should answer my phone with 'previously on the life of Oli'. Sorry for snapping earlier, it's just all so dramatic. What's happening now? Where are you?" He sounds concerned.

"It's a fucking mess, Paolo! I am so lost, no idea what to do. I am literally homeless in London, unless

I stay at Marco's and that just feels strange as it's all so fast," I say in panic.

"Listen to me, you have options. Firstly, darling, calm down. Secondly, where do you want to be right now? Come here to Milan? Stay in London? I can arrange keys to my place for you." I know he's trying to make me see things clearly, but seriously, now I am more confused.

I was having trouble thinking of where to hide, but now I have to think of which country to hide in. "Oh, I've no idea. I mean, I should get out of London, but then the whole reason I am in this is mess is Marco, so should I be running from him too? Plus, I'm due back in Dublin in two days for some TV interview and other work stuff. Maybe I should just head there tonight?" I'm sounding desperate. Before the call ends a second incoming call beeps on the line without showing any caller ID. "Paolo, I have another call, hang on!" I switch lines.

"Is this Oli?" asks an unfamiliar voice in a strong Liverpool accent. "This is Jane Simpson at news-desk of the *Daily Mail*. We're sorry to hear that you've split from Sophia. Is it true that you've already found a new partner? Italian, so the rumour goes..." I end the call and almost drop the phone. I pour another glass of vodka, down it and in panic, call out for Marco.

"What's happened? Are you OK?" he shouts as he makes his way down the stairs.

"The fucking craziest thing just happened! Yes, even crazier than everything else that's happened today." I'm sounding more and more out of control by the minute, as I struggle to light a Marlboro.

"What? What's happened? Breathe, tell me." He's standing in front of me staring into my eyes. Rather than tell him, I reach in to kiss him. We kiss for what feels like forever, until I pull back with a gasp.

"Shit, stop! The fucking papers already know about myself and Sophia. They already know I'm seeing an Italian. They probably already know it's you…" I reach for the vodka again, pouring two glasses.

"What? Say that all again slowly, please. I'm not sure I understand what you said," he asks curiously. Handing him a glass of vodka, I repeat it verbatim, and as I do I see the realisation on his face. "Wait! Who called you? What was their name? What did they say exactly?" he asks slowly, as if speaking to a small child.

"Just what I said, someone, Jane, I think, from the *Daily Mail*. How the fuck does she know? Oh my god, I think I'm going to throw up!" I say, before sprinting through the French doors into the garden and being violently ill. "I am so, so sorry. I think I better just leave… I am so sorry," I say, red-faced, lightheaded and freaked out. As I gather my things, Marco just stares at me. "I need to use your bathroom, to freshen up," I try to smile.

"Wait! What are you talking about? Where are you going?" he asks, sounding almost as desperate as me. "You can't just say what you said and walk out. If this person is going to write something about us, we must stop it before they do so. I don't think you understand how serious this is!" he snaps, as he grabs my arm.

"What the fuck? Let me go!" I pull back. "I don't

know how serious this is? What are you fucking talking about? My sex life is about to get splashed across the papers, in this sordid way, and you say stupid shit like that?" I throw my phone back into the bag and make my way upstairs.

"Oli, stop, please!" he shouts after me, stopping me in my tracks. Well, more honestly, I stop as I realise I have no idea where I'm going or what I'm doing. "We need to think. OK, look at your phone, what number came up when they called? We can call it back and try to reason with them. Or no, hang on… That's too obvious." He pauses.

"There was no number. It came up with ID withheld," I say sadly. "There's no way the papers have word of anything. I mean, come on, how could they? It's only been hours and nobody knows apart from you, me, Paolo, Sophia, her father, and there's no way he would spill the beans. Talk about social suicide!" I say calmly.

"You must remember the journalist's name… Come on, bello, think for fuck's sake!" he rants.

"Jane, Jane, Jane… Simpson! It was Simpson, Jane Simpson!" I sound as if I've cracked some cryptic code.

"Jane Simpson, are you sure? And definitely from the *Daily Mail*, yes?" He is staring into my eyes again. "Ok, so we call the newspaper and ask for this Jane Simpson and see what she has to say. I am not scared of some jumped-up hack, are you?" He hands me his phone.

"Wait! What about Henry? This is such his style…" I'm staring at his name in my phone having scrolled through recent calls.

"What are you talking about?" Marco asks as he plays with fruit in a bowl on the kitchen table. "Henry Duchamp, it has to be. He has every reason to out me and is always chatting with journalists at parties. He is publicity mad and this is a perfect dream." I feel angry, yet relieved that I know what I am dealing with.

"So, I call this Jane person or no?" Marco asks, still looking confused.

"No, no we wait for her to call again and then we…"

He cuts across me before I can finish. "The best thing to do now is deny everything. If you say you have no idea what she is talking about, what can they do? It's all too risky without real proof and it will blow over." He looks so smug, as if he has invented the stiletto. Sadly, having worked within the media, I know what we are dealing with and a paper like the *Mail* won't just roll over and move on.

"No, you're wrong. This story has everything they crave and if they have an insider like Henry feeding them they will know it's true. I need a way to stop him in his tracks. God, I need another vodka, want one?" I ask as I free pour two glasses. As I sip the drink I know there is one person who can help me at a time like this. "Paolo, me again. What do we know about Henry? I mean apart from his polished existence?" I ask, already knowing that Paolo will have something to say. There isn't a person on the scene that he hasn't stored some dirt on and right now I love him for it.

"Oh, darling, with Henry and his lot, I think it's more a case of where to start rather than how to," he laughs. "Well of course his father was caught with those hookers on his jet, but that somehow never made print, if you know what I mean? While his darling mama, well, wasn't she linked to half her friends' husbands? That never made print either," he laughs harder. "Henry, well let's just say Henry's glory days as star pupil at Ampleforth were marred by a slightly less impressive stint selling a mish-mash of drugs at Fabric most weekends. Oh yes, and then there was that hit and run, where he was said to have bragged within hours, about ploughing a poor woman and her young child into a ditch on Christmas morning, having driven at her oncoming Nissan Micra, drunk and at speed in his father's Bentley, before then driving on. The news had made its way from sleepy Hampshire to busy Belgravia, within the hour, but of course that too didn't land in the papers... You see, you have a lot to work with, if needs be. Anything or anyone else you want destroyed today?" he laughs in a bitchy tone.

"I'm sure it's Henry who has leaked the story, trying to out me and place himself as a hero in Sophia's eyes at the same time," I sigh.

"Well, thanks to me, you can now stop the little weasel in his tracks. I must go. Chat later, ciao ciao," he says as he ends the call. Suddenly I am consumed with how to stop Henry on every level.

"Thank God for Paolo, he really is a life saver. I have a plan, but we need someone with a dodgy accent to pull it off," I say calmly. "We need someone, who well, doesn't sound like us. Or, like me anyhow," I laugh, realising Marco sounds very much Italian. "Actually, I know just the man for the job. Do you think Jim would oblige if we made it worth his while?" I ask, pointing to Marco's gardener who is busily sweeping leaves to the front of the house.

Jim is one of those hardworking Londoners, who has a wife, six kids and a mistress, so not much fazes him. Long days are followed by long nights at the Stanley Arms pub, in a place called Bermondsey. Rubbing shoulders with all sorts, Jim was certainly the man for the job, and while his accent may be difficult for most to decipher, he sounds pretty much bang on for a hack, even one from the *Mail*. It always makes me laugh how some of those working at the *Daily Mail* see themselves as non-tabloid and therefore better in some way than those working at say, the *Sun*. As a friend once commented to Nigel Dempster at lunch in Daphne's – "Don't you people see what 'tabloid size' is, or has Rothemere had the *Daily Mail* exempt from such categories?" Luckily Nigel saw the funny side of things.

"Jim, can I ask you the hugest favour?" I say in a voice that can only be described as grovelling.

"Certainly you can, sir. What is it I can do for you?" he asks, wiping his sweaty brow in the sleeve of his Millwall F.C. hoody.

"Well, it's kind of awkward, but there's this guy who is trying to sell a story about me to the *Daily Mail*, and…" I say cautiously.

"Oh, I love this sort of shit, Oli, and yeah, as you've guessed, I may know some people, who know some people." He winks, as he checks that Marco isn't within earshot.

"Oh, oh not that. I mean, what do you mean?" I question.

"I think I've bloomin' well said enough. I'll shut up and you tell me what it is you're after," he laughs.

"Well, I was hoping you could call him pretending to be from, I don't know, the *Sun* or no, better still, the *News of the World*, and say you have information about him and are looking at running the story. You can pretend to be a journalist, can't you?" I smile hopefully.

"So who is this guy, some hooray?" He starts rubbing his hands together.

"Well, he's a spoilt brat, who hails from a family of similar sorts. You know the type, they've never had to work for anything and get away with everything. The funny thing is, his name is Henry!" I laugh.

"Why's that funny?" he looks puzzled.

"Well, you did ask if he was a hooray – hooray by name, hooray by nature." I smile broadly.

"Ha ha, very good, son, very good. So what do you want me to say, and how will this stop him in his tracks?" he asks, as he lights a cigarette.

"Well that part, I am yet to figure out, but he must be stopped as he is planning to out myself and Marco." I sound pathetic.

"You know, I think the best way to do this is the way I thought originally. Not with violence, but with a warning. I can tell him to back down or I'll be going to the press with a story or two of me own." He looks impressed with himself.

"Oooooh, I like it! So you can take your pick of scandals to use, but my favourite is the one about his hit and run with a young mother and her baby…" I fill him in on every little detail regarding the Duchamp family and give him both Henry's number and mine.

"You just consider it done and don't stress yourself over the piece of filth." He pats my shoulder and walks back down the garden. "I'll call you when it's done," he shouts over his shoulder. Returning back inside, I see Marco sitting at the counter staring at his laptop.

"Jim is such a great guy, isn't he?" I smile.

"Baby, I only surround myself with the best. Do you want a drink? Something to eat? I can cook some pasta," he offers.

"You know, I think I am going to head to Dublin tonight. I have to get back for a day or two and I have so much to do before the filming of the TV show starts. Do you mind?" I say sincerely. To be honest, it really does matter what Marco thinks, and while I am pretty sure he isn't too happy with the idea of me doing the show, he knows it's my career and he gets it.

"Bello, you do what you need to do, everything is cool. Besides, I really need to get things in order for a client meeting in Geneva in two days." He reaches out to grab my hand. "We're cool, right? I mean, you're happy with what's happened?" He looks almost nervous.

"Yes, I'm happy. In fact, I think once the dust settles life will be great," I smile.

"Now that Jim is taking care of the stupid media,

let's keep us a secret for a while. What do you think?" He's still holding my hand and I nod in both agreeance and relief. With the TV show about to start filming, the last thing I need right now is this getting out. "So, if I am going to fly tonight, I'm going to need your chauffeur services again, if that's OK?" I ask as I light a cigarette and then stub it out.

"Sure, but when will I see you? Can you come to Switzerland? I will be there for about ten days. We could hide out in a suite at the Four Seasons for days on end." He winks as he clenches my hand tighter.

"Yes, let's do just that. You are an amazing guy, Marco, and even in these few short days I feel closer to you than anyone else before. One thing, can we take it slow and see where we go? After everything that's happened lately, the last thing I need is another mess. In fact, the last thing I need is a mess with you, you are too important to mess up." I lean in to kiss his forehead.

"You know what, to hell with it; let me drive you to the airport. If anyone is worth the hell that is Heathrow traffic it's you!" he smiles, and again I feel like I'm on a cloud.

Approaching the terminal, I get a text message from Jim.

'That's all sorted. Poor little hooray almost crashed his motor when I explained my concerns at his behaviour. You're in the clear son, now you just concentrate on being as good as you can be! Jim.'

As I check in, I have a feeling of relief. Perhaps my real life can finally begin, and boy oh boy, am I ready for it.

Chapter 6

Renards, Dublin

"Seriously, you have to take a hit of this shit, man! Blow your bleedin' head straight off!" screams Kiddo as he pushes a two-euro coin covered in cocaine under my nose for all to see. Kiddo is possibly the most in-demand guy in the club, with everyone wanting to be his friend. He certainly is rough around the edges, but there's a touch of the loveable rogue about him. Good looking in a scary sort of way. Gym fit and sporting a nasty scar on his face which was inflicted by a rival dealer using a Stanley knife, while serving time at Mountjoy Prison. He's tough and rumoured to be very well-connected with all the wrong people, if you follow my meaning. Deep down I think he's a lot less fierce than the image he portrays, like most 'tough guys'. Seven nights a week he does the rounds of the Dublin nightclubs, selling everything from coke to pills and occasionally some puff. Due to his 'business ventures' he's one of the best dressed guys in the city and stores welcome him with open arms most Saturday afternoons when he spends hours, and thousands of euro on Prada, Gucci, Saint-Laurent, and any other labels that suit his mood. Naturally he pays in cash, bags of it.

It's pushing towards 3am and the VIP room of the most famed club in the country is heaving with the bold, the beautiful and the damn right ridiculous of the social scene. As is usually the case in the VIP rooms of most clubs, the DJ pumps out house music to socialites who rub shoulders with shop girls, who date drug dealers and everyone gets along just fine due to free-flowing ecstasy and cocaine. "Holy shit, that stuff is as pure as it gets – unreal!" I say, throwing my head back onto the plush velvet sofa, allowing things to kick in before jumping to my feet in search of some action. After the drama of the last few days, I'm on full party mode and need to let loose. As I push past a group of people I don't recognise they say hi enthusiastically, rather like teenagers waiting to meet their pop idol. Sadly, this lot are just after free drinks and whatever else they can get their mitts on. I am so used to the losers that I encounter night after night, that I appear rude as I blank them. Strangely, my rudeness only further attracts their attention.

Drinks go flying, as myself and two unidentified blonde girls who've crashed our booth take to table and dance to Daft Punk's Around the World. Ice buckets with bottles of Cristal fall one way, while a line of pink-coloured shots go another, spilling over our fellow guests. Do we care? Not one bit. We dance and share a cigarette while trying to remain in an upright position on the tiny table. The place is hopping and the feeling that tonight could be 'the' night is in the air, it's everywhere, you can almost taste it, if only for those of us fortunate enough to be fuelled by Kiddo's endless supply. It's a typical night at the club, in that U2 are holding court at one table, surrounded by female admirers and their usual entourage, while at another, boy band manager Louis Walsh has gathered with a group of young guys, all of whom are looking to be next big thing. Taking over a number of tables is ubiquitous, uber socialite Cindy Cafolla and friends, who are celebrating a friend's birthday, surrounded by a team of good-looking guys and endless rounds of Laurent Perrier Rosé. Then of course there are the girls who spend each night table hopping in search of free champagne, free cocaine and a rich boyfriend or better still, a husband. The sort of girls who look hot in a dark nightclub, but notoriously destroy bed linen with their fake tans and OTT make up.

Most guys who've bedded them woke to quite a shock the following morning when they saw the mess. I once received a text message from a friend of mine which read – 'Help me I think I have woken up on the inside of a wedding cake!' When I asked what he meant he replied – 'Such a mess! Orange sheets, make up all over the pillows and hair extensions everywhere, from the bathroom floor to the bottom of the bed. I repeat HELP!' These girls are in constant demand but remain constantly single as they approach the dreaded age of thirty.

I collapse back into the sofa, down a Jack Daniels and turn to those around me. "Where we heading from here?" ask the group which has rapidly grown larger due to the fact that the club will soon close and everyone is on the hunt for the after-party. That's the thing about being at the centre of the party scene, people always expect you to have an inside track on where to go next, whether it be the next great restaurant, holiday destination or simply a late-night house party. Ever since I became a well-known name I've been torn between two groups of friends – simply Group A and Group B. Group A, or the 'originals' are rich, mostly good-looking and members of some of the most powerful families in the land. Most of whom have been friends of mine for many years and we've shared some great memories. They steer clear of drugs and any sort of embarrassing behaviour, at least publicly, opting instead to enjoy lavish house parties at their parents' country piles. Think long weekends of Pimm's and croquet, rather than long weekends of pills and cocaine, and you get the picture. They remain perfectly relaxed in every social situation, possibly as their lives are mapped and they will go on to run their family empires before retiring gracefully into country life at around forty-five. Then there's Group B, those who work as models, or are associated with the fashion world in some respect. The latter are my new crew. A group that I share very few memories with due to the fact that we are constantly out of our minds on a cocktail of drugs and alcohol. A crew that's drawn together by the fact we're all regulars in the gossip pages simply down to the fact that our constant, if not somewhat twisted on/off dating scenarios make even us confused at times. I think we have all managed to end up in bed together at one point or another over the short period we've been hanging out. It's one of those things that we rarely talk about, mainly as we can't really recall much. Another reason we're friends is that we work together from time to time, on some level. From fashion shoots to TV appearances, it's the same small pool from which the editors and TV producers seek 'characters' to do the do. These are the ones who make it to every store opening, product launch or movie premiere and most nights dance until dawn. These are the ones who fall out of night clubs at 5am on a Tuesday and onward to early houses. Due to licensing laws in Ireland bars are not permitted to sell alcohol outside of the hours of 10am and 11pm unless granted a certain license. The early houses are allowed to open at 7am and despite the fact they're usually dingy, dirty places, for those of us as high as kites they may as well be a five-star hotel. These guys are my best friends at 4am, yet won't even send a text message the following day. Perhaps this is due to the fact that chances are we will re-group the following evening and do it all again. Actually, if anything bad happened to any of us I doubt we would be able to give the police surnames, due to fact we simply don't know them.

The two groups rarely cross for many obvious reasons, but I can feel myself falling more and more in with Group B. "Do you want a smoke?" asks Jesse as she passes me an already lit cigarette. The fact that smoking has been banned in bars and clubs since 2004, doesn't faze her. "If they catch us we pay the fine, right?" she always says in a terribly immature fashion. If I'm the It Boy, then Jesse is certainly the It Girl. Hailing from a properly wealthy, if not rich family, having made their money from her perma-tanned father Nick's property deals in London, Jesse has it all. As an only child there's no doubt that she's certainly Daddy's princess. Everything she wants she gets. For her twenty-first birthday her parents flung open the ginormous gates of their stunning Dublin 6 mansion and allowed 200-plus guests to party for twenty-four hours. Jesse was presented with a white Mercedes SL500 and within weeks the car was totalled, being replaced by a Bentley Continental, at which she moaned as the Bentley was a hard top. Life is one long party for Jesse and I love her for it. Due to my contacts and her looks, she's beginning to make a name for herself on TV, having made the leap from breakfast TV host to MTV, albeit in a small way.

"So where's Marco tonight then, darling? I thought you guys were inseparable?" she asks while leaning in on my shoulder and putting her Gucci stiletto heels on the table.

"Oh, he's to stay in Switzerland for work. Am I not enough for you?" I smile. It's good to be back in Dublin for three days as I really needed to escape London and the non-stop dramas of the last while. When Oscar Wilde said, 'when a man is tired of London, he is tired of life' that man obviously doesn't have to deal the continual SW1 bullshit that fills my days. The fact myself and Marco's relationship has managed to stay out of the news still scares me, as surely it's only a matter of time. Only those that I completely trust know about it and they keep it close to their chests. Oh, and of course reason number two for being here is a TV interview I've agreed to do. One which quizzes its viewers before cutting to an ad break: 'Just what is an It Boy? Join us after the break to find out!' The fact my interview is scheduled to take place in just four hours' time and I'm still partying doesn't faze me. A few years ago it would have, but not now. Having done so many TV and radio interviews I could practically do them in my sleep; besides, hair and make-up will be on hand to transform my face from shooting star to TV star within minutes.

While I shot to fame almost overnight, it was no accident. Having been introduced to one of the country's leading PR gurus at a weekend house party in Co. Wicklow, they set about transforming my life from weekends spent horse riding, to show pony fairly rapidly. In fact, within one week I'd gone from the usual regular mentions in gossip columns or photos in society pages of magazines, to being interviewed and profiled in a number of national Sunday newspapers as 'one to watch'. All highly amusing, if not somewhat daunting. I loved the attention and my agent assured me that I was a hot ticket and set to become a household name fast. She put this down to my lifestyle which involved little more than shopping, socialising and posing for photographs, with the right people at the right parties. While my background can be described as very comfortable, it's a far cry from flying private over commercial and, honestly, I never envisaged my day-to-day life would be so publicly documented, but that's how it panned out once my PR agent took the reins and I was going along for the ride.

Overnight my life changed dramatically. Out of nowhere, suddenly I was everywhere. After all, I was in my twenties and the offer of free flights, cars, and everything else in between certainly appealed. I've always been sociable, but my new life is so full-on that most of the time it leaves me reeling.

"So where are we going from here? Everyone's heading out of town to Dalkey to some house party," Jesse says as she takes a drag of her cigarette and plays with the straw in her glass. She looks complete out of it.

"Dalkey? Darling, you would need to bring sandwiches!" I say, making reference to the distance from the city to the posh suburb. Dalkey is a tiny little place south of Dublin which the property media have dubbed the Beverly Hills of Ireland. Having spent a lot of time in Beverly Hills, I can categorically state that it's nothing like Dalkey. Bono, Enya and other well-known residents call the sea-side idyll home, but heading there at 4am is not for me. In fact, heading there at any time of day would require a very good reason, as it's just a small pretty little village, but what does one do when one gets there? "I've an idea Jesse, baby, why don't we head back to your place and open some wine, smoke a joint and wind down slightly?" I'm realising I should probably try get my head together. Rather than making excuses to the others and explain why we're leaving, I call Tony, my driver, and within minutes he's waiting outside the side door of the club to take us back to Jesse's penthouse at the Four Seasons Hotel.

"Am I only person who lives at a hotel? People are always so surprised when I tell them I live at a hotel," she says, knowing that she really is very lucky indeed.

Arriving at the entrance to the Four Seasons Residences, Tony reminds me to be fresh, dressed and ready at my flat in time to get to the TV studios.

"Yeah, yeah, I'll be there. Stop panicking!" I slam the car door, and we're ushered into the hotel by a handsome Polish concierge.

Taking the lift to the top floor, Jesse orders enough drinks to keep us going for days. "We need two bottles of Bollinger. Do you have magnums? A bottle of Grey Goose, or as Oli likes to call it, Gay Goose," she says as she pinches my ass. "We also need mixers – Coke, Sprite, tonic… Oh, and we may as well have some beers – Becks and Corona. Anything else?" she asks, knowing that we have more than enough already. She has an issue with showing off, but I put it down to the fact that she's just turned twenty-two and her recently found fame. Plus, she really is a sweet girl, so people let it slide. "Oh, I almost forgot – ciggys! Sixty Marlboro Red please. Do you need cigarettes, darling?" she asks me before skipping out of the open lift to her front door, leaving Pawel the concierge somewhat bewildered. *How strange it must be for him to see such a princess in action,* I think to myself, while also thinking how hot his muscular body looks in his super tight uniform.

Once inside Jesse drops her Dior LBD to the floor without any sense of the inappropriate. "I'm so fucking tired!" she moans dramatically. "Darling, do you want a robe too, or are you going to stay suited and booted?" She struts in an overly exaggerated fashion towards her bedroom wearing only Manolo heels and a black La Perla thong. She's in great shape and she knows it. The fact that her shape does nothing for me is accepted by both of us, despite the fact we've never addressed the topic. She knew that I wasn't sleeping with Sophia, but she never questioned why. Perhaps as she already knew the answer. After all, Sophia is one of the hottest girls in the city and not short of admirers, most of whom are pissed off that she's dating me and some of whom make it their business to tell me, usually in a nightclub at way past their bedtime. In fact, one newspaper editor stopped me one night in Lillie's Bordello to tell me he wanted "to shag her" so I should step aside, especially if I wanted press coverage in his paper. Naturally his wife didn't find the story so amusing when I let it slip at a drinks party a week or so later. Myself and Sophs laughed regularly at him and others who attempted and failed. We are very aware that people are jealous of our relationship and we love to play up to them. Anyhow, once the news of our split breaks I'm pretty sure there will be a few smiling faces.

As I sit rolling a joint, Jesse dances her way to greet the room service guy who's at the door with a very large trolley filled with alcohol. Entering the suite he looks shy and keeps his head down. "Where would you like it, madam?" he asks as he attempts to push the heavily laden trolley into the sitting room.

"Oh, anywhere darling," she says in Holly Golightly fashion, as she rushes back towards me, jumping onto the cream sofa. He stands for a few seconds staring at Jesse. He either wants a tip or can't believe his luck that he could even get so close as to check out the half-naked beauty, who is now draped on my lap. "Do you want to join us?" she asks in a sexy low voice making the Asian waiter rush for the door, bumping into a table as he does so and blushing heavily.

"You are terrible, baby," I say as I pass her the huge joint. "Oh look, you made a 'Camberwell

Carrot'!" she screeches. We both share a love of Withnail and I and for those of you who have seen the movie you will get it. For those that haven't I advise that you gather your closest friends and make a night of it. As she smokes I open a bottle of chilled champagne and look at my watch. It's almost 4:15am. The effects of the extra-strong joint are taking their toll on my brain, cancelling out the pills and cocaine of earlier and making me slightly dizzy. "Fuck, I better get my shit together and fast. I am all over the place," I say as I take a swig from the bottle. "Want some?" I offer to Jesse.

"Oh, don't be so mean, open a bottle for me too!" she whimpers in a cutesy voice. That's Jesse; why have one bottle of champagne on the go when you can have two? As we sit drinking our individual bottles of Bolly from the neck, we're silent. That great feeling achieved by true friendship and also the crazy concoction of Class As floating through our system. The smoke is really working and I feel myself sink deeper into the sofa, as Billie Holiday sings A Foggy Day in London Town in the background. Jesse is a modern girl, but she really loves Billie. She hums along to the music as we sit wrapped around each other. "Did you know that there's a real-life con man living on this floor? He moved in days ago and is known to have already scammed millions from stupid people in New York and London. He sets up pyramid schemes or something. Pawel was telling me that he has seen all sorts coming and going from his suite. TV stars, politicians, the lot, all trying to convert their hills into mountains!" she's saying as she stubs out a joint in the Hermès ashtray on the floor.

"Well, he won't have his work cut out here. I mean, practically everyone is stupid and all dying to make a quick mill or two," I say lazily, rubbing my tired and smoky eyes. We drift into our own worlds, silent but very content. So content that we drift to sleep, only waking to the sound of my BlackBerry vibrating on the glass table top.

"Answer your fucking phone, Oli, it's driving me insane. It's been ringing for an age!" she says in a sleepy voice.

As I reach for it I struggle to open my eyes to read the caller ID. "Oh shit. Fuck, fuck, fuck!" I realise I've passed out for more than five minutes and was expected in the TV studios twenty minutes ago. The fact that the TV station is at least forty minutes away only makes things worse. It's Tony who is parked up outside my flat having taken a few hours' break.

"What's the story, big guy? I'm outside, ready when you are! I even got you a coffee, but it may be cold by now," he says in his tough-guy tone. Explaining my situation and location, I hang up. "Shit. Jesse, wake up. I need your help! I have to get my head together. I'm expected on live TV almost an hour ago." I sound frazzled.

"Who? What? Who?" She lifts her head before collapsing again. There's only one thing for it, I need coffee and a strong line of Colombia's finest. As I chop out a large line of coke my hands are shaking uncontrollably, spilling most of it onto the floor; it disappears into the deep pile carpet. That must be at least fifty euro worth I think, as I spill more and more onto the table, greedily snorting it fast in an attempt to level my head. *OK, OK, come on Oli, you can do this*, I think to myself as I down more champagne and walk towards the bathroom to 'freshen up' in the true sense of the word. I look perfect, as I catch a glance of myself, fixing my hair and searching for a toothbrush. Dressed in a deep blue Etro velvet smoking jacket and Saint-Laurent tuxedo pants, I'm possibly slightly overdressed for morning television. Then again, even if I try to dress down I'll still be overdressed for breakfast TV, I laugh to myself. Emerging from the bathroom, I'm raring to go, like a horse at the Grand National, slightly all over the place but ready to run.

As we drive at break-neck speeds through the rush hour traffic, using the bus lanes and breaking red lights, I'm becoming more and more high. I chain smoke cigarettes and continually change the radio stations searching for the right song for my ever-changing mood. As the car approaches the studios I'm feeling as if my body is being pulled in every direction from the cocaine, ecstasy and weed. Am I up or am I down? Truth is I'm a bit of both, depending on the minute. Trying to look and sound sober is not going to be easy.

"Good morning, Oli, my name is Rachel," says the runner at the station. "You really have given us all sorts of headaches this morning. We weren't sure if you were going to turn up. I must have called your phone twenty times!" she whines as she attempts to show some authority over me and the situation.

"Oh, calm down, darling." I stop to catch my reflection in the mirror.

"We need to get you into hair and make-up and…" she says, sounding as if the world is about to end.

"I repeat, calm down or I will be going nowhere near set. I mean, you haven't even offered me an espresso!" I'm pulling rank. "You run along and get me that coffee and I'll walk myself to hair and make-up. Oh, come on, how hard can it be, darling?" I continue as I walk away from her in a daze. While being 'made up' I look through my phones (I always carry two or three – different numbers for different people is the key to a happy life) at photos from the night before which I barely remember being taken. The girl re-emerges to let me know I'll be on after the news, so I can relax a bit. "Sorry, I forget your name, but I guess it doesn't really matter. Eh, coffee? Hello!" I snap without looking up. In a strop, she downs her clipboard and makes her way to get the coffee, muttering something under her breath. "Is she OK? Seems manic," I ask the hair stylist who is busily applying wax to my already perfect blonde hair. "Seriously, don't mess with the hair too much. It was only chopped last week by Philip B in New York and I really only allow him touch it." I'm sounding like an asshole. The hair stylist sniggers and walks away.

"Well then, sir, you are complete. My work here doesn't need to be done." He whips the protective gown from my shoulders, almost taking my eye out of its socket.

Just then, the girl appears again with a mug of black coffee and a Wagon Wheel. "Jesus! Is this instant?" I ask, before spitting the disgusting coffee back into the mug. "I can't drink instant, it gives me dreadful headaches and that's the last thing we want." I'm looking at the chocolate biscuit which accompanies the coffee in disbelief. *What kind of person offers you a Wagon Wheel?* I think to myself before leaving it back on the plate. "So what time will I be needed? I am going to go outside and have a cigarette. I don't suppose you have a split of champagne anywhere in the building?" I say as I walk towards the front door.

"Please stay where you are, Oli, you are on in ten minutes." She's in total panic. Naturally I ignore her and make my way outside. It's overcast and humid in the car park and as I stand there smoking and watching the other guests coming and going, I feel as if I'm ready for bed. Suddenly I'm hit by the tiredness of a week-long, non-stop party. There's only one thing for it, I need to take more coke. Standing there at the main entrance to the studios I snort three large hits of cocaine off my front door key and then lean back against the wall to let things kick in once again. I can see Tony taking a nap in the car and I'm jealous. Seriously, jealous of my driver – the world is going mad!

I bound back into the building full of life and on much better form. "OK, where's the girl? Where are you, darling?" I say loudly as people stare. "Have you seen my girl? Anyone? Have you seen the girl who looks after me?" I ask an elderly lady who is a guest on the same show to discuss her fears of growing old. She looks at me blankly, possibly more scared of her present then her future. "Hello, hello! I am ready as I'll ever be!" I shout down the corridor to Rachel who is chatting on her phone. "Please tell the interviewer that I will not be answering any questions about my book deal. I also won't answer anything about the car crash 'incident' last week in Rome... In fact, they really should know all of this already," I say as I lead my way through to the studio. The last thing I need is them bringing up that car crash. It's one of those things that I'm just not so clear on, but let's just say I was travelling in a car last weekend that knocked a couple off a Vespa moments before smashing into three parked taxis outside the Hotel d'Inghilterra. I have no recollection of it so I have been instructed to remain silent. Now extremely high, I'm not taking any crap from anyone. I'm certainly dishing it out though. "I can only sit with my left-hand side facing the camera. I hate my right side and almost killed the guys in ITV last week for making me sit showing my right side. This sort of thing should all be in the notes if you read through them."

Secretly I'm scared that they may have already heard the rumours of my break-up with Sophs. The more I think about it, the more paranoid I become and in turn more rude. The fact that the news hasn't reached Dublin is simply amazing. Rachel stands looking at me as if I've fallen off a Christmas tree. "Eh, ok.. Well, enjoy yourself and eh, break a leg," she says through a smile as she leaves me with the sound guys.

"We are joined this morning by It Boy, Oliver…" As the camera pans to me it's clear to see I'm not impressed.

"Oh please, I hate that sort of introduction. Can you not think of something more interesting?" I say loudly, stopping the presenter in her tracks.

"Sorry? What do you mean?" she asks, looking genuinely shocked.

"Oh, the whole It Boy thing, I hate it, it's so over. I mean it was fine, but now I hate it. It really pisses me off." I sound, and look like an idiot.

"Please can you mind your language? This is breakfast TV after all!" she says with a smile that doesn't disguise her panic.

I'm in a really bad way, completely out of my mind. Without even realising it, blood begins to emerge slowly from my nose. I can see the look on the presenter's face but assume she's simply baffled by my 'performance'. I can hear her speak but nothing's going in. "There seems to be some blood coming from your nose. Would you like a tissue?" she asks while clearly listening carefully to her ear piece. "So, then, what would you like to talk about? It seems there are a very limited amount of topics on which we can touch." She's looking through her notes, flicking page after page. I can tell she doesn't like me and who can blame her? This is the last thing she needs at ten-past eight in the morning. "Are you sure you're OK?" she continues, now sounding genuinely concerned.

"Oh, come on, you're an experienced interviewer, think of something or do I have to do your job for you?" I say loudly in a disapproving tone as I dab the by now flow of blood which is becoming heavier. "Oh, now this is interesting – have you seen my shoes?" I say excitedly, placing one of them up on the coffee table. "They're Gucci obviously! I picked them up in New York last week. Ostrich skin! Perfect, aren't they?" I ask before falling back into the chair.

"I read somewhere recently that you love to shop. Is this true, and what do you like to buy?" she's asking as if clutching at straws.

"Oh, darling, what are you talking about? I'm so fucking bored. Can I go home now? I really have to leave. I'm sorry!" I'm sounding almost childlike. "Anyhow, it seems to be me doing all the talking here. What do you want to know? I really have to get back to the city soon. Can we move this along?" I'm now sounding rude as well as stupid. My jaws are sliding viciously from side to side and my eyes look as if I'm caught in the headlights of an oncoming car.

"Well I think at this point what we all really want to know is when you last went to bed?" She sits forward.

"Oh, piss off! This is a waste of time. Fuck this, I need to go." I stand up and remove my microphone before throwing it onto the sofa. It bounces and smashes as it hits the floor. In case you ever find yourself doing a TV interview, remember that the sound guys really prefer if you don't touch their microphones. However, if you must, try do it with care. "There's fucking blood everywhere! What the fuck?" I'm shouting at everyone in front of me.

"Having arrived an hour late, it seems that Oliver, eh, he doesn't want to be interviewed this morning after all… So, we will go to an ad break and be back with you in five for our cookery slot!" announces the presenter, sounding almost hysterical.

"What the fuck was all that about?" I ask the floor crew at the top of my voice. "So mundane. Ridiculously boring waste of my time. Plus, my nose is bleeding, it's way too cold in here!" I gather my phones and other belongings.

"We may well ask you the same question," storms

the station manager. "We've already had a number of the tabloids on asking what is going on!" he continues as I push by him and walk towards the door. The fact is I've just publicly embarrassed myself on live television and rather than feel bad, I'm revelling in it. The shortest interview possible, lasting less than two minutes, and the backlash from the media is set to be horrendous. I'm so wasted I don't care a jot.

"Well I'm sorry that you feel that way, but as I have no idea who you are, does it matter? I have a lot of shit going on in my life right now and what just happened is the last of my concerns OK?" I bark, before leaving the station for possibly the last time.

"Oh, Tony, that was a fucking car crash. Can you take me to the Merrion Hotel, I need a drink before this day begins!" I say as I fall into the awaiting Mercedes.

"Oli, leave it out, it's not even nine o'clock." He's pointing at his watch as if I am supposed to take note.

"Oh, yeah right. Better make it one of the early houses on the quays. Now let's see who's still alive," I say, laughing loudly as I scroll through my phone. "God, life is crazy, isn't it? Really, really crazy!" I say to nobody, as the car accelerates onto the busy motorway. Within minutes my phone begins hopping with calls from gossip columnists and such. Before I switch it off, I call Marco to let him know everything is fine. "Of course! I was fantastic, really had them on the edge of their seats! So what time is your flight? How are you? Everything OK? I miss you!" Wired on a cocktail of drugs and alcohol, I just blurt it all out it out, without breathing.

"Eh, yes I'm fine, baby, are you? You sound kind of manic… You sure everything is cool?" he asks, clearly sensing that he's started dating a lunatic.

"Oh, I'm just giddy after the TV thing, you know? Everything is great, everything is fabulous!" I enthuse, as I wipe dry blood from beneath my nose.

"I'll call you from Geneva – have a great day, you special crazy man!" he says before ending the call without knowing how messed up I am.

Without reading any messages, I switch the phone off again. I told you, there's a valid point to having numerous numbers. "Oh, Tony, on second thoughts, I guess I should get home and change before lunch," I sigh as I pop a Xanax and try to figure out what has just happened. Waking mid-afternoon to a flood of messages, a banging headache and missed calls from most news-desks, as well as my agent, Angie, I realise that this time I may have gone too far.

"Holy shit, this sort of crap could only happen to you, bello!" Paolo sounds genuinely shocked. "There's nothing like hanging around for bad news. Get the hell out of there, I'll arrange the perfect hideaway, where you lie low and then when the time is right you rise like a phoenix!" he says confidently. Within ten minutes he texts me the details of my escape to his family's place in Cap Ferrat, a house so magnificent, that it may take quite a while until it's time to become that phoenix.

Chapter 7

The Shelbourne Hotel, Dublin

William Abercrombie sits alone at the Horseshoe Bar, sipping a Horse's Neck and mock flicking through a tatty-looking *Sotheby's Old Masters* catalogue, one which is a few years out of date. Having once been a leading private art dealer, with an impressive client list, lately he certainly looks the part, but is no longer linked to the world he once ruled. Sporting Huntsman tweed and horn-rimmed glasses, it's hard to believe that he's just forty-three. Round in face and figure from too much of the good life, his style and demeanour leads you to believe he's close to, if not just over the sixty mark. Where once he would be enjoying a long lunch at one of the city's leading restaurants, surrounded by 'in demand' sorts who pick up the tab, today he sits alone in the solitude of an empty bar. You see, that's the thing with a scandal, it can either make or break you, it really can. Just look at the Kate Moss cocaine debacle. Having grown up in Glasgow at a time when it must have been difficult to have been gay, not to mention born into the wrong background, he fled to Dublin and established himself as a pseudo toff. You know the sort: everything is so studied that it's transparent, yet still fun. The sort that surround themselves with, and are impressed by those with titles, no matter how lowly or bankrupt they may be. Nobody has ever really questioned his upbringing, possibly as they don't care. However, I think it's more to do with the fact that they won't dare, knowing that he will cut them off. He has been known to go after certain people for as little as them questioning his accent. Anyhow, the scandal which William finds himself embroiled in is certainly the sort that will take a miracle to spin in the right direction.

Just two weeks previous, he was a main player in of one of those truly great pieces of gossip that tend to get around town too quickly. The sort of scandal that even if it can be brushed under the Persian, it never really goes away. Adding to this that like most great pieces of gossip it involves all the right elements; a well-known TV personality, a high-profile solicitor, a rent boy, and a tabloid newspaper. Once a man revered by both those in the art world and international social circles, his life took a serious nosedive within forty-eight hours and he is now very much alone.

Following my rather disastrous TV interview and subsequent incessant media intrusion, I've spent the past few weeks lying low at Paolo's villa in Cap Ferrat. He insisted that I simply needed some down time and he arranged everything for me to unwind. Honestly his villa is possibly the most perfect place on the planet. Despite being enormous, it feels safe and secure from the outside world. "Darling, everyone needs a little Cap Ferrat from time to time, and this is your time!" he said as he handed me the keys. The last few weeks have been unreal, with Angie, my agent, threatening to drop me as a client twice due to the level of calls and questions she was forced to deal with, as I vanished to France. Trying to keep the whole thing from Marco hasn't been easy believe me. He knows that something's up, so I'm putting it down to exhaustion, but that only makes things worse. He has been asking me to step away from the media spotlight for a while and while I really know I should, I simply can't, as I need to work and it's the only work I know. Anyhow, my scandal has calmed somewhat as some two-bit model got engaged to her footballer husband or something, leaving me out of the firing line. I arrived into Dublin just hours ago, to try blend back into the scene easily. I'll attend a number of parties, and also try catch up with one or two friends.

Outside, the temperatures are unusually high but skies remain grey. Torrential rain has emptied the streets, apart from tourists who seem to have come to Ireland ready for the weather and in search of rain. As locals rush along soaked to the skin, without jackets or umbrellas, the French, Italian and American visitors are slow paced and dry. "My darling boy, how so very good to see you!" he exclaims as I walk into the tiny air-conditioned bar. Standing up, he reaches out to hug me, which is certainly unusual, as he isn't known to be tactile. "Now, what are you drinking? You look splendid, please do sit down," he gushes excitedly in an overly rehearsed accent, as he pulls out a bar stool.

"Oh, a Guinness would be just the ticket – when in Rome and all that! So, tell me what's been going on? I've been hearing all sorts, but you know me, I never listen to gossip," I say with a cheeky smile.

"Oh, it's been a very tough few weeks for me, and yes, I'm sure you have heard," he says, sounding well and truly downtrodden.

"Well as I said, to be honest, I haven't heard that much as I tend to ignore this city when I am out of it. In fact, I tend to ignore it when I'm in it!" I laugh. "So, what's so terrible? What has you in this state?"

As he begins to tell me the story, I realise that this isn't the usual sort of drama which surrounds him. Believe me, I'm very used to his calls before eight in the morning, usually in total panic, having insulted the wrong person at a dinner due to one too many ports, or worse again, being asked to leave certain members' clubs and such, due to his drunken and obnoxious behaviour. This sort of thing usually is the result following a successful art sale. As soon as he gets his mitts on his commission cheque, all hell breaks loose. A civilized lunch easily becomes a three-day bender and the mayhem that ensues is usually the sort of thing that's impossible to apologise for. "Oh, I don't even know where to begin. It's all so terrible and a great misunderstanding, you have to believe me," he pleads.

"Listen, I'm not here to judge you. After all, with the craziness that surrounds me, I'm hardly in a position to cast stones, now am I?" I smile sympathetically. Although, I must admit that the suspense is killing me.

"Well, I decided to invite one or two back to mine following a rather great lunch at Peploe's, hosted by Ivor Bancroft-Mills and that solicitor chap Jeremy Mullins. Nothing hectic, just a small group for drinks and what I had hoped would be a few laughs."

As I listen, I can very easily imagine the scene, as many lunches seemed to wind up back at his perfectly appointed townhouse on leafy Raglan Road. However, what had happened on this occasion was slightly more than the norm. Usually, guests made up of fellow art dealers, socialites and some down-at-heel aristos would gather, drink copious amounts of rare vintages, snort a little coke, smoke a joint or two and generally unwind in the privacy of William's immense hospitality. A hospitality that has always been funded by someone, but nobody, not even the most hard-nosed gossip columnists could figure it out. What happened on the night which had shook William's otherwise serene world, was pretty crazy, even to listen to.

"It was, oh I don't know, perhaps pushing nine o'clock, and there were only a few of us still at it. Usual story; others had drifted on to dinner or drinks, having emptied my cellar. For the life of me I can't remember where the little runt came from, but he arrived just after nine and is believed to have been a guest of Ivor's," he begins, sounding both angry and upset at the same time.

"Who? Who's a little runt?" I ask, as I wave at the bartender for another round.

"Well if you'll listen and stop fidgeting, I'll tell you!" he snaps, adjusting his glasses on his increasingly shiny nose. "As you know, Ivor likes to go off-side every now and then and he invited this East European bit of trade into my home under the pretence that he was a friend of his son."

Ivor is the last of a dying breed, the sort that believe they're untouchable and above the law, due to the fact that his family, were once wealthy land owners. Living outside Dublin, in Co. Meath, he describes himself as a farmer. The fact that he's rarely found actually farming the land and instead, spends most days pissed as a fart at either his local village pub, horse trials or in the smarter surrounds of his club in Dublin, seemed to have been missed by him and ignored by others. He believes his wife has no idea about his double life and even on one occasion when he found himself being blackmailed by an escort he had picked up in Paris, she never batted an eyelid when she discovered the bank statements. Their marriage is the sort that can survive anything, simply as she doesn't care what he gets up to as long as they still have a standing socially.

"Anyhow, this bit of trade turned out to be rather handy at first, as he doubled up as a drug dealer. Oh, we were as high as kites, I tell you! Swinging from the chandeliers kind of fun. Coke, ecstasy, the lot! Talk about of out control, I even cracked open a case of damn good Petrus, such a waste!" He's sounding genuinely sad about having wasted such fine wine on such dreadful people. "Anyhow, I hadn't even realised, but they were in and out of my bedroom taking turns on him and at one point Ivor and that Ronan Garvey fool, you know the game show host?" He pulls a face similar to that you make just before throwing up. "Well, they were in bed with him at the same time, doing God knows what, and an almighty row kicked off. I tell you, I was terrified my neighbours were going to alert the police! I almost had a heart attack right there on the spot." He's now sweating badly and growing more and more red in the face. "The last thing I remember was a huge crash and a bang, as one of my Yeats fell off the wall in the hallway as he escaped. Oh, it really is too, too, too awful." He begins to sob uncontrollably into his handkerchief.

"What's too awful? What happened? Pull yourself together and tell me," I ask, now sitting on the edge of my seat. I mean, for a chap that's seen it all in the seediest gay clubs in Berlin, it has to be bad.

"The little runt took photos of us all doing coke and worse, having sex with him and each other! Oh Jesus, that fucking idiot of a TV chap assumed he was sending text messages or something!" he cries. "He threatened to go to the press with them. Oh, he knew exactly what he was up to, he knew exactly who we were and… Oh, get me another drink before I die! Get some whiskey or cognac, or both." He removes his glasses, showing his swollen red eyes, from too much booze and not enough sleep.

"Oh my, that's shocking! The papers would have a field day with it. What did you do?" I sip the end of my drink.

"Well that's just it. What could I do? He wanted us to hand over ten thousand euro in return for the phone, but even then, how could we trust he wouldn't come back for more? Or worse again, he could sell the story anyhow!" As I sit looking at William, I do feel sorry for him, but at the same time

I question why he allows himself to be in this situation. Why are a group of high-profile 'straight' men in his flat, taking drugs and using a gay escort? Surely it's a recipe for disaster.

"Do you fancy some lunch?" I offer, handing him a glass of Jameson Reserve.

"Oh, Jesus fuck! Don't look now, but outside it's Shirley, Ivor's bloody wife!" he says in panic, before jumping to hide behind the bar. As the barman looks on, I watch Shirley making her way into the room, unaware that William is squatting beneath the Guinness taps.

"May I have a glass of champagne? Not Moët!" she asks in overly perfected tones, before settling herself into a table on the far side of the bar.

Trust me, I've been in some strange situations, but this is comedy gold. The Horse Shoe Bar has long been known as 'the' meeting place in the city, and it has been noted that it's a bar where men with no futures meet women with a past. On this occasion, it seems that this man with no future will do anything to avoid this woman and indeed his past. William is sitting on the floor behind the bar and signals to the bemused barman to hand him a pen and paper, upon which he scribbles a note and passes it to me – 'Go over - make conversation. Distract her at any cost'. Saying hello is the easy part, as we had once been introduced at a point-to-point a few years ago. However, what to say next is going to be tough, as she's one of those hard-nosed types who loves her horses more than people, and while she may be a social goddess in the wilds of Co. Meath, her cold manner isn't well suited to life in the city.

"Yes, I only ever come to town when I absolutely must. Dreadful place, so busy and so dirty, and what on earth have they done to this hotel? Where has the style gone? Where are our people?" she quips as she sips her champagne. While she may have been a pain the ass, I tend to agree with her views on the hotel. As a bolt-hole for the country's social elite, the old hotel was slightly shabby, but that was its charm. A hotel that opened in 1824 and has seen all sorts, from the signing of the Irish Constitution, to the employment of Adolf Hitler's half-brother Alois Jnr – nicknamed Paddy Hitler, I kid you not. These days, following a full refurbishment which cost a king's ransom, the charm has all but gone. Highly polished marble floors and other shiny surfaces, just like any other hotel, anywhere else in the world. As one terribly posh Shelbourne old-timer had remarked upon its re-launch, 'Never mind fur coat and no knickers, this is just a fur coat and its bloody fake fur!'

As I struggle to make small talk about my summer, I see William escape around the bar and out the door. Luckily the horseshoe shape of the bar is perfect for such manoeuvres. "Of course, we were in town for the Horse Show. It is after all the last bastion of Irish society, but even it has become tacky..." she bores.

"Really? Sounds great, sorry we didn't meet there..." I say quickly, before making a swift exit. "Jesus, that woman is dreadful! Hardly surprising, that Ivor seeks out more gentile company with other men," I laugh, as I bundle William into my awaiting Mercedes. "Hi Tony, you know William of course. We need to go somewhere low-key... Any ideas?" I ask.

"I know just the place. Do you want food or just

drinks?" Tony asks as we pull slowly into the traffic.

"Food," I say, at exactly the same time as William announces, "Drinks!"

Driving through the rainy city, I can tell that there's a whole lot more to this story and I need to hear it.

"Oh, for God's sake old chap, where are we going?" William moans as he sits, sweating and agitated.

"Almost there now, sir. I think you will be happy with my choice, and you certainly won't bump into anyone you know." Tony is sounding positive. Arriving at Slattery's Pub on Capel Street, is certainly out of the norm, but he's right, there is nobody we know for miles. "Great pub this place, sir, it's one of my regular haunts. I'm sure you'll enjoy it," Tony smiles, as he opens the car door for William, who steps onto the pavement without acknowledging his existence.

Once inside we order a simple lunch of toasted sandwiches and rounds upon rounds of Guinness. The bar, situated on the city's less fashionable northside, is perfect. Busy, but with no familiar faces. In fact, we may as well have been tourists.

"Right, tell me the whole story. Where were we?" I ask.

Before he speaks, he sits forward and looks around to ensure that nobody is within earshot. "Well, naturally we arranged to pay him. In fact, I did. Ivor hasn't been seen since that night and won't return any calls. As for the other two, well, Jeremy stumped up as much as he could in the fear his wife would find out, and well that half-wit Ronan Garvey, if I never see 'her' again it will be too soon," he snarls, making reference to the overly effeminate TV game show host.

"OK, so it's all in order, so what's the problem? I mean with your connections and art collection you can sell a painting and make ten times that amount in an afternoon." I sound confused.

"Yes, that would be a sweet ending to a sorry tale, but it gets worse!" he continues.

"We're going to need two more pints when you get a moment, please," I ask a passing lounge girl. "Christ, OK, go on…" I say calmly, sitting back in my seat.

"Ok, but this cannot go any further, do you understand?" He's looking extremely shaky and I fear that what's to come isn't going to be pleasant. "Well, the thing is, that the editor in question claims the escort never even approached him, but when Jeremy asked, he had in fact alerted him to the fact that there was something to hide," he whispers. "To make it worse, Ivor said he would deal with things, and that we wouldn't be seeing the escort ever again."

As I sit listening I'm not truly following what's going on. "So, what's the problem, well apart from being out of pocket to the tune of ten grand?" I ask.

"Well the thing is, I've been informed that Ivor had him, well, you know, done in, as they say! I really can't cope with it, I haven't slept in days since I heard." He's beginning to fall apart and while I feel sorry for him, I know that I simply can't get involved further. "Look at this." He's showing me a text message on his phone which reads: 'Another ten thousand in twenty-four hours and this will all go away'. Followed by another: 'You're fucking with the wrong people. Pay what we ask by tomorrow or pay in other ways. How much do you value your life?' There's no number or contact details to go with either message.

"Oh come on, are you taking these threats seriously?" I ask in disbelief.

"Well what do you expect me to do? What would you do?" His hand is shaking as he holds up the phone. I must admit if it were me I would simply bite the bullet and contact the police, but I know he'll never do that, as that would open a serious can of worms. "I've also had a number of calls from anonymous numbers, threatening to visit me at home unless I arrange the cash. I simply won't give in to this bullshit!" He sounds strong but his demeanour says otherwise.

The main problem facing William is that while he may have walls upon walls of fantastically expensive art, the rumours are the art doesn't actually belong to him. In reality, his image of a well-to-do art broker is far from the truth and he is in fact exceptionally cash poor. I know that he's really up against it financially and with his lust for the good life, his bad debts are growing, so much so that he rarely answers his phone in fear that it may be a credit card company, bank, or debt collection agency. "Look, my advice is head away for a while. Go see some friends in the UK or head to your sister in France. Anywhere but Dublin! Actually, before that and if you're feeling up to it, I've been asked to drop in to say hi to Peter Suave at his new penthouse, it may be just what you need. If nothing else there will be some great wines, fun company and your face is out there – with nothing to hide. Come on, I promise you'll feel better if you get away from it all for a while," I offer in an attempt to put a smile on his face.

Peter Suave is one of those mystery sorts, having arrived in Dublin relatively out of nowhere a year or two ago. Well, when I say out of nowhere, I believe that he came direct from LA. Driving a purple Rolls-Royce Corniche, and dressing in a style that I am pretty sure the late Gianni Versace would approve of, he certainly stood out in a city which is relatively grey. I first met him one morning as he parked his car on the footpath outside the Westbury Hotel, when he was moving into one of their finer suites for the foreseeable. At six-foot-six, he stood, dressed in skin-tight stonewashed jeans and a leather jacket with a huge Medusa on the back panel. Smoking a Monte Cristo, his mirrored aviator sunglasses and silver hair slicked back into a pony, made people take stock. We chatted that day as his car was being dealt with and we ended up spending the afternoon at Bruxelles Bar, where it transpired that we had a number of mutual friends. Since that day we've been close. In fact, I introduced him to his current girlfriend Tatiana, a twenty-five-year-old Russian model who claims to be from a 'powerful family in Moscow'. Although unclear where she gets her money from, she alludes to the fact that her father is a private banker. Having bothered to look into this, it seems that her father is the most low-key banker ever, or possibly not a banker at all, as nobody within my banking contacts has heard of him. The rumour is she's a hooker and a busy one, who works in an upscale boutique on Grafton Street in an attempt to disguise her true career choice. Anyhow, these days she doesn't need to spend her own money, as since landing Peter he lavishes her with whatever her heart desires, from Cartier to Mercedes-Benz. Despite the more than thirty-year age gap, they seem genuinely happy.

His vast wealth comes from his family oil business in Texas and he really is a walking, talking JR Ewing, albeit a more JR meets Liberace. Anyhow, this afternoon he's having a small get-together at his twenty grand a month rented penthouse, situated on Merrion Square. While I may be trapped with an almost suicidal William, that doesn't mean I'll be missing Peter's party. "So, will you come along and try to be happy, even for an hour or two?" I ask.

"Oh, I can't bear society at the moment," he replies through bloodshot eyes. Bloodshot from non-stop drinking and nothing more. "Who will be there? Ghastly people I suspect," he continues, sounding like a spoilt teenager.

"Who knows? Let's freshen up, and show face!" I take full control of the situation.

Arriving at the ultra-modern penthouse, the mood is light and breezy and the views are beyond. "Peter, you know William?" I ask, already knowing that two had become friends, due to the fact that Peter's millions were perfect for William's never-ending supply of off-market art. Dotted around the vast drawing room are some of the sales: Monet, Picasso, and a very rare Lichtenstein, all supplied by William and his spider's web of contacts.

The gathering is slightly more than I had first thought, and as I look around the room I see faces that I know, or at least knew before they had visited their surgeons. You know the look, it's hard to tell if she's thirty-five or sixty-five. Young girls looking older, older women looking younger, yet somehow they look the same age due to the stretching of the skin and removal of any life-lines. "Don't worry, most of them will be leaving soon," Peter informs us as he offers to show us around. The place is unreal, wrap-around terraces with outdoor hot tubs overlook the entire south city, while inside the six bedrooms have walk-in closets, saunas and steam rooms. There's a gym, staff accommodation, and in one unused room, referred to as the 'art store', lies more art that is yet to be hung. Against the walls of the otherwise empty room must be close on twenty million euro worth of master pieces.

Waiters work the room, carrying trays of Dom Perignon. "No, sir, we are only serving champagne or vodka today, as Tatiana doesn't like coloured drinks," smiles a handsome Brazilian. *Tatiana has wasted no time making the place home*, I think to myself as I remove two glasses from the tray.

"Well, what do you think?" I ask William as I hand him a drink.

"Oh, it's typical I guess. Not my sort of thing at all. Pure new money on every level, including his hideous guests," he moans loudly, making people stare.

"It doesn't stop you quaffing his champagne or flogging him more art that he doesn't need or understand," I say coldly. If there's one thing I can't stand it's those that befriend people only to slate them behind their backs. Trust me, the number of people I know that sit lunching together day-in, day-out, when one or both are constantly bitching about the other, is comical. It's usually the same sorts, ones who have it all, well, at least on the outside. On the inside they resent everyone who is prettier, richer, funnier or has, I don't know, say, access to a larger yacht or can hop the line at Les Caves du Roy. Seriously, 'anything you can do, I can do better' isn't just a song! "You really need to pull yourself together or at least pretend to," I advise. We settle into a large cream sofa and watch as Peter works the room and winds things down.

"Everyone, can you please listen," announces Tatiana in her sexy broken accent. Dressed head to toe in Chanel, she's certainly adjusted to her new life easily. "We are going to move the party into the beautiful five stars Shelbourne Hotel whenever you're ready. Drinkies are on Peter!" she laughs.

"Oh, for fuck's sake, what are we doing here and what is that tramp banging on about?" William asks as he casts his eyes over the room. "A grand gathering of the great unwashed. Give them a Louis Vuitton handbag and a tan and suddenly it's Monte fucking Carlo!" he hisses.

"You are more than welcome to stay here if you wish," Peter offers. "There are one or two going to stay back, but to be honest I want to clear the rest. Mainly Tat's pals who seem to be unable to balance on their heels, and they're damaging the fuck out of the floor!" he says in a strong Texan accent, pointing to the damage their stilettos have made.

Looking around I can see what he means; in between the ageing legal sorts and friends from horse racing circles, are tanned, long-limbed models, who despite the fact that their modelling career has so far amounted to wearing a bikini on Grafton Street mid-January, for some product launch or another, look down their freshly powdered noses at those 'non-models' gathered. Also standing in a corner taking in the scene are a group of guys who can only be described as bulldogs; you know the sort, square shaved heads, no necks, stonewashed denim, leather jackets. The sort that clearly look as if they're involved in something dodgy. I watch as they watch the scantily clad girls and expensively dressed men in the room. They stand coldly, not speaking with the other guests, and whisper to each other suspiciously. I'm sure to many they would be described as typically East European.

"Oh, it's like a bad scene from Prêt-à-Porter in here, I need some air," William says coldly before walking out onto the terrace.

"Is he OK?" asks a genuinely concerned Peter. "Should I go after him? I've heard on the grapevine that things aren't so good," he continues, all the while puffing on a huge cigar. Watching, I see William chatting and laughing with a group of the sorts he was bashing just moments ago. *Even at his lowest, he can still go lower*, I think to myself. "Of course you know Tatiana," Peter says with a wink, as she sits beside me on the large silk sofa. Of course I know her, after all I was the one who had introduced them, even if I regret doing so now. Since moving in on Peter she's become every inch the new-monied bitch possible, creating dramas with some of the city's most prominent socialites, and going as far as changing the way Peter dresses. As if his OTT style couldn't be topped, today he is wearing python skin loafers with a matching belt. You know what they say – never marry beneath you, as they will surely end up on top of you. Hopefully the sound of wedding bells isn't on the cards any time soon.

My first encounter with her was at a club called Spy at around 3am, where she cornered me for longer than I'd enjoyed and quizzed me about almost every guy in the room. In almost military precision, each question leading back to one thing – money and who had the most of it. While, she certainly is attractive, she's far from a beauty. Blonde highlighted hair, high cheekbones, fake tan, and long limbs, all put together pretty well thanks to Peter's Centurion and an eye for what suits her. Dublin had rapidly become awash with girls like Tatiana, all in search of a new life. Very typical really, someone, most probably their mothers, had told these girls that they are stunningly beautiful, even though they are far from it, and to go get a rich stupid man in the west. The fact that most of them work for the minimum wage in mind numbingly boring jobs, rather than modelling for Dolce and parting on the FTV yacht, doesn't bother them. I often mention amazing parties in Monaco, or such-and-such having just taken delivery of his latest giga-yacht in St Tropez to see Tatiana salivate. She can't resist it, the mere mention of anything to do with billionaires seems to be her cocaine. While places like St Tropez and Marbella have always been home to hookers from the east, Dublin is now red hot and on their radar.

"So Oli, tell me, it is difficult to be a gay here in the Ireland?" she asks with a snide smile. "I mean, if we in the Russia now, I would not even do the speak with you in public, you know it?" she continues.

"What are you talking about?" I smile curiously.

"You know, in the Russia there are no gay mans. It is not allowed to be a gay. It is actually forbidden by the Putin because we like only the real mans in Russia, you know it?" She's cold and contrived.

"Well that's a shame for Russia, but not so much for Ireland, England, Italy, the US… Oh yes, I've met so many out and happy gay Russian men around the globe. Most of whom have zero desire to return to the grey and cold that is the motherland," I laugh.

She doesn't laugh with me, but rather stares coldly. "Yes, it's true what I've been hearing about you lately, you are the fucking dreamer, Oli," she says, reapplying her lip gloss.

"Yes, and from meeting you again just briefly today, it's true what I've heard about you too, Tatiana." I smile a fake smile. "I mean come on, I've only met you a few times and I can tell you're clearly not Russian. So darling, where is home? Latvia? Lithuania? Moldova? Come on, you can tell me," I laugh. "Oh, and for the record, I most probably won't be speaking with you in public again. For you it's bad to be seen chatting with someone who is gay, well, for me it's a case of social suicide to be spotted engaging with someone, well from, well from the third world," I say without any hint of apology.

"You think you are the smart one, yes? Well you know nothing about me. Zero, nyet! I can fuck you up!" she snaps, before standing suddenly, leaving me to jump to my feet too.

"The point is, I don't care where you're from, but your reaction shows me that you clearly do. So that answers my question perfectly. Just so you know, nobody in this town gives a fuck where you guys are from, as none of them have ever, or will ever go further east than Switzerland. Just remember that," I smile before walking away, realising that she won't let me have the final word.

"Don't walk away from me, you asshole!" she screams, making most of the gathered guests take notice. I continue out to the terrace where I find William surrounded by a mixed group of young guys, possibly gay, and older women, definitely overly flirty meets borderline horny. Just as I attempt to sit down Tatiana barges towards me. "Get the fuck out of here you disgusting shit of a person!" she orders. "Nobody speaks to me that way that you do, do you hear me? You think you are smart, mister, do you? I will show you smart when I call my brother and his friends to come over and beat fuck with you!" She sounds deranged, but her lack of basic English amuses those seated.

"Oh, brothers, yummy. How many?"

William sits up in excitement, removing his sunglasses for dramatic effect. She stares at him coldly as if issuing a warning, before looking back at me. "I hate guys like you, thinking they know everything. Thinking they can fucking…"

Just before she can finish, Peter steps forward. "Tatiana, what the hell is going on?" he barks, scaring her into submission.

"Oh, baby, this guy is like so very rude. He saying

very disgusting things to me and about my family." She actually stomps her foot.

"Look, Peter, all I did was ask where she's from, as I simply don't know. Is there a problem?" I ask before standing up.

Hearing the commotion, two of the burly 'bulldogs' appear on the already crowded terrace and make their way towards our table. "There is problem here, Tatiana?" one asks in a very heavy accent. She walks towards him and whispers into his ear. Suddenly chaos ensues, which is very typical of so many similar girls I've had the misfortune of encountering. The drama for drama's sake sort, twinned with the fact that she's clearly as high as the moon. In an attempt to defuse things Peter suggests that Tatiana and her party move onward to the hotel and to his awaiting bar tab.

"Oh, this is all so horrid, it really is. If this is the new Dublin, I am going to have to relocate to where these people are not. Perhaps I shall live in the east, after all it seems that all east is now here in the west," William says as he brushes by Tatiana and her dodgy-looking friends. The fact that he may really need to relocate soon, is lost on the guests who laugh at his quip. The room and terrace empties out pretty quickly, leaving only a select few. That few includes myself, William and one or two daughters of bankrupt aristocrats. The sorts who still manage to dine out on their by-now defunct family name. They are lapped up by the likes of Peter, who due to his American upbringing believes that any sign of a decent family tree means class.

"Oli, I'm so sorry about Tat's behaviour, it really is

out of order and I'll be speaking with her later about it. Are you OK?" he's asking, genuinely concerned. The thing about Peter is that while he may be addicted to Tatiana and her pleasurable ways, he knows that I'm his friend and he values that above and beyond. He's not like the rest, who simply want me on side in order to get them guest-listed at clubs or parties. Peter values the real friendship we've built over time. Besides, he's not really one to have problems getting into places as he is on every list imaginable. Seriously, he is the only man known to have others removed from their tables at say Bagatelle in St Tropez, mid-July, just by arriving without as much as a reservation. Money talks and all that.

"Oh look, it's fine. She just went a little crazy when I asked where she's originally from. I thought Latvia, but she insists she's from Moscow and from a very powerful…"

Before I can finish, Peter stands up to show me an iPhone which is on the table. "You know, I was led to believe she was Russian too, but then I found this phone and it contains a heap of photos from her home town in Belarus, something she likes to keep hush-hush. I haven't bothered to question her on it, as I simply don't care. It's not as if she's marriage material, now is it?" He laughs heartedly. That's the thing with rich guys like Peter, they see girls like Tatiana as play things. Expensive play things, but play things nonetheless. He passes me the phone to scroll through, and there amid endless photos of Tatiana wearing little more than bikini bottoms, are photos of a simple grey-looking town, one I clearly don't recognise, and a place that she clearly wants to forget at all costs.

"So Peter, are you saying there's no wedding plans on the horizon? Oh, poor Tatiana will be devastated," I smile. "I'm pretty sure she has already visualised her big day with your big cheque book!" We laugh.

"Are you OK there, William? You don't seem to be yourself at all," Peter asks, having clearly noticed that he has been off since arrival.

"Sorry but I need to go, will you excuse me please?" he says, quickly making his way to the elevator.

"What the hell is up with him?" Peter asks as he leans in to top off my drink. "He's an odd one, Oli, no doubt about it!" he continues, with a curious expression on his face.

"Look, I need to speak with you privately, can we move to where people are not?" I ask, gesturing towards the hallway. "I don't really know where to begin and what I am about to tell you must, and I repeat, must, remain between just us OK?" I say calmly.

"Go on, I must say this turning out to be quite the day," he smiles.

"You know that the story going around town is that William and his high-profile pals may have gang raped a young male escort, don't you?" he asks, with a facial expression packed with disgust.

"Fuck no! That's not the story at all," I say dramatically.

"Well I tell you, Oli, that's what I've been told and I have it on good authority. Between us, Tatiana knows the guy in question and she's been filling me in on things. Apparently they used him and then didn't pay. Oh, I don't know, Oli, you know me, I don't care what people get up to, but not paying a hooker, well, it's bad business all round." He sounds sincere.

"The fucking lying asshole! That's not the story at all. He's been blackmailing William to the tune of ten grand claiming he has photos of what went down. On top of this, he and his cronies have been calling and texting William, demanding a further similar payment or things will escalate. They paid the first ten grand and they still haven't handed over the phone." I'm trying to fight William's corner, although I'm not really sure why, as I know if it was a reversed situation he wouldn't stand by me. "Also, as you may, or perhaps may not know, William has no money and the others aren't willing to chip in."

"So what do you expect me to do? Drag Tatiana over the coals? It's nothing to do with her really, now is it?" He's relighting his cigar, filling the space with expensive smoke.

"Nothing to do with her? How sure are you that she isn't linked to this whole thing and those guys aren't here working with her? They really don't look like the most pleasant sorts now do they? Peter, you really can't be involved in this." I am beginning to panic, having realised that this whole thing is starting to look like a set-up. It's far too coincidental and what William was saying now makes sense. They targeted him and his crew, knowing there was money to be made. In fact, my money is on the fact that Tatiana targeted me to start with. Thinking back, she was extremely insistent on becoming close to me and my circle. Once positioned with Peter, she had access to where she needed to be. "We need Tatiana here and we need to speak with the escort and see what he has to say," I suggest, jumping to my feet dramatically.

"OK, OK. Calm down, kid. Why don't you fill me in on every detail, before I drag Tatiana into this further?" He offers me a seat. As the remaining guests make their way home we sit talking for an hour, trying to figure out how to handle things.

Lifting his phone, he calls William. "It's Peter Suave calling, is everything alright?" he asks, as if not knowing a thing about the biggest piece of gossip to hit this town in years. "Yes OK, stay there and we'll see you in ten." He ends the call. "OK, Oli, we've to meet him at the Merrion. Look, if I can help I will, but I'm doing this for you. I'm not sure that lot deserve rescue," he says, making a valid point.

Walking to the hotel, the weather remains unusually humid and the sky overhead is as dark as death. While our world is spinning rapidly, the humdrum of commuters making their way home from work is a stark reminder that our lives are so very different to theirs. I often notice it, usually when falling out of a restaurant drunk at 5pm, straight into their disapproving glances and stares. I guess if I had to sit at a desk nine-to-five in some dull-ass job I'd resent those that don't too. As we stroll I can sense eyes on me, and I'm pretty sure it's down to that breakfast TV fuck-up. *Who knew so many people were awake so early to see it?* I think to myself. William is sitting at a quiet corner table in the Cellar Bar. A bar that attracts the city's social elite, as well as politicians and visiting dignitaries due to its location directly opposite Government Buildings. It's a place where

William once held court, centre stage at the bar, regaling his entourage of high tales from his jet-set lifestyle.

"OK William, I'm not going to beat around the bush, so I need you to tell me everything that went down that night. Then and only then can I decide how to proceed," Peter says sternly.

William looks to me for assistance, I offer none. "The thing is, why are you offering to help? With respect, how exactly can you help me?" William asks in his usual snooty tone. I swear to you, I'm beginning to wonder why we are here at all.

"So you're telling me you have the next instalment that they're hounding you for? You have access to ten grand? Sorry, there seems to be a misunderstanding," Peter sips his whiskey and stares coldly. Truth is, Peter really can just stand up and walk away, as he owes William nothing. In fact, I get the feeling that deep down he rather dislikes him, especially following their last dealings on the sale of a Kandinsky. William tried and failed to double his commission, almost losing the sale completely once Peter was alerted to the fact. That's the thing about William; he has many enemies and due to his day-to-day demeanour, many more waiting in the wings. "Look, I'll give you the money, but only as Oli here is a good guy, and he's explained things." He leans in close to William. Meanwhile, William gives me dagger eyes, realising that his secret is out. "Don't look at Oli, he only told me in an attempt to save your sorry ass. I'm the one speaking with you, so look at me," he continues without removing his gaze. "So, here's the deal. You have something I want and don't worry, I'm willing to pay you the market value, plus a little something for your time." He sits back in his seat, knowing that he has William's full attention.

"And what is it you want?" William asks wearily.

"In your hallway you have a set of Picasso drawings. The ones I've tried to purchase twice now. I don't suppose they're worth too much, but let's say I feel it's the right time to sell, wouldn't you agree?" he smiles falsely. As I've already explained, the art that enhances every inch of William's townhouse is the property of someone else. The owner is so elusive that I don't even know who they are. "So, what do you say? Do we have a deal?" He finishes his drink.

"I've explained that I can't sell them, quite simply as they don't belong to me!" William rants. "Well, I'll leave it with you to think over. If your answer is what I'm hoping for, I can meet you at 10am at the Shelbourne to conclude." Peter is already standing and ready to leave. "Oli, I'll call you later. William, please give this offer some serious thought, as from what I believe, it's a truly life-changing situation we find ourselves in." He leaves us.

"Well that is me well and truly fucked! Thank you, Oli, thanks a fucking bunch!" he snarls, before Peter has even left earshot.

"Actually, you know what? Fuck you, and fuck the mess you're in! You actually deserve to be where you are, as you are a nasty, twisted, ungrateful prick!" I stand up. William sits looking wounded, knowing that he has possibly just ruined his last real friendship. "Take, take, take, that's all you understand. I'm trying to help you here, and considering you've never helped me, even when I've needed you, from here on in you're on your own," I snap. "Seriously, thinking about our friendship, it's all one sided... Right down to the times when you have chosen not to introduce me to so-and-so, as in some fucked up way you feel that your circle of snobbish, bankrupt pals are better than me. Newsflash – where the fuck are they now?" I really am letting rip. I stand up and gather my things, leaving him staring at me like a lost dog.

"Oh, to hell with you, to hell with all of you!" he shouts, which only attracts the attention of others in the bar. He is rapidly spiralling out of control as he knocks over a wine glass in an attempt to leave before me. I don't hang around.

At home, I cancel my dinner plans and decide that it's time to chill. Seriously, I can't remember the last time I was able to just stay home and enjoy some down time. As a city Dublin may be small, but that doesn't mean it's tame. In fact, I think I party more in Dublin than anywhere else on the planet. Here someone is always ready to meet for drinks, no matter what hour it may be. After the drama of today, the last thing I want is to entertain people further, on any level. After a long soak and an even longer joint, I'm zoned and ready for bed. Standing in the drawing room of my flat, I call Marco, noticing that Gianna Nannini sings Sei nell'anima on MTV. There really is no escaping Italy, I smile to myself as the call is diverted to voicemail. I don't leave a message – I don't know about you, but I hate answering services, even ones that belong to those close. I extinguish about twenty candles and turn in. I don't remember falling asleep, and for the first time in years I manage to wake late the following morning.

Looking at my phone, it's almost ten. As I make coffee, I send a text message to William to see how he's feeling. Don't get me wrong, I'm not backing down for what happened last night, but I believe in clearing the air when needs be. He doesn't reply, which is hardly surprising. We have rowed many times before, and he can go days without speaking, let alone apologising for his behaviour. I don't really have time to dwell on things as I am supposed to be packing in order to leave for London.

Standing in my dressing room, I'm facing my usual dilemma: what to wear, not to mention what I need to bring with me. Dividing my time between two cities is becoming a chore, as I tend to buy clothes for each city and then I can't remember which tuxedo is where. I am contemplating hiring a PA who can handle matters like this. Piles upon piles of clothes face me and I'm starting to panic. Just before I begin to tailspin, Peter calls. "No, I haven't heard a word from him since yesterday. He was on very bad form and we exchanged words," I explain. Peter, has clearly had enough of William and his rudeness, as he is currently sitting in the Lord Mayor's Lounge at the Shelbourne awaiting William's arrival. At already almost an hour late, Peter is pissed.

"What kind of fucking asshole misses the chance to solve a mess like his? To hell with him, I'm out of here and won't be offering my help again!" He sounds really angry. Realising that William may well and truly be about to blow it, I try to contact him one last time. His phone goes unanswered.

As the plane taxis into position at Heathrow, I switch my phone on to receive a string of messages, mainly from Peter asking me to call him urgently. Once inside the terminal building, I'm standing at the carousel awaiting my six pieces of Hermès luggage. I call Peter and he answers almost instantly. "Oli, where the hell are you? Have you heard about William?" He sounds stunned.

"Heard what? Did he meet you? What's the fuck's up now?" I ask, half distracted as I see one of my bright orange bags making its way towards me."

Oli, are you somewhere where you can talk? You may need to sit down," he says calmly.

"What the fuck? Tell me, what's happened?" Suddenly he has my full attention.

"His body was found this morning. Poor guy, hanged himself in his bathroom. His cleaning lady discovered him, just hanging there. Can you imagine?" His deliverance is clear but I need him to repeat what he's just said. Just as soon as I've gathered my luggage I'm making my way to the Aer Lingus desk to book the next available flight back to Dublin. Sadly for William, his funeral, which takes place at University Church on St Stephen's Green, is a small affair, extremely small in fact. A handful of friends gather, but there's no sign of any family. Standing next to Peter in the almost empty church, I look around at those who have shown up and there's no sign of anyone that's involved in the scandal that drove William to his demise. Somehow, I genuinely feel that he's in a better place now. He was always a troubled soul, looking over his shoulder, trying to keep up with the persona and the lies he had created so many years ago. The one thing that does interest me is the fact that the phone with the photographs is still out there somewhere, and with respect to William, whoever has the phone knows that the other far more high-profile guests present on that night are the ones where their blackmail cash lies.

Chapter 8

Eaton Place, London

"OK Oli, we're ready to start filming in five, four, three, two, action!" says Sandra, the producer of NQOCD, a TV documentary which I've been signed to for a British network. The whole idea is that I'm followed by a camera crew for one week in order to see how I live. In reality, this 'reality' show is completely staged, like so many others I've participated in. Unlike the others, this one begins the second I've opened my eyes. Actually, this one is starting and I haven't even closed them, having fallen home thirty minutes ago, just before they arrived. As I sit in the drawing room of my newly rented flat, sipping what appears to be an orange juice, I'm on flying form and certainly look the part. Dressed in a navy Loro Piana polo neck and Tom Ford jeans, I'm feeling confident. Confident, but still drunk. The fact that my juice is 90% Grey Goose only further helps my mood. The fact that it's not yet eight-thirty, I've already taken a line of coke and only day one, scares me.

"So Oli, what are you up to today?" she asks as I reposition myself in a leather armchair.

"Well, you know today is going to be pretty crazy, so I do hope you can keep up!" I say with a cheeky grin down the barrel of the camera. "I've to get to Chelsea for a haircut then a massage at the Mandarin Oriental, before heading to Gucci for a fitting. All this before lunch at the Ivy with cousin Izzy. Busy, busy, busy!" I take a large sip from my glass.

"Hang on, hang on… Stop!" comes a voice from the corner of the room. "The sound levels aren't right! Sorry guys, give me a minute, will you?"

I top off my glass and fix my hair in the huge Louis XV mirror. "Hey Oli, are you drinking vodka?" a scruffy, yet weirdly attractive camera man asks.

"And what if I am?" I smile back cheekily. "Would you like one? Feel free to help yourself." I'm pointing to the vast selection of drinks on the marble table.

"Don't mind if I do! I was at a mate's birthday last night, and feeling rough as a badger's arse. I'm Matt, by the way," he laughs as he pours himself a rather generous Stoli. "Cheers, pal! I fuckin' love this stuff, best vodka there is!" he says as he knocks the triple shot back.

"Well you know where it is, as I said, help yourself," I smile. "So, how long will it take to start filming? I'm kind of anxious to get going." I sound like a true diva.

As we sit waiting for things to be sorted myself and Matt chat and continually refill our glasses. He tells me about his ex-girlfriend whom he refers to as a 'slag'. "She shagged my best mate, man. I caught them at it in my fuckin' bed! Can you imagine?" He's already starting to sound drunk.

"That's terrible, sorry… Sandra, will this take long? May I talk to you for a minute?" I ask as I walk out into the hallway.

"Oli, what can I do for you? Sorry about the delay, it shouldn't be much longer than five minutes," she smiles as she takes in the rest of the flat.

"Don't get any ideas, darling, we are only filming in here. Just because I am happy to be filmed twenty-four-seven, doesn't mean I want to show you the contents of my bathroom cabinets. If this is going to take a while, I may nip out for ten minutes to pick something up. I was expecting a delivery but have been told I must now pick it up," I smile back.

"Honestly, we'll be ready in five minutes. Please can you just take your position again?"

Ignoring her, I pretend to go freshen up, but nip out and make a dash to The Antelope pub on nearby Eaton Terrace. Awaiting my arrival, my dealer Dave, AKA Disco Dave. We exchange pleasantries and five hundred pounds before I hot foot it back to 'my position'.

"Oh there you are, Oli, we thought you'd done a runner!" Sandra laughs hysterically.

"Are you OK Matt? You seem a bit… I don't know? A bit wasted!" I laugh.

Matt is now slumped over his camera with vodka in one hand and an almost burned-out cigarette in the other, just staring at the floor. "Oh hellooo matey, you alright?" he slurs as he reaches out to a nonexistent ashtray.

"Sandra, is everything OK?" I only ask as I spot another member of the crew pour himself a drink. "I mean come on! I nipped out for ten minutes and you guys have raided my flat?" I shout. Realising the potential seriousness of the situation, Sandra attempts to calm me down.

"Oli, I am so, so, so sorry. Get up, Matt, for fuck's sake! This has never happened before, and I think perhaps we should arrange some coffee to sober everyone up! Get the fuck up now, Matt!" she snaps, as a nerdy-looking girl who hasn't spoken at all, approaches to test the light or something.

"Oh relax, I'm just kidding!" I laugh loudly. "As for coffee, it stains your teeth. Plus, who needs black coffee when you can have… white!" I say dramatically, as I place the huge bag of coke on the table. Pushing the carefully selected fashion and interior design books, as well as a pretty floral display out of the way, I frantically chop out line after line of coke, before opening a bottle of Louis Roederer and insisting that everyone joins in. Within minutes, work is on hold as both Matt and his sidekick Freddie drink champagne and snort a line or two.

"Are you sure this is cool?" asks Freddie as he wipes the white from his nose.

"It would appear to be, wouldn't it?" I say with a wink. "So, now all that awkward crap is out of the way shall we start filming?"

"I am not happy about this one bit, to be honest. It is most unprofessional and if it ever gets out we will all be in serious bother," Sandra panics.

"Oh, shut up will you? It's just a bit of fluff to loosen the mood," I say as I offer her a rolled-up fifty-pound note. She declines. "I really think we should take the filming out onto the street, this place is not exactly exciting, now is it?" I ask.

"Oh, I think it's lovely. You really are very fortunate to live in such a fantastic home," says the nerdy one.

"Look, let's get out of here. You can follow me around – a day in the lifestyle!" I enthuse as I gum some coke and once again fix my hair in the mirror.

"Fucking love this idea, man. In fact, I fucking love you!" Matt says as he tries to hug me. "

I never, ever hug in cashmere, sorry." I pull away. "OK, so shall we walk and talk? Or shall we take it as a given, we'll chat as we're chauffeur driven," I joke. To look at me it would be very hard to tell I was high as a kite and more worryingly pretty pissed.

As we drive towards Chelsea in rush hour traffic, my ego is out of control. While I pretend to detest doing TV shows, secretly I love the attention the cameras and a crew of four bring me. I mean, there is something slightly unusual and attention-grabbing about arriving into Gucci, or say, Patisserie Valerie, or somewhere mundane like that with a full film crew in tow. As the cameras roll Sandra does her best to capture some TV gold. "So Oli, where were you last night? Anywhere fun or just the norm?" she asks ever so condescendingly.

"Oh, I hit up a party at Hermès, then on to The Orangery at KP for Hesky Bannon-Scott's 30th birthday bash. It was so amazing! The Cardigans played, as a total surprise, and one or two royals passed out! Can I say that? Is this live?" I laugh, knowing that I'm really on cocaine talk mode.

"Who is Hesky? Can you tell our viewers?" she asks with a smirk.

"Oh, darling, everyone knows Hesky, well, anyone of note that is," I say coldly with a stare. "She's like the girl of the moment – rocked in at number one on *Tatler*'s Most Invited this year. She has this fab little shop in Belgravia that sells the most amazing shoelaces. I guess you could say she ties the shoes of one or two high-profile Qataris, as well as one or two emerging oligarchs," I smile, as I wipe my non-stop dripping nose. I'll take you to see her during the week if you behave yourself."

Arriving at Daniel Galvin's salon, we troop in to be told that filming won't be possible due to the fact other high-profile customers are in situ. That's it, my crew have to sit outside until I re-emerge looking fresh. "Thank God for that! I've only been with them an hour and already I wanna jump!" I explain to the girl who is washing my hair.

"Why, what are you doing with them?" she asks innocently.

"Oh, they're just following me around as they want to see what my life is like!" I'm sounding cocky.

"I don't mean to be rude, but why? Who are you?" Yet again, sounding innocent.

"Seriously?" I walk away in disgust. That's the thing with no sleep, a lot of vodka, the odd line of coke and a camera crew. It can turn even the most humble into an idiot. I mean, how is the girl washing my hair supposed to recognise me? It's not like she was going to be in the VIP at Boujis, now is it?

As I sit awaiting my haircut I call my agent, Angie, to check in. In every successful socialite is at least one fierce agent and in London mine is Angie, a woman so revered that she can she really should be living at Number 10. Mid-forties, yoga fit, only dresses in black and only consumes white foods and drinks. Of all her clients, I know she has a soft spot for me, perhaps due to the fact that I arrange flowers to be delivered to her every Monday morning, and am in high demand. "Listen, baby, I can't handle this lot today. Are they for real? Non-stop stupid questions, I swear I think they are laughing at everything I do and not in a good way. This is a set-up, I can feel it," I snarl suspiciously. "Also, I am beyond warm, I've totally worn the wrong outfit, perhaps I should try change at Gucci? Oh, I don't know, Angie, help me!"

"Seriously Oli, I do love you, but sometimes it's just a tiny bit like babysitting! Just relax, you've signed the paperwork, now you must do the work!" she snaps, sounding business-like as usual.

"Seriously, they want to follow me into Gucci to a fitting? Someone shopping, who the hell would think that's interesting or glamorous?" I ask in genuine disbelief.

"Not everyone shops at Gucci, or has even ever been through their doors!" she laughs.

"Oh, can you call them and ask them to leave me alone until this afternoon? At least then they can capture me at the shows. I mean, Fashion Week would be interesting to a viewer, no?" sounding like I truly care. The fact is I'm in dire need of some time alone and of some sleep.

"So you want me to call the crew that you are actually with and instruct them as to what you want? Are you insane?" She's now sounding pissed off and slightly baffled.

"Well if you're too busy get someone at the office to do it. Isn't what an agent does? Isn't it why I am paying you?" I'm genuinely feeling hard done by.

"Oh, while I have you on the phone, an offer has come in for you to appear on Celebrities Living Wild. It's a new show where ten celebrities are sent to live on a desert island, with little else than the clothes they arrive in. The fees are good and it would be a really great way to find yourself, Oli," she says almost excitedly.

"Find my-fucking-self? I'd rather find myself in a suite at the Four Seasons, darling. Are you sure you really know me at all?" I say before hanging up.

After about ten minutes Sandra arrives into the salon to ask what's going on, having received Angie's call. "Well, it's self-explanatory, it's just as Angie said. I need some time alone, I've a few things to do, you know. None of which will make for great TV. So let's regroup and hit the shows." I'm taking control of the situation.

"You're booked for one week starting today, so we can't really allow that, Oli, sorry." She's sounding less cheery than a few hours ago.

"OK, well can you wait until I at least get my hair sorted? Thanks," I say as I return to look at my phone. It's only morning one of day one and already the idea of being followed non-stop is pissing me off. It isn't only annoying but also extremely difficult. On top of this I'm suffering from severe paranoia and am sure they will edit things to make me look crazy. Jesus, at this rate it wouldn't be too difficult to achieve. *'Man gets hair cut then massage and then goes shopping!' Hold the fucking front page*, I think to myself.

After over an hour I'm ready to leave and when I arrive at the crew's van the mood has changed dramatically. "We've spoken with your agent and she agrees with us. You must do the show as contracts have been signed and a schedule must be kept," Sandra says, sounding very much in charge.

Buying me some time, I suggested that we meet for lunch in forty-five minutes at the Ivy. "I can just see you guys there as I must go to an urgent meeting and again, they won't permit filming. It's with my lawyer, I'm sure you understand," I shout over the sound of nearby road works, as I try to hail a black cab.

"Ok Oli, the Ivy in half an hour, we will call ahead to clear the filming. Don't be late!" she shouts after me as I hop into a taxi which hasn't fully stopped.

"Where to, gov?" the driver asks.

"Somewhere away from here… The Goat in Boots on the Fulham Road, please!" I reach for my phone to call Paolo. "Where are you? Come to the Goat, I'll be there in five minutes," I say before he can even say hello. Realistically I'm about twenty minutes away from the bar but knowing that even if Paolo was next door it would take him an age to show up, I always pretend to be just arriving wherever we are meeting.

Sitting at the bar drinking a Hendrick's and tonic, I

pick up a copy of the *Sun*. 'Fears as Socialite is taken into rehab for the Second time this Year' reads the headline, accompanied by some dreadful photos of Gussy Henderson-Blake-Scott falling out of a taxi in the West End. *Oh, Christ. Poor, poor Gussy,* I think to myself as I skim through the article. Gussy is an old friend who has inherited a shed load of money following the death of both his parents, when their private jet came down in the Swiss Alps. He was just thirteen years old at the time and has since spent his time being expelled from Eton, Le Rosey and other high-profile schools due to "unruly behaviour", or drug abuse to you and me. An only child, he inherited their entire estate on his eighteenth birthday and to celebrate he had a three-week party taking in St Tropez, Ibiza and New York for a select few of us. Following which, he took us to Santorini for a month to recover. To this day I don't think he is allowed through the doors of the Four Seasons in Manhattan. His inheritance has been reported to be in excess of two billion pounds. A figure he laughs at, claiming it to be closer to three. Now at twenty-five he is four years my junior and despite our constant rows, I consider him to be like a brother.

Opening the paper, I continue reading the article which lists myself, Paolo and one or two others from our circle as 'close friends'. "Jesus fuck!" I say out loud.

"What's that, Oli?" asks Matt the barman.

"Oh nothing, Matt, sorry, just something I'm reading in the paper."

"I thought it was the name of one of your creative cocktails," he laughs, making reference to the fact that I constantly ask for strange drinks.

Just then, Paolo arrives and it's as if the news of Gussy is light compared to his latest drama. "Ciao darling! I swear driving in Chelsea is getting worse. I just knocked some fool off her bicycle on the King's Road. She came out of nowhere and landed on the bonnet of my brand-new Lamborghini!" he says as he rifles through an oversized Louis Vuitton bag searching for his phone.

"Shit, is she OK?" I ask, genuinely concerned.

"Oh she's fine, she bounced and shouted a little bit, so I gave her two hundred pounds and told her to buy a stiff drink and new set of wheels. I think she must have been a lesbian, she was very sturdy." He's sipping my drink. "Oh yummy, we'll take two more of those, Matt, darling, when you're ready!" he says without flinching.

"Have you seen the paper?" I ask as I hold up the front page.

"I know, poor old Gussy, he really needs to donate that money to charity or something," he says, sounding cruel but at the same time making sense. Ever since Gussy inherited his great wealth he has lived life on the edge. "I knew this was coming, I met him only last week at the Save the Polar Bear Ball at the Dorchester and he was wired. Seriously, I couldn't even get a full sentence out of him. What rehab is he in this time, does it say?" He continues searching for his phone. "Call my phone please, will you? Where are we lunching?"

"Well that's just it. I'm filming that TV show today, or at least supposed to be, but I had to escape. Would you like to join me for lunch at the Ivy? My cousin Izzy was supposed to be coming, but she just bailed via SMS, the bitch!" I'm sounding slightly desperate.

"OK," he says without question.

"Seriously? You'll come? Oh, Paolo, I love you!" I say as I hug him.

"I know you love me. Everyone loves me, darling. Now tell me about this show, what's it all about? What's it called? I need to know what I am appearing on," he laughs.

"Well it's called NQOCD which means…"

"Not quite our class, darling! I know what it means. Do you think I live under a rock?" He sounds offended.

"Well, yes, of course you get it, but I mean, will Joe public?" I ask.

"Who cares about Joe public? They love having to find out what an acronym means, it makes them feel smart at dinner parties. Clever move on the TV people's side," he nods as he finishes his gin.

"Well anyway, they're following me around to see what life is like for people like us," I say, still trying to make sense of the concept myself.

"Well surely it should be called PLU then, no?" he smiles cleverly.

"PLU?" I ask.

"Think about it, blondie… Now what time is lunch?" as he stands up and checks himself in a large mirror.

"It's now, and we're late!"

"Well call them and tell them to calm down as you've secured some serious international TV totty!" he says as he pops his Fendi sunglasses on.

At the Ivy the mood is fun, mainly thanks to Paolo who is playing up to cameras like a true pro. "So you boys are off to the shows this afternoon, yes?" Sandra asks excitedly.

"Well that rather depends. We have been known to ditch Stella McCartney if say, James Middelton was nearby!" he laughs hysterically.

"So you have a crush on James then?" she continues, knowing that this is really what her bosses want.

"Darling, have you been asleep for the past forty-eight months? Everyone wants a bit of Jimmy! And now with the beard… divine!" he gushes.

"Anyhow, there is no sign of James in here, so yes, we will attend a show or two," I say, trying to get things back on track. It's clear that 'on track' isn't really what the crew are looking for. They want totally off track, derailed, huge crash and numerous fatalities.

"So Oli, do you dine here regularly?" she asks as she looks around the busy dining room, which today counts David Furnish, Tara Palmer-Tomkinson and some chap from EastEnders as diners.

"Not so much actually, it's a bit high profile for my tastes." I'm trying to sound cool but instead sounding stupid.

"What do you look for in a great restaurant then?" she queries.

"Honestly Sandra, these sort of questions are

boring me to sleep, so imagine what the poor viewers will think? I mean, if you want to talk restaurants why don't you interview that fucking AA Gill guy or whatever his name is? I'm off to the loo and before you ask, no, you can't follow me. Come on Paolo, I need to talk to you – in private!" I say, sounding like a spoilt brat.

"Seriously, we need to make this more exciting!" I'm chopping out a huge line of coke on the toilet seat.

"Is that enough? I mean you did say exciting," Paolo quickly points out.

"Fuck it, darling, you're right, let's do it all," as I chuck the rest out, spilling most of it on the floor. As we stand there waiting for things to kick in, we both rub the remainder of the cocaine on our gums and try hard not to laugh when we hear someone farting in the next cubicle. Once the coast is clear we return to the table, pay the bill and gather ourselves.

"OK, so we're going to do Temperley, Christopher Kane and Nicole Farhi! Are you ready for some fashion fixing?" I ask, sounding far more upbeat.

"Why have you chosen these three, Oli?" Sandra ask in her usual mundane tone.

"Oh, it's like an eeny meeny situation really. Oh, we get invited to every single show from here to Hong Kong, so it's rude not to show up. Naturally we can't be bothered to hit them all up, so we just pick at random. Besides, it's Alice's first show in London after a three-year absence. She's been showing in New York for the last six seasons in case your math isn't too good, so we've gotta support our girl and welcome her home. Plus, she gets the best crowd – Peaches Geldof, Mischa Barton, Jacquetta Wheeler, Laura Bailey, Rosamund Pike and Edie Campbell. Edie's actually walking for Alice so it will be a great show!" I say excitedly and sincerely.

"Sorry, who is Alice?" Sandra quizzes.

"Are you serious? Alice is Alice Temperley! Alice, Alice, who the fuck is Alice?" I laugh as myself and Paolo collect our coats. "Honestly can you believe these guys? Talk about clueless!" I whisper into Paolo's ear. "We'll go in Paolo's Batmobile and you can tail us, OK?" I say as we walk out of the restaurant, much to the delight of the awaiting press.

"Oli, can we get a pic of yourself and Paolo for the *Daily Mail*?" asks a staff photographer from the paper, followed by another from *The Express* and another from Condé Nast. As the paparazzi are busily snapping away, the film crew are rolling. I swear it's like a circus and it isn't even three o'clock.

"OK, that's your lot, chaps!" I announce loudly. "We have shows to get to and people to shake with," I'm taking a bow. The cocaine may have woken me up but boy oh boy am I behaving strangely for lunchtime. As we try to climb into Paolo's shiny black Lamborghini Murcielago I can see the cameramen getting extremely excited.

"Is this your car, Paolo?" one of them asks, sounding like a giddy teenager as he takes a photograph on his phone.

"Well of course it's my car, darling. Do I look like the sort of boy who goes around stealing sports cars?" he says before slamming the large butterfly door shut. With a roar of the engine we're gone, leaving the film crew still gaping in awe.

"They have absolutely no idea where we are going. Come to think of it, do we?" I laugh so hard my head hits the dashboard.

Chapter 9

London Fashion Week – Philips de Pury Building

Screeching to a halt and almost taking out a number of fashionistas in the process, we arrive early for the Temperley show. Once we've managed to find parking for Paolo's beloved Italian machine and reconnected with the camera crew, we're ready for show time, and by show time I am of course referring to the 'Oli and Paolo Show', which goes ahead on a daily basis, with or without a camera man.

"Oh, I really think we should make a pit stop at The Punch Bowl for a quick drink, I totally need one after that journey. Seriously, we were nearly hit by about three white van men, all looking at me when they should have been watching the road. I am beginning to question why I spend millions on my cars, when I can't even drive them properly in this city!" he says in all seriousness. In Paolo's head they were of course looking at him and not his car. "Plus, if nothing else, to allow that lot to calm down." He's making reference to the fashion darlings who are giddily gathered in front of the impressive building. "I've to meet my man and there's no way I'm doing that here!" he says as he dials his coke dealer's number. "Jeff hi... Yes, an eighth... Ten minutes, Punch Bowl on Farm St... Ciao, darling." He ends the call. Paolo likes to keep things short when it comes to making deals, whether it be a deal for a Picasso, a rare Rolex, or a bag of cocaine. Another thing he is consistent with, is that he calls everyone darling. I guess it keeps things simple and means he never has to remember anyone's name.

As we sit at the bar it's clear to see that it's the bar of the moment, having been bought and completely renovated by Guy Ritchie and Madonna just a few months previously. Once a quiet pub for posh Mayfair locals, it's now the chosen boozer of Princes William and Harry as well as Jude Law, David Beckham and Leonardo DiCaprio to name a few. This afternoon is a different scene completely, as there are only two other customers, both of whom look like they may be awaiting Jeff's arrival too. Eventually he shows up looking more like a City banker than a dodgy dealer. "Afternoon boys, mine's a Midleton if you're buying," he says as he pulls out a seat to join us. "Paolo, I'm heading to Ibiza at the weekend so anything you need will have to be sorted before I jet, alright?" He's sounding very business-like. With a handshake and a quick drink, the deal is done and we're on our way.

As usual it's something of a bun fight trying to get through the throngs of fashionistas and press gathered at the entrance of the show. "What is it with fashion folk? Why must they always stand in your way?" Paolo asks as he continues pushing forward. "Move, bitch!" he snaps at an emaciated girl who has decided that wearing a large red telephone box on her head was a good idea. "Honestly, these people… Talk about trying too hard, and most of these losers aren't even invited to the show, they just pose for the photographers in the chance of making Vogue Diary!" he moans as we make our way inside.

Sandra is standing with a clipboard and looking impatient, like an embarrassing teacher on a school trip. "Oh, there you are Oli, where have you been? We really need to catch a few shots of you mingling and maybe a quick chat with the designer if you can set that up?" she says as she tugs at my arm.

"Seriously, can you stop doing that! This is not the sort of cashmere one pulls." I'm removing her hand from my sweater. "So start filming and follow me around, but if you think I'm going to try get a chat with Alice today you must be high!" I say rather ironically. "Oh, hi darling, I'll be over in a minute!" I shout over the crowd to Alexa Chung, who's swamped by photographers. "I've no idea where Paolo has disappeared to. I must find him before we can begin," sounding as if my life depends on it. In fact, my life kind of does depend on it, as my coke buzz is wearing off and in its place is a thumping headache plus that creeping feeling of paranoia. Not helping is the fact that his phone is going directly to voicemail. As I work the room on my own I can feel the cameras almost on my shoulder and a sudden flush of blood to my head. "Seriously, can you stop for a moment? This really is too much. It's way too warm in here and…" Before I can finish, I collapse to the floor. The last thing I remember is seeing a waiter within reach carrying a tray of champagne and as I reach for a glass I hit the deck bringing the tray and its contents down too. While fainting is a pretty awkward thing to happen at the best of times, I wake to find I'm still being filmed. "Where am I? What the…?" I ask, sounding completely disorientated.

"Oh, be careful of the glass!" a handsome French waiter urges, pointing to the smashed champagne glasses.

"Are you OK, Oli? What happened?" Sandra asks, as wired Matt the cameraman films from over her shoulder.

"Seriously will you fuck off, you stupid bitch!" I'm trying to get to my feet with the help of two burly security guards. "I'm calling my agent and putting an end to this immediately," I snipe. "You're putting so much pressure on me, it is not normal," I continue, much to the amusement of the other guests.

"This is gonna make fucking amazing TV! Career changing, for both us! You got any more of that marching powder, mate?" Matt asks. He's ignored.

Suddenly Paolo reappears, having heard of the commotion. "Darling, what happened? Let's get you out of here." He puts his arm around me.

"But Oli…" Sandra whinges, sounding more and more desperate.

"Listen, we're done here for today, OK?" Paolo says sternly. "You can see that Oli isn't well and needs rest." He ushers me through the crowd outside to the fresh air.

"Holy shit! What happened?" I ask, genuinely feeling shook. "One minute I was chatting to the camera and being fabulous and the next, boom!" I take a drag on a Marlboro Red.

"Oh bello, it's all very Pats and Eddie, I think we need to get out of here and reboot!" Paolo reaches for his phone to call for a driver. "Let's leave the car where it is and go to the only place on earth that can fix a situation like this – The Ritz!" Most people may have decided that going home, taking a bath and going to bed was the answer, but not Paolo. "The Ritz fixes everything, everyone knows that! All you need is to escape from this circus, it's all too much." He sounds genuinely concerned. "How much are they paying you anyhow? No matter what it is I'll double it if you stop now," he says sincerely. That's the point, unlike Paolo and others I know, I'm not stinking rich, and have always had to work in order to survive. While I take his offer as that of a caring friend, there's no way I'm accepting it. "I've called Julia and she will arrange to collect some clothes for you. Oh, and I've also sent her to Space NK with a list as long as Naomi Campbell's legs!" he says of his trusted housekeeper and confidant. As I wait in the Rivoli Bar I look at the scene in front of me.

In utter confusion and more possibly exhaustion, I've managed to order a selection of drinks, not knowing what I really want. I sit sipping a glass of Barolo one minute, some still water the next and then espresso macchiato the next. The array of drinks is a true reflection of my mood, I'm clearly all over the place and need time out. I sit gazing at the fantastic art deco interior of the bar; stunning Murano chandeliers, set into gilded ceiling domes. Animal print chairs and lots of lacquered wood panelling make me feel as if I've been transported back in time to a far more glamorous era. Don't get me wrong, I've been in the bar before of course, but this time I'm really taking in my surroundings, as if my wired state has heightened my awareness of everything and everyone. From the windows, I can see the evening light coming from the Piccadilly Arcade, while the bar staff busy themselves with tray after tray of champagne cocktails and martinis. Paolo seems to be gone for an eternity as he busies himself organising a room for me to unwind in. When I say a room, I do in fact mean a suite. That's the thing about Paolo, he never does things by halves. "I've booked the Prince of Wales Suite for the night. We shall send out for whatever we need, order in whatever we want and spend the evening watching movies! How does that sound?" he asks, sounding proud of himself. "It is my favourite suite in the hotel. I once stayed for over two weeks while the townhouse was being painted, oh, but never tell anyone. People can be so judgmental, especially at five grand per night." He sips his wine.

"You really are a great friend P," I say as I lay back into the sumptuous sofa.

"Darling, we are much more than friends, we are family, just like Sister Sledge!" he laughs. "Anyhow, sorry to dampen the mood but have you seen the evening paper?" He reaches for a copy of the *Evening Standard*. "They're linking Gussy's latest rehab stint to royal circles. It also says that he's been partying with one or two Greek shipping heirs, and we know who," he says, sounding all Ms Marple. "I'm telling you, darling, if this mess gets any closer I'll jump. It's a true 'iceberg straight ahead!' situation and I'll certainly be man overboard," he sighs.

Once we reach the suite I can feel my mood change. Gone are the stresses which have plagued me all morning and in their place is a sense of calm, a feeling of serenity. Paolo isn't lying when he says the suite is beyond fabulous. We're greeted by our very own personal butler who shows us around. "Not every suite comes with thirty Jo Malone Lime Basil & Mardarin candles, I sent out for them." Paolo smiles smugly as we walk from room to room. It really is enormous, complete with a vast drawing room opening into a dining room, two en-suite bedrooms, a staff kitchen, and views over Green Park.

"I can totally see why you had found it difficult to check out last time." We stand looking out over the park below.

"Now, perhaps you should take advantage of the situation and pop along to the spa for a detox massage?" he says as he hands me a robe from the bathroom. "That will take you just over an hour and will give me time to catch up with some emails I've been meaning to reply to for a week. When you come back we can order in and watch movies. Sound good?" He flips his MacBook open.

"Well, how can I refuse? What will I do about the TV crew? What about Angie? Should I…?"

Before I can answer, he raises his hand. "Look, Oli, I don't mean to sound rude, so please don't be offended, but you look like crap. No, no you really do, totally and utter shit," he says sternly. "Don't worry about the small stuff. I'll call them and explain that if they leave you be for be for a day or two you will emerge glorious! Now go, or you'll be late," he smiles.

As I lie on the massage table, I slowly start to drift off to sleep, before the treatment even begins. Waking after an hour, I feel like a new person.

"Drink your green tea and try not to drink an alcohol this evening. You will wake tomorrow feeling fantastic. Now I will leave you for a few moments to relax," the pretty masseuse says calmly. For once in my life the last thing I want is more alcohol. I feel like I'm ready to begin a whole new lifestyle, one of health and fitness, that involves early nights and regular meals. That's the thing about a great massage, you feel like you can change the world, well, at least for those first few minutes afterwards.

As I walk back to the suite I feel as if I'm floating. I've completely zoned out from everything that's going on, or supposed to be. Opening the door, I can hear Paolo is having a heated argument with someone on his phone. "No, no, no, you listen to me, you idiot! I am telling you, if you even try to proceed I'll have you fired and your dreadful newspaper shut down!" he snaps. "You really have no idea who you're dealing with. Oh really? Well perhaps Google my family and then talk to your boss." He flings the phone onto the large striped sofa.

"What's going on now?" I ask, sounding slightly stoned.

"This whole thing with Gussy is becoming a circus. They are now trying to link us to his mess. I am so fucking furious!" He's dialling a number into his phone. "Hello Papa, I think we may have a situation. Can you talk?" he says calmly as he walks into the dining room.

As I sit, our butler Gerald appears with a silver tray, upon which sits a bottle of Dom Perignon Rosé and two glasses. "Compliments of the house, sir." He quietly places the tray and pops the vintage cork. As I wait for Paolo to re-emerge I decide it would be rude not to at least take a sip. After all, it's a gift and I've never really considered champagne to be alcohol. *Plus, we all know what Madame Bollinger famously said,* I think to myself as I finish off the glass.

"Oh, is that champagne? I so need this right now!" Paolo says as he downs the glass in one go.

"Jesus, can you relax? You're ruining my hippy trippy state. Surely it can't be that bad?" I'm lying back into the sofa as Gerald tops off my glass.

"Well, if you consider photographs of you, me and Gussy partying hard at Nikki Beach a few years ago no big deal then yes!" he shouts as he helps himself to the bottle. "I mean, being photographed at such a tacky beach club is bad enough, but apparently they have access to photos of us doing coke and they are willing to publish!" he says quietly so Gerald can't hear.

"What? Who has photos of us? Who took them? I don't believe a word of it!" I say as my chilled mode rapidly becomes frantic yet again.

"I took a call earlier from some chap at the *News of the World* who says that he's been offered the photos and asked if I had any comment. Well, I think you heard my comment when you walked into the room." He starts pacing the suite again.

"I think you are overreacting. Leave it to your father's legal team, they'll sort it. Can you imagine the scandal if it did make print!" I sit forward, now too starting to get genuinely worried.

"It must be someone we know. I mean, who would have photographed us just hanging out? It doesn't make sense," he questions as he begins scrolling through his Facebook friends list on his laptop. "Anyhow, I must try stay calm. Papa knows all about it now and he is talking to our legal people in Milan to try get it stopped. Oh, I need something stronger than this," he says before calling for Gerald. "Oh, there you are, darling. I think we're going to need some much stronger. Could you fetch a bottle of Suntory The Yamazaki? The twenty-five-year-old!" he says as he sits down beside me. "I swear, if this story breaks it will be the kiss of death for my new label. All my hard work and time, for nothing," he says solemnly.

In truth, Paolo is set to launch his new fashion label within just weeks, but as for his hard work and time, well between you and me, he has a whole creative team in Milan and Florence doing the real work, but don't ever tell anyone.

"Your whiskey, sir." Gerald presents the prized Japanese single malt.

"I know you're not supposed to be drinking but will you join me? I've spoken to the TV crew and sorted everything. You are free for forty-eight hours and then back to work." He takes a glass from the silver tray and hands it to me.

"OK, but we aren't going out. We can stay 'home' and have a few drinks, order some food and watch those movies as planned. That is my best and final on the subject," I smile. As I say the words I know that I'm fooling nobody. Within an hour we were already through the bottle and Gerald is off in search of a replacement.

"You know, darling, it is so nice to just stay in like this, isn't it?" Paolo says as he lights two Marlboro Reds, handing me one. "I mean, this is what normal people do every night. It's not so bad, so why are they always moaning?" The fact that we're sitting in one of the most expensive hotel suites in the world, drinking one of the most expensive bottles of whiskey, has obviously escaped him somewhat, but that's what I love about Paolo. He isn't showy, flashy or spoilt, he's just very, very privileged. "We need some music in here, and also Gerald really needs to put out that fire, I'm super hot! I mean, who needs a fire in September?" He's pulling his sweater over his head dramatically, messing his perfectly tousled hair in the process. As Paolo reaches for the television remote to switch on MTV or some other music channel, I decide to send a text message to Marco. I'm not sure if it's the whiskey or the fact that I'm genuinely feeling worried about everything that's happening, but I can't help myself. It's been almost eight weeks since we've spoken, following yet another manic row at a party in Rome. We are together one year now and I swear to you we have spent most of those twelve months fighting. This time a rather public row that began at Dal Bolognese, and continued for many hours back at my flat on Via della Croce, much to the annoyance of my Russian neighbours. To be honest I don't really know what the row was about, it just seemed to start and not stop. That's the thing with myself and Marco; two very passionate and at the same time stubborn people. Sure, there are upsides to our tempestuous relationship. The sex for one is beyond, as is our social life, but when we fight it's out of control. Full-on proper crazy fights where items of furniture get smashed and terribly hurtful things are said. After accusing me of being 'crazy', he's told me not to get in touch, but as I said, I can't help myself.

'Hey Marco, it's Oli. I miss you x' is all I can muster, and before sending it, I read it ten times, as if by doing so it will validate the message somewhat. After forty minutes and another half a bottle of whisky there's still no reply.

"Fuck it, P, let's go out! Where are all those invitations you were showing me earlier? Let's get dressed and go see what's what." I jump to my feet.

"OK, but on one condition. Will you eat something first? When did you last eat?" he asks, sounding like an overly concerned nurse.

"I'm not at all hungry, but something light perhaps. We could always bypass the food option. It is Fashion Week after all. Where's the coke you picked up earlier?" I ask as I check my phone again.

"Will you stop with the phone? It's starting to piss me off," Paolo snaps before he removes my BlackBerry from my hand.

While I shower he makes it his business to order some 'light bites' from the extensive room service menu. Being Paolo, this order is made up of two full trolleys of food, none of which is consumed. "Oh, there you are, I thought you'd been washed down the plug hole." He's sitting chopping out very large lines of cocaine on the table.

"Sorry, I just needed to wash away the day, you know?" I say as I tighten my bath robe and check myself in a mirror.

"So, one lump or two?" he laughs, passing me a rolled-up fifty-pound note.

"I really think tonight is going to be fun. It's just over a year since I first met Marco and I really thought he was the one, but I guess not. I say we get our party mode on and go find a replacement. One each!" I snort two lines of the coke off the table and reach for the TV remote to turn up the volume.

"Oh, I love this fucking song!" Paolo gushes as he dances around the dining table to Poker Face by Lady Gaga. "I think this should be filed under super gay sounds! P-p-p-p-p-p-p my poker face," he sings loudly, mimicking what she's doing in the video clip. Once the second bottle of whiskey is finished, we're asking Gerald to fix us some espresso martinis. After three each we're wired to the moon, although it's hard to tell what we were buzzing on, as the concoction of alcohol, cocaine and caffeine is pretty potent. We both dress in this season's Gucci, and we're really rocking our inner boho sixties vibe. "I wasn't really sure about this collection at first, but the whole hippy aristocrat thing is seriously growing on me. I love all this fringed-belt detail," he says as he stands in front of the mirror for perhaps the tenth time.

"Yes, baby, we are super stylish. Why can't more people have a clue when it comes to selecting pieces from Gucci each season? I mean you're only supposed to pick certain pieces, unless you're a Russian. The head-to-toe look is very nasty. If only more men could follow our lead." I'm sounding more and more like Zoolander by the second. "So, where to first, my stylish hippy friend?" I ask as I knock back a shot of chilled raspberry Stolichnaya, before attempting the awaiting martini.

"Oh, I think we should really show face at the *Vogue* party briefly, then onward to Burberry, and perhaps a little action at Boujis?" he suggests as he continues to dance, spilling martini everywhere as he does. We really are ready to go, which is quite a feat, seeing as only hours ago I was almost dead.

Zooming through the evening traffic in a chauffeur-driven Maybach, Paolo is truly on form. "What are we doing in this thing?" he asks the driver, who up until now hasn't spoken much. "I mean, no offence but it's hideous. What sort of person buys a Maybach? Talk about attention seeking!" he says loudly. The fact Paolo is an attention whore only makes things funnier. "Is this your car? If so, I'm sorry, but you need to see a therapist!" he instructs the smiling driver.

"No sir, I'd need to work a lifetime to be able to afford a car like this," he replies in a sexy, gravelly South London accent.

"Gosh, now that really would be a waste of a life, wouldn't it?" Paolo smiles, before snorting up a small amount of coke from a solid silver cocaine snorter. "Fab, isn't it? I found it at the bottom of my croc Birkin, I had it made in New York ages ago. It's a copy of a 1920s one by Tiffany, or at least I think that's what the guy who sold it to me said." He places his latest toy under my nose.

Arriving at the *Vogue* party, it really is a feast for the awaiting paparazzi and their lenses. Everyone from Ivanka Trump to Hamish Bowles have gathered and are doing their very best to air-kiss as many people as possible in very cramped surroundings. "Oh wow, it really is the party of the week. Alexandra sure knows how to do things!" making reference to the magazine's editor, as he takes two glasses of champagne from a passing waiter. As we too air-kiss and flirt our way through the party I start to feel very unwell. I begin to feel beads of sweat forming on my face and my temperature drops rapidly. Holding on to Paolo's arm as he works the room, I'm getting severe stomach cramps, and the last thing I remember is seeing models Jasmine Guinness and Georgia May Jagger chatting with Nicky Haslam. Attempting to say hello, I collapse again. From there I don't remember a thing, which is just as well, as I'm not so good when it comes to such dramatic scenes. Waking at the Whittington Hospital, I'm completely destroyed.

"Oh, thank God you're OK! I really thought we'd lost you," Paolo cries as I open my eyes. I try to speak but my mouth is so dry that it's impossible. "Here, drink this. Don't worry, it's just water," he smiles as he places a plastic cup to my lips.

"What the fuck happened?" I ask, sounding completely dazed.

"You collapsed again and you've had your stomach pumped." He grips my hand. "How are you feeling now? You really gave us all such a fright."

"Oh, P, I've no idea how I'm feeling. I just know I need to talk to Marco. Please can you call him and let him know what's happened? Perhaps leave out the bit about my stomach being pumped. I mean, that may be a TMI situation." I'm attempting to sit up in the bed. "Oh, Jesus, it happened at the *Vogue* party, didn't it?" I ask, half knowing the answer. "What time is it? I really need to get out of here and sort my life. If this ends up in the papers… Oh fuck, they'll link this to the Gussy story, I'm sure of it!" I'm now panicking.

"You've to try to calm down. Nobody can write anything as nobody knows what happened. If anyone asks I'm going to say that you had severe food poisoning, OK?" He places extra pillows behind my head.

"Rather ironic, don't you think, considering the huge amount of room service food at the suite." I crack a smile.

"While you were resting I was thinking, you really should write a book. No, seriously you should, like a guide-book to fellow socialites. How to survive a *Vogue* party, literally," he says sweetly. Now I know what you're thinking, a party hosted by *Vogue* is far from a 'simple thing', but for Paolo attending these events had been the norm since birth, so please forgive him. "You rest some more and I'll go contact Marco and see what's up his ass," Paolo smiles. "Darling, I don't want to upset you, but I did hear he was spotted in Paris last week, lunching at L'Avenue with Alessandra. It could be nothing, but seriously, you need to take time out of all this and decide what it is you really want. I really think you should take that trip to Spain you were planning. Go alone and take time out." He kisses my head. "Oh, I've already told the doctor that you don't require a lecture on alcohol and drug abuse. So if he comes knocking, stay asleep!" He kisses my forehead again and leaves the room.

As I lie here staring at the ceiling, I feel angry and sad as I can't help but picture Marco and Alessandra lunching at L'Avenue, a restaurant that we too have dined at numerous times. What the fuck is he playing at? To be honest right now I have no energy to even think about it. I thank God for sparing me, yet again. *Onwards and upwards,* I think to myself, as I feel the pain in my stomach. I re-adjust to a more comfortable position and I take Paolo's advice. I think a few days in Spain may be just the ticket. As for now, it may not be in The Ritz, but rather ironically it feels like heaven.

Chapter 10

Marbella, Spain

Waking in unfamiliar surroundings is nothing new for me, as over the years I've managed to go to lunch in Dublin or London and wake up in St Tropez or Ibiza, waking in a different country with no recollection of how I got there. Apparently, I've missed out on some seriously impressive jets, even though I was on board. There have been times when I needed to call reception to see which hotel I had woken in and which country. You can imagine the shame but at the same time fun of asking the receptionist which Four Seasons I had slept in. This morning is slightly different, as I wake alone and I know where I am, or at least in which country. Having rented the stunning beachfront villa in Marbella, I'm at least sure of my location, but having spent the previous day drinking and partying hard I've no idea what the villa actually looks like. Lying in bed, all I can hear is the sea lapping on the shore and the rather annoying song of some birds who seem to be taunting me. I've that sinking feeling which creeps in when you know something terrible has happened, but thanks to too many Jack Daniels it's delayed in reaching you. "Oh fuck, fuck, fuck!" I say aloud as I lie staring at the ceiling. Reaching for my lighter, I raise my head, light a Marlboro Red and collapse back onto the stack of pillows. Rather than staying in the thick of Marbella madness, I've opted to stay in the far more chilled and exclusive Los Monteros area, a part of the Spanish millionaires' playground that counts Antonio Banderas as well as many other members of Spanish society as residents, so I am pretty sure my behaviour on night one hasn't impressed anyone.

Lying here, I try to remember the day and more importantly night before, but nothing. I sit up and look around the room. My iPhone has no battery power, on the floor my Tod's, which were originally sand coloured are now almost black, and my white Saint-Laurent jeans, well, they're soon to become cut-off shorts due to what looks like either red wine or blood staining them badly. I pray it isn't the latter. Standing up my head feels as if it will fall off as I walk across the ginormous bedroom towards the equally expansive terrace. It feels like a chore, one which I may be unable to complete. I slowly open the large glass doors and step outside. The terrace is perfect, complete with a hot tub and uninterrupted views of the Mediterranean. Well, there is one interruption, being an extremely sexy gardener who has removed his t-shirt shirt and is busily clipping a large lemon tree. It's a surreal feeling, as even though I've paid a fortune to rent the house during the height of the holiday season, I've no idea what or who awaits me downstairs. I feel as if I'm a guest in someone's house, who fell home drunk as a lord and was banished to his room.

As I shower I hurt my brain as I try to remember what happened. Even the slightest detail would be an achievement, but still nothing. Well, apart from the fact that I arrived early in the day and picked up a hire car in the form of a black Mercedes-Benz 500SL before hitting the N340 coastal road with the roof down. Instead of stopping by the villa and checking things out, I drove straight to the Marbella Club for lunch as I was running late to meet my dear friend Sal who always knows how to cheer me up. Sal is one of Marbella's most prominent art dealers and socialites. Having blown in from New York via Madrid twenty years ago, she is the one to go to if you are on the hunt for a rare off-market Picasso or Monet. If she hosts a party you know it will be beyond! With access to the richest and most powerful people in Europe, if not the world, she is a force to be reckoned with.

Sal awaits my arrival at MC Café, sipping chilled Laurent-Perrier and chatting with two young guys from Paris who are at the next table. Both possibly models and less than half her age, they're hanging on her every word. Set on a white sand beach, with amazing views of both the sea and the drop-dead gorgeous wait staff, she manages to outshine both, dressed in a shocking pink Dolce & Gabbana halter top and circulation-stopping tight jeans. Her perfectly tanned skin enhanced by honey blonde hair, at 54 she looks roughly fifteen years younger, due to the odd 'touch up' of Botox and enough money to cover any of life's stresses in fabulousness. While the weather is typically hot, the atmosphere is perfect. Overly large silver fans blow a refreshing breeze from the beach towards diners, carrying on it the scent of the sea. As I arrive she introduces me to her new friends, who while being hot, don't catch my attention. We dine light; a simple squid salad, two bottles of champagne and a whole lot of essential gossip from her ever hectic world. Actually, truth is, she's more interested to hear my news.

Yes, as you've figured out I took Paolo's advice and I'm in Spain alone, as myself and Marco have broken up yet again due to the fact that my partying is, and I quote, "worrying". He's also less than happy with the fact that I did the reality TV show and worse, the amount of media attention it's brought. In fact, he's getting pretty tired of the media intrusion on every level, even when it's simple things like me opening up my wardrobe to some style supplement or another. They're so interested in our relationship that they've begun stalking us in a way. Well, at least that's how he sees it, so most evenings we just fight over the most stupid of things. It's a catch twenty-two, as it's my job to be so out there in the press, but trying to have a private life is getting more and more stressful. Anyhow, we're on an 'official break', which as you know really means it's over. I tried to listen to Paolo's advice when he told me to step back, and if it's meant to be it will go full circle, but I'm so fucking exhausted by it all and perhaps it's time to call it a day. All crazy when you consider the way Sophia and others got hurt in order for us to be together.

"I'm serious, this time it's over for good! We just keep coming back to the same place and it's a boring place, baby, I'm sure of it! Whenever I ask him if we can talk, he shuts down and this time has vanished completely," I insist, removing my Tom Ford sunglasses and looking her in the eye to emphasise my point. The fact she hasn't removed hers only makes my point somewhat half arsed.

"Oh, I've heard this all before, darling," she says as she places her hand on mine. "We have been here before, no? I can't keep telling you that dating Italians is like trying to run up a downward escalator. What do you mean vanished? He is Italian, so have you tried calling his mother? I mean isn't that where all Italian boys run at any given opportunity?" she laughs, as do the two French guys who are somehow half listening to our conversation. I give them a stare, they look away. "If it really is over, why won't you allow me to introduce you to a friend of mine while you are here? He's handsome, very jet-set and fantastic fun!" she says as she reaches for her jewel-encrusted Vertu phone to show me a photo. "Actually, let's do this the old-fashioned way. Are you man enough to go on a blind date?" she gushes as she flicks her hair for the boys' amusement. Having met her billionaire husband, investment banker Dieter on a blind date, she referred to this style of hooking up as the old-fashioned way.

Personally I've always thought blind dates are for the desperate, but what the heck? If the Louboutin fits and all that... After lunch we relax at the super exclusive private beach, ordering jugs of Pimm's Royale and planning my date. Well, Sal makes the plans, I just nod in agreement. Anything for an easy life is my mood du jour. From there things are slightly blurred. I do recall having cocktails at Pravda in Puerto

Banus and meeting some Middle Eastern friends of Sal's who insisted on taking me to legendary nightclub Olivia Valere, where we drank Jeroboams of Dom Perignon rosé and danced on tables. Oh, and my car was safely parked at the Marbella Club, before you ask, but that is all I can remember.

Stepping out of the shower I walk onto the terrace again to take a proper look at the gardener, but he's nowhere to be seen and the heat of the midday sun is not helping the situation. I return indoors to search for my sunglasses, a phone charger and a cure to the fear which is getting worse by the minute. Arriving into the kitchen I look fresh; dressed in a white Ralph Lauren polo shirt, white tennis shorts and Stan Smith trainers. I'm greeted by two uniformed maids and a cook, all curious to see who is staying this week. "Good morning, sir, I am Ana, the house keeper. Is everything OK for you? Is there anything you require?" she asks in perfect English. She is a typical house keeper in that she's middle aged, round in figure and isn't wearing a wedding ring. She has a caring, honest face.

"Very pleased to meet you, I am Oli," I say as I shake her hand and smile as wide as the hangover allows. "I'd kill for a bottle of cold Perrier with some lemon and three painkillers. Last night was possibly too much fun," I say as I walk from the kitchen out to the pool. "If you could have someone change the flowers throughout the house. I'd asked that only cream roses be in place. I hate coloured florals, they hurt my eyes!" I continue, trying to pretend to myself that flower choices are all I have to worry about.

"Of course, sir, and here is your water and pills,"

she smiles, placing a silver tray down beside my chair. Pouring the water, she looks worried.

"Is everything OK?" I ask, sensing the worst.

"Well, sir..." she stumbles.

"Oh please, Ana, call me Oli, I can't be dealing with such formality at this early in the day," I say, realising it was already afternoon.

"Well sir, there was a matter with the police, if you remember?" She looks at me sternly.

"Police? What happened with the police?" I ask, sitting up in my seat like one of those meercats you see on TV shows.

"There was an incident with your car at the Marbella Club, sir," she continues.

"You came home with two policemen. Don't you remember, sir?" she asks as she wipes the back of a chair with a cloth.

"Oh please, Ana, stop with the 'sir' thing! No, I don't remember! Can you explain further?" I'm now really freaking out and feeling that perhaps tan Gucci loafers would better suit my look.

"You have to go to the police station today. You attacked the night porter at the hotel at five this morning. He is OK, but you must go there," she says before walking back inside. As I sit there listening to the cicadas which are making so much noise, I feel my head will implode, total panic is setting in. Why would I attack someone? Why couldn't I remember this? How had the police allowed me to go home?

"Ana, do you have an iPhone charger?" I call out, as I go to make the necessary calls.

"It's all OK, Oli, calm down. Luckily you actually missed when you threw the plant pot at him. They wouldn't give you the keys to your car, and quite right too. What were you thinking? Drinking and driving is never ok. Get dressed and I'll come collect you. Text me the exact address and I will be twenty minutes, I am just finished at the hair salon," Sal says before hanging up.

"Ana, where are you? I need my clothes. Where are they?" I shout from the kitchen to the entire house. Thankfully after all the drama I managed to retrieve my luggage from the boot of the car, even if I had no recollection of doing so. I change my shoes and stand at the gates of the impressive villa waiting for Sal to arrive and I listen to twelve voicemails on my phone. None of them from Marco, despite me sending him an SMS before departing London. There are continual security guards on patrol which make me feel more scared than safe.

"Ok, you have some serious explaining to do, darling. Perhaps we should grab coffee before going back to the hotel to get your car. You're lucky that they will allow you to enter the grounds. Seriously, what were you doing? The Marbella Cub is 'Marbella', if you can't hang out there, you may as well be in Torremolinos!" she says sternly.

"I really have no idea? All I know is that I had a row with someone; I thought it was the security guys at the house. Oh, Jesus, I need Marco for this sort of thing, but he would probably freak out more than me!"

Arriving at the Marbella Club, Sal makes it her business to handle things. "Wait here and whatever you do, don't attempt to drive it away!" she says with a smile. She has a fantastic relationship with the powers that be and I hope she can persuade them to not press charges. As I sit patiently in her Bentley Continental I watch preppy-looking guys arrive with well-dressed women and white golf buggies deliver rich American guests to and from the beach. After about ten minutes she emerges from the front of the hotel carrying an envelope. "OK, you're very lucky that you didn't actually make contact with the porter, but you must pay for the plant pot you broke while attempting to. The manager says that it's all on CCTV – you arrived in a taxi at 04:50am and demanded they hand you over your car keys, but when they refused you went all Naomi Campbell. I think you need anger management or at least a champagne control course! Now, here are the keys, your car is parked over there – follow me to Marbella," she says as she pulls away slowly out of the car park.

Get me out of here, I think to myself as I drop the roof and start the engine and in doing so the stereo blasts out Touch Me by Rui Da Silva at crazy levels, which in turn makes heads turn in my direction. Let's just say that this is not the sort of place where loud thumping music is welcomed. The fear is now mixed heavily with shame and a realisation that I may still be drunk. "No drinking today," I say aloud, as I reverse slowly out of the parking space as silently as I can, as if trying to creep away.

After two hours sitting in an extremely warm police station I'm handed a piece of paper, which, after reading, basically explains that I am free to go with just a warning. "Oh, I think I should just go back to Dublin or London or anywhere away from here,

Sal!" I whine.

"Let's go have a quiet lunch somewhere and unwind. It's not the end of the world. You really are a crazy guy but nobody died! Anyhow, we have to set you up with your new man," she says with a wink.

Sitting at the Puente Romano, I am stunned. What has just happened? I've split from Marco just weeks ago and already my life is a mess. "I really don't think I can go through with this date idea, Sal. Please can we just forget about it?" I ask, pulling a sad face.

"Absolutely not! I've spent the past few hours organising it and you can't back out now. Besides, wait until you see Henri's stunning mansion. He has the largest house on the Golden Mile! You don't think I am setting you up with just anyone, do you?" she smiles, raising her champagne.

"I'm not even single, darling. Should I really be meeting someone new?" I ask, sounding pathetic.

"Look, I'm tired of this game you play, Oli! You moan and moan about Marco and when I try to arrange for you to meet someone new, you moan further. Dinner will be fun and I have to go anyhow as I have convinced Henri to set it up." She signals to the waiter.

"Tell me about him. All I know is that he has a mansion on the Golden Mile and I don't even know what the Golden Mile is. Perhaps if I knew a bit more I could be more interested."

"OK, he is slightly older than Marco, but he looks good. He doesn't work so much these days, he doesn't have to! Homes in Marbella, London, Monaco, New York..." she says excitedly, like some sort of coked-up real estate agent.

"You really think that's all I want? More homes? I have everything with Marco, but there is just something not right. He isn't being honest with me about something... Oh I don't know, Sal, is it wrong that I am even considering going along to this dinner?" I ask, sounding both needy and immature.

"Listen, honey, it's a fucking dinner! There will be many other guests there too you know. I've just dropped the hint to Henri that you are young, free and single! So, best not to mention Marco tonight, OK? I mean nobody needs to hear about him, especially not tonight!" I sit looking at the sea, listening to her advice and think, *What could the harm be? It's just a dinner...*

Back at the villa I decide to take it very easy poolside. After my behaviour the day before, I feel some tanning, swimming and relaxing is a perfectly acceptable way to spend the afternoon prior to a civilized dinner. On the sound system Gabin 'Slow Dancing' plays as I sip an iced tea and read through a copy of *GQ* which was left for me by Ana or one of the other maids. Stopping, I flick through my phone and spot that Marco has been photographed and tagged on Facebook at a lunch party in London by a mutual friend of ours, Auriela Soames. Auriela is the sort of girl who upon hearing of myself and Marco's split would be either trying to turn him straight again, or worse, setting him up with a twenty-two-year-old Brazilian go-go dancer. I'm fuming! For fuck's sake, Marco doesn't even use his Facebook page, having once told me it's a "pointless load of bullshit for people wanting to try convince themselves of their own popularity". I jump into the pool and spend twenty minutes swimming back and forth, all the time thinking of what was going on in London. How, if he couldn't even reply to my text message, could he be lunching? *To hell with it,* I think, and I send a text message to Sal – 'Really looking forward to this evening! What should I wear? Xx'

That is it, if Marco is out having fun, then so am I! I dry myself with an oversized Hermès beach towel and as I look up the gardener is back in view. "Buenas tardes!" He waves from across the pool, and all I can see are biceps.

"Hey man, how are you?" I ask.

"Please, my English no good, sir. Sorry…" he replies, looking shy, yet at the same time beyond hot.

"That's OK. You finished work for today?" I ask very slowly as if speaking to an alien. He walks towards me and I feel incredibly nervous. He must be all of twenty-three with a body of a guy who works out every day of the week. On his leg, a large tattoo of a lion's head and while his light blue polo shirt is clean, it's clear to see he's sweating from the afternoon heat. You know when they talk of how macho and masculine Latino men are? Well this is walking talking proof!

"I am Pablo, sir, very nice in meeting you," he says holding out his strong hand for me to shake.

"Really good to meet you, I'm Oli," I say with a wide smile, as I remove my shades.

"You are enjoying your time?" he asks, seeming to flex his biceps as he does so. "You need anything you can ask me, I am here for you, sir," he smiles before walking to the pool-house. "You can find me here.

It's where I live..." Is he flirting with me or just very friendly? What is going on? I sit down pretending to read the now upside-down magazine and spend the next few minutes watching the pool-house door which is open. Inside Pablo is probably stripping off and taking a shower after a long day working hard in the sun... *My mind is racing and it's only day two*, I think to myself with a cheeky smile. I fix my hair using my phone screen as a mirror and suddenly Marco's Facebook lunch isn't the main thing on my mind.

Just then my phone beeps with an incoming SMS from Sal – 'Darling let's just say sexy formal ~ but not formal formal. Pick you up at seven-thirty! Xx'

Chapter 11

Marbella, Spain

"Thanks Ana, you really are too kind. Are you sure I can't bring you with me when I leave?" I joke as she leads me to my dressing room, where my entire luggage has been unpacked, pressed and arranged. "If you need anything else, sir, please just call." She gestures to the phone on the wall. Would you like me to arrange a drink while you dress?" she asks, sounding super-efficient yet at the same time motherly.

"Oh yes, a Campari and soda would be great, thank you." As I sort through my wardrobe I try to make a decision as to what would be appropriate attire for 'sexy-formal'. Before I have time to make such life-changing choices my phone starts vibrating and on the caller ID is Marco. "Hey, what's up?" I say calmly as I pick up. "Hello? Can you hear me?" I ask, walking out to the terrace in search of better coverage. There's nobody at the other end, just loud music and people laughing. I hang up the call and try to call him back, but it diverts to voicemail. I don't leave a message. To hell with this, if he can be out partying what am I worried about a casual dinner for?

Honestly I feel as if this time myself and Marco may have finally hit the proverbial brick wall. We've a tempestuous relationship most of the time but for the past few weeks we've been fighting a lot, over the simplest of things. So much so that I've been staying back at my own place most nights and when we do stay together the only action the bed gets is eight hours' solid sleep. Having only been together one year, it's sure been a rollercoaster ride. One minute extremely passionate and fun, the next, worse than fighting, there's silence. Marco can vanish for days and reappear without explanation. Usually showing up full of passion suggesting a road trip or holiday. Quiet weekends spent in Lugano, staying with friends or at the Hotel Splendide Royal, which has over time become our bolt hole. Long weekends walking or biking, followed by massages, long lazy lunches and that all-important passion. It's as if once we're in Lugano nothing bad can happen. Pausing for a moment to think of Lugano and the happy times we've shared there, I sip my drink and I can hear voices coming from below my terrace. Stepping outside I can see it's Pablo and a friend chatting at the pool-house. Staring slightly longer than I should, I duck back indoors when he spots me. What the fuck is going on? I'm acting like a stupid love-struck teenager. *What am I doing?* I think to myself.

Looking in the mirror, I fix my hair and notice that I'm blushing. How typical of me to want the very obviously straight and muscled gardener. After about three outfit changes and five cigarettes, I decide to keep it simple and wear a Dsquared2 tuxedo with a fitted white Gucci shirt underneath. I leave the shirt open to my chest, for the 'sexy' bit. Dressed and ready, I make my way downstairs and out to the pool to get some fresh air. OK, OK, and to take a look at Pablo. He's sitting with his friend who looks like his twin. Both dressed in white V-neck t-shirts, baseball caps and shorts, I feel like I'm backstage at a Dolce & Gabbana show.

"Hello, sir, good evening!" He waves enthusiastically from across the pool.

"Oh, hi Pablo, what's up?" I sound vague. "I didn't see you guys there. Beautiful evening, isn't it?" I walk slowly towards them.

"You look very well, sir. I think very much stylish!" he says in broken English, standing up to shake my hand. "This is my cousin Bruno, he is just making the visit for a few hours. I hope is OK?" he asks politely.

"Nice to meet you, Bruno, you are welcome to stay as long as you like," I say, sounding borderline flirtatious. "I'm going out soon anyhow," I quip, in order to quell any hint of flirtation. "So you guys must work out together, you look so similar," I say, now sounding ridiculous.

They both laugh, as Pablo lights a cigarette. "You look good too, sir, I saw when you were swimming." As I thank him for his kind words I almost faint. Here it is again, the feeling that begins deep down in the pit of your stomach and grows and grows until you feel butterflies and then almost hit the deck.

"So what are you guys up to this evening?" I'm asking as I'm trying to move things along quickly.

"Oh, we are having no plans, just maybe drink one beer, maybe smoke a cigarette. No great plan," Pablo says, sounding almost sad. "Bruno wants us to go to a bar but I think not tonight. I want to stay home and sleep. So I will be home all night…" He takes a drag on his Winston. "And you, sir, where are you going? Somewhere very special I think because of your dressing."

"Oh, I'm going to a dinner at some guy's house, no idea why really," I say, sounding unsure of what I'm doing. The truth is I've no idea what I'm doing. As I stand here dressed and ready to party I feel lost. "I partied a little too much last night so I think tonight I will try to behave myself." I laugh hysterically.

"Yes, I hear you had a fun last night, sir. I hope everything is OK for you now?" Pablo asks with what seems like genuine concern.

"All OK, Pablo, and please call me Oli. 'Sir' makes me feel so old," I say as I stroll back towards the villa.

"Have a very good evening, sir – sorry, Oli. If you need anything later you know where I am!" He salutes to me in military style.

As I walk to the front gates of the house I call Sal who is already pulling up outside. "Well, is this sexy-formal enough?" I ask as I mock pose in front of the car, a Mercedes G-Wagon registered in Monaco.

"Ha ha, darling you look perfect. You always look perfect! I want you to do me one favour before dinner, OK?" she asks as she reapplies her lipstick in the rear-view mirror.

"Of course, what is it? And just how many cars do you have?" I ask.

"Reach behind your seat, there's a bottle of Bollinger in a gift box. I picked it up for you to leave for the night porter at the hotel. We can stop off on our way to Henri's and if you behave yourself we can have a drink at the bar," she says reassuringly. "I've spoken with the general manager and he's willing to accept your apology. I told him you were going through a tough time and he's fine as long as you behave from now on," she says before we inch our way onto the motorway from the slip road.

"As long as it's a quick drink! I'm not so comfortable going back to the hotel at all," I say, checking my phone signal for the tenth time in as many minutes. At the hotel the night porter is off-duty so I leave the bottle with a note for his attention and after one quick glass of champagne it was time to meet Henri. "So did I tell you about my gardener Pablo?" I ask as we walk to the car. "He is divine! I was..." Before I can continue Sal cuts across me.

"Darling, I am sure he is a great gardener, but you can't hump the help – enough of that talk!" she snaps, although I know she would secretly do exactly the same thing in my position. Actually, between you and me, she was banging her personal trainer for months before she realised that he had stolen a Rolex from her Knightsbridge townhouse. Quite the scandal, so much so that said personal trainer was sent packing back to Lithuania without as much as a reference. A situation that left many out of shape and sexually frustrated women in the SW3 area.

"So what do I need to know about Henri before we meet?" I'm genuinely interested.

"Well he's slightly older than Marco, with silver hair, collects Ferraris, and art. He has two yachts, seven homes and is single, but maybe not for long." She winks as she opens the driver door and climbs in.

"OK, interesting, but just how old is older?" I ask as we drive around the roundabout and into the ultra-exclusive area known as the Golden Mile. Passing the famous landmark that is Mosque King Abdul Aziz it's clear that this section of Marbella is different to any other.

"This is possibly some of the most expensive real estate in the world. Myself and Dieter are in the middle of buying a plot here to develop next year. You would not believe the drama, in order to do so," Sal says casually as we approach a set of large gates with a crest in the centre. As the gates slowly open we're greeted by two security guards who scan the registration plate on the car and then signal us forward. Not one, but two large guest-houses on one side, a two-storey garage which stores almost thirty Ferraris and other cars in the other.

"This place is unreal! Are we in Beverly Hills?" I ask excitedly. In front of us stands a team of uniformed staff – enough to make Downton Abbey look shabby.

"Just relax, don't think about Marco and enjoy yourself," Sal says as she hands her car keys to an Indian parking assistant.

Once we scale the mountain of candle-lit steps leading to the doorway we're greeted by more staff and ushered into a hallway where other guests including minor European royalty, diplomats and one or two well-known faces from the social pages of *Hola!* magazine are gathered, sipping Cristal and catching up on the summer gossip. Marbella like most places has a 'scene' and it begins in early July and runs through to mid-September. Like so many other similar places, there's a very small pool of people, so within a few minutes I am the centre of attention. After a string of introductions we finally arrive next to Henri, and as he turns to greet me I'm actually surprised. He's everything Sal has described him to be; distinguished, well-dressed, handsome with a kind smile and after a few minutes of chatting I discover he's funny too. "It is my complete pleasure to meet you, Oli," he says as he places he hand on my arm and walks me outside to the garden. "So, this is my home and you are very welcome. If you need anything at all just let me know. We won't be dining for another hour, so perhaps we can sit and talk for a few minutes before joining the party?" He smiles warmly.

"Yes of course, and may I say your home is like none I have seen before, you have immense taste." I'm for once in genuine awe. Every last inch of the manicured garden is perfect, an ozone-treated swimming pool surrounded by large Diptyque candles, while sculptures by Giacommetti and Jeff Koons are dotted cleverly between topiary and ornate furniture. As soon as we're seated, a waiter arrives with a bottle of Dom Perignon, a bottle of Evian and some strawberries. "You may notice that we're drinking DP, I am serving Cristal to my guests, but personally I prefer DP, especially the '85. If you would prefer Cristal, just say." He instructs the waiter to pour.

"Dom Perignon will do just fine, thanks," I say, raising my glass to salute my host and new friend. As we sit sipping our drinks, three beautiful Dachshunds come rushing to greet us.

"Oh, here are my boys Charlie, Alessio and Mele, I do hope you like dogs?" he asks as all three all jump at the same time onto my chair. "I sometimes think I prefer them to people!

"These guys are just beyond fabulous." I lay back and allow the most 'designer' of designer dogs to jump all over me.

"Perfect! I like you, Oli. It's hard to find someone like you, who also loves my boys. However, they will destroy your jacket, but please don't worry, I will have it brushed down before we return inside," he adds, as he makes eye contact with a member of his staff. "So, Sal tells me you are only in town for a short time. Where are you staying?" he smiles as he lifts one of the dogs, I think Alessio, from my lap.

"I've rented a great house right on the beach at Los Monteros, do you know it?" I ask.

"Sadly not. I don't really know anywhere outside of this area," sounding slightly arrogant. Arrogance isn't something that usually interests me, but this man certainly has the goods to back it up.

"Oh, I see. Well, it really is a very nice area and the sound of the ocean is so soothing at night." I take a large sip from my glass. The fact that last night I hadn't even remembered coming home let alone the sound of the sea made me cringe inwardly.

"Yes, I agree, I sometimes sleep on my yacht far out in the middle of the sea for that very reason," he continues. These kinds of statements would usually make me want to run, but something about Henri ensures me he is a genuine guy. He isn't showing off, but rather just living his very fortunate life to the max. He reminds me of Paolo and how he will be in fifty years' time.

"Where do you keep her?" I ask, making reference to the location of his yacht.

"Well I have one here in Marbella, actually in Puerto Banus. It's the only reason on earth to venture to that part of town. It's so terribly trashy, I don't even think it is good enough for the 'jet-set' crowd anymore, and I can't stand them! My second yacht is moored in Monte Carlo," he says without flinching. He claims to be fifty-four, but in reality I think I could add at least another decade on top. Dressed in a navy blazer, white shirt, pink jeans and Gucci loafers without socks, he certainly looks every bit the Euro jet-set gent he claims to detest. "Tonight is a pretty formal affair as you can see, so perhaps you would allow me invite you to lunch tomorrow?" He sits forward in his seat. "You really are very handsome, but I am sure you know that already." He's looking into my eyes as he places his hand onto my leg.

"Yes, lunch could be fun, I guess." I feel my face turning bright red. "Oh, look what you've done, you're making me blush," I say, in order to compensate for my changed complexion.

"Oh, I thought it was just your Irish skin after the sun," he teases. He certainly is charming, with a good sense of humour. "Of course you know there are a lot of Irish living down here? None quite as wealthy as they used to be from what I hear. They sure are a crazy lot when they start drinking. They got slightly out of control at some charity ball thing and were almost air lifted out of the Marbella Club for life. I'm not sure they understood the ethos of the hotel sadly," he continues as he shakes his head. Don't get me wrong, usually I would stand up for my fellow Irishmen, but on this occasion I agree with him totally, having already heard the story from a number of well-placed sources. "So, may I ask, are you single or has some lucky guy already snapped you up?" he asks while leaving his hand on my leg for slightly longer than necessary.

"Oh, it's a very long story, one which I won't bore you with now." I sound vague.

"Not to worry, you can tell me all about it over lunch tomorrow. Now perhaps we should return inside and mingle a little bit before dinner." He stands up. "It really is a pleasure to meet you, Oli, here's to a great night and a new friendship!"

Back inside it really is a who's who of Europe, all gathered in small groups of two or three and all looking as if they're chatting in extreme confidence. On one side of the room are three bitchy-looking gay guys from Italy who stare at my every move. Eventually one of them makes it his business to introduce himself. "Hi, Giancarlo, and you?" He extends his limp wrist in exaggerated fashion, as if the fake Cartier Ballon Bleu is too heavy.

"I'm Oliver, how do you do?" I say calmly.

"Who are you here with? Where are you from? Are you new in town?" he asks before glancing back at his friends and smiling.

"Wow so many questions! Are you a cop?" I say, just as Sal grabs my arm to introduce me to a friend of hers from Madrid.

"This is Celestina, one of my dearest and oldest friends. We lived together in New York while she was at Condé Nast," she gushes. Celestina is certainly the perfect friend for Sal, as she too has landed one of the richest men in Spain, an industrialist known to all as Dodo. Despite having homes dotted around the globe, these days they travel it on their giga-yacht *Kaput*, hosting and attending the finest parties. She looks radiant, in a shimmering silver Cavalli dress and rocking the body of a twenty-five-year-old.

"While you are in town you must come to *Kaput* to have dinner. Sal tells me you are recently single, so we are just going to have to find you the perfect match, now aren't we! If you will excuse me I must find Henri," she says with a cheeky smile.

"Isn't she fabulous? Talk about a hot lesbian!" Sal says, taking two glasses of champagne from a passing waiter.

"Did you just say lesbian?" I don't know why I'm shocked. It really does take a lot to shock me, but this was truly shocking. Her husband, who's a bit of a dish, is standing not so far away and they seem to be blissfully happy.

"Oh, Dodo knows all about it, he has a few girls on the go too. It's the secret to a happy marriage, but if Dieter tried it I would have him rolled in one of my Persian carpets and left in the hills above Marbella! Easy, no question. The hard part would be trying to select which carpet as I love them all." She sounds serious. "How did you get on with the Spice Girls?" she asks, gesturing towards the three Italians who are now watching our every move.

"The Spice Girls? Why are they called the Spice Girls?" I laugh, almost spitting some seriously fine champagne.

"Well look, there's Scary, for obvious reasons. The blonde is Sporty, clearly not so obvious, and number three is Posh, apparently. In fact, he's known as Posh as he's possibly the furthest thing from posh imaginable. Rumour has it he comes from a very bad background in Milan and his mother was, or perhaps still is a hooker. They're three of the worst queens alive, yet somehow they manage to get invited everywhere," she says in disgust. "Stay away from them as they will want you out of the picture pronto. As far as I know Posh has been trying to land Henri for months, but no dice!" Looking at the trio, I try not to laugh. They really are just like bitchy women – grouped together snarling at people, their emaciated and tired bodies wrapped in pashminas. All carrying Birkins, wearing dodgy-looking Cartier watches and bracelets, and they have crazy, crazy eyebrows. Seriously, I mean insane! As I watch, they stare back with a venomous look. They bring new meaning to the adage 'Italians do it better'... "Come on, let's move over here out of their grasp!" Sal says as we both laugh loudly.

As we are called to dinner Henri grabs my arm and asks if I'll sit next to him, having already changed the table plan just moments previously.

"Of course, Henri, it would be my pleasure," I smile as we cross the huge hallway passing a collection of Warhols. The dining room is magnificent, complete with a retractable roof for nights just like this. In total thirty-two guests sit for dinner and the table is itself a masterpiece using the ocean for inspiration. Festooned with deep blue orchids and an interesting collection of shells and other nautical objects, it's completely candle-lit by ten large silver candelabras.

Arriving at my seat, I'm greeted by Posh Spice, AKA Giancarlo. "Excuse me, have you switched the name place cards?" he says sternly in an overly camp heavy Italian accent, before swiping the card from the table to read it. "There has obviously been a mistake, as I always sit next to Henri at dinner. You will need to find another seat!" He pulls out the chair and takes my place, leaving me standing like a fool as everyone else sits down. "Seriously, move away from here and from me before you cause a scene!" he snaps, clicking his fingers. The truth is that he's the one causing a scene as most of the other diners have noticed. I'm not usually one to allow someone to treat me this way but when in someone's home I opt to be the quiet dinner party guest, unless the occasion calls for it. Noticing my situation, Sal and one of the waiters comes to see what's happening.

"God, this is awkward, Giancarlo has told me I must move and find another seat, although my name card is, or at least was in that place and Henri has just asked if I would sit next to him." Seriously, I'm genuinely shocked by the situation. "Look, it's OK, I'll sit somewhere else, maybe next to you?" I ask as we look down the long table to spot a free seat. Obviously the only available one being in the middle of the other two Spice Girls. "Oh well, Sal, c'est la vie and all that. I think it's a sign that I shouldn't even be here."

Being in between Sporty and Scary is just as scary as it sounds. Trust me, I've had some run-ins with bitchy queens over the years, it's kind of par for the course as they say. This, however, is a totally different level. "I see Giancarlo is very insistent that he be placed next to Henri," I laugh to the caustic duo.

"Listen sister, we have been, eh – come si dice? – researched you, and now we tell you, just that you are not so welcome here. You will never be a welcome here, do you get it? We are the very select group of Europe's best, one in which you do not have an area, do you understand me?" Scary says in the most broken of English, living up to his nickname but sounding stupid.

"Oh, you're so right, I have no intention of spending my time in the company of desperate power bottoms like you three. In fact, you're the sort of homos that make people lie about their sexuality." I'm smiling at an extremely elegant lady on the far side of the table.

"What a fuck? Do you have ideas who you are talking with, bitch? Giancarlo is ready about to move in here to the house with Henri and he will get a wedding, so you can, eh, fly back to London or whatever grey city you come from!" he snipes. I truly am shocked and as I look around for Sal I can see she's deep in conversation with Dieter who has arrived late.

"You really should learn to speak English, it's a first-world language after all. But I know that your sort only ever speak one language, American Express! In fact, you're just a glorified go-go dancer that needs to go-go away from me." I feel like I'm lowering myself to his bitchy level.

"Good evening, ladies and gentlemen, my friends." Henri is standing at the head of the table. "It is my complete pleasure to welcome you all to my home for the first time this season. Some of you for the first time and others, well forever." He sounds gracious. As he addresses the room, I can see Giancarlo, who has by now removed his dinner jacket, typing frantically into his phone with no regard for Henri or anyone else. "However, before we begin I do have one thing to fix. Please, where is Oli? I did ask if you would sit next to me at dinner. Perhaps Giancarlo could be a gentleman and return to the seat which was designated for him and Oli could sit here?" He smiles warmly to the gathered guests.

"I guess you girls were right, I certainly don't belong here. I belong there, right next to the host. Do enjoy your evening," I say before walking away.

"That was all terribly embarrassing. Please accept my apologies, Oli. It seems I have some cleaning up of my guest-lists to work on." Henri sits down. While it was slightly awkward, it sure was worth it to see the look on the faces of the Spice Girls. "So Oli, I was thinking about lunch tomorrow, would you like to meet me at my yacht and we can lunch at sea?" he asks as he leans closer.

"That sounds perfect and I am sure it will be." I notice Giancarlo is staring at us.

"Do not worry, I can see him too and as soon as

we finish dining this problem will be eradicated." True to his word, after dinner Henri makes it his business to say goodbye to Giancarlo for the last time. There are some raised voices and slamming of doors before Henri returns and asks a select few including Sal, Dieter, Celestina, Dodo and myself to stay on for drinks by the pool.

"Darling Henri, what was all that dreadful business with the Spice Girls?" Sal asks.

"Oh, you are terrible! But I think it's the last we will see of Giancarlo and his backing dancers. They ran up a tab under my name at Olivia Valere last weekend, so obviously darling Olivia called me to check it was all OK. Naturally, we decided to leave them to reach close on two thousand euro before she broke the bad news. Can you imagine the fun when they had to try and settle the bill with three credit cards, making up the balance with cash!" he laughs heartedly, almost spilling his drink. "I had hoped he would come clean about the incident this evening when I asked him, but sadly he denied it all." He sounds disappointed.

"Anyhow, Henri, who needs their sort when there are fabulous men like Oli in the world?" Sal says as she squeezes my leg.

"I really must be getting home; I promised I would behave this evening. It's been a great success, Henri, thank you, but it's time I got to bed. It is so great to meet you and if your invitation still stands I will see you at 12:30 in the port," I say sincerely.

"Allow me to organise a lift home for you. Wait just a few moments and they will bring the car around,

OK?" He picks up the telephone to organise things.

Once I say goodbye to Sal and the other guests, Henri walks me to his awaiting Rolls-Royce Phantom. While staff rush here and there in order to close the house for the evening, Henri pulls me close to him and kisses me while nobody is looking. In fact, I don't think he cares who is looking. I pull back slightly and he passes me his card with a list of phone numbers. "You have more numbers than me!" I smile.

"I have more numbers than most, darling, and you can reach me on any of them at any time. I will send the car to collect you at noon tomorrow if that suits?" he asks before I step inside.

On the way home, I sent him a text message. 'Looking forward to tomorrow. Sleep well x' It's the first time since meeting Marco that I haven't thought of him for hours. As I undress for bed I notice that the light in Pablo's pool-house is still on… *Tomorrow is another day*, I think as I close the shutters to the terrace.

Chapter 12

Marbella, Spain

Lying in bed I feel a rush, not the usual sort of rush from too many martinis or strange pills popped in dark clubs at 4am, this is different. In fact, rather than waking feeling terminally hungover, I am feeling fresh and ready to take on the day. Believe me, this is a first. I call down to the kitchen to order some coffee and water and as I do, I can see that there a number of missed calls and messages flashing on the screen of my iPhone.

'Looking forward to seeing you later! The car will be with you at noon. H x' – I smile as I read it. A string of missed calls, all from the same London number. One I don't recognise, so therefore don't care about, and then there it is: a text message from Marco. Before I even open it, my mood flips from one of calm to one of calamity, dropping the phone and smashing the screen as I do so. "Fuck!" I shout loudly, as I stare at the screen, which looks just like Pistoletto mirror. With an efficient knock, Ana enters the room carrying a large silver tray with two bottles of Evian, two glasses, two cups and a large pot of coffee. Oh, and the most amazing cream roses – she has been listening.

"Good morning, Señor Oli, I hope you had a perfect sleep." She's smiling broadly.

"You know, I really did. The best sleep in years, now that I think of it." I'm sounding almost surprised. "Why have you brought two of everything? Are you joining me?" I laugh.

"Well, señor, I always think it is better to bring two of everything and not assume you came home alone. This is Marbella after all, sir!" she winks, as she places the tray onto the huge bed. I tell you if I had an Ana living with me 24/7 my life would be fantastic. She's a trooper and the more I get to know her the more I like her. "Oh, what happened to your phone? What a mess!" She holds her hand out. "I will send Pablo to get you a replacement immediately, yes?" she's asking in a tone that is almost telling.

"Well, there are a number of messages I must read, so that would be fantastic." I hand her my American Express card and scribble down the essential details, as I realise that I'm sounding overly excited. The prospect of having a reason to chat with Pablo far outweighs the new handset. It even outweighs Marco's message. Sipping the coffee, my mind is racing. Just what could Marco want? What time was the message sent at? Was he drunk, or has something happened? Just like that, my mood had changed. "Ana, Ana…" I call from the stairs.

"Señor what has happened?" She rushes into the

hallway three floors down.

"How long will Pablo be?" I sound slightly manic.

"Not long, sir, he will be back in maybe twenty minutes. Is everything ok?" she's asking as she ties her apron around her rotund waist.

"OK, let me know when he gets back please as I have some very important business to deal with," somehow turning a simple text from Marco into a life and death. As I shower I'm in two minds, one which is thinking of the day ahead with Henri, knowing how perfect it will be. That's the thing about dating older guys, they really have seen it all and know exactly how a date should go. However, killing the mood is the fact that I need to know what Marco wants. What is in that message? I stand in the wet room, staring at myself in a mirror. Even at a time like this I find fault with my body. "I must say no to carbs at every opportunity, I must say no to carbs at every opportunity, I must say no to carbs at every opportunity," I say loudly, as if it's my new mantra – actually, perhaps it is.

Reaching for a towel I open the door and through the steam I'm greeted by Pablo who is in my room leaving my new phone by the bed. "Oh, good morning, sir – sorry, I mean Oli," he stutters nervously with a flash of his killer smile. "I did not know if you were in…" He smiles as he hands me the box containing the phone as well as my credit card.

"Oh, you are very kind, Pablo, thank you. And to answer your question, I'm out!" I laugh, although I feel my comedy is lost on him. Dressed in his uniform of polo shirt and super short shorts, he looks better each time I see him. "I like your Nike," I say, making reference to his bright green Air Max. Me, I'm dressed in, well, just a towel and I while normally it would be an awkward situation, it's not.

"Would you like me to help you set up the phone? I have some time if you need," he smiles again. There is definitely tension.

"Well, eh, OK, that would be cool." I'm sounding like a giddy teenager. I walk to the other side of the bed and pull a white V-neck t-shirt over my still-wet body.

"So what are you doing today?" he smiles.

"Well, I am meant to be having lunch with someone I met recently, but to be honest I would much rather stay here by the pool and swim, tan and relax." I pull a sad face.

"You do not have a girlfriend? Or maybe boyfriend?" he asks as his face blushes.

"Ha ha, well no. I guess, for the first time in a long time I am alone," I laugh. There's an almost awkward silence, but only for a moment.

"I do not think you will be alone for long time." He blushes more. What the hell is going on here? It's way too difficult to call. Is he flirting or do I just wish he is? He sits playing with the phone as I dress and pour some water. "Eh, this is your new phone all ready, I hope. I am sorry for I ask the stupid questions." He looks nervous.

"Thanks," I say as I take the handset. "Don't be silly, your questions are normal and I am not offended. So, what about you? You must have so many girls wanting you." Now I'm blushing. Jesus, I sound like that dumb teenager again.

"Ha ha, yes maybe you are right, but I am not a rich man, you know, I am just the gardener. The girls like a man with money and fast car…" He looks sad again.

"Are you kidding me? Women like you! Look at yourself, you are hot!" Now we both blush. "To answer your question, I am gay and single," I say with a smile.

"Well Oli, I do not think you will have the problem to finding the right one for you if you make open your eyes. OK, I better now leave you to be ready for your lunch meeting." He stands up and stares at me slightly longer than he should, before turning to leave the room.

"Oh, Pablo, please, where are my manners?" I say as I hand him twenty euro for taking the time to get my phone sorted.

"Honestly, I cannot take this. I am sorry." He hands the note back to me. As he reaches the door he turns and smiles. "You know, maybe we can have one beer later, if you want to and if the meeting at lunch is not much fun and you like come home. You know where you find me, maybe we can play a game?" He closes the door. Play a game? What the fuck is going on? Somehow his broken English makes me want him more.

I switch on the phone and there it is, Marco's message – 'Did you try to call me? I have a number missed calls from a private number.'

That's it? That's what I smashed a fucking phone

for? I don't even bother to reply as my mind is racing following Pablo's mysterious exit. There's only one person who could make sense of all this.

"Darling, I can't talk for long as I am late for Ashtanga. How's Marbella? Still tacky?" Paolo sneers into his Vertu.

"Oh please, everywhere is tacky, the trick is to avoid the tack," I laugh back.

"Yes, perhaps, but we are wasting words now and I don't have time!" he warns. I explain my Pablo situation and without hesitation I get the answer I was expecting. "And the problem is where? Go to the lunch with Henri and see what happens. It's not as if the gardener guy is going anywhere!" he laughs. "Besides, bello, we both know what's on the cards, don't we? Now that I've solved another of the world's most important issues I must go." The call ends without as much as a 'ciao ciao', which is typical of our friendship.

Dressing for lunch, I sip a glass of Pingus and listen to Nina Simone sing My Baby Just Cares for Me. I'm in no real hurry to get ready and instead top off my wine and walk out onto the terrace to see Pablo starting to clean the pool. He has his polo shirt off and the glisten on his tanned skin shows his hard work. Yes, I want to stay pool-side for the afternoon, and what's interesting is that Pablo knows it. My problem now is to figure out if he's playing a game as I am the guest, or is he really interested? Downing my wine, I notice the time is approaching noon and as I make my way downstairs, I stop to look at myself in the hall mirror – white Saint Laurent jeans (miraculously looking brand new again thanks to

Ana), a navy Ralph Lauren polo, and a slightly newer than new looking pair of Superga. *Simple, elegant and chic,* I think to myself as I gather my keys and wallet.

"Ana, has my car arrived yet?" I ask, popping my head around the kitchen door.

"Yes, Oli, it is just at the gates. Is there anything I can arrange for you for this evening or are you staying out?" she asks warmly.

"I'm not too sure yet, but no, I don't need anything special, thanks Ana. I'll see you later."

Outside the gates, sits a black 1970s Bentley which conjures images of glamour and style just by its very being. "Good afternoon, sir," smiles a handsome, uniformed, if not somewhat ageing driver.

"Aren't you warm?" I ask, making reference to his attire.

"No, sir, I am used to being dressed this way," he says in a London accent.

As the car pulls away from the villa I feel as if I'm floating on air, or perhaps a magic carpet. The wine has certainly kicked in and the fact that I've skipped breakfast may not be the best idea. "Where are we going?" I ask.

"I am taking you to the marina at Puerto Banus where Henri is waiting onboard his yacht. We are a bit early so I will drive slowly if that is OK with you, sir? Henri likes things to be just so," he says through the rear-view mirror. Unlike the rest of Henri's vast staff, this man is easily approaching sixty and he's clearly straight. I must admit that there were one or two that I assumed to be gay among his household staff. I don't know why it makes a difference if one's staff are gay or straight, but when you see a very rich, older gay guy and a team of staff that look like Abercrombie & Fitch models one does raise an eyebrow, if you know what I mean?

Arriving at the port, it's clear to see why so many people I know avoid it like the plague. Hordes of day-trippers pose beside parked supercars, trying to look convincingly like the owners, apart from one small but rather important clue. Aston Martin owners rarely sport Aston Villa jerseys. Not to mention enormous beer guts and dodgy tattoos. Yes, this is the part of Marbella that even those who choose to call this part of Spain home, hate. It's as if all eyes are on this tiny marina, whether it be those spotting cars, those selling coke or those selling themselves.

All this alongside Tom Ford, Roberto Cavalli, Louis Vuitton, and other stores which pop up and then close down each year along the front line. As the car inches its way along the narrow street people stop and stare. I guess that even amidst the endless parade of brand new Lamborghinis and Ferraris that circle the port repeatedly in search of admiration, a great old Bentley still steals the show. Pulling up to one of the marina entrances, the driver lowers the window to chat with security. "Now, sir, one minute until the gate opens and I will deliver you directly to the yacht."

Pulling alongside Henri's yacht, it's at the farthest point of the jetty and it towers over the other far-from-small vessels moored next to it. Registered in Valletta, *You Don't Say* is stunning. Over five levels of beauty, it's hardly surprising that Henri has the largest yacht on the costa. Next to it, normally impressive craft sporting British and Irish flags, look like dinghies. As one would expect, a full team of good-looking, uniformed staff greet me, as Henri floats around on the upper deck chatting on the phone. "My dear boy, you are most welcome!" he exclaims as he makes his way towards me, slipping as he misses the last step of the stairs. A pink shirt, sleeves rolled, navy chinos and tanned bare feet, his relaxed approach is certainly attractive. "I am so happy you are here." He places his hand at slightly higher than knee level on my leg. "Now, what would you like, champagne? A martini?" He waves to another member of his staff, who is possibly better looking than the last. "What about we have Krug '88? I'm sure you will want it," he smiles. I can tell that he's already been drinking, as not only is he unsteady on his feet, but he sounds drunk. "How have you been since we last met? Discovering the charms of charming Marbella?" he asks, as the champagne is poured and a silver bowl of chilled mixed berries is placed between us.

"Well I only saw you last night, remember? So, I'm yet to see what this place is all about," I smile, knowing that perhaps my answer seems rude.

"Last night, yes of course I remember. What a rude thing to say!" He puts on a pair of Cartier sunglasses. "I was hoping to take us out of the marina, but would you be OK if we lunch right here? The whole effort of moving this big girl can be immense," he sighs, at the first-world problem. In reality I think the task seems huge as he is wasted, but who am I to talk? To be honest, I'm dying to have a snoop about inside, rather like Marilyn Monroe in

Some Like it Hot, when she goes on her date aboard her supposed millionaire's yacht.

As we chat, mainly about how well connected he is, he name drops badly from members of the British royal family to certain world leaders that are so obscure that I daren't question him. As he rambles on I'm beginning to see a very different side to him. Empty bottles of champagne are removed and replaced at quite an alarming rate, even for me.

"Can you excuse me? I really need to go freshen up," I smile.

"Certainly, Javier will show you where you need to go." He struggles to stand.

Inside, the yacht is as magnificent as his home. Simple cream on cream, with deep carpet and an impressive array of photographs, mainly black and white. Silver frames featuring Henri with everyone from Maria Callas to the Duke of Edinburgh, and strangely, a large photo of him standing with Naomi Campbell and Kate Moss at some fashion week or another. I mean, nothing strange about darlings Kate and Naomi, but since we met he has told me about five times how he detests the fashion scene and avoids it at all costs.

"You really have impeccable taste!" I beam as I return to the table.

"Yes, I think I do, but it's always nice to be complimented on one's style, even if one knows it already," he smiles, somewhat coldly.

"I especially love your photos, so fascinating! You and the supermodels is my favourite, I'm impressed," I enthuse as I sit down.

"Oh please… Of course you are. Of all the wonderful people I'm captured with on film, you pick the two vacuous ones," he sighs.

I must say, I'm taken aback and just sit silently behind my shades. Usually I would just tell someone what I think of them and storm off, but for some reason I'm uncomfortable. More champagne is poured and quickly downed by Henri, before being refilled. The next ten minutes are so fucking strange. It's like sitting with an out-of-control angry alcoholic, who is ranting under his breath. We chat, albeit mainly about Henri and his fabulous life, but his tone is dreadful, like a spoilt teenager throwing their weight. Worse, it's that of a snob, and in my experience a snob is the most insecure person imaginable, not to mention unbearable. It's as if I'm lunching with a completely different guy to the one I met previously.

"People like you are everywhere in places like this," he announces out of nowhere.

"People like who?" I ask, genuinely confused.

"Guys, girls, more guys all looking for someone to pay their life tab," he snarls. "You know, every week I get inundated with offers of sex, offers of love, offers, offers, offers…" he rambles.

"I have no idea what you're talking about, but for the record I am certainly not offering you anything," I say calmly. The fact that I was considering offering both just hours ago now makes me angry. "In fact, it's hardly surprising you get those offers, if you search for love on gay dating sites and such," I say rudely, as I wipe the lens of my shades in a napkin. Oh, I forgot to mention that I spotted him on Gaydar this morning (where he's apparently aged 51), when I was snooping to see if there was any sign of Pablo. Sadly there wasn't, or perhaps that's a good thing, as I tend to find guys who use dating sites are the worst type of all, big muscles perhaps, but big queeny attitudes to go with them.

The more he drinks the worse his attitude becomes. It can only be described as crazy and my presence seems to be making things worse. I sit listening to him ramble on and on about some clapped-out royal, one that even those who are interested in such matters would find dreary. "And of course I know Valentino, he really is such a bore…" he continues. He seems irritated, as if something has happened prior to my arrival, or perhaps he's just a bad drunk. In an attempt to lighten the mood things turn for the worse, when I bring up the subject of relationships. "I am beginning to feel as if you are regretting inviting me to join you," I say genuinely. "I can go if you want, it's not a problem." The scene may be pretty, but the atmosphere is dire. I actually feel ill.

"Stay, go, do what you want, boy. If you aren't happy with my hospitality, you can leave whenever you want. You are not a prisoner. Perhaps you prefer to eat lunch at one of those dreadful restaurants?" he comments snidely, without looking at me but waving his hand in the direction of the port. I'm totally dumfounded and not sure what to say.

"So, you know about my relationship status, yet I don't know anything of yours," I say in an attempt to lighten the mood. I take a large sip from a glass of white, Chablis if my buds serve me well.

"Well, I like to keep myself to myself you know, and I hardly know you, so that question is rather personal…" There's an overly dramatic pause. "Seeing as you've been as bold to ask, I have been through a very bad time and now I don't trust anyone. Nobody. Fact. Period. Actually, I don't want to be with anyone again on that level. My life is now destined to be that way. I will live alone for the rest of my days." He removes his sunglasses and wipes his eyes, although there is no sign of tears.

"Oh, I'm sorry, I didn't mean to pry, you don't need to continue," I smile almost sympathetically.

"No, no, now I must, seeing as you've pressed me. I was seeing, well, I guess more than seeing, I was in love with an English chap, who has betrayed me terribly. Not only did he sleep with anyone and everyone from here to Los Angeles, all on my credit cards, but he also, it transpires, has a wife and a child who live right here, up in the hills in some horrid little village. I have only just found out that I have been supporting them for years!" His eyes fill with tears. "Anyhow, he left me and before he did, he asked me to give him half a million euro in order to begin his new life." He sounds bitter and looks angry. "You're all the same, each and every one of you! All of you wanting my fucking money, my bloody cars, yachts… And you show no shame either," he shouts. I remove my shades, but before I can react he's off again. "Actually, who are you to ask me these fucking questions? I am so insulted, but not surprised that you show such little compassion. I mean, who are you anyhow? Some socialite bimbo… What do you know of life or society? Oh, I don't want to continue this conversation, really, why have you asked these questions? Now I no longer want lunch!" He throws a crystal glass to the ground, followed by his monogrammed napkin, before standing up and storming inside. *What the fuck just happened?* I wonder.

I down my wine, which is instantly refilled as soon as I do so. It's as if the staff have been instructed to get everyone who steps onboard completely hammered. After about ten minutes, and the remainder of the wine, I ask Javier if he can fetch Henri to see if all is OK. "I am sorry, sir, but Henri will not be returning today. He has asked me to arrange a car to bring you to wherever it is you need to go," he smiles.

"What the fuck? Please can you go find him?" I snarl. I don't care who he is or thinks he is, I'm not tolerating this bullshit any longer. I mean, it's not as if I am stuck for a lunch date. Seriously, this is the trouble with these rich old ones, while they may be surrounded by the very best of everything, but from experience, most of them are miserable and slightly nuts, from too many long days drinking too many vintages on their own or in the sort of company Henri had just described. I am, however, shocked that someone who has such good manners one minute, can act this way the next. I gather my things and leave. "I don't need a car to take me anywhere, and please pass a message to Henri, tell him to delete my number from his phone and seek help for his alcohol addiction!" I shout to Javier, once I am back on solid ground. Walking along the port, I feel ill. An illness resulting from what's just happened, and also my surroundings. How can it be that every time I meet someone that could be the next chapter, they turn out to be such a disappointment?

The fact that I wasn't even looking for the next chapter only makes me feel worse. Somehow I end up stopping at News Café, ordering a gin martini and finishing it in seconds flat. Looking around, it's truly hell on earth; the place isn't too busy, but it has somehow attracted the sort of people that should be banned from air travel. I reach for my phone to text Paolo. I've been told he is only contactable by SMS today due to "insane work levels" – 'Paolo, get in touch. I've just been asked to leave Henri's yacht! He flipped out and smashed the whole place up!!! X' OK, so my text is slightly OTT but I am trying to get his attention. Before placing the phone down, I dial Sal's number. "Sal, what the fuck is going on? He is bats! I've just been booted off his yacht! Why did you think I would even want to get involved with someone like him?" I ask.

"Jesus Oli, what did you do?" she barks from a lunch party in the far more suitable surroundings of Sotogrande.

"Me? What did *I* do? I arrived for lunch on his yacht and he was steaming, so much so he broke a glass before he broke down in tears and then vanished. The man has problems. I don't need this shit right now! I'm going back to the house to relax by the pool." I end the call. She's clearly pissed, as despite the fact she may like him, it's super clear to see that any future art sales he may give her are far more important. Seriously, art dealers are nothing more than gypsies in Hermès, when it comes down to it. They look a certain way and want the world to see them in a certain way, but at the end of the day they would have you shot, for the commission on a decent Richter. With non-stop wine, very little food and that last martini, my brain feels as if it's suspended in booze and I'm feeling slightly drunk, but again, somehow I end up stopping for another drink further along the port at Sinatra's. Another martini and this time all I can hear are Irish and English accents. Looking around, the place is a mix of flash, dodgy-looking men with trampy-looking women.

"Are you Oli? It is you, isn't it?" asks a woman who is so tanned that she makes Donatella look pale. Her accent is hard to place, but it's not pleasant. Do I know this woman? Why is her arm around my neck? As she continues to talk at me I zone out. Her accent is one of those nondescript English accents, from a place like Coventry or Birmingham. A Jeremy Kyle accent as they're often referred to. "Can we get a few photos with you? I'm here for my hen party so you can't say no!" she orders, as she drags me to meet her friends.

"I told you it was him! Oh, we love you, are you going to buy us a few bottles of champs?" asks her equally tanned and equally brash friend. Posing for photos, I feel as if I have been transported to a different planet. It's almost two o'clock and everyone is drunk. As they look at the recently snapped photos on their phones I make a dash for it before they've noticed. Attempting to make my way out of the marina, very definitely for the last time, I'm almost hit by a teenage girl and an octogenarian, who can barely see over the wheel of his Ferrari F430 Spider as they come speeding in to join those already showing off.

Once I reach the villa, all feels sane. In fact, it feels heavenly. From the madness of Puerto Banus, the villa feels a million miles away. The sound of cicadas is all that interrupts the afternoon tranquillity.

"Ah, Senor Oli, you are back early! Is everything OK?" asks Ana.

"Yes, thank you. Everything is fine, I just want to take it easy and relax in the sun," I say, scanning the pool area in search of Pablo. Even without realising it, I do it.

"Would you like anything? Are you hungry? I can arrange some lunch perhaps?" she asks as she follows me out to the terrace.

"No, no everything is fine." I spot him busily working at the far end of the garden. "Why don't you take some time off? Come back later, I'm pretty sure I can entertain myself for a few hours! In fact, you could take the evening off and come back in the morning," I smile.

Once I change, I return to the pool where I lap for ten minutes without stopping, in search of stress relief. Eventually I stop and rest at the deep end, placing my head on the side of the pool, allowing myself to float, suspended and light. The temperature must be in the mid-thirties and, while slightly unbearable, it sure beats the usual scenario back home. My view is Pablo, who has by now spotted me and is walking up the garden towards me. Again, without realising it I fix my hair and place my shades over my eyes. "Hey Pablo, how's your day?" I ask breezily.

"Nice day for the swim, it is too hot no?" He looks perfect, sweat glistening on his skin and a polo shirt that looks just the right amount of scruffy.

"You know, Ana is finished for the day so you can too, if you want?" I say, or more realistically, I ask.

"I have one or two things more I must do to be finish and then, well yes, why not? Thank you, Mister Oli," he smiles, before walking into the house to get himself a cold bottle of water. I shower and settle into a crisp white lounger to soak up a few hours of sun, all the time keeping an eye on his movements. Movements that can only be described as hot. You know the way some people can make cutting grass look sexy, while others, well they make it look like cutting grass. I chain smoke and drink a cold Coronita. As I'm about to zone out, Jose Feliciano starts to play La Copa Rota at the highest volume possible right across the garden. "Is ok? You like the music?" Pablo shouts over the noise.

"Si, bravo!" I shout back as I raise my hand, even though I'd rather something different. As much as I try to escape what happened with Henri, I can't and the more I think about it the more worked up I get.

"Paolo, why didn't you reply to my text?" I say angrily, before he has had time to answer his phone properly. "It's been almost three hours!" I continue.

"Eh, hello some of us work!" he snaps back. Now, when Paolo uses the word 'work', he clearly uses it loosely, as his idea of work is selecting fabrics or exotic animal skins, for his soon to be launched accessories line. And when I say soon to be launched, I mean sometime soon, as he has been working on it for almost three years now. In fact, when I say working, I mean wearing the pieces he has commissioned.

"There was a huge drama with Henri, like crazy shit!" I rush.

"Why is everything you do so dramatic, bello? Can you not just have a calm day from time to time and give my brain a rest? What now?" he says wearily.

"Well, that's just it, I have no idea. I arrived for lunch on his yacht, he was fine. Kinda drunk, but friendly drunk, you know? Then, out of nowhere he started insulting me, before he snapped and left me alone at the table, instructing one of his staff to tell me he wouldn't be returning." I sound deranged.

"Well, look, why do you care? You don't even want to be with him, you told me so much only yesterday! I have to go as I am going into a meeting, so stop panicking over nothing. Remember, you're only playing games until Marco clicks his fingers," he says correctly.

That's the problem with everything right now. I thought by escaping down here I would be free, but I can't escape him, as much as I want to. At least Sophs had the respect for herself not to contact me since our split, well, apart from one drunken night when she sent a slightly too long text saying how much she missed me. I didn't tell you at the time, as I thought I should let it slide.

"Hey, Oli, I am finished now. Would you like a Coke?" Pablo asks from behind my sun lounger.

"Fuck, man, you scared me! Sure, to the Coke, but maybe with a little Jameson?" I laugh.

"Yes, I can get this for you, but I cannot drink

alcohol when it is working time," he smiles.

"Well I won't tell if you won't. So make it two whiskeys and one Coke." I pull myself upright and walk over to the edge of the pool. He returns carrying just what we need and sits next to me, removing his flip flops before placing his tanned feet into the water.

"Cheers, is correct, yes?" he asks with a broad smile.

"Yes, it's perfect," I smile back.

We just sit silently, staring at the water, and sip our drinks. You know that feeling, when you both know what the other is thinking but are too shy to say it. It's a bloody great feeling, one where you're scared but aroused. "You had the good day?" he asks as he reaches for his Winston.

"No, it was shit. Really shit in fact," I laugh, taking the cigarette he offers.

"No, what is happened? Do you want to tell me it?" he asks.

"It's so boring, just a lunch date with someone who was really wrong for me," I sigh before taking a drag of the cigarette. He stares at me and I feel nervous. Not scared, but excited. That feeling when someone you really want looks into your eyes.

"Ah, OK. What is the wrong thing with this date?" He kicks the water gently.

"Oh, the guy was a big disappointment; too old, too drunk, too rude, too crazy…" I drift. "We were supposed to have lunch on his yacht, but, well it didn't happen." I pull a sad face.

"Oooh, a yacht… this is very good." He sounds

slightly wounded for some reason. Perhaps it's jealousy. "I only see the big yachts in Puerto Banus, I have never be inside. Maybe one other day," his simplicity becoming more and more attractive.

"Well, I'm happier to be here than on the yacht." I feel myself blush as I say it.

"Ana has really gone to home for this day?" he asks as he finishes his drink.

"Yes, I told her to take the afternoon off. Maybe another drink?" I suggest, as I wave my almost empty glass. Watching as he walks towards the house, I'm swamped by how much I want him. OK, so he seems to be straight and too hot to be true, but it's not as if it's the first time I've been in a situation like this. Life can be funny at times, I tell you, when it takes you by complete surprise, meeting someone who blows you away just by being near you. One time, I ended up in bed with a Polish plumber that was working at my house. Seriously, one minute he was fitting the bathroom, the next we were naked in bed. Well, to be honest it was after three days of him working at my place and a lot, I mean, a lot of tension, similar to the way I feel right now. Unlike the plumber, Pablo isn't married with three kids, but you get the point. Arriving back at the pool with a bottle of whiskey, and strangely a packet of Lays, I can almost feel the tension getting stronger. "So, what's your place like?" I ask boldly.

"You mean my house where I live, or here, this pool house?" he smiles curiously.

"Is there a difference? I thought you lived over there?" I say, pointing to the pretty bougainvillea-covered pool-house tucked away in the corner of the garden.

"No, it is only my place for when I working. My family live in the Mijas, up in the mountain." He sips his drink and pulls a face. "Too much whiskey?" I laugh, knowing that my measures are large, even for the free-pouring Spaniards. I swear to you, I'm not trying to get him drunk, and I'm beginning to hope I don't need to. "Do you want to smoke, eh, how do you say... joint with me?" He smiles again, as he pulls a pre-rolled smoke from his Winston packet. We sit with the sun slowly dropping into the sea and Jose Feliciano still strumming away on his guitar. A song I don't recognise, but will certainly remember after today. I don't know about you, but I'm obsessed with music, from jazz to opera and just about everything in between. Apart from blues, I can't stand blues. I mean, life can be blue enough without having to listen to the likes of Muddy Waters droning on.

"This is good smoke!" I say as I exhale deeply.

"I can get you more, if you want? I like to finish my day with one or two marijuana cigarettes, it makes my sleep too good," he smiles, his eyes already looking hazy.

"They make you sleep well," I correct him, although it goes unnoticed. "Wait here, I want to give you something," I say as I make my way into the house. "Don't move!" I shout excitedly. Inside I change my t-shirt, fix my hair again, spray a little Acqua di Parma and bring the smashed iPhone out to the pool. I had noticed that Pablo was using an old Nokia, so why can't he have my smashed but only two-month-old iPhone? "Hey, you want this?" I ask as I pass him the phone.

"Seriously? Is for me?" He jumps to his feet like a kid on Christmas morning.

"Sure! All you have to do is get the screen replaced and make sure you delete my photos," I laugh.

"You are the best guy, Oli, really, I serious," he beams.

"Look, it's just a phone and, well, you're a cool guy too. We cool guys have to stay together," I say, realising how it sounds once the words leave my mouth. "So, let's go see the pool house," I say as I jump to my feet, getting a head a rush as I do so and falling backwards into the pool. We both burst out laughing, as he helps me out of the water. I am tempted to pull him in with me but his strength pulls me up before I can. Inside we waste zero time in ending the tension. I watch as he pours a glass of Coke and without thinking I reach out and touch his arm. As we lock eyes the glass overflows before smashing to the floor. With that we kiss and he pushes me back onto the bed. Now, I know how books like this usually tell you all the details of a sex scene. Usually doing so in a way so flowery that they seem like a load of bollocks, so I'll spare you. Let's just say that it was hard, rough, sweaty and over way too soon, which clearly shows me that Pablo is, as suspected, 'straight'. As soon as he finishes, he pulls away, as if realising what he's just done. There it is, that dreaded tension once again. We just lie here silent, staring at the ceiling, both feeling bad about what's happened, but for two very different reasons. While I feel bad as I know it won't happen again, he feels bad as he, well…

"So, what we do now?" he asks in a voice that wants me to leave. "You know I must go to meet my girlfriend very soon," he says without looking at me. I just lie there, having spent the last few minutes hoping I was wrong, wanting him to relax and maybe even go for round two. Now I see it for what it really is; a pool boy who saw an iPhone and maybe more coming his way if he played the game.

Or perhaps a guy who was curious and once the experiment was over he felt ashamed. "Yes, you really should go get her, I am going to head out after all. Goodbye, Pablo," I say as I light one of his Winston and leave. While I should be feeling low, instead I laugh to myself as I walk by the pool to the terrace. I'm not sure if I was Pablo's first gay experience, but I doubt it. Why am I so sure? Well, let me tell you, the amount of guys just like Pablo that I've met and ended up with for NSA would be quite alarming, if it wasn't so frequent and international. As our world gets smaller with thanks to apps such as Grindr or Romeo, just who is into what seems to change hourly. As I sit watching the light on the pool I'm truly glad that I'm single and ready to leave Marbella after just a few days. When it's to time to return to reality, it's time. The only problem I face now is what is my reality? Where to next?

Chapter 13

Unicorn Restaurant, Dublin

The million-euro traffic jam attempting to park in the tiny laneway outside the Unicorn makes passing tourists stop and stare. Ferraris, Bentleys and Aston Martins noisily awaiting their turn to be told that there's no space and they have to back up. The whole thing just reminds me of the fun I'll be missing in St Tropez this weekend, having decided to return to Dublin, after yet another attempted make-up, which became a huge row with Marco just days previously. "Oh, I've tried to be calm, but it's not working, darling. He won't listen to my side of things…" I say, trying to remain upbeat. Paolo really is a dear friend and I know that he wants me with him for a fun-filled early summer weekend, but I can't face it. "Anyhow, Paolo, I'm just about to have lunch, can I call you later? OK cool, ciao ciao!" I hang up the call and glance at the chaos taking place all around me. The sun is shining and it seems that everyone in the city wants to be on this terrace. OK, so it's not St Tropez, but it isn't all bad, as it's a rare hot early May afternoon, the skies are azure blue, the Bollinger is flowing and while many of the other diners at the restaurant may not be to my taste, they certainly are entertaining, as they try to balance on their five-inch Saint-Laurent heels or attempt to navigate the Italian menus, resulting in orders being bottles of prosciutto and plates of prosecco. *Who cares about St Tropez? Life is good*, goes through my mind as I sip a Campari soda and await my lunch guest, fellow socialite Tamara Roxcroff.

Tamara is the type of girl that manages to make a simple task such as entering a restaurant a big deal. Dressed to kill in a white Gucci mini dress with bright pink Fendi heels and clutch, she certainly looks fantastic. With possibly the longest and most tanned limbs in the city, her mere arrival sends men into a sweat and women into a rage. She stops by at least four tables on the bustling terrace to air-kiss and flirt with admirers before finally landing beside me at the 'star table'. The star table is in every restaurant in every city in the world, well at least the ones I frequent. It's the place that has not only the best views of the other diners, but also the one place where other party-hungry diners will gravitate towards as lunch rolls into dinner. It's the place where clever restaurateurs place certain people, like me.

"Sorry I'm so late, darling, I am utterly frazzled!" she gasps before taking a large sip from a glass of San Pellegrino. "My stylist was late this morning, which in turn made me late for yoga, which in turn left me late for my hair appointment and so on… Anyhow, you look fab, who's here? Anyone of interest?" She's spinning around on her seat to check things out. Naturally there are a few well-known faces already in situ. At a corner table nightclub owner Robbie Fox is wearing shades and nursing a hangover while chatting into his phone. At another, U2 manager Paul McGuinness sports a Panama hat as he lunches with theatre boss Michael Colgan. Sitting inside and out of the sun, Maurice Donnelly is joined by his constant companion Bruno. Maurice, a successful businessman turned part-time TV show guest, made his millions from a string of low-end, high-price delis. You know, the sort that sell vegetables with dirt still on and market them as 'organic'. He's always with his Brazilian assistant Bruno, who at just twenty-one and at over twenty-five years his junior seems to be a vital part of Maurice's empire. The truth is they are lovers, having met on a gay dating site, and most people have figured it out.

Meeting Maurice on his own, he will talk about the women in his life, and when surrounded by all male company he becomes some sort of macho idiot, claiming to have bedded half the female population of Ireland. He's gay and everyone knows it, but nobody really cares, which would possibly be more crushing to Maurice's ego than having to come out. "Of course my stalker is here, dining solo as per." I gesture towards a corner table where Peter Donohue sits alone. Not the most popular chap in the city, he is somewhat obsessed with me. Having asked my agent, Angie, on numerous occasions to arrange a radio interview with yours truly for his beyond embarrassing weekly radio show Pure Irish Style, and having had each request declined, he's gone all cray-cray which really is rather amusing. The reason I've declined his offers is simple, I don't like his show and it certainly isn't the right fit for me. It's the sort of two-hour slot that features, oh, I don't know, so-called well-known TV continuity announcers or no-name models, telling listeners about their so-called fabulous lives. Also Peter uses the word 'exclusive' in his promo clips and advertising for the show, so I'm sure you can see my point.

In fact, looking at him now there's no way I could possibly be interviewed by him. Considering his show is supposedly all about style, his fashion sense is rather bizarre; stuck in time and totally passé. Right now he's wearing the same black suit which he seems to wear every day, shiny from way too many trips to the dry cleaners. Twin this with a receding 1990s hairstyle and a personality that is borderline loony tunes, and you get the scene. Lately he's been writing the most ridiculous, borderline libellous articles about yours truly in a little newspaper column that he managed to get his name on, having begged the paper's editor into submission. A column he believes to be red hot, just because he attempts to slate well-known people, usually those who have also said 'no fucking thanks' when he's come knocking for one of his 'exclusive interviews'. In reality the column is a lame attempt to boost his profile, as the fact is nobody really reads it, or at least nobody in my circle. Honestly, he has been pretty scathing in his rants about me, but amusingly I've never seen one of them. Each time he lets rip I find out weeks later from some taxi driver or hairdresser, who feels it their business to tell me that I should knock him out. I've never spoken with him, or at least I don't think I have – it's hard to remember what goes down in nightclubs at half past something in the a.m. All I do know is that he's a miserable sort, and even those he considers to be his friends have taken time to bitch about him to me at one point or another. Seriously, people feel compelled to tell me of their 'experiences' with him. Of how he never gets his wallet out, or how he has sofa surfed his way through his annual summer sojourn to Marbella, without ever giving his hosts as much as a bottle of champagne as a thank you gift. Also, on top of this there are rumours that his financial situation isn't great and no matter how much he brags about his success, those rumours continue to spread like wildfire. "You know I heard somewhere that he had to sell his beloved Porsche on a car website, I think it was either that or the finance company would take it!" I say smugly to a disinterested Tamara.

Yes, life for 'yet to be married' Peter is far from glamorous, so I turn my gaze back to far more glamorous Tamara who is staring at possibly the loudest table of all. Seated bang centre of everything and all female, they are making serious noise as they laugh and screech at everyone and everything. Ten middle-aged women dressed just like their daughters have gathered to see and be seen. Loud, rich and although a little bit past it, on the hunt for men. "Really, look at them," Tamara says as she removes her oversized Dior shades in order to take a proper look. "If my mother went to lunch dressed like them I would simply die." The fact that they're only ten or fifteen years older than her doesn't seem to faze her. It's going to be her day and nobody is going to steal the limelight. Before we even order lunch she decides to make a quick phone call to her ever-efficient cocaine dealer. "I think it's time to kick start this lunch, baby!" she says, jumping to her feet. Pacing up and down through the other tables, laughing and flicking her hair in an over-animated fashion, she knows that all eyes are on her. Despite the fact it's only two-thirty, it's show time for Tams, as she's known.

One of the city's in-demand party girls, she works part-time with leading interior designer Moira Kelly-Byrne who heads up a design team responsible for most of the capital's on-point bars and restaurants. When I say part-time, I mean one morning a week. She once told me that it's all she can handle, as the concept of working full-time scares her. I kid you not. Born in South Africa to Dutch parents, her family relocated to Dublin in the 90s as her diplomatic father was posted here and he too became something of a socialite, known for his lavish hospitality and his equally lavish home on Herbert Park. Anyhow, she's become something of a household name, well at least with those that still read the social diary sections of the Sunday papers. Diaries that were once essential reading and taken pretty seriously, by everyone from government ministers to emerging It Girls. Tams makes regular column inches due to her non-stop partying, and one or two high-profile romances. In fairness, she makes more column inches every time she gets dumped. Anyhow, work simply doesn't fit into her world and even though she may not have the bank balance she requires, she always gets by. How does she do it? The answer is simple; men seem to see it as their duty to pick up her tabs, whether at restaurants, nightclubs or Prada. I must say I do admire her for her ballsy approach to life.

The party is in full flow and the staff at the restaurant know just what their wealthy diners want – music volumes continually rise, with the party soundtrack being supplied by Hôtel Costes, resulting in more orders of Gavi di Gavi and more clothes being shed. Within minutes a rather dodgy-looking chap arrives by motorbike and comes straight to our table. Sitting down momentarily, he makes small talk about the weather, and with a quick exchange of €400.00 the deal is done. We are still to order any food and it's now suddenly the last thing on our minds. "I'll have penne a la vodka, but ensure chef uses Grey Goose or Chopin, I can't stand basic vodka even in pasta. Oh, and another bottle of Bollinger," I tell the amused waiter.

"I need a quadruple espresso ASAP!" Tamara barks as another waiter passes by already laden with empty plates.

Dressed in Dsquared2 jeans, a white Dolce & Gabbana t-shirt and Gucci shades, I must admit, I know I look good, even if it did take me almost two hours to leave the house. Plus, compared to the other guys seated around me, I shine. Wearing ill-fitting suits, having escaped the office for the afternoon, or their dressed-down 'trying to be cool' chinos, loafers and open-neck shirt looks are never really going to cut it. While Tamara makes a trip to the powder room, I'm looking at the other diners and acknowledge one or two with a fake smile. Having been dubbed the 'It' boy by the media and propelled into the social limelight overnight, it not only gives me a feeling of superiority, but also makes me very much aware of just how little style there is in the city.

Buckets of money, sure, but style, no. Waiting for a 'refreshed' Tamara to emerge from the loo, I observe the behaviour of the other diners. Some struggle to hold a knife and fork properly, which I must admit is one of those things that really creeps me out, while others repeatedly order bottles of Sauvignon Blanc as they're afraid to attempt the pronunciation of anything else. Most are completely overdressed – as if they're in a night club or attending a formal evening event. The 'Puerto Banus brigade', as they're known. Having only ever wanted to holiday in the Spanish millionaires' playground since childhood, now they can, as their husband's property dealings have afforded them the opportunity to buy a second home in the area. Of course they like to keep this on the down-low, yet somehow manage to tell anyone who will listen about 'their stunning mansion by the sea' after one too many champagne cosmopolitans.

"Oh my god, you simply won't believe who's just arrived!" Tamara shrieks as she bounces back to the table. "Joanne Browne! Just saw her driver letting her out of the car. Fuck, I really hope she doesn't see us. Oooh, I wonder who she's meeting?" she continues nervously and annoyingly.

"Relax! You are totally ruining the mood. I told you to hold off on the coke until later, and now you're super paranoid. I doubt Joanne will even want to join our table after what you did," I tell her in a calm yet assertive tone. Joanne and Tamara had been very close friends for many years, attending all the right parties, not always with all the right people, but they always had each other's back. True social teammates, both in search of rich, powerful men and not afraid to let their desires be known. However, that all changed in the space of one afternoon when Joanne returned home early from a Paris shopping trip to find Tamara in a rather awkward situation with her husband, investment banker Mark. Having started out as a model, Joanne quickly made a name for herself when she moved into PR. She landed a job with a leading estate agency and helped to market the growing property boom. She became a force to be reckoned with, especially when it came to knowing which high-end properties were about to hit the market before anyone else. Something which has come in very handy as her love of property dealing, is rapidly becoming a notable business. Also, Joanne's ability to integrate herself into many social circles from ambassadors to those controlling the country's leading financial institutions, means that she is red hot when it comes to real gossip. However, she isn't the most popular girl in town, due to her non-stop and clearly obvious search for a millionaire spouse. Of the time it took to find her own husband, there are many rumours that she busied herself with the husbands of others, resulting in plenty of enemies on the tiny Dublin social scene. Most of whom simply leave a party if she arrives, or as on one occasion a wealthy, self-made sort made it quite clear to the Maître D at the Four Seasons, either she left or he did. Naturally Joanne backed down and made a quick exit.

Having met Mark at a July 4th party at US Ambassador's residence, she pursued him carefully and finally he popped the question. Ever since her wedding, which of course took place in Marbella, directly followed by a second, less high-profile ceremony and party on Ibiza, life has been very different. Dressed in a Chanel suit, with large-logo Chanel shades, she certainly looks the part of millionaire's wife, as she's escorted to her table by Giorgio, the restaurant's affable owner. All the while Tamara's eyes follow her intensely. "Maybe I should go over and say hello?" Tamara suggests in utter panic. "I know she's seen me and it's not as if we are kids. Yes, I'm going to go say hi and be the bigger person." In Tamara's mind the fact that she'd been caught at her best friend's home with her best friend's husband was just a total mix-up. "Nothing happened, I swear to you, how many times must I say it? We were simply having a fucking glass of wine when she walked in. Hardly high-octane lovemaking. Hardly an affair," she moans, trying to convince herself that being in the home of her best friend with her best friend's husband is completely normal. "I'll just nip to the loo and then say hi."

Just as Tamara is out of sight Joanne's lunch date fellow developer Michael Farrell arrives and is on everyone's radar as he makes his way inside. He is the sort that people like to see, mainly as he's constantly sending bottles of wine and champagne to friends at other tables and not afraid to press the flesh in true politician style. Of course, there have been rumours that he had wanted a political career, but life sent him into bricks, much to his annoyance. Joanne and Mark befriended him whilst buying their stunning home on Elgin Road in nearby Ballsbridge. A neighbourhood once known for old money, but now due to the economic boom a place where new money clashes very loudly with old. White Range Rovers are fast becoming the norm in this leafy part of the city. Once the stomping ground of judges, surgeons and the fading aristocracy, now it's rapidly being snapped up by property developers, who are mostly referred to as builders by the old guard. The thing about the two classes is that the new money doesn't care about the old money or their values. They've arrived and they're showing off. The fact that most of them will be bankrupt within five years and gone again doesn't seem to matter. Wonderful gardens are being pulled up and replaced by 'shop to order' landscapes direct from the Chelsea Flower Show. Hideous mansions are popping up alongside perfect examples of Victorian, Georgian and Edwardian architecture.

The fact that Joanne and Mark's monstrous house has been nicknamed The Pitz, goes over their heads completely, perhaps by choice, as they are aware that they are certainly blow-ins. Where once old Bentleys, Volvos or racing green Range Rovers were the chosen modes of transport, now it's more about the Bugatti, Ferrari or Lamborghini. In fact, they want anything as long as it's flashy, despite the fact that it collides with the elegance of the original residents. It's well-known that the old school reject party invitations from their new neighbours and one resident went as far as to write a letter to papers complaining about her new-monied neighbours and their lack of taste. Some others see it as a perfect opportunity to downsize by selling their large Victorian mansions to the new sort for hugely inflated prices.

Joanne looks cool, calm and in control as she sips on a glass of champagne. A strong comparison to Tamara who emerges from the loo looking like a rabbit caught in the headlights of an oncoming car, having decided that the best way to deal with Joanne's presence is to take a fresh hit of coke and then make her approach. However, somehow her plan has backfired, leaving her looking completely strung out. Making her way through the restaurant, I watch as quite possibly the worst thing happens. She bumps directly into Sylvia O'Rourke, a woman who has social climbed her way from a pink bungalow in Co. Leitrim, to a four-storey over basement on Wellington Road, as well as a position of power heading a charity for terminally ill children. A woman who, despite humble beginnings looks down her perfectly re-structured nose at most people. However, she has many reasons to hate Tamara, but mainly because she's been having a rather public affair with her husband David, a self-made millionaire, who had made his fortune through less than above board property deals in the South of France over the past decade.

Tamara, now completely high and face to face with her nemeses, has little choice but to continue towards Joanne's table with her head held high. As she approaches, Joanne signals to her not to come any closer. "I just want to say hi, darling." She tries to move closer. "I really miss you and was wondering if you wanted to catch up later?" She sounds utterly desperate.

"No, I certainly do not," Joanne says sharply. "You are nothing more than a sad drug-addled bitch with ideas way above your station. Stay away from me and my family or you'll regret ever meeting me," loud enough for most to notice.

Stunned, Tamara turns to walk away from the table realising that the entire restaurant has heard every word. Mortified, she makes a beeline for me, extremely shaken by both encounters. "She is an utter bitch! How did you ever allow me to hang out with her?" she asks in an attempt to make herself feel better. "I mean look at her, head to toe in Chanel. It was only like yesterday that she was asking me for fashion advice and despite my best attempts she always got it fucking wrong." She is determined to shake off what's just happened and get her fabulous day back on track, re-applying her Chanel lipstick before pretending to eat her salad, pushing it around the plate like a spoilt child for ten minutes before giving up. "Oh, I need another quadruple espresso ASAP," she orders loudly to a passing waiter.

Lunch rolls on and many of the other diners are involved in a spot of table hopping, and we're now busily holding court for a mix of models, socialites and those all-important rich men. Endless bottles of Bollinger are being popped as gifts from various admirers. I watch as Tamara gets more and more animated with the mix of champagne, espresso and cocaine, so while others look on she urges the staff to crank up the music so she can dance and flirt with a group of admiring American dot com guys, who are at the next table. "Let's all go to the garden of the Four Seasons and continue the party," she announces much to their delight.

"That sounds cool, baby! We're staying at the hotel, so that works, right?" says one of them to his crew, with a gleeful face. With chiselled good looks and a smile so white I'm glad I have my shades on, he clearly sees a good time ahead. The fact that they're staying at the Four Seasons was registered by Tamara within minutes of introducing herself.

Just then, my phone beeps with an incoming text message. It's Paolo. 'You're totally missing the best beach day. The party is off the charts, but everyone wants to know where you are. What about this – if I organise the flight, would you join us here tomorrow for lunch at Voile Rouge? Marco is leaving tonight so it will be fine. x'

Totally confused and with my lunch date currently on another planet, I reply 'Why not! I need to get the fuck out of here ASAP! x' After all, I'm only home in Dublin three days and so far it's proved rather dull. With three long months of summer stretching out before me where would I rather be, stuck here with this aging deluded lot or lunching at Le 55 in St Tropez one day and at La Terrazza in the Hotel Splendido, Portofino the next? It isn't much of a contest, as I look around at the people sitting at our table. Is this really the best Dublin has to offer? Is this it for the next three months? *Absolutely not*, I think to myself as I start mentally packing my Hermès overnight bag in my head. Unlike the rest of the diners, Joanne's lunch is short and business-like. As she's about to leave she makes her way towards me and kisses me on the cheek. "I just wanted to say hi, I'm dashing to the airport as we are having dinner in Madrid tonight with some friends of Mark's. Thank God we have the PJ; I don't know how people use commercial airlines. It must be pure hell. Are you going to the Louis Vuitton dinner on Wednesday? I'll call you next week and we can have drinks somewhere beforehand." She glides towards her awaiting S-Class. Her presence is brief and hasn't even been noticed by Tamara, who is like a yo-yo back and forth to the loo.

At seven o'clock a fleet of cars arrive to pick up those wanting to go to the hotel. I'm really in two minds about it. The friendly Americans are so impressed with Tamara's entertaining ways that they insist on picking up the lunch bill, so I guess it would be rude to not buy them at least a drink. Tamara and two of the Americans are insisting that I join them and literally drag me to an awaiting Jaguar. Once inside they ask if I'm looking for a guy or a girl for the evening. "Well, having taken a good look at the options I think I'd rather be single if it's OK with you."

As the car whisks us through the evening traffic to cool and calm of the Ice Bar at the hotel, I'm already regretting my decision. Tamara is once again in need of pumping music and almost causes the driver to crash as she leans forward to adjust the already loud car stereo. As soon as they arrive 'Team America', headed up by a chap called Conrad, begin ordering bottles of Grey Goose and Magnums of Krug, while Tamara heads straight to the loo to freshen up again, returning full of life and ready to party. While others look on, Tamara is unaware that her behaviour is somewhat out of control for 7pm in a five-star hotel. I'm surrounded by this OTT crowd, all boring each other with tales of their wealth and bragging about who has the most expensive car in the car park. I'll tell you who, the leasing company. A strange mix of investment bankers, car salesmen and property developers, all flashing their cash, as if in a modern-day survival of the fittest demonstration. Their antics are naturally greatly admired by Tamara and the rest of the overly dressed women at the bar, who down vintage champagne that they can't pronounce. "It takes around two million a year just to run my personal lifestyle, not taking into account my cars and houses of course…" bores one of the nondescript middle-aged chaps at the bar. Clearly he's been dipping his nose into Columbia's finest all afternoon.

While I chat with two women who want me to act as MC at an upcoming charity lunch I notice one of the Americans slip something into Tamara's drink. "Oh relax, you are always finding fault with people," she snaps as I try to warn her. "These guys are fantastic and Conrad has already asked me to go to the Hamptons this weekend. His family are very Connecticut, Upper East Side, so what's not to like? Who knows, he could be the one!" she's gushing. Despite being uber-confident, mainly due to her coke habit, she's like most girls her age; desperate to be married. Sadly, unlike most other girls, she has one major obstacle, being that she'll only marry someone super rich. Super rich and party loving, as in order to maintain her day-to-day life, she needs someone who will not notice her out-of-control ways. Surely she can't believe that some guy she met just a few hours ago, and is clearly out for good time, as well as out of his mind, could be the one?

"But I saw him dropping something in your champagne. Don't drink it, that's all I'm trying to say," I advise calmly, as I hand her a replacement glass.

"Oh, fuck's sake, Oli. Lighten up, darling; it's just half an ecstasy to help the party flow. Ever since you and Marco split you've been no fun at all. Zero!"

Heading outside to make a phone call, I don't return to the bar, but instead I use the hotel's chauffeur service and head straight home to prepare my luggage for St Tropez. Tamara, fuelled on a mix of drugs and alcohol, doesn't make contact again that night.

Early the following morning I'm sipping espresso when I take a call from a very distressed Tamara. "Darling, where are you? The worst thing has happened! Help me!" she's sobbing into the phone. "I can't remember a thing after you left and I've just woken up in a suite at the hotel. There are champagne bottles everywhere and Conrad is... he's bloody gone!" She sounds both upset and completely out of it.

"I'm at the airport about to catch a flight to Nice. I did warn you about those guys. You really need to start being more careful," I offer.

"The worst bit of all is I'm pretty sure he wasn't the only one to come back to the room. I think... oh God, I think I'm going to throw up." She is sounding loopy. "I think I did a threesome, but I can't really be sure... And wait for it, you are going to die! He left a note which says," she clears her throat, "thanks, you were great. Look me up if you make it to New York, and beside it is €500. He thought I was a hooker. A high-class one obviously, but still a fucking hooker! Plus Dino, my new coke dealer, has switched his phone off. Please help me, Oli!" she sobs.

"Sorry darling, my flight is being called. I'll hit you up from the other end." I swear to you, I'm trying not to laugh out loud. "Get up, get a shower, get a coffee and get the hell out of there!" As I board the flight I smile, knowing that Tams will use the money wisely. Perhaps she'll buy shoes, or perhaps a good lunch. Actually, who am I kidding? That cash will go to her VBF on the motorbike for more marching powder, which is the only fuel she needs. Rather ironic that I'm heading to St Tropez and leaving a very St Tropez scenario behind... More importantly, I wonder if the contents of my overnight bag are going to be enough for my stay. Hopefully not...

Chapter 14

The Four Seasons Hotel, Dublin

"Another day, another lunch!" exclaims fundraiser Marie Higgins as she reapplies her Tom Ford lipstick in the mirror of her compact.

"Oh, I love your dress, where's it from? How much was it? Animal print is huge at the mo," Patricia Henderson asks in truly gauche fashion. Poor old Patsy has been on the social scene longer than cocaine, having blown in from Yorkshire over forty years ago, and is struggling to remain sober, following her overindulgence during the free-flowing pre-lunch champagne reception. That, and the fact her surgeon has prescribed some seriously strong painkillers, following yet another attempted eye lift just days before. I say attempted as it's clear she still has a lot of work to do in order to look her desired age of thirty-five. In reality she should be still lying on her back recovering, while watching daytime TV. Actually at well over sixty, perhaps she should take the daytime TV option on a daily basis, rather than trying to cling to her position on the social scene.

"Oh yeah, thanks, I picked it up in Puerto Banus last month. I always pick up a few bits down there for the charity season. You know, so far this year I've saved starving children, rescued some elephants, built a school in Africa, pretty much solved the homeless issue and it's only June!" smiles Marie smugly, while winking at a Polish waiter who is young enough to be her grandson.

Every city in the world has a Patsy and every city in the world wonders why. You know the sort – once something of a big name, hosting and attending the best parties, but then somehow due to paranoia or whatever else, they manage to create dramas which alienate everyone close. They spend the rest of their life trying, at every opportunity, to get one over each and every one of them. As an onlooker, the funny thing is those they wish to attack, have forgotten about their existence and moved on. I sit listening to the bullshit taking place all around me and long to be anywhere but here. After a great week in St Tropez, I find myself trapped at this excuse for fundraising, because my agent, Angie, booked me for the job, thinking charity work is essential for one's popularity. While I am all for charity, personally I am of a different belief. Having sat on a number of charity fundraising committees, I can tell you that endless meetings over cocktails, lunch or dinner to discuss ways of raising money is clearly not the way forward. Especially when so much money and time is wasted organising crappy events for people that only attend in some vain attempt to get snapped and appear in the social pages of one low-rent magazine or another.

I mean come on, if you want to support a charity just write a fucking cheque and do it without a circus to award yourself. Anyhow, I'm here, I'm tired and I've been asked to present the prize for best dressed, which, by looking around is going to be a needle in a haystack situation. Why, oh why do women dress like this? Full-on ball gown scenario and as I glance at my watch, I can see it's only half past noon.

"Oli have you met Richard Godson? He is the man who put this whole gala together," Patsy gushes, as she presses her tanned arm on his.

"No, I don't believe I have, how do you do? Well done on the bash, looks like it will be fun." I try to sound sincere.

"Richard is Marie's husband, and the pair of them are utterly amazing, raising all this money for those poor little kiddies in Africa!" She smiles a daft smile.

"Actually, this lunch is for Moldova, Patsy," Richard says, holding up a flyer for the lunch, which clearly has the word 'Moldova' across it in bright red lettering. "If you'll excuse me, I must greet the Lord Mayor." He smiles falsely before sliming his way towards more important company. Listening to Patsy ramble on, it's clear to see that she has the hots for him, which is understandable. He is tall, with a great smile, shiny black hair, oh, and is not short of cash, which is possibly his most attractive feature, especially in Patsy's surgically enhanced eyes. Although, nobody is quite sure where the money comes from, or rather where it came from almost overnight.

It's not quite Lake Geneva money, but enough for him to drive a Bentley and for Marie to have gone from a Renault Clio to Range Rover overnight without flinching. The rumours circulating are that Richard has conned one or two high rollers into investing heavily into a planned boutique hotel which is yet to materialise.

"Their new house in Rathgar is divine, have you seen it?" she continues.

"Darling, does their new house resemble a boutique hotel by any chance?" I laugh. "Seriously, I've no idea who any of these people are? All I know is that their wealth has emerged out of nowhere and has certainly become the talk of town. On top of this, I've been warned to get my fee up front, or face months chasing Marie. I must speak with her, as the rumours are far from good," I say sternly, scanning in an attempt to spot her. It shouldn't be such a hard task as she's dressed as if she escaped from a zoo, after all. On top of this, I recently was forced to read an article in some in-flight magazine or another where she opened her closet as well as her safe to brag about her love of everything expensive, including her love for Van Cleef & Arpels. Seriously, I almost needed to use the sick bag, it was so horrid.

"No, don't be crazy, Marie is fantastic! She has no worries financially as Richard has buckets, and I mean buckets of money. Old family money, you know the sort?" She starts to gently lick her lips. While personally I feel the friendship between Patsy and Marie is odd, it's one that seems to work. Possibly as they both need each other on one level or another. Marie, while in demand, is relatively new to the scene, and Patsy is somewhat a shadow of her former social self, so requires Marie to keep her in the loop. The thing that not many know, is that Patsy has been having secret meetings with Marie's beloved husband for months, and ever since her divorce from Nick, tortured husband of almost twenty-five years and father to her three daughters, who will undoubtedly be forced into the same social scene. Patsy has kept herself busy with many husbands of her close friends or their sons from time to time. In fact, the final straw of her already broken marriage to Nick was beyond funny. Pushing the boundaries, she liked to try new things sexually, whether it be outdoor sex, dogging, or mile high. She and her Romanian gardener chose to do it in the panic room in the basement of her house but sadly got trapped. The room was installed after a rumoured kidnap attempt and Patsy often bragged about her impenetrable safety device. Once inside the metal box that is the panic room, the doors closed and wouldn't open again. They were trapped inside until Nick eventually arrived home from work six and a half hours later to find the pair naked, well, apart from Patsy's stilettos and feather boa. The funniest part of it being that Patsy told me afterwards how dreadful the ordeal was once she realised that she didn't even like the gardener. Six hours is a long time to get to know someone and when they started talking instead of fucking, well, she lost her sex drive. Soon after this she lost her husband.

Where once Patsy was the toast of the social scene, driving a Porsche, living in a desirable postcode and being on every possible guest-list in the land, since the divorce, she has been unable to hold on to a man as long as she has her by now almost embarrassing six-year-old Porsche Boxster. The car, or rather the age of the car, is the one thing that really gets under her skin. Although we aren't really close, I've been forced on more than one occasion to listen to one of her rants, when she's spotted a rival socialite driving a brand-new BMW or Aston Martin. Having always had a brand-new car as soon as the clock struck midnight on New Year's Eve, her by now tatty-looking wheels are one thing she wishes to upgrade, but sadly her divorce settlement doesn't include annually. It does, however, include a substantial chunk for her general upkeep. I think she gets an annual allowance of fifty thousand for cosmetics and a further thirty or so for 'maintenance'. I have no idea either, but assume she means spay tans and such. She spends five days a week with her hairdresser, getting her jet black, almost midnight blue hair blow-dried or treated to yet another deep condition. However, weekends that begin on a Thursday evening in the bar of this very hotel, sipping vintage Bollinger, and end on a Tuesday with dinner in some low-key, out-of-town bistro, sipping bottles of twenty-euro rosé, don't come cheap, especially when you see fit to pick up the tabs of others around you just to save face.

Wednesdays are all about recovery mode, at home curtains remain closed, and she can be found on the sofa, usually dressed in a bath robe, eating her own body weight in Häagen-Dazs, as she tries to sort out the various rows that have taken place over the weekend, which naturally are all of her own doing. However, like many others in her position, come every week she is in dire need of her divorce cash, and before stepping out of bed is online checking that it has been deposited to her bank. Nine times out of ten it's there, and life is fine, but once or twice there's been a 'mix up' with the transfer and all hell has broken lose. "No funds means no fucking fun!" she screams into the phone to her nearest and dearest. The irony that her closest friends are in fact her dearest is somehow lost on Pats. Week in and week out, her routine is the same; lunches, dinners, cocktails and parties, most of the time enjoyed by those whom she rarely knows and all of the time paid for by her. The result is always the same – a blur of a weekend surrounded by a party hard group, made up of random sorts in nightclubs who sip Grey Goose and DP, dance on tables and then wind up back at all-night parties in her beloved Dalkey home, much to the annoyance of her neighbours. In her mind people still look up to her as someone to be taken seriously. This, as I am sure you already know, is the most dangerous type of deluded madness possible.

While she works hard at portraying an image of wealth and success, those she wishes to impress have moved on and rarely even mention her name in the day-to-day. I secretly believe she knows that the ones she obsesses about don't give her a second thought, which results in her creating dramas week after week in order to lash out at them. Again, sadly her 'dramas' have become something of a laughing stock to all concerned, with most not even raising an eyebrow, and the lack of brow movement has nothing to do with Botox. As I look at her across the table busily gossiping with some guy I've never met, I hear my name being announced by someone who has an accent as fake as Patsy's tan. "It is my great pleasure and utter honour, to welcome It Boy Oli to the stage, to select and present the award for Best Dressed. Having flown in from St Tropez especially for the occasion, please put your hands together for…"

Marie drones in an accent that she struggles to control. Making my way to the stage, I sense that most of the women gathered are trying to get my attention.

"Looking fab, Oli! Come join us for bubbles later?" an unidentified blonde screeches as I pass her table. Yes, she said bubbles! It's beyond me why grown people use such words and it drives me bloody insane!

"Good afternoon ladies and gentlemen, and welcome to the eleventh annual Help Moldova Lunch!" I say enthusiastically to a loud applause and flashing cameras. "I'm literally just off the plane and leaving again this evening. It is an absolute honour to have been asked by the committee to help select the most stylishly attired amongst you, which has been a tough job, let me tell you," I smile and fake wipe my brow. Truth is, like so many other similar events I haven't even looked around the room as Marie has already selected the winner and all I have to do is announce the name. "And the winner of Best Dressed goes to... Patricia Henderson!" I say excitedly, although my excitement is almost at an all-time low. How the fuck have I ended up presenting crap like this? I can see Patsy making her way to the stage to collect her prizes, stopping by almost every table to air-kiss and shine. Her award for being selected includes a huge, hay fever-inducing bouquet of horrid flowers, a voucher for a weekend at some country house in Cork, and a dress by an Irish designer I've never heard of and can hardly pronounce... Blathnaid O'hEalaighthe or something? "You are so, so deserving, I must say," I utter as I present the flowers. Dressed in the tightest DVF wrap dress I have ever seen, she looks like a ready-to-burst sofa cushion. In fact I think every outfit choice I have ever seen shows off her large snake tattoo which seems to wrap itself from her left shoulder all to her right thigh. Something I'm pretty sure she must think as ghastly as the rest of us.

"I am totally and completely shocked by this award. I spent only a few minutes getting ready for this lunch, and as I always say, less is more and more will follow!" She's going into full-on Oscar night territory. "But seriously, this lunch is so important and raising money for these poor kids in Africa is always top of my list. Here's to next year!" she screams before almost falling off her Gina heels. To me, she epitomises the whole charity circuit – only moments before, she had been pulled up on which charity event she was attending, yet it didn't register. What does register is the assembled group of photographers from the various magazines and news desks.

"Patsy, can we get a few snaps for *On the Town* magazine diary pages?" asks Randy, a middle-aged snapper who certainly lives up to his name. His look is seedy playboy – albeit on the low-rent side of playboy. A tatty leather jacket over a washed-out AC/DC t-shirt, tight faded blue jeans and cowboy boots, that look as if they have been through some of the world's most historic moments. Naturally Patsy knows how to pose, having once been one of Yorkshire's most in-demand models way back when, and as she loosens her dress to reveal her enormous cleavage Randy gets slightly over excited. "Wow! Beautiful, darlin'! Really work it, like you own it!" he pervs, as a group of young girls watch on in shock.

"Imagine she was your grandmother!" laughs one leggy blonde who must be all of nineteen.

"Don't hate me 'cause you ain't me, girls!" Patsy snaps at the gathered group of next season socialites. Making our way back to our table, she's is on form, acting as though her winning first prize has come as a shock. "Oh, thanks guys, it's just a little Diane von Fürstenberg number I threw on last minute." She waves to a table of women who look as if Patsy is their fashion role model. There it is again, that mix of ball gown meets Marbella beach attire. What the fuck is going on in this city? Of course between you and me, the dress obviously wasn't a last-minute decision but instead is out on 'loan' from a store just off Grafton Street and will be dry cleaned and returned tomorrow.

Arriving back to her table, Patsy's mood is shattered when she spots her main enemy on the scene, Leslie Dunphy, chatting with Marie and Richard by the bar. Rather than be the bigger person and let it slide she sits staring and loudly ordering more and more champagne for her guests. "Oh, we must get out of here soon, suddenly the edge has gone off this event!" she announces to her invited friends, who all seem content to remain in place, especially as they are yet to eat. The funny thing is that Patsy and Leslie used to be best friends, but like so many others in the tiny social circuit they came to blows and haven't been able to resolve the matter since. The matter in question is of course, being a man, each one thinking that the other had slept with him and each one eternally blaming the other for taking away the love of their life. Truth is Charles

Singcroft, the hedge funder in question, didn't sleep with either of them. I mean, why would he, when he's surrounded by beautiful young girls every day and night of the week and is also fifteen years their junior? Anyhow, the stand-off is more of a laugh-off as far as I'm concerned, with Patsy directing idle threats and dagger looks across the room at Leslie.

"That's it, I'm going to leave! This is supposed to be a classy affair and she isn't classy. Look at me, I am classy!" she barks loudly enough for Marie to take notice.

"Darling what's wrong? Is it Leslie? I didn't invite her, she's her with some English guy. He's actually very sexy, look over there," Marie says, making her way towards our table. Without realising it, she may have just said the very thing to make Patsy flip out completely. As Patsy discreetly reaches for her glasses – something she rarely does in public, as she believes that if someone relies on glasses, even Tom Ford, they are old, in fact they're ancient.

"I'll be right back," she says as she makes her way directly towards Leslie's date. "Well hello there," she says in a sexy voice as she stands next to him at the bar. Marie is right, he is a bit of yes please, looking rather like a young Carlos Souza. "Just a word in your ear, handsome – watch your back with Leslie. Nothing good ever comes from her company, trust me, I know first-hand. Plus, you're way too sexy for her." She's gently stroking the lapel of his blazer. "Wanna join my table?" she says, removing a strawberry from her champagne and taking a sexily executed bite. From where I'm sitting all I can see is a look of bewilderment on his face, before he leans in and whispers into her ear. "Well fuck you! Fuck off, you sad creep!" she screams loudly enough so that not only Leslie hears, but I'm pretty sure the drivers waiting in the car park too. As the room turns towards the chaos, Patsy lashes out, firstly throwing her drink and then slapping him hard across the face. Never been one to avoid her working-class background, in fact she dines out on it, today she is living up to her image. I stare as she storms in my direction with a face like thunder, while behind her Leslie makes her way back to her date. "Let's get the fuck out of here now!" she barks. "You lot can stay if you want, bunch of nobodies!" she snipes at her guests. "I'm going into the bar, it's where the real party will be!" Again, so loud that everyone hears. I swear, I want the ground to open up and swallow me whole. Without hesitation I follow Patsy out of the busy ballroom and into the empty bar.

"What the fuck is going on? Jesus, you couldn't let it be, could you?" I snap. I'm not sure if it's tiredness, a hangover or the fact that I'd rather be at home knitting my own sweater than here right now, but she is really getting on my nerves.

"I'm going to have him, I swear it. And no, I don't mean sexually, as clearly I'm way too good for him. He's an Audi and I'm, I'm a fucking Lamborghini!" she snarls and she raps her fake nails on the bar top.

"Miss Henderson, what may I offer you? Your usual Bollinger?" asks the handsome Mauritian barman.

"Thanks, darling, and I think we need some Goose shots too," she laughs in a nauseatingly flirtatious way, as she plays with her hair extensions which makes me feel uncomfortable every time she does so. I mean, I'm all for some flirtation but this is just wrong. It's like granny hitting on everyone she meets, assuming they all want a piece of her. The barman delivers the champagne along with two elegant, yet tiny shots of vodka, and before the shot glasses are placed on the bar Patsy grabs one and then the other, downing them both in seconds flat. "Actually, bring us a bottle of the Goose. I need something stronger than fizzy after that load of crap!" she moans.

"What the hell happened? What did the handsome one say?" I ask, stupidly realising my mistake as I do so.

"Handsome? Who, that sleazy guy at the bar? Jesus, Oli, you must be drunk, or desperate. He told me that I wasn't his type, as I was too old!" she whispers.

Seriously, what the fuck do I say to that? Option one is to agree with her and then have to listen to her talk about her fabulous self all afternoon. Option two, explain that he may genuinely like younger women and get an ice bucket over my head. "Actually, I really think we are better out of there, it's a hideous group of people anyhow. Yes, even the ones you invited. I cannot stand that Fergal, or whatever his name is. He's the sort that gives gay guys a bad name." I cover my mouth as if I am going to gag. Fergal is fast becoming one of the country's leading fashion designers, having crawled his way out of somewhere in the midlands, and started making a name for himself as the go to chap for that ball gown/Marbella look. Today is really his day, as a sea of tacky shimmering dresses surrounded his every turn.

"Fergal is cool, if you don't like him it's your problem. Everyone else wants him at their table. Are you jealous? Is that it?" Suddenly I'm in her firing line.

"Oh, please. Jealous? Of that filthy-looking ex-rent? Does he ever shower?" I laugh loudly as I take a shot of vodka. "You know, today has been a bore from the start, so the last thing I need is more crap. I'm going back to the lunch to find Marie and to get her cheque book shaking," I say as I turn to leave.

"Don't you dare fucking walk away from me! Come back here or I swear you're finished, removed! Don't walk away from me…" She sounds even more desperate than I'd thought. I take her by surprise when I turn to walk back towards her.

"Are you threatening me? Is that what is going on here?" I look straight into her eyes. "You need to get a grip, darling, you're delusional. You do realise that nobody and I mean nobody takes any notice of what you say? Where are all your real friends, the ones who were there at the beginning? You drive everyone away and surround yourself with people who hang on your every word," I continue, knowing that she is ready to explode. "While you waste your life partying with people who are clearly using you, it's no secret that you want to be back you the 'in crowd', but sadly the 'in crowd' have outed you and moved on. So, eh, if I'm finished or removed or whatever it is you said, well that's ok with me. I'll go sit with Leslie and her hot guest. Thanks for the vodka," I say with a wink before heading back to the lunch. If she wants to try her games on me, it's fine, I'll leave her anxiously typing into her phone, alone in an empty bar. No doubt she will round up some of her freeloading entourage to make her feel popular.

Back in the ballroom, I can see why I spend such little time at these events. It's all about the ego and very little to do with the charity. I see Richard holding court with a group of similar sorts. All middle aged, ill-fitting suits, impossibly garish ties, and all looking very impressed by his tales from a recent golf trip to Portugal. In Richard's mind he's at the top of his game and by attending charity events and hosting tables that cost well into the thousands, he gets the justification he craves. "Richard, where can I find Marie? I really must see her before I leave," I ask casually.

"Come with me, we need to talk," he says in a tone that is far from friendly. "Listen, we don't like the way you operate. Demanding payment is not how we roll." Seriously, he actually said 'not how we roll'. I'm trying not to laugh. "You'll be paid when Marie is ready to do so, and she isn't ready now. We're sick of people like you demanding money from us. Sorry from a charity, have you no shame?" he snaps, while still smiling broadly in order to save face.

"Who the fuck do you think you are? You may think I'm impressed by your bullshit charitable ways and your wife posing for photos in some shitty magazine telling the world about her 'blessed life'," I laugh.

"What are you trying to say?" he asks, inching closer to me with a look of disgust covering his tanned face.

"Well, judging by the look on your face, I think I'm being very clear. You must remember Richard, that working within the media, especially in the area I do, I hear an awful lot of stories, and your name just keep coming up. It's as if the world wants me to notice you," I say, taking a glass of champagne from the bar. "I suppose it would be rather bad luck if I gave one or two editors the idea to do some digging. I mean, come on, almost overnight you land a Bentley, a D6 mansion and, what is it you do again? You run a string of newsagent's, right? Alas, that's not my style. I don't give a fuck where you get your cash from as long as you run along and get mine now," I smile falsely for all to see. "I would say donate the money back to the charity, but with so many questions over where the money actually goes with these charities I think I best take it and spend it wisely," I continue smiling. I swear to you, I've never seen anyone move as fast as Richard upon realising I'm not bluffing.

"Here's your fucking money! Marie has asked me to say that you're overrated and certainly over-paid." He hands me a fistful of rolled-up cash.

"Oh cash, perfect. I was worried about the possibility of a rubber cheque," I laugh falsely.

"The fact that you're gay, well, I've no idea what Marie was thinking. We steer clear of your kind as much as possible," he says, attempting to be cruel.

"Oh, now that is interesting, as I tend to avoid your lot too. Crooks, that is." I down the champagne. "And for your information, I'm booked to attend events globally, but never once have I been advised to demand payment on the day. It really says more about you than me. Dodgy is as dodgy does. Let's just say, if I count this money and there is anything missing, I won't return but rather press send on an informative email to those ever pesky editors… As for being gay, you have nothing to worry about, Dickie, I like my men rich, not just entry level. Ciao!"

Passing the bar, I spot Patsy surrounded by her usual entourage of thirsty twenty-somethings, all downing shots of vodka and making way too much noise for mid-afternoon. Standing chatting to the other drivers, Tony spots me coming and puts his jacket back on. "Oh, Tony, you don't need to wear the jacket, it's so warm!" I say with a smile.

"That was quick, I thought you'd be hours," he says as he starts the engine.

"It was long enough," I sigh. "So, where to now, Chief?" he asks me through the rear-view mirror.

"St Tropez, I think… Yes, let me make a few calls, pop home and grab a bag and then out to the airport if you please," I say as I throw the fistful of cash onto the seat beside me. "I really don't know how that lot don't wind up doing time for multiple murders," I laugh.

Arriving at VIP handling at the airport, I can see Paolo's jet already waiting on the tarmac. "Oh, a glass of champagne, perfect," I say to a pretty girl who is designated to keeping me happy before take-off. Oh, and yes, of course I sent the email to the powers that be at one or two national papers. I did it as my charitable deed to society! Let's just say their house of cards came crashing down pretty rapidly, front page of almost every newspaper within just days. In fact, once the story was investigated many, many well-known sorts lost their shirts. Richard had managed to con millions from his circle. Last I heard, he had skipped town and Marie was busily trying to flog her beloved jewellery to anyone who would still speak to her.

Chapter 15

We Love to Party magazine Offices, Dublin

"Can I see you for a moment in my office please, Oli?" asks Martina O'Hagan, with a beyond nauseating smile. Having landed her dream job as office manager at the busy HQ of the somewhat trashy weekly magazine, she's an important cog in the wheel which seems to turn twenty-four-seven. As previously explained, I may be surrounded by some seriously rich friends, and move in a fast-paced glamorous world, but I still need to work, even if my job choice is something of a joke to others. As often happens once you become even slightly famous, people become intrigued and want to know more. It's one of those positions which Paolo has encouraged, as he believes to know nothing at all is a waste of time. 'Do you respect the Hilton sisters? Exactly, nobody does,' he says at any given opportunity. So with his advice ringing in my ears and following a tedious lunch meeting with the editor Mark Edwards, I'd accepted the request to pen a weekly diary of my life. Little did I know that this diary would soon become the hottest column in town, complete with some light-hearted gossip and a few photographs of me either on a private jet, at a fashion show or hanging out with certain well-known types at one party or another.

Following a lavish lunch at twice Michelin-starred Restaurant Patrick Guilbaud, I was well and truly on board and ready to open up my life in full colour print, even if I wasn't sure that anyone would be interested. It was a serious lunch, you know, the sort that expense accounts are created for, and only seem to happen when people really want you, whether it's to have you on their team, or your help with something, or of course, sex! Anyhow, the lunch was a bore; making small talk with Mark was like pulling teeth. I mean, apart from the fact that we had zero in common, he's from some part of the UK I've never heard of, as I am not a regular viewer of TV shows such as Jeremy Kyle. In fact, the entire meeting was dreadful and from what I could gather, when we spoke of him growing up in the UK and how he set up the magazine at the right time to capture the Irish wealth, I could tell that he was somewhat ashamed of his upbringing. Clearly resenting those he wanted to interview and feature, due to his humble less-than-glamourous beginnings. The fact that I had zero interest if he had been conceived and raised in a skip, didn't register with him, instead he continually asked if I knew such and such and if I would have any problems 'turning them over'. Jokingly I pretended to misunderstand him and assume he meant sexually. Again, sadly my humour was lost on Mark, who sat red-faced, with an expression that clearly wanted the ground to open. Funnily enough, after about twenty minutes of listening to him whining on, I too wanted the ground to swallow him whole. The thoughts of looking at his face on a weekly basis made me feel rather ill, but it was a job and I needed one.

After a few weeks it became clear that the job suited me, and according to my weekly fan mail, I suited it. Now well into the swing of things, I am sitting flicking through a copy of *Harper's Bazaar* and sipping a cappuccino. All in all, the mood is good and I'm on form. To be honest, I enjoy the atmosphere of the office, although I very rarely make an appearance, apart from attending the mandatory team meeting every Monday morning, and then dropping by for an hour or so to file copy on Fridays. So far my relationship with the team is pretty much how it should be and while the job may have been something to aspire to for others on the social scene, to me it's nothing special.

"What can I do for you, Martina?" I ask as I close the door of her beyond-small office. You know those cubicles that they call office space within modern buildings, dreadful air-conditioned cells. Chuck in a straitjacket and you could be in an institution.

"You look great, Oli, I love your jacket," she beams.

"Thanks – Dsquared2. So what's up?" I smile falsely.

"It's been brought to my attention that your contract with us is almost up for renewal and I just wanted to see what your plans are moving forward?" she asks as she pours out two glasses of water, passing me one. She refers to the magazine as 'us', which makes me laugh inwardly, I mean come on!

"You know, there are rumours circulating. Talk is that we may be losing you to Italy. If that's the case we wish you well. However, we are happy with the way things are going and ideally would like to extend the contract for a further six months. Naturally with a pay rise if that sweetens the deal," she continues with a confident smile. To look at, she's nothing special, I guess in a way she looks as an office manager is supposed to. Dressed in a navy trouser suit, from somewhere nondescript like Marks & Spencer, her hair is in a bob, one which needs attention, and she wears red heavy plastic framed glasses – you know the sort they sell in your local pharmacy, usually as part of a two-for-one offer. Her fashion faux pas aside I've always felt that I could trust Martina. She, unlike most people in the busy office seems to be genuinely kind-natured and sensible.

"Well, the truth is, and I really need you to keep this between just you and me, ok?" I start and she nods in agreement. "The truth is, I am in a relationship with an Italian guy and things are going really well, so perhaps that's where the rumours are coming from. I certainly enjoy working with you and would love to continue as things are. Plus, the pay rise will help with my Alitalia bills," I joke. She's one of the first people I've told about my sexuality and while I feel rather relieved having told her, I'm slightly worried.

"Wow! Well, that is certainly big news. Good for you!" she smiles, as she gathers her diary and fixes papers on her desk. Nervously playing with the tassels on my Berluti loafers, I lean forward across the desk and take a deep breath.

"Please, I trust you will keep this to yourself. I haven't even told my family, so it's best kept on the DL." Standing up, I smile and leave the room. *Perhaps today is going to be a bloody great day,* I think to myself. Minutes later, I'm on the phone to some pretty annoying PR girl who is begging me to attend and cover some fashion show at some boutique on Grafton Street. Seriously PR people are like the fakest of the lot, all over you and sickeningly so. I mean, are they so clueless that they think people actually believe their crap? "Yeah, yeah, Louis Vuitton handbags and some Dolce vintage pieces… I get it. I'll try to stop by but no promises." I hang up the phone before she starts insincerely asking how my family are keeping. As the call ends, she's still reeling off the jaded names on her guest-list. Looking up, Martina is patiently standing by my desk.

"I can see you're busy, but could I have another very quick chat?" she pleads, as if I am going to shoot her down. More of that 'workplace' insincerity. Man, it drives me nuts! Walking to her office, I can feel the eyes of one or two of the editorial staff on me. Always the same ones, the straight guys who look at me as if I have fallen off a Christmas tree. I can't help myself; I openly flirt with them just to see them panic. This certainly isn't a place where I belong. Not only because I look different to the rest of them – I mean seriously, off-the-peg suits? Hackett as a designer label? *I'll be the judge of that,* I smile to myself. Anyhow, they're all set to extend my contract so I can do insincere too. Best of all, I'm heading to Capri in a few days for a week of little more than shopping, tanning and lunching.

"So Oli, I've just spoken to Mark and we're delighted to extend your contract. Also, he sends his congratulations on your news and would like a word with you if you're not too busy. He wants you to write your story of 'coming out.' A heartfelt tale of the journey that took you to arrive here today out and proud," she says happily, as if delivering the winning lottery numbers.

"What the fuck are you talking about?" I ask before standing up. "Less than ten minutes ago I asked you to keep this information to yourself and now Mark wants it to be bloody front-page news? Are you fucking kidding me?" I storm out, and pace the short distance to Mark's equally dreary office, which rather comically doubles as a board room. Not the most popular chap in the building, he sits, dwarfed by his overly large, yet clearly cheap flat-pack desk. His lack of popularity isn't due to him being the boss, but rather because of his manner. He's comes over all timid and weak, but underneath it he's ruthless and at worst a sneak. As one would expect of someone in his position, he spends almost every waking hour in his tiny office with views over the city. A city he clearly thinks beneath him. Weirdly, he obsesses over the Ballsbridge neighbourhood, or rather its residents. One of the best addresses in the country, crammed with judges, surgeons and such, as previously explained, it's also become home to the 'new sort', and they fascinate him. The ones who are bussed around in Maybachs, Bentleys and private jets. They sure get under his skin and he spends his days trying to wipe them out. Strange really, as I've always assumed that a chap like Mark, who clearly comes from where he does, would salute those who made a better life for themselves. *Isn't jealousy a dreadful infliction?* I often think to myself.

A difficult person to please, he likes his power to be known and regularly let's his voice be heard when the going gets tough. Right now, it's my turn to let my voice be heard. "You want to see me?" I enter his office unannounced. Staring at Martina, I let her know that she is next in the firing line.

"There you are, Oli! Martina has just told me your great news. Well done you!" he says in a truly condescending manner. "Although, I guess it isn't news to many people," he grins. "It will make such a great story; the readers are really going to love it. Your colourful journey and experiences will be just what people need to read right now. I'm thinking two thousand words should do it with lots of detail. Lots of funny and sad moments. You really are a chameleon; Madonna has nothing on you when it comes to reinvention. I'm guessing she is an idol of yours?" he winks. I'm just staring at him as if I'm going to jump across his less-than-stately desk and punch his lights out.

"Are you for fucking real?" I bark. "There's no way this will be appearing in your magazine. There's no way I am sensationalising my sexuality in order for you to boost your sales. This is real life – my life. How dare you even suggest such a thing!" I snap, before turning to Martina. "And as for you, what on earth were you thinking?" I'm furious.

"Perhaps you should head home and relax. Have a think about it all and I am sure you will see the wood for the trees." He's still smiling like a Cheshire cat. "The story will get out eventually one way or another, so better the devil you know and all that. Take a few days off, get your story together and we will arrange a photo shoot to go along with it. How about Thursday or Friday? Can we shoot at your place, Oli? Martina, will you look after that?" he says as he scribbles into his notebook. A notebook he never leaves down, or out of sight. A notebook which is believed to be filled with scathing pieces of gossip aimed at wiping out certain folk. "Let's get the details of your article sorted and then we can look at the new contract," he says assertively, letting me clearly know that my future at the magazine depends on my performance.

At my desk I gather my belongings and I can tell that others in the office know something serious has just happened. Walking out, I feel a mixture of anger and fear. Having started the day perfectly, now everything is a mess. Everything is all over the place and my upcoming trip is the last thing on my mind. Reaching for my phone I hit Marco on speed dial, but I get his Italian answering service. I light a cigarette and hail a cab; feeling completely stressed, I head for the safety of the Cellar Bar at the Merrion Hotel, a place which has become something of a second home over the years. I down a Manhattan, and try to plan just how to tell my family the news before the media beat me to it. Calling my brother to invite him for dinner seems a good starting point. "No Alex, nothing serious, I just want to see you and to catch up. How about seven at the Merrion? Great, see you then." Placing the phone on the bar, I order another Manhattan and repeatedly try to contact Marco but his phone is switched off. Remembering that he's en route to LA, I realise that this is one of those things that I'm going to have to do alone. While most of my life is organised and somewhat controlled by others, be it agents or public relations firms, this was one of those things that I'd have to deal with myself.

Evening comes all too soon and I'm dressed in a black Gucci suit with a crisp white shirt. I certainly look good, but my suit isn't acting as protective armour as I sit sipping a glass of Meursault, and wait nervously for Alex to arrive. There's been zero contact from anyone at the magazine which leaves me feeling at ease, but also stressed as to what could happen next. Ever punctual, Alex arrives exactly on time, looking tanned and refreshingly healthy, having just returned from almost three weeks sailing in the Adriatic. "I'll have a gin and tonic if you're offering – Hendricks naturally!" he says as he gives me a hug. "So what's the news then? Anything exciting going on? You know, I haven't missed this town one bit for the last few weeks," he says as he pulls out a bar stool.

"Oh, nothing much, but I'm starving. Let's move to our table!" I say quickly, sounding anxious. Having scanned through beyond enough holiday photos from his trip, we order. The waiter arrives with two complimentary glasses of champagne. I down mine in seconds flat. I'm sitting trying to listen to Alex's news and also trying to figure out how to tell him mine, without making it too dramatic.

"Well I think I'll spend next month in France then maybe head to Ibiza late summer, if you want to join us. There are eight of us so far and we've chartered the most amazing boat…"

"I'm gay!" It just blurts our as I down the last of the champagne. It's at this very moment the entire dining room falls silent. "Well, aren't you going to say anything? I mean, you heard what I just said, right? Even the people at that far table in the corner heard me!"

"Wow! I'm not quite sure what to say really. Good for you, I guess," he says calmly. "It always amazes me why gay people are forced to have to tell people about their sexuality. I get that it's society's fault and all that but, imagine if every straight person you met had to tell you that they're straight! Jesus we'd be here all day," he laughs. I'm quite shocked by his relaxed attitude.

"Is that it? You have nothing more to say? Did you already know? Did you suspect? Shit!" I'm the only one who's shocked.

"Never really thought about it and you always had the hottest girlfriends so I just assumed you were straight," he smiles and shrugs his shoulders. "Anyhow, like I said what difference does it make? Whatever people do in their sex life is really up to them, but it doesn't change the person they are in everyday life, now does it? I mean, yeah, you wear a lot of cashmere and have a strange obsession with Tod's driving shoes and live in a house which is like something out of World of Interiors… I guess they could all be clear signs of homosexuality, but if based on those grounds, then I am as gay as a goose too!" he laughs loudly. "Oh, to hell with this, let's get drunk to celebrate your royal gayness!" He attempts to get the waiter's attention. "Oh, there you are, we'll have a bottle of Krug '85 and two glasses." As the waiter pours the champagne I explain the real problem. Truth is I'm far more concerned by it than the 'coming out' part. Somehow the news of the very publication for which I work wanting to 'out' me this coming weekend is far worse. "What? Surely, they can't do that to you. That must be along the lines of sexual harassment or something?" he says angrily.

"They have let it be known that if I fail to cooperate with their plans, they may not renew my contract and furthermore will probably run the fucking story anyhow!" I sigh, feeling genuinely hard done by.

"Well then you must get on the phone and arrange to meet Mum ASAP. I think she will be in town on Friday evening for the opera. Perhaps a good opportunity to spill the beans? Not really an opportunity as such but with time rapidly running out you have to tell her before some shoddy tabloid headline does it for you," he says, trying to sound relaxed but freaking me out even further.

"Yes, you're right I'll call her first thing tomorrow before I talk to anyone else. What about the bloody papers though?" I ask.

"Well, it sounds like this Mark guy is a snake and you already know that he has a tabloid background which runs through and through, so he'll run the story with or without you. If your contract being renewed depends on it, then fuck it and go with it. But make sure you get that new contract up front," he advises. Following my news, we skip dinner and return to the bar where we talk for hours. So much so that the final bar tab was just under eleven hundred euro, so you get the mood. Waking the following morning, I'm hit with not only the worst hangover known to man, but also I've to call my mother Caroline and break the dreaded news. She's currently enjoying a week in Juan-les-Pins with friends, so my call is sure to ruin that. Again, I think of Mark and how much I want to knock him out.

"Hey Mum, it's Oli. How are you, darling?" I'm sounding as upbeat as possible. As I begin to speak I bottle it and rather than tell her all, I opt to let her know that I'll be joining her at the opera on Friday evening and at a planned dinner afterwards at Peploe's, a restaurant my family counts as a 'favourite'. Ending the call, I'm standing in my kitchen overlooking the garden and I'm completely distracted, as I'm also expecting a camera crew from UK society magazine *Fabulous Lives* to arrive later to do an 'at home' feature.

Having already planned every last detail, I mentally work through the house again in my head trying to decide which rooms are to be photographed and what must be arranged. I'm interrupted as my phone rings. "Good morning Oli, it's Martina at the office. Mark wants to know if he can meet with you this morning at around eleven?" she asks sheepishly.

"I don't really see the point of a meeting, as he already knows my feelings on the whole thing," I say coldly. "Tell him I'll see him at noon, as I have a million and one things to do. Before you ask what they are, let's just put them down as personal matters. You know, the type of things that shouldn't become office gossip." I slam the call to a close. My answering machine is flashing to tell that there are twenty-one new messages. Pressing the play button, I stand silently in my hallway.

"Hello Oli, this is Enda Mulally at the *Meteor*. We're running a piece tomorrow about your coming out story and were wondering if you have anything to say on the matter? The rumour is that you have a partner in Italy. Paolo or Giorgio or something? Anyhow, can you call me back when you get a chance? Planning to run the story tomorrow so don't leave me hangin'. Thanks pal." *Pal? Who the fuck uses the word pal? Nice to see you have managed to do your research,* I think to myself and delete the message. So now even a free sheet wants to damn me. The *Meteor* is one of those free papers they hand out to rush hour commuters, which only cheapens the whole thing further. How the fuck do they know? Seriously the media is like Chinese whispers with journalists spilling beans rapidly, even to rival press.

"Ok Oli, come on, it's showtime," I say loudly to myself.

Staring at myself in my dressing room mirror, I'm ready for anything and capable of everything. Dressed in Gucci jeans and a Dolce & Gabbana t-shirt with Superman printed on the front, I know that today is going to require all the powers of a super hero to make it bearable. Outside, my driver Tony is sitting on the bonnet of the shiny black Mercedes enjoying the early morning sun. "How are we today then?" he smiles as he puts his shades on. "Where we off to first? To get coffee?" he continues, opening the door of the car for me, as a group of tourists look on.

"Yes, strong coffee would be a good start!" I sigh.

Arriving at the nondescript magazine offices, my feelings are mixed. Both nerves and anger well up inside me, but I must remain calm in front of my colleagues. I walk the full length of the editorial office keeping my head down, to avoid making eye contact with anyone, which could lead to dreaded small talk.

"You can tell Mark I'll see him as soon as possible. I don't plan on hanging around!" I snap at Martina, who somehow is acting as if she's in the injured party.

"Oh, hi Oli! How are you today? Great t-shirt, I love it!" she says nervously. However, our fake friendship is very much over so I ignore her completely. Sitting at my desk, I feel all eyes are on me once again. Even when they try to stop working, a journalist's curious nature gets the better of them.

"Oh, good morning Oli," says Bridget Cumiskey, a woman who has found herself working at the magazine, writing a weekly column about the storylines of the various soap operas. She deems her position below her both socially and intellectually and she usually sits further down the room, but today she's right beside me.

Out of all the people in the office, I like Bridget the most. While we're very different, on every level, we've become quite friendly over the past few months. She knows that something's up. There are no jokes, no fun, no usual banter. In fact there's very little chat at all, as I sit opening invitations for various events. "You know what?" I say loudly, to nobody in particular. "I'm so over this town and these stupid parties night after night. The whole thing has become such a bore."

"Cigarette?" Bridget asks. Outside and not one to miss a trick, I can see her eyes dancing as she awaits the juicy news.

"Oh, to hell with it, you're going to hear sooner or later," I tell her.

She moves closer to hang on my every word.

Pulling heavily on her cigarette, I can see she clearly needs her teeth whitened. "Oh, for God's sake. So you're gay – big deal! It certainly explains why you are always so well dressed," she says in an attempt to make me feel better. I have no idea why people always make that reference about gay men being well dressed? They really need to take a closer look at what passes for style in gay bars in every city in the world. If you want I'll write the article. "Yeah, tell that prick Mark I'll interview you and we can do it your way, with you getting final approval," she says on an outward breath of smoke. "Jesus, he's such a cunt, isn't he? At least with me doing it, it'll be less of a drag and you'll get to keep your job," she says, looking pleased with her solution.

As we return inside I come face to face with a furious, red-faced Mark who was carrying a copy of the *Meteor*. "Have you seen this? Have you?" he says as he pushes the paper into my face. "A whole fucking page about you. It's even plugged on the front! You and your big fucking story! I ordered you no to speak to anyone. I fucking ordered you! I wanted it as an exclusive!" he shouts, as everyone turns to look at the commotion. Walking through the office I can see that every last one of them has their head buried in the low-rate free rag, and then, there it is, lying open on my desk, yet another copy of it, complete with photos of my house, of me looking worse for wear as I down a bottle of champagne on the back of some yacht at the Cannes Film Festival, me and some It Girl or another falling out of L'Equipe Anglaise back in the day, and a load of bullshit purporting to be a story.

"Lovely house," smiles a fashion columnist called Julie who is sitting opposite. At least I think her name is Julie…

"Yeah, thanks." I shake my head. Seriously, I'm trying my best to remain calm, as WW3 is about to kick off in Mark's office. Martina emerges and signals to me that it was time to meet with him.

"What the fuck are you up to?" he screams from his desk.

"I may very well ask you the same question. I'm so stressed by all of this that I haven't slept a wink and all you care about is the story." Just then, my phone rings.

"Do not answer that!" he orders.

"Oh, piss off!" I snap. "Hello? Speaking, who is this? Oh, darling, hi. I am going to have to call you back in a few. I have something that needs cleaning up this end." I end the call. "Never, ever tell me when or when not to answer my phone, do you understand me?" I glare. "Now, before you continue whining, let me tell you that this is not a story. This is a fucking nightmare and the fact it has landed itself in the *Meteor* is most likely down to your inept staff. Who the fuck have you spoken to about my personal life? Whoever it is has obviously let it slip. My advice to you, Mark, is to get up off your skinny arse and go out there and find out, before I call my lawyers!" I'm inching towards his desk, staring him in the eyes. I can feel the blood pulsing through my veins.

"Ok, OK, we need to calm down," he says, realising my anger and lifting his phone to call backup. "Now that the story is in the *Meteor* we look stupid. However, we can still come up smelling of roses. If you give us the exclusive story. The real story. You know, how free and liberated you felt when you met, eh, what's his name? How your life is complete now, etc.," he gushes like a giddy schoolgirl.

"Before you say one more word," I cut him dead. "As this is my 'story' I think I should let you know the way it's going to go. Firstly, the matter of my contract. Not much has been said about it since my first meeting with Martina. If I agree to give you my story, I want that contract drawn up and signed off first."

"Sure, OK," he smiles, again scribbling into his notebook.

"Will you fucking look at me when I'm speaking to you! I haven't quite finished," I bark, noticing that he's anxious to speak. "I'm not going to write the piece, as it doesn't feel right having to even do this, but Bridget Cumiskey has suggested she can pen it, and will interview me over lunch somewhere."

He sits back in his chair, staring at me. "Well Oli, haven't you been busy. Fine, let's nail it today, send Bridget in here," he orders to Martina. "We need to act fast on this as it is already Thursday and we need to get photos taken, etc. Pick a restaurant and get working, the pair of you," he says, treating the story as any other piece of social gossip.

"And my contract? When will it be ready for me to sign? I mean, you're lucky I'm not charging the magazine for the 'exclusive' interview." I look up from my phone.

"I'll have Martina sort it and we will chat later

when you have done the interview, now get going, time is running out. Tick tock, tick tock."

Having been featured in many papers and magazines many times, usually for all the wrong reasons, I'm used to being the talk of the town, but this time it's different. This time I don't want the story to appear, furthermore I really don't want to even do the interview, but feel well and truly trapped.

*

"Oh, this is very swanky, isn't it?" Bridget blushes as she's ushered into the dining room of the Four Seasons.

"Is it?" I sigh.

"I know you're nervous, but this really is a lovely treat. I've never been here before. Oh, look, is that Ryan Tubridy?" she asks as she waves at the renowned broadcaster whom she's never met.

"Can you just calm the fuck down?" I order as I sit.

"Yes, you're right, just go at your own pace and it will flow easily enough," she suggests, as her head continues to spin, taking the whole room in over and over.

"Oh, I think a very large gin will certainly help the situation," I smile to the waiter. "It's so strange being interviewed by you, but at least it's you and not someone else. One of those blood hungry vultures that are dotted around the office, awaiting their chance of a cover story. Aren't they the most pathetic of all?" I laugh, although I don't mean it. Looking through the menus, we're aware that lunch is being paid for by the magazine. "A bottle of Montrachet '82 and some still water, Italian if possible," I say coldly.

"Oh, you are funny. 'Italian if possible'." She laughs a goofy laugh. "Seriously, that has to be the most silly thing I have ever heard!" she continues.

"Yes, almost as silly as that pleather handbag you carry constantly. Seriously, it should never have been allowed to leave the Asian sweat-shop it was created in. Buy yourself a new bag, for fuck's sake, I can get you discount at Chanel if it's the money you're worried about. In fact, you need an entire overhaul. Take a day off and sort yourself out," I smile cruelly. "As for the water, I prefer Italian or French water. I don't see why that's an issue. You really are terribly pedestrian, aren't you?"

Once the sommelier has poured the wine, Bridget takes a huge gulp, almost downing the entire glass, unaware of its importance. "Now, shall we begin?" she asks cautiously.

"Oh, to hell with it, go on then, but be warned I'm not some rookie, I won't be swayed to answer anything that I feel uncomfortable with. Got it?" I say sternly.

To start with the questions are dull, dull, dull. Where did you meet Marco? Have you always known you were gay? Is it difficult growing up gay and in the closet? Nothing heavy, just dull. Just as I am easing into a second glass of wine comes a bombshell. "They've specifically asked me to ask you about your sex life." She looks embarrassed, as she nibbles on the end of her Bic. "They want to know what it was like the first time you had sex with a man. Did you feel free?" she blushes.

"Feel free?" I swear I almost spit Burgundy all over the table linen. "Of course free, I'm not a hooker! Seriously, I'm not answering any questions of a sexual nature, as I said. It's not my style. Having dated many of the city's most beautiful women, I had never made comments about whatever sexual experiences may or may not have taken place, so why should I do so now? I'm fucking serious, Bridge. If they're going down that strada, then I'm not saying another word. The whole thing sounds so tacky, so cheap. I know you're just doing your job, but just tell them I wouldn't answer that." I lift my phone to send a text to Marco.

"Oh, it's just… They really need this to make it stand out, you know?" she stutters.

"Stand out? Stand fucking out? It will no doubt be plastered across the front page, what do they want? A tit shot?" I snarl.

The rest of the interview drags on, with stupid questions about the gay scene, life in Italy, why I love shopping… Seriously, it's that sort of trashy magazine after all.

"Oh my god, I'll be shot! How on earth did we spend that amount of money on two starters and two tiny bits of salmon?" She reads through the receipt over and over.

"Oh, just pay it, will you? I'm just going over to say hi to Camilla Ashford. Do you know her? Oh, of course not, sorry, I'm not thinking," I smile.

Once the bill has been settled, seriously I think it took the combination of two credit cards and cash, I call my driver to collect me. "You will need to book a taxi, as I'm certainly not going in your direction." Once in the car I call the office to speak with Mark, only to be told that he's unavailable for the rest of the day. Fucking typical, he has his story and I am persona non grata. "Oh, to hell with it Tony, can you drop me in Grafton Street? I think some retail therapy is required for this Capri trip!" The whole ordeal of the past few days has really taken it out of me, but at least I will soon be with Marco, which makes everything OK.

Chapter 16

Merrion Square, Dublin

Waking at 05:55 the following morning, I do so with a jump. You know, the sort of shock that wakes you like eight shots of espresso? I'm lying in bed and my mind is reeling. How am I going to come clean about my news? And what should I wear to deliver the news? The last one is kind of obvious; always wear something strong and black to deliver important news. Luckily I have a perfect Tom Ford tuxedo which will suffice, so that just leaves the other far more important dilemma to sort. As I shower I'm feeling so nervous that I may actually throw up. Knowing I've to tell my mother my big gay secret this evening is making my stomach flip repeatedly, and my head ache intensely. It's something that can only be understood by any gay guy or girl who is ready to come clean. The fact I'm not even close to ready only makes it worse. Going to tell loved ones something so huge with a gun to one's head is never clever. How will Mum take it? What if she's genuinely hurt and upset by it all? Will she speak to me again? I try on six different white shirts and as many pairs of similar Dsquared2 jeans, and in the end opt for the first ones selected. Really my head is spinning as I call for my car and ask Tony to drop me the magazine.

As the car inches along the street Madonna and Justin Timberlake '4 Minutes' plays and I find myself singing along, not that I know the words, but four minutes to save the world sounds about right given the circumstances. I'm staring at the blue sky and can feel the warm sun on my face through the open window. It's one of those great early spring days when you can feel the seasons change and there's finally light at the end of the tunnel, at least weather wise. We stop at Donnybrook Fair on Upper Baggot Street where I pick up a cappuccino and a croissant. I really don't know why, but I always buy a croissant and every time I do, it ends up uneaten and in the trash. *If they don't have my contract ready, there's something serious up*, I think to myself, as I attempt to sip the overly hot coffee. "Jesus, why the fuck do so-called baristas burn the milk? Every time!" I moan to Tony who is being his usual cheery self.

As the car pulls up outside the dreary 1970s office building, I can see the 'faggettes' standing at the entrance, staring at my arrival. Honestly, they really shouldn't be allowed gather there. The sight of five overweight, balding men smoking at the front of a building is bad enough, but the shiny polyester suits, un-tucked shirts and top buttons clearly undone is hardly the image any company wants to portray. Then again, I'm not entering Vogue House, now am I? Oh, I call them the faggettes, simply because they chain smoke and are notoriously homophobic. Plus, I've absolutely no idea of their real names, or even which company they work for. Before stepping out of the car, I decide that I'm no longer allowing Mark to treat me the way he treats everyone else. Step one, I call his office – "Mark Edwards please," I strain, trying to disguise my voice. Strangely by doing so I come across all Yorkshire, just like Mark.

"Who shall I say is calling?" asks the voice at the other end.

"Tell him it's a personal call." I'm deadpan serious.

"Mark Edwards!" comes his chirpy voice, which somehow today sounds like Tony Blair.

"Is my contract ready?" I sound the far end of chirpy. "I've left numerous messages for you, so I can only imagine that you didn't receive them?" I continue coldly.

"Oh yes, there are messages here I am yet to deal with. You're not the only person I have to deal with, you know?" His tone dives from chirpy to failed sarcasm.

"Well perhaps, but I'm pretty sure that I'm the only person you are 'outing' against their will this week, or are you planning to destroy a few other lives as well? Either way, I don't care, we had a deal, which sounds to me like you are going to break," I say, remaining calm.

"Who said anything about breaking the deal? You really are very dramatic. I guess it comes with the territory," he laughs.

"Excuse me? Comes with what territory?" I ask,

knowing exactly what his remark means. "I'll be at the office in five minutes and I want either you, or someone who has a clue to meet me and show me this contract!" I end the call.

Arriving into the office I'm greeted by Martina who has been asked to 'deal with me'. "Hi Oli, how are you?" she smiles pathetically. "Mark says that the contract will happen, it's just a bad time of year for us as there are a lot of people on holiday and nobody to do the paperwork," she attempts to explain nervously.

"Bullshit! Utter bullshit," I snap. "It's pretty obvious what's happening here. He made a deal with me, forcing me to do the interview, and now has completely gone back on his word. I'd like to say I'm shocked but it is exactly the sort of shit I see in this place week in, week out. I really wish I'd never done the fucking interview. I wish I had never told you anything. This really is all your fault and you know it!" I shout, making the entire editorial department take notice. "Now if that's what you people have dragged me in here for, I need to leave. I've to go get things organised, as next on my list of fantastic things to do this week is tell my mother my news, before you do. Tell Mark I want that contract on my desk the minute I return from Italy next week and also tell him that there is no way he can make the article sensational. No mention of my mother, as she hasn't even been told about all this shit, and no mention of sex whatsoever. You got that? Perhaps you should write it down! Better still, hand me a permanent marker and I'll write it across your shiny forehead!" I snarl.

It's already approaching noon and I'm due to meet my mother, Caroline, for drinks at six-thirty. Before this I have to squeeze in a lunch date with my friend Edward Cavenagh at Dylan Hotel, a place currently so hot you can burn yourself just by ordering a champagne mojito. Myself and Ed have been friends since forever, having met at one party or another. Neither able to remember exactly where, we imagine it was in a night club at 4am possibly doing tequila shots or lines of coke or both. Anyhow, we've seen a lot of water pass under the bridge since. Having been through almost everything together, there's absolutely no reason why Ed shouldn't be involved in this drama too, especially as I was on hand when it was his turn to come out two years previous.

"What the fuck am I going to do?" I ask as I down a glass of Laurent Perrrier in seconds flat. "Honestly, I haven't really slept since all this began," I stress.

"All what began? You being gay? Jesus, so you haven't slept in thirty years?" he laughs.

"I'm serious, this is all out of control and I don't like things being out of my control, as you know." I'm sounding manic.

Noticing how fast I am drinking, he refills my glass. "You have to try stay calm and focused. It's happening whether you like it or not, so grab it by the balls and go with it. I think I'll just have a Salade Nicoise as I'm out again tonight," he says without breathing.

Over lunch I play with my salad and down almost two bottles of champagne. "Look, it's like this, if your mother flips out we'll be nearby at Bang having dinner so just join us there. My phone will be on, so text me and let me know. Oh, and don't stress about that thing in the *Meteor*, nobody reads that paper, especially not people we know. Seriously, taxi drivers and those who take public transport to and from the city. Not really our scene, now is it?" he laughs, before paying the bill. Moments later I'm standing in line at Craft Dry Cleaners and suddenly I feel as if the entire world is slowly turning against me. Even the women working at the cash desk looks angry. "I'm so sorry, I can't find my ticket…" I say, sounding almost childlike.

"Well we could be here all day then, couldn't we?" a middle-aged rotund woman who is next in line retorts.

"I hope not as I have a lot of things to do," I smile, having missed her tone. "It's a tuxedo… I think it was dropped in last Friday. It's Tom Ford…"

"Aha, here it is! That was easier than usual, you're in luck," she smiles. "It's a lovely suit, are you off somewhere nice this evening?" she asks, as she wraps it.

"I am going out, I know that much. Where I will end up is anyone's guess." I wink from behind my shades.

With time running out before I meet Mum, I call my brother to see what time he can get to hotel. The last thing I want is to be hanging around with time and alcohol to hand. "I'll be there by around seven. Just relax, it'll be fine, as long as you choose the right moment. By the way, I told Charlotte, and she's totally cool with it all. I'm telling you, Mum will be too!" he says calmly.

Charlotte is my aunt, a woman who seems so unflappable that I sometimes wonder how she does it. I've never seen her let things get to her and even if they do she rarely lets it show. Her approval already makes me feel slightly better. Back home, I check the time and it's almost four. I fix myself a Negroni and stand staring into my somewhat excessive wardrobe. I keep drinking but I'm certainly not showing signs of being drunk. I must be standing here for about ten minutes before I check myself and realise the chosen outfit is already hanging on the back of the closet door, having been picked up less than an hour ago. Seriously my head is all over the place. I hit play on the stereo and on comes The Rolling Stones, Sympathy for the Devil. With the three large sash windows open over the street below, I blast the volume as far as it can go, noticing a guy walking his dog on the far side of the street looking up at the scene. I take an extra-long shower, fix another drink and lay my suit, shirt and shoes out. The whole thing feels as if it requires military precision. Like I'm getting ready to go into battle, one I am sure I'm going to lose.

Downing the drains of my drink, I look at a bottle of Veuve Clicquot that's chilling in the fridge door. If ever there was a 'Nerve Clicquot' moment, this is it, but I close the fridge and make espresso instead. Making a call to the Beverly Hills Hotel, I need to talk to Marco to calm my nerves. "Can you put me through to Marco Rossini please? I believe he's staying at one of the bungalows," I say quietly, to the overly happy and efficient receptionist.

"Certainly, sir, transferring your call, please hold and have a nice day!" with possibly the most candied Californian accent possible.

"Pronto." Even when he's in the US he still remains

extremely Italian, possibly even more than usual.

"Pronto yourself, baby!" I laugh, already relaxed by the sound of his voice.

"Well it's almost time to meet Mum. I'm shitting myself but I just needed to hear your voice before I go and do this," I sigh.

"Everything will be fine, bello. You'll see, that within a few hours you will be totally relaxed and those dreadful people at the magazine will mean nothing to you. Trust me, ok?"

Although I'm not exactly sure it will be as easy as all that, the fact that Marco is on my side makes me feel ten feet tall. "Ok, I better go. I'll text you with the result of my evening later. Ciao ciao," I smile before ending the call.

Arriving in the hall of the Merrion Hotel where my mother is staying, I feel numb. A feeling that refuses to leave no matter how hard I try to smile. Sitting on the terrace I spot her chatting with some friends. Dressed in a perfect midnight blue Dior evening gown, she looks fantastic. *Here goes nothing,* I think to myself as I walk through the large open windows onto the bustling terrace. The evening sunshine is warm and among those sipping cocktails are a mixture of well-known property developers, TV personalities and wealthy Americans. As I make my way to the table I'm forced to exchange small talk with those I know.

"Good evening, Mum!" I'm desperately trying to sound upbeat, leaning in to kiss her on the cheek.

"Oh hello there, handsome!" she says, standing up to introduce me to her two friends. "Oliver, you remember Monica and Susan? You met at my birthday party last summer," she explains, at the same time waving to the waiter. "We're on champagne, would you like a glass or something different?" she offers.

"I'd love a Negroni and a large bottle of still water." I'm trying to remain calm. While they chat I can feel both palms of my hands beginning to sweat. "Any idea when Alexander and Charlotte will get here?" I ask.

"Oh, darling they're here already. Been here hours, myself and Charlie even had a sneaky lunch at Guilbaud earlier. Thought we would make a day of it," she laughs.

"Oh, what room are you in? I'll pop up and say hi," I say, knowing I must talk to Charlotte on her own. "The Merrion Suite, in the main house, naturally. Do pop up and tell her to get a wriggle on, we're expected for drinks in thirty," she smiles. Now I feel worse, as it's clear Mum is obviously having a fantastic day, and my news is sure to shake things to the core. How has nobody mentioned the piece in the *Meteor*? Perhaps Ed is right, and nobody within our circle could have read it, I think to myself as the elevator soars.

"Well, well you're looking good!" she says, opening the doors to the impressive suite. "It's all going to be fine. Trust me, come in and have a drink," she continues while pouring me a glass of champagne. As I stand at the open window overlooking Merrion Street and Government Buildings opposite, I feel it may be easier to just jump.

"Oh God, how am I going to do this? What's the

plan of action? I don't think I can sit through the Magic Flute with all this going on in my head. I mean seriously, who the hell comes out to their mother at the Magic Flute? You couldn't script it!" I say, downing the glass of champagne in one.

"Try to relax, it will be fine. You know your mum is cool. Half of her friends are gay for god's sake. Just get through the opera and let it happen over dinner," she says confidently, grabbing my arm.

"I've decided that I won't lie to her anymore. If she asks about who I'm dating, I'll be honest. It's wrong to lie about this stuff and it has gone on long enough. Oh, I think I'll have another glass of champagne, if you don't mind," I say reaching out the empty glass towards her.

Arriving at the theatre, there's something of a traffic jam. As our car awaits its turn to deliver us to the door I spot a group of press photographers huddled together outside the entrance. Stepping out of the car there's the usual requests for photographs, and then from out of nowhere Billy O'Reilly from the magazine sticks his head through the flashing bulbs. "Here, Oli, can I get a photo of you and your ma? The photo-desk want a few snaps to go with the piece," he barks in a thick Kerry accent. So thick, luckily Mum doesn't understand a word.

"No sorry, we're running late, so no photos tonight," I say, ensuring Alex walks Mum through the door. If he can't get myself and her together he can't get his shot. Inside are plenty of familiar faces and old family friends gathered for pre-drinks, and while Mum and Charlotte instantly work the room, I'm joined by Alex by the bar, where we drink more champagne in an attempt to remain calm. During the performance I can't concentrate and the entire opera is a blur. In fact this is a blessing, as from what I've seen it looks bonkers, not my sort of thing at all. Honestly, the sort of opera that requires LSD to make it bearable.

Outside, I smoke a cigarette as we wait for the car to collect us. "Who knew there were so many chauffeurs in the city? That traffic jam is crazy, surely we would be better walking?" Mum laughs. In fact she has a valid point, as the restaurant is a short stroll along the park. I am just so accustomed to being driven everywhere, that the idea of walking has become alien.

At Peploe's, the atmosphere is fun, upbeat and busy. "So, how is everything with you then? Looking forward to you week in Italy?" Mum asks.

"You have no idea how much I need this break. I'm counting the hours until the plane roars down the runway," I smile.

"Oh come on, life isn't so bad is it? I mean, you're always at some glamorous party or another," she winks. "It's hard to keep up with you. How is Sophia? She's such a great girl," she adds. It's true, I've never been short of beautiful women on my arm, so much so that Mum has had a hard job keeping up with exactly who I am dating. It was hard enough for me to keep track of at times. All that changed when Sophia came on the scene.

"Well actually, I'm not seeing Sophs anymore. It just didn't work out," I lie. Jesus, I'm still lying, and I'm about to deliver the truth, or at least I hope I can.

"Really? Oh, that's terrible news. Tell me you haven't hurt her, or did she finish it? I genuinely thought you guys would marry." She's shaking her head. "So who's the next girl out of your little black book then? I trust you haven't been cheating on her, have you?" she questions.

"Nobody, that's it! There are no more girls in my little black book. In fact there are no girls at all," I sound almost angry. Charlotte and Alexander do their best to pretend to be engrossed in conversation, but are both clearly showing signs of anxiety having overheard my words.

"No girls? So are there any boys?" she continues in a deadpan tone, sipping her Kir Royale and looking through the menu.

"Oh, here goes nothing. No, Mum, there are no girls. There haven't been for quite some time, well, apart from Sophia. I am in a relationship with an amazing Italian guy called Marco, and it's serious. So serious that I had to end it with poor Sophia," I blurt out, without breathing. "There, I've said it and there is no going back now, is there?" I ask everyone, but mainly myself.

"Are you joking? Is this some kind of wind-up?" Mum asks, quickly pulling away from me.

"Oh, now come on, it's hardly the end of the world. Nothing has really changed, has it?" Charlotte sympathises.

"Hang on a minute, you knew about this? How long have you known?" She's sounding both shocked and angry.

"Look Mum, this hasn't been an easy thing to do,

and I've been living with the fear of this day forever," I say firmly.

"I don't think I can sit through dinner, I think I may need to leave and go to the hotel. Where's Tony and the car?" she continues, before standing up. The mood at the table has suddenly gone up in smoke.

"Listen, sit down, I'll leave if at least for a few minutes," I offer. Realising that there's worse news to be delivered, I stand up and go outside to get some air. "But look, Mum, before this all gets out of control. Please try to remember that I'm still the same person who walked into this restaurant with you twenty minutes ago and that this is even more of a big deal for me than it is for you." It's very true, coming out seems to be about so many other people rather than the one who has to stand up and be judged. Standing on the front steps of the restaurant surrounded by those grabbing an inter-course nicotine fix, I wonder what will happen next. What will happen when I tell her about the bloody article which will hit the newsstands within 48 hours?

"May I bum a cigarette?" I ask a French guy who is chain smoking and has been having a heated conversation rather loudly on his phone.

"Sure man, no sweat. Bloody stupid smoking laws... Eh, nice suit by the way," he says as he offers me his box of Dunhill. After ten minutes I return to the table and sit once again beside my mother, who by now is looking slightly more relaxed.

"Look, it's been a shock and I'm not good with things like this being sprung on me as you know, but what can we do?" she smiles. Just then, the sommelier

Frederic appears at her side holding a bottle of Bollinger. "Oh, darling Fred, you better make it a bottle of pink, as Oli has just told me some wonderful news, that he is gay!" she leans in to kiss me on the forehead. "Come on, Charlotte's right, it's not the end of the world, now is it?" she gushes.

It's clear that most of the other diners are glued to the antics at our table which I must admit is nothing new for me, as ever since I became a well-known face, I have had to get used to strangers speaking to me as if they know me, or random people asking for photographs. A fact that still amuses me, even after a few years. During dinner I tell her of the stresses that the planned magazine article has put me under during the week. "Well perhaps we should get someone to have a word with them. Perhaps a stern call from Hugo will make them back down," she suggests. Hugo is the family solicitor and has become well used to dealing with the legal sections of many Irish media outlets on a regular basis.

'See, I told you everything would be OK,' Alex texts from across.

"You will come in for a night cap, darling," Mum insists as we arrive at the hotel. "I think we could all do with one," she says, linking my arm and walking through the doors. A round of espresso and Armagnac is ordered, before we settle into one of the large sofas in the main drawing room. "I must admit that I'm rather shocked by tonight's events, but, whoever said that life would be dull?" she laughs as she fixes her dress and removes a cream Louis Vuitton wrap, filling the warm air with her scent, Hermès, Eau des Merveilles. We sit talking until it's almost time for breakfast. As we talk I tell her all about Marco, show her photographs and explain how I have always known that I was gay, but was too scared to be myself. She is kind and understanding, which makes me feel lucky. So many other guys I know have had a terrible time when they were in my position.

Walking the five-minute distance to my house along an empty street, I smile. *All you need in life is for the people that matter to be happy*, I think. Stopping for a moment to light a Marlboro, I look up at the magnificence of Government Buildings, and the sense of relief makes me see that sometimes we worry so much over the things we can't control, and sometimes in the end those things weren't even worth worrying about to begin with. Once home I call Marco, who despite the time, picks up. "Tell me you are all still alive?" he asks through a gravelly, sleepy voice.

"Yes, all present and correct. In fact, I feel great. Just wish you were here right now. Mum thinks we should take legal action, but I'm more inclined to just leave things as they are and not bother Hugo. Do I really need a load of legal nonsense? To hell with the rag, it's clear to me now that they are not my sort of people after all," I say as I light another cigarette.

"You should sleep, bello, you don't want to look tired when you arrive in Capri! We can now start the rest of our lives – finally," he says and I can tell he's smiling.

"What time is it? I think I'll try to sleep for an hour or two. Will you call me at ten to wake me?" I ask as I finish my drink and stub out the cigarette in a somewhat overflowing ashtray that I pinched from Senequier a while back.

Waking at nine, I try to call my mother but the phone is unanswered.

"Hey, what's up? I tried to call Mum but she's not picking up," I say to Alex who is clearly hungover at the other end of the phone.

"Who? What? What time is it?" he asks, sounding flattened. "Eh, she said she was leaving early, to get her hair done and shopping or something... Then on to some lunch in Co. Meath," he continues. The way he describes my mother's busy social calendar, makes me realise once again that I didn't lick my party loving ways off a stone. "I think she'll be fine with everything, but will need time to adjust. Best to leave her alone for a few days," he advises. After all the drama, the stress, and the worry, I decide to spend the day at home alone, packing my luggage and trying to keep my mind off the dreaded article which is by now being printed.

Arriving into Dublin airport at 5am, I have a nervous yet excited feeling about seeing the paper. Checking in, I go straight to the Gold Circle Lounge and pick up a pile of Sunday newspapers as well as a copy of *We Like to Party*.

'EXCLUSIVE – The Day I Told My Mother I Was Gay – The story of how socialite Oliver came to terms with coming out!' reads the headline, complete with a huge picture of me at some party clutching a glass of champagne looking wasted. *Jesus fuck! People must think that's all I ever do is drink champagne and party*, I think to myself as I scan the article which takes up four pages. Reading it, I'm furious. Not only have they ignored my request not to mention my mother, but have done so in the headline. Worse still is the fact that in the article itself they've made up quotes. 'The first time I slept with Marco it was so amazing. I felt so free.' I would never, ever say something so tacky. "Fucking low-end hacks!" I say loudly, which gets one or two stares in the otherwise tranquil lounge. Not only is this not true, but also manages to make the whole thing look cheap – like a kiss and tell. The fact that it has made front page news on three of the leading newspapers will surely make Mark happy. I keep my head down as I have something to be ashamed of, and on the flight I can truly sense and almost hear the other passengers gossip about me.

At Da Vinci Airport, Marco greets me. Well, he greets a half sober version of me. Stupidly I spent the flight going through the article and the trash in the other papers over and over, resulting in me getting more worked up and thanks to the free-flowing vodka, more messed up. As I emerge through the crowd there he is, dressed in a navy polo shirt and jeans, Gucci loafers, and a huge white smile. I don't know why, but I run towards him, dropping my bags and grabbing him tightly, as if we haven't seen each other in years. Suddenly I'm sober. "It's all OK now, bello, you're home!" he whispers into my ear, before gathering my luggage and driving us to his place. As we drive we're silent, the sort of silence that feels comfortable, and can only be achieved once you are completely at ease with the other person. He drives his Maserati in a typically Italian style, erratic but under control. On the radio Gino Paoli sings Il Cielo in Una Stanza, and the traffic is heavy.

Once home I'm almost licked to death by Marco's second love, Camilla, a beyond adorable British

Bulldog. "Let's toast the future!" He pops a bottle of Perrier-Jouet and we step out onto the roof terrace. "Our life is now ready to start properly and our first step is going to be breakfast in the garden of Hotel De Russie," he smiles confidently, knowing that his plan will make me happy. "We're booked to stay at the Capri Palace this week. No stress, no newspapers and no hassle – pure escape!" He looks so proud of himself, having organised the perfect much-needed holiday. True to his word, the following week is just that. A care-free time with zero stress and a whole lot of love. I've often wondered how you know if it's the real thing, if it's love. Oh, I still don't have the answer, but all I can say is those few days spent with just Marco, well, it's as good as it gets. Endless days tanning, swimming and the obvious bit merged into one long relaxed sunset. In my entire life, I have never been happier. A happiness that is hard to understand at first, but when you just go with it, it's bloody great.

*

Arriving back in Dublin, I must say I feel ill. There comes a time when you need to move on and this is one of those times. Having stopped off for breakfast at the Dylan, I head straight to the office to see if my now overdue contract is awaiting my signature and also to attend the weekly editorial meeting. There are mixed reactions towards me from fellow staff. Some people keep their heads down and their eyes on their work, while others go out of their way to greet me, like I'm an Olympian returning with gold medals. As I had suspected all along, there is no contract awaiting me on my desk. In fact, my desk has been cleared and while my things are still here, it feels like it is ready to be occupied by someone new.

"Oh, good morning Oli and welcome back. How was Italy?" Mark smiles falsely.

"It was just the ticket. Thanks for asking," I say calmly without looking up.

As the other members of the editorial team gather in Mark's small office I look at them; all worriedly holding scraps of paper with their ideas for the week jotted on them. Ideas that have been pulled from other publications such as *Cosmopolitan*, *Hello!* or such. They sit patiently, as if about to be interviewed. All awaiting their turn to pitch their plans to Mark, hoping that he'll get equally excited by their offerings. Sadly, he very rarely does. After the meeting I return to my desk and within minutes Martina is by my side. "Can we have a chat in the office when you have a moment?" she asks, before walking away. Could it be that without even having to ask, my contract is ready? "I really hope you had a good holiday. You look refreshed," she says falsely.

"I sure did and I am ready to put this behind us and get back to normal," I smile genuinely.

"OK, well while you were away there were some changes." She looks worried. "Mark and the accounts department have had word that our budgets are being chopped dramatically and the bottom line is that we will not be extending your contract going forward. I'm terribly sorry." She looks smug.

"You're sorry? Why can't you people just be honest? You were never going to renew my contract, were you? From the minute Mark heard that I was gay

I've noticed serious changes in attitude towards me. One that I'm sure other magazines and papers will find most interesting once this gets out. You do know that most people consider this rag to be one of the most homophobic titles on the newsstands?" I say sternly.

"I'm not sure what to say. I'm really sorry, Oli," she continues. "They've told me that they will continue to pay you for any contributions you make but it's just that with the new girl starting here next week we just can't have your name on the page too." Somehow she is trying to sound sympathetic.

"Let me get this straight. So there are budget cuts, yet you will continue to pay me for any tit bits of gossip I can offer, and any other help, say, like hard-to-get phone numbers and such that you may need. I mean come on, let's face it; between the lot of you, your contact books are rather dull. To make it worse, or perhaps funnier, you are willing to employ someone new to front things? I've never been treated so badly in my life and without a hint of shame on your behalf. It's shocking! As for your new face of the diary page, well I do hope you've selected someone more suited to this rag." I stand up, open the door and walk out. I don't even bother to clear my desk. "Well that's that then Bridget. As I predicted, it's game over! Take care of yourself, I hope you see just what type of low lives you're dealing with," I say, gesturing towards Mark's office door.

And just like that it's all over. All the stress, sleepless nights and worry have been for nothing, apart from one thing, I'm free to start my life and stop writing bullshit about people I would cross the street to avoid. As Tony drives me to lunch at the Unicorn I call Marco. "Well, I am officially unemployed and you know what? I love it!" I laugh.

Chapter 17

Ailesbury Road, Dublin

"Oh, darling I detest showers! They ruin my book, dilute my wine and extinguish my cigarettes," Paolo says loudly as he turns his back on Joanne Browne. He's clearly growing tired of the conversation if not the company. Joanne is after all one of the most important socialites and philanthropists in the land, at least in her own head. The fact she married her rich husband Mark within a month of meeting him has shocked nobody, as it's always been clear that she was on a mission to bag a rich spouse from the get-go, having dated and lost a string of high-profile lovers along the way. Mark's divorces from his three previous wives were well documented in the press, due to the whopping settlement amounts he was forced to pay out each time. Despite the fact most people avoid her at any cost I genuinely like her and find her to be fun company, if not borderline bonkers. We'd met many years ago while she was working as a hostess at a nightclub frequented by the city's richest (usually married) men. Back then she was more in need of charity than the type to sit on the board of one. She lived in a tiny studio flat which would have left Kelly Hoppen lost for design ideas.

It's a rare occasion, as I've convinced Paolo to join me in Dublin for Horse Show Week. He rarely comes to town, but the prospect of escaping the overheated and overcrowded Med is a good incentive. We're guests at a garden party being hosted by one of the most distinguished hostesses on one of the most distinguished roads in the city. "I swear that woman you left me with would bore for Europe. Don't do it again, bello! She's been telling me about her new bathroom and how expensive her shower is. Do I look as if I am sort of the person to share an interest in someone's bathroom? Shoot me now. I am not joking!" he continues as he extinguishes one cigarette and instantly lights another.

"Oh, she's not so bad really, she's adjusting to becoming super rich overnight," I smile.

The fact is that this party is pretty lame, being made up of a very mixed bag of guests. Where once Google Maps could have zoomed in on some pretty posh folk, these days the once exclusive strip of real estate is home to property developers, entrepreneurs and new-monied types. All jostling for position against some of the country's oldest and most respected families. Where snobbery has always played a major part in the day-to-day life of its residents, now there's a new level on which to base the good the bad and the damn right out of place. These new 'locals' arrived with the flick of a switch, when Ireland was overtaken by the new breed. The sorts who befriend the powers that be in the country's leading financial institutions and who arrived into the best addresses, built hideous new builds next to grand Victorian and Georgian piles without any concern for anyone or anything. The fact that most of them will be bankrupt and gone within five years doesn't seem to faze them one bit. Today in an effort to welcome her new neighbours and I suspect to make up numbers, Nancy Collins-Jones has invited them to sip cucumber martinis and nibble canapés by her pool, as a post-Aga Khan Trophy treat. The problem is the two tribes certainly don't mix. So much so that the old guard gathers on one side of the pool, dressed in understated, borderline vintage Hermès and pearls, whilst the new money crew are on the other, dressed as if they've run through Harvey Nichols covered in Sellotape.

Gucci clashing with Dior, Versace clashing with Chanel and Louis Vuitton, well, clashing with everything. The louder the prints, the larger the logos, the higher the price tag, it's all on display. All the height of bad taste, none of which seems to register with the wearers. On one side of the pool talk is of horses and the crazy property prices in the area, on the other it's of such and such and his new Gulf Stream or the fact that some flashy daft property developer had gone completely over reserve at a recent auction of modern art at Sotheby's, not knowing what he was buying and making himself something of a laughing stock. This piece of gossip amuses both tribes at least. The mood is sombre due to the great divide and I like everyone else can sense it. Adding to this the fact that Paolo would rather be bobbing on a yacht off Panarea with some

DSquared2 models and Marco's flight being delayed and you will understand my mood.

It's a humid, overcast evening and while the gardens of Nancy's home are exquisite, it's hard to find anyone fun to chat with, so myself and Paolo seek refuge by the edge of the pool where we chain smoke Marlboro Reds and bitch about everyone and everything. Rows of uniformed staff stand still like statues holding trays of cocktails, champagne and wine. Just as we think we may have to throw ourselves into the water in order to get some entertainment things gets interesting. "Seriously, look at Tamara, she's wearing almost nothing. Looks like a hooker, but then again if the Philip Treacy fits and all that…" Paolo says as he peeps over his Dita sunglasses disapprovingly. As usual he's right, she may be wearing Hervé Leger but she looks like she's ready to go to work the yachts in St Tropez. She is as usual cautiously hiding from Joanne, following yet another of their recent 'run-ins' at a charity lunch. She manages to be at the opposite end of the garden to her at all times. If Joanne moves, then so too does Tamara, with almost military precision. We sit watching the scene and try to decide how we can escape.

"Do you have any idea who I am?" comes loudly from inside the imposing red-brick mansion. "I am here to see someone of little importance and then I will be gone, now get out of my way this instant!" The overly posh tones become a vision in white Gucci storming by a waitress which sends glasses of chilled Chablis flying. Seasoned socialite Lizzy Gunne is not to be messed with. Having climbed her way from a humble background to the position as the undisputed queen of the Irish social scene, albeit it only in certain circles, magazines and newspapers, she has never been close friends with Nancy, so she really has some nerve barging into her home. Pushing sixty but with the help of her trusted surgeon looking closer to forty-five, she is one of the most loved and respected party people in the city. The fact that old-school Nancy looks down on her only further makes for her popularity. In fact, it's been noted on occasion that she has the power to make or break those wishing to join her gilded group of all-female charity fundraising crew, who party harder than women half their age. All eyes watch as she pushes through the guests, before finally landing her hand on Tamara's shoulder. As usual she's completely unaware of what's about to happen as she chats with two handsome members of the British Equestrian team. "We can either do this here or you can come inside with me!" she announces to the gathered party but directs at Tamara.

"Oh, hey Lizzy, you look fantastic! I didn't know you were here…" Tamara says in overly plumy, if not practiced tones, while flicking her hair and looking around for anyone who may be able to help. While all eyes are on the pair it's clear that not even the hostess is willing to get involved.

"You've been seeing my husband for long enough and I'm here to put an end to it," she says, before producing a phone from her suit pocket. "I've seen all of your sordid messages and while at first I felt ill, now I realise that not only are you sexually deranged – seriously gather around if you want to see the sort of filth this tramp uses to steal other people's husbands!" She's offering the phone to the other guests who decline her invitation. Naturally nobody dares come forward, except for Paolo who is ready to snatch the phone from her hand, only that I pull him back sharply. "Most importantly you have done me the biggest favour imaginable. I've known of your 'affair' for a while now. If I can call it an affair. Quick sex in dodgy hotels in exchange for some diamond earrings, or holidays in the South of France at my home where you spent the entire week on your back. In fact, Charlie has been at it with a few others too, so you're not so special. It's all on the CCTV which I had installed at the villa without him knowing. It makes for some seriously disturbing viewing and I'm thinking of posting copies of it to all involved and their other halves. So what have you got to say for yourself? Come on, we're all waiting!" It's clear that Lizzy has been drinking, and who could blame her?

"Have you no shame?" Tamara asks in an attempt to gain the upper hand. "Storming in here uninvited and making such a scene. Honestly is nobody going to have this woman removed?" she asks in desperation as she looks around the garden. "I mean look, I'm pretty sure when Frida Giannini designed that suit she was aiming for a much younger customer!" Tamara adds in true bitchy fashion, while taking a sip from her cocktail. That's the thing about Tamara, she certainly can tell her Gucci from her Pucci, possibly as she spends her days studying *Vogue* as well as books like the Louis Vuitton Guides in order to know just what to say and when.

"You fucking whore!" screams Lizzy as she pounces forward, pulling at Tamara's hair and making a charge towards the makeshift bar area. As the bar staff move out of the line of fire the pair continue to cat fight. Tamara's hair, made up mainly of clip-in extensions is being pulled out, leaving her looking ever so slightly worse for wear. All sorts of profanities, none of which are suitable for a garden party, certainly not one in this neighbourhood, can be heard before they vanish, head first into the pool.

"Oh, finally something fun!" squeals Paolo as he flings his drink into the air. "Darling this is fantastic, leave it to trampy Tamara to bring the party to the party and typically we have front-row seats!" he says as he reaches for his iPhone to capture the moment on camera. He's never been Tamara's biggest fan ever since they met. They both went after the same guy at Nikki Beach in St Tropez one afternoon and following a lengthy and costly battle Tamara won. The guy they both wanted was a Calvin Klein underwear model who played them both for hours. Endless bottles of champagne were consumed before he announced that he was straight. A guy's sexuality is not usually something to get in Paolo's way but this time he didn't stand a chance. Since that day he detests her. As Lizzy struggles to make her way to the side of the pool guests rush to help her, leaving Tamara to her own devices.

Tamara's problem is that everyone already knows she is a notorious bed hopper, so help isn't forthcoming. Standing at the far end of the pool Joanne Browne begins to clap loudly. "So Tamara, perhaps my paranoia is just after all. I think it's time you got out of here and started to run!" she says, sounding extremely scary. Well you know what they say – you can take the girl out of the nightclub and all that… As Lizzy emerges from the pool she looks every day of her true age.

"Here, boys, get me some towels and a fresh drink!" Tamara screeches from the pool. "Is nobody else getting in?" she laughs as she removes her dress over her head before swimming towards us, clearly she's high as per usual.

"Ugh, you really are too much. Is no man safe?" Paolo asks in exaggerated fashion.

"I think you're pretty safe, you queen," as she blows him a kiss.

Nancy is standing at the far side of the pool and she gestures to her staff to help Tamara out of the water. "I think it's time you gathered your belongings and left my home. You are never to cross my path again, you hideous woman! No, do not offer her a towel," she barks at a Czech waiter who seems excited by the scene.

"Well, New York, London, Paris and Milan have Fashion Week and here in Ireland we have Horse Show Week! It's almost just as dramatic!" I say to Paolo, who is by now beside himself with giddiness. As the waiter refills glasses in an attempt to regain some normality, I receive a text message from Marco who has finally landed and is already settled in the tranquil garden of the Merrion Hotel. 'Hey baby I'm at the hotel and have a surprise for you! Sitting in the garden with a Pimm's… Find me xx'

"That's it! Our escape plan is in place," I say with a wide smile. "Let's go find Nancy and make a dash for it." I'm pulling Paolo by the arm. Outside there's something of a traffic jam, as each driver tries desperately to get into pole position to be ready to collect at a minute's notice. All that is, apart from mine. "Where the hell is Tony?" I ask myself aloud as I reach for my phone, noticing the battery is about to die for the second time today. It's like trying to find 'Where's Wally?' Rows and rows of black Mercedes S Class and BMW 7 Series. I call Tony's number and it's diverting to voicemail. "There's only thing for it, we'll have to get a cab! Brace yourself, Paolo!" I say assertively. Anyone would think we were about to go into battle. In way we were, on two levels. Trying to find a taxi during Horse Show Week is an almost impossible task. Worse than that is trying to get Paolo into one.

"We are taking public transport? What the actual fuck is happening here?" Paolo questions with genuine panic in his voice. For as long as he can recall life has always been about stepping in and out of chauffeur-driven Rolls-Royces or Bentleys. Taxis are very much on his 'public transport' list and something which should only be used in emergencies. As we stand at the side of the street I try in vain to hail a cab but nothing wants to stop. Making matters worse is an imminent thunder storm which is casually brewing overhead. "I cannot believe the way this day is turning out! We should get the, ahem, taxi and go directly to the airport and back to Italy in time for dinner!" Paolo says in utter disgust as a dirty-looking Toyota pulls up. "You cannot be fucking serious? I refuse! I actually think I may throw up! White Saint-Laurent jeans and this?" The thing about Paolo is that unlike anyone else, when he says something he genuinely means it. Life for him is extremely different to that of anyone else I know.

Using the bus lane, we speed past the standstill traffic along Merrion Road. Paolo is hanging out the window, talking into his phone loudly in French. He looks like one of those funny dogs who do the same thing on every car journey. With his mop of super shiny black hair blowing in the wind and oversized shades, he was certainly every inch of the jet-set star the media claim him to be. Hanging up the call he looks at me and makes a funny face. "Bloody more problems with the staff in France! Oh, how can you bear this? The smell! The plastic seat covers! It's too hideous to even be funny!" he says, deadpan.

Arriving outside the hotel we're relieved to be back to almost normality. Marco sits alone at a table on the corner of the terrace. An ice bucket containing an unopened bottle of Krug and some mineral water is by his side, while a dish of strawberries, an espresso and copies of *L'Uomo Vogue*, *Tatler* and *Condé Nast Traveller* are strewn everywhere. He's chatting into his phone as we make our way to greet him. "Ciao Ale, parlare presto…" he says before standing up. Looking at him I still feel the same way as I did that night when we first met. Dressed in a fitted pink shirt and faded jeans, he's by far the hottest guy at the hotel and he's all mine. He hugs me tighter than ever before. It's only been a few days since we've seen each other in Milan but it feels like an eternity. That's the thing about finding your soulmate, when you're alone for even a day or so, you miss them constantly. I've never had that feeling before with anyone else. I must admit that it scares me. "It's so good to see you. I've missed you too much," he whispers into my ear.

"OK, OK, enough already you two, let me have

some of the love!" Paolo says loudly, so the entire terrace turns to look. As the waiter pours champagne Marco sits smiling from ear to ear.

"Why are you smiling?" I ask.

"Oh, no reason other than because I can see you." He's sounding slightly cheesy. "And touch you!" He reaches out and touches my face.

"Honestly if this shit is going to continue I am getting the next flight off this funny little island!" Paolo threatens.

"Don't worry, P, we'll calm down after a few hours, I promise," Marco says as he raises his glass.

"So, guess what I have in my pocket?" Paolo asks with a cheeky smile.

"Oh, seriously it could be anything with you, darling," I say teasingly. Just then he produces a mobile phone and places it on the table. "Well, what's with the phone?" I ask, genuinely curious.

"This phone contains what will soon be the talk of the town … Yes, Oli, this is Lizzy's phone, the one with all the messages from her husband and Tamara!" he gushes. "So, shall we see just how she manages to bed so many powerful men? What does she offer?" He's already searching through it.

"What does he mean?" asks a confused Marco.

"Oh, it's a long story but let's just say this afternoon has been something of an eye-opener for us."

Paolo sits staring at the phone and then bursts out laughing. "Oh my, she really is a dirty bitch. Look at this photo!" he says, offering me the phone. Poor Tamara would die if she knew what we were looking at. There she is dressed as a dominatrix standing with her stiletto-heeled boots on Lizzy's husband's privates. As if this isn't bad enough, there's a string of text messages with explicit details of what the pair were going to get up to and had already gotten up to. Lizzy's husband, Philip, is a high-profile banker with a reputation of being a ball breaker, if you pardon the pun. He likes to portray a wholesome image of the consummate family man at any given opportunity, most recently having invited a certain Sunday newspaper's style section into his magnificent country house in Co Wicklow. Pages of glossy photos of him in his gym or cooking with Lizzy. You know the sort of thing, carefully placed antiques, a highly sought-after art collection and of course beautiful Golden Retrievers here and there. The fact that Paolo had a bit of a run-in with Philip on his last visit to Dublin only further fuels his desire to ensure the phone lands into the wrong hands. Philip may have wanted the public to see him as someone to look up to, but in fact he's a homophobic nightmare of a being. Paolo's run-in with him was at a charity gala at the Shelbourne Hotel. He made it clear that he was intolerant of gay guys, even though Paolo could most probably buy the bank he works for and have him fired if he truly wanted.

I can see his eyes dancing as he skims through the various images and text messages on Lizzy's phone. "There's no way you could do anything like that to Lizzy. She's a sweetheart," I say half testing Paolo to see what his intentions are.

"Well she means nada to me, bello, and she'll probably be happy to see the two of them publicly shamed." He sounds menacing. "Will you excuse me? I just need to make a few calls. I think I'll try to get a massage. Back soon…" he says, placing Lizzy's phone into his pocket as he walks towards the bar.

"He really is a crazy kid, no?" Marco asks, reaching for something inside his bag on the chair. "I told you that I had a surprise for you and here it is, baby. It is kind of like a one-year anniversary gift." He hands me a large white envelope. As I peep inside I feel like a kid on Christmas morning. It's a brochure for possibly the most beautiful yacht I've ever seen. I look from the photos back to Marco and he smiles. "We pick her up in Portofino on Saturday and we sail to St Tropez for a party. From there we can do as we please for ten days. Are you happy?" he asks, although he clearly can see that I am.

"Happy? Baby, I've never been happier. Even without this amazing gift. Seriously, I have never been more alive than I am right now!" I really meant it. Life is full for the first time and every day is filled with excitement, knowing that I've finally made the leap to be who I was born to be. Sharing day to day with this amazing guy is just the cherry on top.

"That's not all. As Paolo is staying at your place, I've checked in here – booked a suite for us for tonight. I mean it would be a great shame to miss this moment and I am so fucking horny!" he says as he downs his champagne. "Hold tight and I will be right back," he winks. As I wait for both of them to re-emerge I take a call from my agent, Angie, to let me know that I've been offered a monthly column in a society magazine which will chronicle my partying and jet-set ways.

"Oh, that sounds like fun! Would I have to actually write it? I mean, it does sound time consuming," I say, genuinely sounding concerned.

"Think of the money, Oli, not to mention the profile. The magazine is on sale right across Europe and could be handy for opening doors!" she says excitedly.

"Personally I find that doormen are usually the best option for opening doors, darling, but I am always interested in the financial side of things, so let's see what they're offering." I end the call and take a sip of champagne. Isn't life the funniest thing? So many ups and downs, so much time wasting stressing about things we can't change. I mean, look at me now, sitting here, out and proud, with the man I want to spend my life with, and new work opportunities coming my way. I'm not spiritual, but, it's as if the universe wants me to know it feels my mood.

Scanning the terrace for any familiar faces, there aren't any. Like most civilized societies in August everyone is out of the city at either their country house or on the back of a yacht in the Med. Plenty of tourists, but no locals apart from two detestable gay guys that I avoid at every cost. I use the term 'local' rather loosely, as they live roughly three million euro below local property value away from the hotel. You know the sort, once they make any sort of money, they splash it on all the wrong things, and by doing so only show their true colours even more. Both hairdressers, they're known as the scissor sisters, and they've worked their way up from sweeping floors to opening their own salon, 'Jazzy Cuts', a few years ago. Now I think they have two or three others in their 'empire'. Luckily they haven't spotted me, as if they had they'd be already at my table drinking my champagne.

As Marco makes his way back to the table I can see them staring at him intensely. As their eyes follow him they suddenly realise that he's joining me. "Darling, I think we better move fast as there are two dreadful people about to make their way…" Before I can finish they arrive at our table uninvited and completely in my face.

"Well, look at you all tanned! Where have you been, ya bitch? Hi, I'm John and this is my boyfriend – sorry, fiancé, Sam. We're celebrity hairdressers. Who are you? You're bleedin' gorgeous!" John says as he pushes his hand out towards Marco, almost knocking two champagne glasses to the ground in the process.

"I am Marco and I am Oli's…"

"He's my friend. My friend from Italy and we are actually just about to leave, so have a nice afternoon," I say, removing my shades in order to make eye contact with Marco.

"Of course ye are. Funny how every time we try say hello you have to leave suddenly. You're too important, or at least that's what ya think," Sam says in a true bitchy tone.

"We knew her when she was a nobody," he adds as he attempts to pull out one of the heavy chairs and sit down.

"Sorry, she? Who are you referring to?" Marco asks, genuinely confused.

"Her!" they say in unison as one points in my direction and the other checks the bottle of champagne to see what's left to drink.

"Pay no attention, Marco. The truth is I don't know these two at all. They are constantly doing this." I'm sounding angry.

"Who the fuck do you think you are? We all know about the way you operate. You're a fucking nobody, goin' around lookin' down your nose at everyone. The bleedin' state of ye!" Sam snaps. Suddenly Marco stands up and orders that they move away from our table. At six foot two and with a strong, muscular build he isn't the sort to be messed with.

"Oh relax, Rambo, were only buzzin' with yiz! Come on, let's get pissed. We gettin' another bottle of this? What is it, cava?" John asks as he waves for the waiter. "We'll take another bottle of fizzy, thanks handsome!" he says to the shocked French waiter.

"Certainly. Another Krug and how many glasses do you require, sir?"

"Eh hello! Four obviously! Jaysis, how do some people even get a job?" Sam laughs out loud.

That's it, I can tolerate most things, even hideous people such as Sam and John, but I cannot stand rudeness directed at waiting staff. "As I said, we're actually just leaving but thanks all the same," I say as I gather our belongings and stand up.

"Oh, whatever, ye ungrateful dickhead! Go on, run along… Be careful with this one, Mark, he'll probably try get ye into bed!"

Marco, sensing my disgust turns back to the table

and says, "Boys, you hardly think he hasn't already. I thought you hairdresser sorts have all the gossip. Haven't you heard the latest? We are getting married in a few weeks. Very nice to meet you both." He leaves them both gob-smacked.

"You are too funny, baby," I laugh as I look back at them, scowling at me.

"Not as funny as it will be when they get their bill for that bottle of 'cava'!" he laughs, before grabbing me close as the elevator doors close silently. The funniest thing about meeting the scissor sisters is that within days the story of our impending wedding has made the social diary of that rag, the *Meteor*, which makes myself and Marco laugh for days. Sometimes life is just too easy.

Chapter 18

Gstaad, Switzerland

It's the day before New Year's Eve and the entire ski club which counts Valentino, Roger Moore and Mr 'Jet-Set' Taki Theodoracopulos as members is buzzing with the bold and the beautiful, all enjoying a long and lazy lunch as the year winds down. In between courses there's the usual table hopping with all talk of the night ahead.

"Darling, see you at the Palace later?" roars Jacks Thompson-Walker as she works the room, dressed in a full mink coat and Chanel ski-boots, heavily tugging on an unlit Montecristo.

"Yes, where else?" I smile, raising my glass.

"She does realise that her cigar isn't lighting, right?" Marco questions.

I smile and shake my head. Jacks' behaviour is certainly the sort that would only ever be accepted during the festive season at the Eagle. Perched on top of Wasserngrat, a private mountain serviced by a private ski lift, the Eagle is possibly the world's most exclusive club. In order to join you must be invited, then undergo the gruelling vetting procedure of the terrifyingly discriminating committee and then, and only then, you wait up to three years before they'll accept your membership fees or push you off the piste. You know when they say money can buy you anything, well that certainly doesn't apply in Gstaad. At the Eagle, celebrity sightings are the daily norm, it's the sort of place where it's not unusual to have kings and queens dining next to film stars and political heavy hitters. It's fair to say that Jacks' full-on party attitude would most certainly have been enjoyed by ex-club president Vicomte Benoist d'Azy and club founder the Earl of Warwick. Jacks is one of those truly out-there London 'It' girls who seems to jump from party to party without ever having to pay for anything. Designers send her clothes each season, in the hope she'll wear them, or more importantly be photographed wearing them. Airlines send her first-class tickets, although like many others, she tends to hitch a ride on private over commercial. Her choice of car changes weekly, from Bentley to Porsche to Range Rover, quite simply as each luxury car marque wants her to be seen behind their wheel.

Life became something of a media circus for Jacks when she fell face-first out of the Met Bar (way back when the Met was cool) with just two international playboys to hold her up. She was the original panti-less flasher for the press, as she struggled to climb into a Hummer outside the club, showing so much that the editors of the red tops had to blur certain areas of the photos, if you know what I mean. Her antics led the way for such behaviour, leaving the likes of Paris Hilton et al trailing behind in beyond boring copycat fashion. The fact that she's known to have an in with royal circles, only makes her more interesting, at least to those trapped at the news-desks of the *Daily Mail*. In reality she's a nice girl, but her addiction to cocaine is no secret and by lunch time most days she's as high as a kite. Yet somehow she attracts some of the world's richest men, all of whom love her rather OTT sense of fun and endless tanned legs. Today is no different, as she bounces around air-kissing and laughing for all to see and hear. She is the essence of a true party person, born to do it, but sadly she doesn't quite know when to stop.

I'm sitting enjoying a low-key lunch with Marco, who looks hotter than ever, dressed in a navy Moncler turtleneck sweater, and sporting a tanned face. I watch him chat with some guys from New York who are 'Eagle virgins' and seem to be in awe of everyone and everything going around them. Hedge funders who look like they're doing a shoot for Brooks Bros. Broad white smiles and shiny, preppy haircuts. Guests of a host that seems to have vanished, not that they've noticed. They're fully loaded and they're sure enjoying the ultimate 'I've made it!' lunch invitation; constantly taking selfies and posting every detail to Facebook and Twitter. While Marco detests social media, much to my amusement he's being forced to pose for their photos, as they ask his expert opinion on where to hang out in Europe during July and August. "Like, where do the really hot chicks and, ya know, celebrities go? Is Ibiza still cool?" asks a guy who looks as if he's fifteen years old and would most probably scare easily of the scene on the Isla Blanca.

Seriously, I don't think I've ever been happier. I'm sipping on a glass of Brunello, following a wonderful, yet simple lunch of spaghetti with white truffles. We're in great company, joined by two friends from Rome who are in the same mood, having spent the past two weeks skiing, eating and drinking too much. Francesca, one of Marco's oldest friends and her husband, Piero, are such easy company, and we're guests at their perfectly situated and designed chalet. Francesca is fast becoming one of Europe's most important collectors of futurist art, while Piero is involved with a leading F1 team, but rarely speaks of his work. It's funny as everywhere Francesca goes she gets hit on by art dealers hoping to obtain a slice of her wealth. Today is no different, as a portly-looking Milanese chap has been doing his utmost to offload a Modigliani and one or two 'overly seen' works by Fontana, but sadly for him he's getting nowhere. As a couple they're both super well-connected, yet super easy going, a complete joy to be around. I watch as they check something out on an iPad, constantly laughing and touching hands. They really are the perfect couple, almost as perfect as myself and Marco, I smile inwardly.

Looking around the room I think of how much fun a gossip columnist would have if he could gain access to this haven of society in the sky. It's the sort of place where you spot the beyond handsome Arki Busson, hanging out with similar sorts, or effervescent Tarama Beckwith lunching with Giancarlo Giammetti and Valentino. In fact, one of today's familiar faces is Geoffrey Moore, who's a 'life member' and therefore a very much sought-after lunch date. He's chatting on his phone at the 'Moore table', named after his father, Roger. He waved to Marco as we arrived and shouted something about a lunch party on New Year's Day.

"What do you want to do tonight, baby?" Marco asks, grabbing my hand from across the table.

"I'm not so sure? Perhaps, and dare I say it, a night at home? Movies, vino and bed sounds kind of totally tempting." I can see that's the plan Marco wants to hear. Sadly, in Gstaad a night off from the social scene is pretty much unheard of, the same way as it is in Monte Carlo.

"Oh no you don't!" Piero cuts in. "We're going to Rialto for dinner with some fantastic friends from London and then guess what? We'll end up in GreenGo!" he jokes as he waves his napkin in the air like a teenager at his first rave. "It's been arranged and the booking includes you two love birds so that's it sorted! Plus, we should probably start getting ready to head back." He downs his cognac. The Eagle is fantastic but in order to get back down the mountain many lunches have been cut short as the lifts close at 16:45 sharp. After that you're on your own, so to speak, which is never a good idea after so much wine.

As we say goodbye to a table which includes a number of Guinnesses, a Rothschild and a host of blonde girls from London, all looking to be twenty-one or so, Jacks bounds over to me clutching a bottle of Krug and demanding we share a glass. "How long are you boys staying?" she asks while flicking her honey-blonde hair and looking around to see which eligible guys are within earshot.

"Oh, we're leaving for Milan on the third. As

much as we adore Gstaad, it's almost time to get back to the city and to reality," I say while raising my glass to toast Jacks and the year ahead.

"Seriously, who needs reality? Actually, what is reality?" she laughs. "Oh come on, darling, stay longer please – I'm here until early February," she moans, as if her extra-long winter break is a pain in the ass. Of course she's staying until February, as it's well-known to be the month when Chopard, Bvlgari and de Grisogono hold their lavish jewellery sales at the Palace. A string of glamorous parties aimed at supplying girls like Jacks with endless joy. The sort of joy that can only be showered on them by admiring billionaires, even though Jacks certainly has the bank balance to buy them herself. But who on earth buys themselves jewellery? "Will we see you tonight after dinner? I really want to have a blast. New Year's Eve is all well and good, but I much prefer to party when you are not expected to. Tonight will be divine! OMG is that Charlie Bettencourt?" she says without taking a breath.

While the snow is coming down heavily outside, it's clear that it was being snorted up at the same rate by Jacks and her band of followers inside. With that, there's a loud crashing sound followed by rapturous applause. "What the fuck?" she screeches, before hopping onto the chair to get a better view.

"Please, madam, can you get down?" asks a waiter who goes unnoticed.

"Oh, how funny, how bloody funny!" she wails. "It's Bianca, she has totally broken her chair and pulled the table over at the same time! I have to go rescue her, darlings. See you boys later, no excuses!"

Making her way back to the drama, myself and Marco give a knowing look. It's clear that we want a log fire, movies and bathrobes rather than champagne, tuxedos and more of the same. Any more debauchery and we may be entering Riot Club territory.

As we make our way back down the Wasserngrat, he leans in close and whispers in my ear, "Do you know that I love you?" What would usually be a cheesy moment feels so right, and yes, I do know it. I've felt the same since the first few times we'd met, but it's nice to have it confirmed. As we arrive into the bar at the Hotel Olden for much-needed hot chocolate with Armagnac, I look around to try and find a quiet corner. That's the other thing about Gstaad, being super social it's hard to find a quiet moment. We settle in at the bar and for the first time in days we're alone. "Do we really have to do it again tonight?" he's mock yawning. I know that Marco loves the scene here, but even for a couple like us that are very used to going for weeks on end without a social break, Gstaad is taking its toll.

"If you really need to stay home, stay home. I can go along to dinner and skip the after-show." I pat him on the head, ruffling his shiny black hair.

"My hero," he smiles. The fact is, all I want to do is sleep so it really does make me a hero, I guess.

Dressing for dinner, I light a large Jo Malone Pomegranate Noir candle in the bathroom. The matchbox I use has a slogan on the side which reads 'Gstaad – Come up, slow down'. I'm certainly up, but there's no sign of slowing down any time soon.

Leaving Marco fireside sipping a whiskey, he looks

so sexy – white towelled bathrobe and navy cashmere socks, showing his tanned, gym-fit legs. It's hard to tear myself away from what could be a perfect night in. Sitting down to dinner with Francesca, Piero and their two friends, Hugo and his wife Aurelia, I receive a text message from Jacks who seems slightly manic. 'Darling do you have a number for supplies up here in the hills? It seems all my guys are in St Moritz fuelling the Russians! Loulou and Bianca are coming to the Alpina for drinks, then onward to The Palace at midnight – join us? Xox'

I read the text then delete it. While Jacks is fun to be around, once she's started her party she becomes somewhat unbearable. As for her two sidekicks, well let's just say they aren't to my taste. Bianca is possibly the loudest and most obnoxious 'girl-about-town' to have ever crept out of Essex via South Ken, following a stint on some reality TV show or another. Her father is a self-made multi-millionaire having made his fortune in scrap metal or something similar and believes that everything his princess wants, she gets. So much so that not so long ago she had an affair with art dealer Charles Costa, who was Jacks' on/off boyfriend of three years. The one guy Jacks adored, even if he had treated her so badly. Bianca cheated behind her back and just before things became common knowledge she announced that he had tried to rape her. A case that predictably never made it to the police, but worryingly almost made it into the tabloids. However, somehow Jacks remains her friend. The last time I had the misfortune of meeting her was outside the London EDITION, where she was pulling at her blonde hair extensions while shouting at a traffic warden for ticketing her illegally parked bubblegum-pink Bentley Continental. Need I say more?

As for Loulou, well, nobody really knows too much about her, apart from the fact that she's French and exceptionally rude. I've been told that she is in fact a high-class call girl, but as dear Paolo had once questioned, "High-class, are you sure?" Possibly most embarrassing of all is a rumour that she repeatedly called the editor of *Tatler* to demand they do a feature on her and her fabulous lifestyle. It never happened. The idea of spending the evening listening to the three of them screeching at each other and splashing Cristal makes me feel ill. As I delete her first message I receive another. 'OK where the fuck are you? Delivery has landed and we're at the chalet. Skipping dinner natch! Come here and join us. You know you wanna darling! xx'

I choose to ignore the message yet again and switch my phone to silent in order to enjoy dinner, which turns out to be rather good fun. It's the sort of evening I need, low-key and hassle free. Aurelia is stunningly beautiful, dressed in Vionnet and rocking some serious ice from Van Cleef & Arpels. She works in television in the UK and by the time we've reached coffee she's insisting I go to a meeting in London about presenting a lifestyle show of my own. You know the sort of thing, covering the string of fashion weeks which kick off almost as soon as I get back to the UK. "You're perfect for it and you've already done heaps of TV, so it's a walk in the park for you," she gushes while taking a group selfie. As dinner comes to a close we, like most people in the tiny village, are heading to GreenGo to dance until the world runs dry of champagne. GreenGo is as essential to the Gstaad as Jimmy'z is to Monte Carlo. On any given night of the season you can spot royalty dancing next to pop stars, who down Dom Perignon with regular faces from FTV, who chase the sons of billionaires, who clearly enjoy the attention. This is a place where Gstaad's new and old gather every night and let loose.

"Good evening, how great to see you again!" beams Romano, the club's host. "Now to get your evening started a little festive gift from us to you. Is Marco not joining you?" He ushers a waiter to deliver our little gift; two huge ice buckets filled with all sorts of treats from a bottle of Cristal Rosé, a bottle of Grey Goose Citron and some bottles of Evian and mixers.

"No, can you believe he's having a night off, at home watching movies," I smile as I sit down. I reach for my phone to text him and see if he's still awake. I know that as soon as everyone has settled in, I can probably make my exit and be fire-side with my man to enjoy some down time. Plus, the mountain air sure does make me horny.

Before I can escape, Aurelia sits beside me offering a glass of champagne and a kiss. "I hope you're as excited about our TV idea as I am?" she smiles. The truth is, while I'm honoured and curious about the idea, I'm not too sure I want to be away from Marco and real life so much.

"I'm just not sure if I want to start the year flitting between London, New York, Paris and Milan." I'm sounding pathetic.

"But isn't that what you do normally?" Piero laughs as he leans in to top up his vodka soda.

"Plus, I thought you had a special love for London Fashion Week, no?" Francesca winks.

She was right, after all London Fashion Week was where I'd first met Marco, but it all seems so long ago now, as I sit now with his best friends who have become my best friends too.

"Actually, speaking of Marco, would you guys mind if I call it a night? I'm shattered and would love to go chill by the fire. I'm pretty sure Marco's flat out in front of the TV, so I can surprise him." Making my way out of the busy club, I take a call from Jacks. "Jesus Jacks, you're bloody persistent, what's up?" I ask as I wave goodnight to Jim Leblanc, the resident DJ who is pumping out a great set.

"It's not Jacks, sorry, this is Bianca. You have to come at once! Something terrible is happening to Jacks. She's lying on the bathroom floor moaning but not moving. Fuck, just get here!" she screams into the phone, sounding even more hysterical than usual. The problem with girls like these is that it's hard to decipher what is an actual emergency and what's a cocaine panic.

"Have you called emergency services?" I ask, trying to hear her over the strains of Chic's Forbidden Lover. "Where the fuck are you exactly? Call a fucking ambulance!"

"We're at the chalet, just get here now!" The phone line goes dead. In a panic I try to call Marco but his phone diverts to voicemail. Seeing my distress, the doorman organises a car to take me to the Thompson-Walker chalet. I'm trying to call Marco again, this time leaving a message. As the car makes its way slowly out of the village I fear the worst, knowing that Jacks has been partying solidly for at least four days. I'd seen her numerous times and each time she was in a state, even pre-lunch. I try to call Jacks again but now her phone is also going straight to voicemail. After what feels like an age we arrive at the chalet and I call the intercom. Without anyone answering the gates slowly open and we drive onward. By now I'm scared of what may be awaiting me, and I'm chain smoking. Parked in front of the house are a number of cars including a classic Rolls-Royce Corniche, a Mercedes SLS AMG and a number of Range Rovers all with English plates.

At the front door stands Loulou clutching a bottle of Stolichnaya and dressed rather ironically like a call girl. "Shit, what took you guys so long? Come on, help us, man, this is serious!" she screeches as I push her out of the way.

Inside, house music is pumping out of the kitchen and large Byredo candles are lit everywhere. "Bianca, where are you?" I shout as I make my way up the main stairs to the first floor.

"We're on the top floor in the bathroom, hurry!" she screams, sounding as if she may explode. Reaching the bathroom door, Bianca is standing looking like she already knows the truth of the situation. Pushing the door open, I see Jacks lying on her side wearing a blood stained open bathrobe and knee-high Gucci boots. Her nose is bleeding badly and there's blood marring her usually perfect hair. In fact it's everywhere. The pristine all-white bathroom looks like a scene from, I don't know, CSI Miami, or one of those police TV shows.

"What's the latest on the ambulance? Has anyone called one? What's she taken? Come on Bianca, for fuck's sake!" I'm shouting like a lunatic.

"Eh, no I haven't called the ambulance just yet. I was waiting for you, to see what we should do. We can't get the police involved in this, you know? What about the newspapers? I can't be named!" She's sounding as pathetic as ever.

I pull my phone out and call emergency services. Staring at Jacks lying on the white marble floor, I feel so sad. Her life may be charmed, but boy is it lonely. Having never had to work, life is filled with endless booze-filled lunches, parties and meaningless affairs. One night we were guests at a party for French *Vogue* at Hôtel Costes and she told me how she was scared to grow old alone. I'm pretty sure it was just cocaine talk, but looking at her now, I feel so sorry. Sorry that she may not get the chance to grow old at all. That night in Paris was pretty wild; even after leaving a string of after parties, she wanted more. As we sat at Café de Flore taking ecstasy at 10am, others sipped café au lait and stared in shock. Her behaviour that morning scared me, as she was like a wild animal. Loud, brash, rude and craving attention from complete strangers. Seriously, to see a girl who has it all succumb to nothing – a mess.

I lean in close over her, but it's hard to tell if she's still breathing. "Where the fuck is Loulou and what did you guys take? I need to know so I can tell the medics!" I'm shouting at Bianca.

"Just the usual, a little coke, a little vodka… Eh, I think Jacks may have used some MDMA too." She's like a teenager who's been caught drinking alcohol for the first time.

"Listen, you crazy bitch, go and get Loulou immediately!" I order.

Bianca says nothing, but as if in a trance goes downstairs to do as I say. There's nobody at home, not even the housekeeper, who from memory, is always floating about making sure everything is in order. Finally, as I'm just about to give up hope I can hear the ambulance coming in the distance. Suddenly everything starts happening so fast, as the medics take control of the situation. I swear to you, I'm ready to faint. Bianca and Loulou are nowhere to be seen, having both fled the scene, like the bitches they are. *It's hardly surprising*, I think to myself as I take the stairs down to the hallway. Despite roaring log fires and the plushest of furnishings, everything feels cold. The two of them have literally vanished, being more concerned with the possibility of bad press than their friend's well-being, which sadly has always been the case. I'm standing at the foot of the staircase and I call Francesca to ask her to bring Marco to me. I light a Marlboro Red, and even though I am in shock I know I must quit smoking as my New Year resolution.

Looking around, the chalet is stuffed with Old Masters and 18th-century furniture; it's a perfect example of the more impressive homes in the area and includes Valentino as a neighbour. These sorts of details are what made both the *World of Interiors* and the *Sunday Times* Style magazines giddy when they interviewed Jacks at home only last year. Right now, they seem to mean absolutely nothing. When it comes down to it, it doesn't matter whether you're on Carrara marble or cheap linoleum, when you fall down, you fall down. All these thoughts are rushing through my mind as I wait for the bathroom door to open.

Just then, Marco comes rushing up the front steps followed by Francesca. "Baby, what's happened? Are you OK? Where's Jacks?" he's asking and squeezing me close, so close I can't really breathe. Before I can answer, the bathroom door opens and Jacks is lifted out on a stretcher to the awaiting ambulance. She looks so tiny, wrapped under a pile of blankets.

"We need to take Ms Thompson-Walker to Zweisimmen Hospital. Her condition is extremely serious. We advise that you make contact her next of kin and let them know," a female medic is requesting calmly.

"Can I go with her or should I, should we follow in the car? Marco, you haven't been drinking, can you drive us there?" I beg.

"Yes, of course! You can make the calls en route." He hands me his phone.

Marco's rented Mercedes jeep is parked outside with the doors open and the engine still running. Speaking with Jacks' father, I'm numb and somewhat lost. "I'm terribly sorry to call so late, but there's been an accident in Gstaad and we're taking Jacks to hospital. She is in good hands..." It all sounds so stupid, but I'm not sure how to deliver this sort of news. Having had a few drinks, I now feel utterly sober. I'm sure he's aware of her lifestyle, but I'm not sure he knows just how out of control it has become. "I really don't think she's going to make it. I've a very bad feeling about this," I say to Marco and Francesca as we follow the ambulance out of the large gates, and passing the twinkling lights of the boutiques in the village, it's all a blur.

The clock reads 02:43am and as a doctor walks towards us we can instantly tell he doesn't have good news. "I regret that Ms Thompson-Walker didn't pull through. She died just moments ago. We did everything we could, but now I need to speak with her family," he says sternly. He remains calm, before apologising once again and returning behind closed doors. Although I've always known that Jacks was a flame waiting to burn out, I didn't think I'd be the one at her side when that time finally came. Myself and Marco stare in silence. Even though he'd never been her biggest fan, I can see it's hitting him too. Francesca, not sure what to do, offers to get coffee, leaving us to try to figure things out. Naturally the police are going to have to be informed and both Bianca and Loulou questioned. My white shirt is blood stained, as are my hands, and I swear to you I'm ready to hit the deck. Of course, in turn the media would need to be dealt with, but for now I just need a hug.

"She's gone. I knew it would happen. I felt it. Oh, how are we going to tell her father?" I say, holding back the tears, but then I can't hold them in any longer. Suddenly like a wave it hits me and I sob for Jacks. I collapse to the floor uncontrollably.

I don't think I've ever been so upset by anything. Perhaps the idea that it could be almost anyone or all of us, scares me to the core. Even though she drove me insane most times, I know she was a good person. There on the floor, in the hallway of the hospital, I'm out of control and there is nothing Marco can do can help. "Shit, why Jacks? Such a great soul surrounded by such bad people. Just look at the way her two best friends left her to die on the fucking bathroom floor. Those two bitches have sponged everything – her contacts, her wardrobe, her boyfriends and now her life." I feel the tears soak my face. It's beyond disgusting and totally upsetting. "Fuck, I can't do this! I need to get out of here. I need to go home." Marco helps me up and I'm shaking uncontrollably.

Looking to the clock on the wall, it reads 03:34 and I realise that it's New Year's Eve. Arriving back at the chalet, I walk straight to the bedroom and close the door.

Marco hands me a glass of water and a Xanax before taking my phone and switching it off. "I'll call her father, you stay here," he says calmly. As I lie staring at the wall I know that I'll be once again linked to a scandal of epic proportions, even if this time I wasn't part of the mess.

Within hours I'm woken by Marco who tells me that as suspected, there's a media frenzy and he's been avoiding calls from almost every newspaper possible, all of whom are tying my name to the story. As usual with Chinese whispers, the story that's reached London is that I've been partying hard with Jacks for days on end. One journalist went as far as to say that he has been offered photographs of us doing cocaine together at some party only days ago. Upon realising the level this lot will sink to in order to run a story, I leave my phone switched off and ask that Marco does the same. The result being a string of headlines that will most certainly require the attention of both the Thompson Walker's lawyers and ours, but for now all

I am concerned with is meeting Jacks' father and trying to explain the real story. What a way to start a new year.

Printed in Germany
by Amazon Distribution
GmbH, Leipzig